Also from Indigo Sea Press

Novels by Sherrie Hansen

Night and Day

Maple Valley Trilogy
Stormy Weather

Water Lily

Merry Go Round

Wild Rose of Scotland Series
Thistle Down (a prequel novella)

Wild Rose

Blue Belle

Shy Violet

Sweet William

indigoseapress.com

Love Notes

By

Sherrie Hansen

Hope, joy, peace, Love, Sherrie Hansen

Veracity Books
Published by Indigo Sea Press
Winston-Salem

Veracity Books
Indigo Sea Press
302 Ricks Drive
Winston-Salem, NC 27103

This book is a work of fiction. Names, characters, locations and events are either a product of the author's imagination, fictitious or used fictitiously. Any resemblance to any event, locale or person, living or dead, is purely coincidental.

Copyright 2012 by Sherrie Hansen

All rights reserved, including the right of reproduction in whole or part in any format.

First Veracity edition published
April, 2016
Veracity Books, Moon Sailor, and all production design are trademarks of Indigo Sea Press, used under license.

For information regarding bulk purchases of this book, digital purchase and special discounts, please contact the publisher at
indigoseapress.com

Cover design by Lonnie Arnevik

Manufactured in the United States of America
ISBN 978-1-63066-395-7

To Aunt Pat and Uncle Frank Decker, who regaled me with stories of a honeymoon spent in a cabin on Bear Island Lake, tales of colorful cabins named after ladies, and Almond Crusted Walleye eaten at a lodge overlooking the lake. Thank you, Pat, for letting me be "lazy" while I relax and write on your deck every summer. Frank, your boat conking out while we were out in the middle of the lake was perfect. Getting stranded was fodder for a great opening scene.

"If it were not for hope, the heart would break."
~ Thomas Fuller ~

*"As I was wandering over the green
Not knowing where I went,
By chance I saw a pleasant scene -
The cottage of content."*

Chapter 1

The wave hit the boat hard on the port and disappeared into a frothing swirl of white. Tommy Love tightened his life vest and squinted at the pastel-colored cabins scattered along the beach and in the forest off the starboard side. "That's the place?" he yelled over the wind.

"Yep. Rainbow Lake Lodge," Billy yelled back as the motor strained to beat off the whitecaps slapping at the bow.

Tommy peered through the haze of pine and birch trees blocking his view of the top of the hill and felt a surge of joy. He'd been dreaming of building a house in a spot like this since he was a kid stuck in a trailer house on the edge of Miller's Swamp.

Now, it was finally going to happen. He shielded his eyes against the sunshine, but all he could see was a part of the roof. Not that it mattered. Billy had assured him the old lodge was nothing a bulldozer wouldn't take care of in quick order, and he'd already had an architect look at aerial and topographical maps so he could draw up tentative plans for the house he planned to build on the site. Still, he was curious. The pastel, rainbow colors she'd used on the cabins were a little too cutesy for his taste – thankfully she hadn't painted the cedar and stone cabin by the water. "Come in a little closer, Billy. I want to see if the cabin nearest the lake is big enough to convert to a boathouse."

"Hope might be home," Billy said. "What if she sees me? Or recognizes you?"

For starters, maybe he could stop feeling like he was sneaking around and make the woman an honest offer – face to face. "You're sure there's no way this Hope person can make a go of the place?"

Billy tried to bring the boat around. "Not if God Almighty himself came down to earth and managed her finances."

Tommy ignored the pin pricking his conscience and tried to picture himself relaxing in his very own Finnish sauna or sitting in his leather recliner, his guitar cradled in his arms, with one of northern

Minnesota's most picturesque views to inspire him. It had been years since a parcel of land this big – this private – had come on the market anywhere in the vicinity of Embarrass, Minnesota. It was perfect.

Except for the smidgen of guilt in the back of his brain. Tommy Love and the Love Notes was practically synonymous with making women's dreams come true. It wasn't in his nature to dash anyone's hopes. But this wasn't a normal situation. Billy had crunched the numbers – if he said there was no way this Hope woman could hang on to the place, then Tommy was inclined to trust it was so. Hope Anderson was going to lose the place one way or the other – he'd be a fool to let something he'd been dreaming of since he was a kid slip through his fingers because he felt sorry for the woman. No sense both of them being frustrated.

"Don't worry about Hope Anderson," Billy said, fussing with the throttle. "Once she gives up this unrealistic dream of renovating the lodge, she'll be free to move on and do something useful with her life."

"I'd like her to have an extra ten grand over market value. Can you do that?"

Billy looked pained, but he nodded, took another swig of beer and burped like it didn't bother him. "She'll be fine. With that kind of money she could go back to school and get trained to do something she'd be good at. You know. Like a school teacher, or a nurse."

"There's a huge demand for nurses," Tommy said, trying to put a positive spin on the woman being forced from her home. "They can practically set their own salaries. And live in whatever part of the country they want to."

"She wouldn't need any training to work at the nursing home in Embarrass," Billy said. "They're always hiring – caretakers, aides, cooks, people to do laundry. Those kinds of jobs come naturally to a woman."

Yeah. At minimum wage. Tommy felt a flicker of pity. He was starting to wonder if Billy was telling him the whole story or if the truth was a little more complex than his old friend had let on. He knew Billy and the board of directors at Embarrass National Bank planned to call the Anderson woman's note, which would force her to sell. As Tommy's Realtor, Billy stood to make a hefty commission on the resale. Unless her loan balance was a lot steeper that lending ratios typically allowed, Hope Anderson would walk away with a lot of money when he plunked down market value for Rainbow Lake Lodge.

His eye caught the flash of a blue jay flying from the shoreline, up the hill, closer to the buildings. "It looks like she's done a lot of work on the cabins already. You're sure she can't turn things around?"

"There's no way she can run this place all by herself. If the resort wasn't out in the middle of nowhere, if the Andersons had left the place in decent shape when they died, she might – might – have pulled it off." Billy steered a little closer to the beach. "But the way things stand – the insurance money she got when her husband died is long gone. If it weren't for that old outhouse, she wouldn't have a pot to – "

"I get the picture. Turn around and make one more pass, will you?" Tommy said. "It's hard to get the lay of the land from this perspective."

"She can see the lake from the lodge. She's gonna get suspicious if we keep doubling back." Billy cut the throttle and let the boat float as free as the choppy surf would allow.

"I just want to check out the –"

"There she is," Billy said, pressing the starter and frantically urging the boat away from shore.

She was walking down the path to the cabin closest to the shore, her long hair fluttering around her face in the wind. "She's holding on to something," Tommy said, squinting. "Looks like a shovel."

"Turn around," Billy hissed at him. "If she sees you –"

"She probably doesn't even know who I am," Tommy said.

"Yeah, right," Billy said, riding the waves like a cowboy on a bull as he steered the boat against the wind. "She grew up in the eighties right along with all the other screaming teeny-boppers who were always hot on your trail."

There hadn't been a groupie on his tail since he turned forty, and that was eight years ago. As for teeny-boppers... "Middle-aged housewives and grumpy old men would be a lot closer to the truth," Tommy said, wishing that he were still a star and not a hitless has-been. Like it or not, his fans were getting old. The baby-boomers who'd loved his music as teen-agers and young adults would be dying off faster than fruit flies before long. That's why he needed a new hit. A strong, up beat, cross-generational, mega hit that would make today's teens love him as much as their parents had, way back when.

He glanced back at the shore. Hope had her hand to her brow, watching the boat. He could understand why this Hope woman would want to stay on at Rainbow Lake Lodge even though she'd lost her husband – she might not have any money, but she must have a lot of memories wrapped up in the place.

Did that make it wrong for him to want the one thing stardom hadn't given him? He lived in one of the biggest mansions in Nashville, but he'd never really had a home. He had a star on Hollywood Boulevard, but no children to carry on his name; a list of friends who read like the nominations on Grammy night, but no family; a staff to cater to his every whim, but no one to love.

A rogue wave slapped the bow. Tommy grabbed the gunnels and held on. All he really wanted was to have a place to call home again.

Billy looked over his shoulder, revved the engine, and bucked as the front of the boat surged into the air. "She's looking at us. She's coming this way."

"You're going to bounce me out of the boat or tip the thing over if you're not careful," Tommy yelled. "It's gonna be hard writing a new hit single if I'm at the bottom of a lake blowing bubbles."

"It could ruin everything if she sees us out here. It's not like we can pretend we're out for a swim. It's October. It's freezing cold," Billy yelled back.

Tommy watched as Hope Anderson waved at the boat in a neighborly sort of way. Billy was beating such a quick get-away that she was a mere speck on the shoreline by the time he pried his fingers from the gunnels, raised his arm and waved back.

"It's for her own good," Billy said. "She just doesn't know it yet."

"She ought to be able to do anything she wants with the money she'll make," Tommy said, trying to soothe his conscience. "I'm sure I could make her see that if I just had a chance to talk to her."

"I told you I'd take care of it," Billy grumbled, easing off the throttle once they were far enough from the shoreline.

"I'm not out to hurt anyone." *Was it his fault that he had the wherewithal to make his dream a reality and she didn't?*

"Why don't we drive over to the airport and take a spin in your plane? Fly over the property once or twice," Billy said.

"Good plan."

Billy grunted and turned the boat to the west. "I think I'll head back to the shoreline where it's not so choppy. It'll take a little longer to get back, but we'll have a smoother ride."

Tommy grabbed the gunnels, anticipating the surge of power that would rock the boat when Billy cranked up the throttle.

Nothing happened.

"Is something wrong?" Tommy asked.

"The engine died," Billy said. He turned the key. The engine sputtered and coughed. He fiddled with the choke, pulled out the throttle and waited for the engine to kick in.

Nothing. The boat listed toward the shore, then bobbed back toward the center of the lake, caught in a current, pushed by the wind.

Billy tried to start the engine again. And again. And again.

"I smell gas." Tommy scanned the horizon. They hadn't seen another boat the whole time they'd been out on the lake. Nobody else was dumb enough to be out on a day like today.

Billy punched the starter. The boat responded with an ominous whine.

"The check engine light is on." Billy fumbled around in his pocket and pulled out his cell phone. "No signal."

"Grab an oar." Tommy ordered, picking up the first of the pair and stabbing it into the water. "We can row her in."

"In these waves?"

"We have to try!" But after a few seconds, he could see it was futile.

"I've never had any trouble with this boat," Billy said, fussing with the starter again. The whines had faded to a series of snapping, crackling, and popping noises – the kind that didn't leave a good taste in your mouth.

"We're dead in the water," Billy said.

"You've got to be kidding."

"I can't believe this is happening." Billy slammed his fist against the steering wheel.

"Did you tell anyone we were coming out here?" Tommy asked.

Silence from Billy. Plenty of noise from the waves crashing into the boat.

"We have to do something," Tommy said. "We could be out here all night."

"The lodge is the only place anywhere near the water on this side of the lake."

Exactly the reason he wanted to buy the place. "You'd better pray that this Anderson woman can hear me when I start yelling," Tommy said.

"I'd rather freeze to death that let that woman rescue me. Assuming she even knows how to start a boat."

"What would you suggest?" Tommy said, wondering how much worse the weather might get before someone discovered them.

"We'll drift ashore eventually," Billy said, kicking the steering wheel.

The boat was drifting – but not toward shore.

"Right. An uninhabited, bear-infested island in the middle of nowhere." Tommy said.

"Be quiet so I can think," Billy said.

"There's nothing to think about. It was twenty-five degrees when I woke up this morning and the wind is getting stronger by the minute. We have to do something."

Chapter 2

Hope jabbed her spade into the crumbly soil, scooped out two heaping cupfuls of dirt, and dropped in a daffodil bulb. She was tamping the earth back into place when she heard something – or thought she did. The wind had really been howling for the last hour or so.

She pulled her hat down over her ears and sank her blade into a spot about four inches to the right. Normally, she wouldn't be outside when the weather was so raw, but this time of year, the term *nice weather* was relative. When you knew that things were only going to get worse, it made sense to take advantage of every "semi-nice" day you were fortunate enough to be blessed with.

She lifted her head and tilted her ear in the direction the wind was coming from. There it was again. Or was it? During the last month there had been sightings of bear, moose, even a cougar nearby. She hoped it wasn't a wounded animal.

She'd probably imagined it. She sang a few bars of *How Great is Our God* and tried not to jump when a cluster of brittle leaves skittered across the yard in a wild frenzy of motion. It was almost as though summertime knew its time was at an end and was mourning out loud.

She dropped a tulip bulb into the next hole with a renewed sense of urgency. Much as she loved living at Rainbow Lake Lodge, there were times when being all alone, out in the middle of nowhere, was a little frightening. As if to prove her point, the wind stopped to catch its breath. For a second, it was so quiet she could hear her own heartbeat.

Dig, scoop, drop, pat. There were only a few more bulbs in her basket. If she could put up with the wind for a few more minutes, the job would be done.

She stopped to make sure her hole was dug to exactly the right depth, made a circle of six crocus bulbs, and checked to make sure she had the pointy ends up. These were precious bulbs. They were going to grow, and she was going to be here to enjoy the blossoms, and that was that. There was no way she was going to let Billy Bjorklund take

Rainbow Lake Lodge away from her after all she – and David – had done to save it.

If she'd known the bank was going to cut off her funding, she never would have spent fifty dollars on something as frivolous as a little spring color. But she hadn't known, and she had the bulbs, and they weren't going to do anybody any good in the bag.

"Help!"

This time, the sound was unmistakable.

"Help!!"

A jolt of adrenalin shot through her muscles as she scrambled to her feet and looked toward the lake.

A boat. Probably the same one she'd seen earlier. She shielded her eyes and saw someone standing at the bow waving what looked like a white flag. Without stopping to think, she flew down the hill to the dock, jumped on board and untied David's speedboat.

The engine turned over the first time. Thank God. She'd tried to keep the boat up just like David would have. It had been his pride and joy. The boat bobbed wildly in the choppy waves as she nudged it away from the dock and pointed the bow in the direction of the other boat.

She had strapped on her lifejacket and had just cleared the dock when she hit the first white cap. A spray of water drenched the back of the boat. The person in the other boat was waving and trying to communicate with her, but she couldn't hear a word he was saying over the roar of her engine – and the wind.

Wave after wave slammed against the hull of the boat, her back slapping against the boat with one sickening thud after another as she headed in his direction. The wind felt even wickeder than it had on land. She hated being out on the water in weather like this - if Sharon had come out yesterday like she'd intended, she'd have had the boat out of the water already. But she hadn't, and someone was in trouble. What choice did she have but to go to their rescue?

That was when she caught a glimpse of what looked like a second man – or woman – hunched in the bottom of the boat. Her pulse quickened and a shiver ran down her spine. What was she getting into? She hoped someone hadn't been injured. She'd assumed all they needed was a simple tow. Now she wondered if she should have taken the time to go back to the lodge and call for help, or grab the radio. David never would have...

"Thank you!" The wind blew the man's voice across the waves.

She couldn't see much of the man's face thanks to his hat and sunglasses, but she could see that he was tall and broad shouldered. His khakis and leather jacket looked a bit out of place with a lifejacket over the top, but all in all, he looked respectable enough. Still, she felt wary as she cut the throttle and eased her boat within eight or ten feet of theirs. She didn't dare get any closer – both boats were rocking so wildly that subtle movements were next to impossible.

"The engine stalled," the man shouted over the din.

The other boat bobbed helplessly in the water. She fought to keep hers from ramming it. She motioned in the direction of the person in the back of the boat and tried to ask what was wrong, but the wind snatched her words away faster than she could spit them out.

"Seasick," the first man said.

She nodded and tried to maneuver away from his boat's erratic movements. "If you turn the key back on, you'll be able to steer even though the engine's dead."

He nodded and went to the driver's seat.

She threw him one end of a sturdy rope. "Tie it off. Do you have the anchor down?" They may have tried to secure their position, but the water was so deep in this part of the lake that the boat was likely adrift either way.

The man lopped the towline around a sturdy hook at the bow and yanked in the anchor.

"Where did you put in?" She yelled and hoped the wind carried her voice far enough for him to hear.

The man motioned to the east.

The only thing in that direction was the public access. Figured. No one who lived on the lake would be stupid enough to be out in weather like this. She eased the throttle back and bucked as the weight of the other boat strained against the taut line.

The lead creaked and groaned but held. Thank God! She began the arduous task of slowly towing them in, praying that the line was strong enough to survive the pull of the waves and the weight of the boat.

"Steer into my wake," she yelled, trying to ease her fears with a show of bravado. She'd never really rescued anyone before, although she'd been along when David had - certainly not in this kind of weather.

One more thing she could put on her mental resume of things she'd learned to do on her own. Not that being out on the lake in gale force winds was something she'd dreamed of doing. Crazy people. They'd be lucky if they didn't get them all drowned. The dock was still a half-mile off and anything could happen in a wind like this. If the line snapped, the force of the break could make the line ricochet back with enough speed to slice through a leg or an arm as easily as a knife through butter.

"Thanks," the man in the other boat yelled across the waves, the wind snatching half his words. "We would... cold by morning."

"Yes." She nodded in case he hadn't heard her, and squinted into the sun. There was something so familiar about the man.

"You live around here?" she yelled.

He shook his head no, maybe because he didn't, maybe because he hadn't heard what she'd asked. If he said more, she couldn't make out his words. With the glare of the sun in her eyes, it was hard to tell if he had even tried to answer.

She shrugged her shoulders and reluctantly turned her attention to navigating the boat toward the other side of the cove. Her arm muscles were already screaming from trying to keep the boat on course. "Keep me safe, Lord," she whispered, hoping it would calm her nerves.

She glanced over her shoulder and saw the man struggling to follow the winding path she was cutting through the water. It might have been a fun ride in the sun back in late July, but on this cold October morning, it dragged on dangerous, tedious foot after foot until they reached the dock.

The dock. She hated this part. The timing was so tricky it had even made David nervous. She'd hated even being in the boat when David had done it, charging toward the dock like a mad steer, waiting until the last second to swing around.

Her hands shook and she gripped the wheel until her knuckles were white. What was she trying to prove anyway? She should have called the sheriff, told him there was a boat in trouble out on the lake, finished planting her daffodils, and gone inside for a hot shower instead of storming into the middle of God-only-knew-what like she was some sort of Wonder Woman.

She held tightly to the steering wheel, craned her neck around and prayed he could hear her. "Unhook the tow line when I swing around. Okay?"

He nodded and grabbed the knob where the boats were joined. She cut the engine and yelled over her shoulder to make sure he understood. "It will only go slack for a second. Don't get your hands tangled in the line." If he hooked toward the dock and didn't undo the towline in time, their boat would crash into the pier, and hard.

The two boats were close enough that she could see he was as green to the procedure as she was. Comforting thought. But this was the way it had to be unless he wanted to swim to shore. And the man definitely wasn't dressed for a dip. He wasn't even dressed for boating.

She said a prayer, gunned the engine and headed straight for the shore. The dock rushed toward her like a freight train, except that she was the one who was moving, maybe too fast, maybe too slow. How was she supposed to know? She nodded, yelled "Now", and pulled sharply to the left. A second later, she felt the line go slack. She cut her speed and turned to watch as the other boat glided toward shore. The man reached for a piling, lopped a rope around the post and jumped onto the dock.

She cut the engine. "We did it!" she yelled, her voice shaking almost as much as her hands.

"Man, am I glad you heard me!" he called back, still sounding oddly familiar. "Will you be okay?"

"I'll be careful." Funny - he didn't look like anyone she knew from town, yet she was almost sure she'd seen him before. Where? She hovered thirty feet or so off the shoreline until the stranger turned and waved one last time. The man in the bottom of the boat pulled what looked to be a plaid blanket around his neck but made no effort to climb out of the vessel.

She thought about them several times during the cold ride home. Her instincts told her that something fishy was going on. Why would anyone venture out on the lake in weather like this – on her end of the lake in particular? She certainly hoped it had nothing to do with Billy Bjorklund.

She looked across the lake to the lodge. No point in worrying about the unknown when there were so many known facts to fret about... for starters, unpaid utility bills, a kitchen that didn't meet code, a litany of unfinished jobs, and a bank that no longer believed in her.

She cut the engine when the dock was close and let the boat drift along side until it bumped into the old tires lining the edge. The first winter after David's accident, some men from church had taken care of getting everything ready for winter. She'd headed back to Virginia to spend some time with her great aunt Myrtle. The second winter, she'd managed on her own with a little help from Sharon. This year's unseasonably warm weather had lulled her into lethargy. She should have had the boat out of the water, her wood cut and stacked, and her bulbs planted by now.

She tied off the boat, climbed out and looked up the hill to the lodge. The flowers she'd planted would look wonderful from the water come spring, assuming the deer didn't eat them first... and that she was still here to see them.

"Welcome home," she whispered. If she could just make it until spring... She could hardly wait to see her daffodils in bloom, to see the lodge bustling with life again. Seeing the resort come alive with children, families, and activity again was the whole reason she and David had worked so many hundreds of hours to renovate the place. Reopening Rainbow Lake Lodge was the only way she knew to preserve David's legacy.

If Rose Bjorklund had remained in control of Embarrass National Bank, she never would have allowed any of this to happen. And Billy... well, Billy Bjorklund could go eat worms. There was no way, no how she was going to let him chase her away from her only remaining tie to David and his parents. Not now. Not ever.

Chapter 3

"So that's the widow who's in so far over her head that she doesn't know which way the sun sets?" Tommy yanked the blanket away from Billy and pulled him to his feet. "She seems pretty competent to me."

"So she knows how to drive a boat." Billy leaned over the side of the dock and coughed. "Stupid blanket's covered in dog hair. Brian always used to take his mutt out on the boat before he moved to California. Idiotic –"

"I hate feeling like I'm doing something underhanded," Tommy said. "Why can't we drive up to her front door, ask to see the place, and make the woman a reasonable offer?"

"Trust me," Billy said. "This may seem cut and dried to you but it's a lot more complicated than that."

"I'd like to understand," Tommy said, planting his feet in the middle of the dock.

"Fine. Take a crash course in banking and finance law and we'll talk."

"Or, maybe I should find myself another realtor - one who doesn't work for the bank. Maybe then we can talk."

"You wouldn't even know about this place if it weren't for me," Billy said, swooshing his arm like it was no big deal. "If I hadn't told you this place was coming up for sale, you wouldn't have stood a chance of getting it. Places like Rainbow Lake Lodge never come on the market. You know it and I know it. They're sold to someone with connections to the seller or to the banker long before the news ever goes public."

"So I owe you one. That doesn't mean we should have to sneak around, acting like fugitives, hiding under blankets–"

"There are protocols of banking that I have to observe," Billy said. "Rules, regulations, timelines set down by the government – that I have to follow whether I like it or not."

"So it's the government's fault that Hope Anderson can't know that I'm interested in her property."

"No," Billy said, throwing his arm around Tommy's shoulder and guiding him toward dry land. "It's yours. This is a very delicate situation. Under any other circumstances, I never would have involved a buyer at this stage of the game. But you live in Nashville, you happened to have a concert at Indian Bay and you said you wouldn't be back up this way until spring."

Fine. So Billy had done him a favor. A few favors. Well, quite a few. He still had to live with himself.

"Hey – we've been friends since, what, third grade?" Billy said, patting him on the back. "You know me better than my own mother does. There's no way I'd ever steer you wrong."

Tommy shoved his hands into the pockets of his leather bomber and let his shoulders relax. Billy's attitude about certain things - women, for one - might be a little archaic, but he'd always been an astute financial advisor and he shared his family's longstanding reputation as an excellent banker.

"Trust me," Billy said, walking up the hill to the wooded lot where they'd left his pick-up and the trailer for the boat. "I know what needs to happen and when it needs to come down. Go back to Nashville, do your thing with Vince and the boys, forget about Hope Anderson and leave all this to me. That's what I'm here for."

"I'll get the truck." Tommy stretched his hand toward Billy, who dropped the keys into his open palm. Billy could spout all the platitudes in the world, but if Tommy wasn't absolutely convinced things were on the level by the time they wrapped things up at Billy's office, he'd ditch Billy, rev up the Porsche, and head out to Rainbow Lake Lodge to get the real story from Hope Anderson. In the flesh.

"Sure." Billy punched him playfully in the arm. "Back the trailer down into the water just as far as you can."

Tommy climbed behind the steering wheel of Billy's truck and conjured up an image of Hope Anderson that was the best he could do given the fact that he'd only gotten to see her from a distance. She was smiling, thanking him for being the impetus she'd needed to move on. *Leaving Rainbow Lake Lodge had been painful for her at first,* she said in a soothing tone, *but now that a couple of years had gone by, she felt nothing but gratitude that he and Billy had had the foresight to force her hand.*

Chapter 4

Hope peered through the maze of branches outside her front window and watched for Sharon's Dodge Ram. The woods were generally so quiet that she could hear vehicles approaching from half a mile away. Not today. The winds had quieted down a little since earlier when she'd been out on the lake, but they were still whipping up a storm. She could feel it in the air.

She finally heard a car jostling over the potholes in her driveway. She'd planned to have a few loads of crushed rock delivered before winter, but that was going to have to wait until she got things straightened out with the bank.

Sharon's car came into view and Hope frowned. *What was Sharon thinking?* She grabbed a sweater, swung open the front door and met her at the bottom of the steps. "There's no way the armoire is going to fit in your Hyundai."

Sharon wouldn't even look her in the eye. "I've been trying to say this nicely all week, but you won't listen. I simply do not feel comfortable dragging away an heirloom that's been in your family for over two hundred years."

"I'm sorry if I'm putting you in an awkward position. But as I keep telling you, I'm going to need the space for tables and chairs when I reopen," Hope said, trying to sound unscathed even though she was about to sell something that was so precious to her it hurt. "Wait. I'll get a tape measure. Maybe the hatch is bigger than it looks."

Hope had never been good at bluffing. She supposed having an honest face was a good thing – unless you were trying to keep the whole town from finding out about your problems.

"The armoire is not going to fit in the car," Sharon said, walking up the steps to the massive log-and-stone structure that was Rainbow Lake Lodge. "Even if it would, I'm not taking it."

"I have to leave room for the dance floor and a juke box, and a play area for the kids..."

"So put it in your bedroom," Sharon said. "It would be a great place to store your sweaters."

"I never should have lugged it all the way up here in the first place," Hope said, pulling out the top drawer. "Grandma would be mortified if she knew I'd carted her prized antebellum period armoire up north to this old pole shed. I should have sold it to that dealer in Charleston when I had the chance."

"So it doesn't match your North Woods decor. It's the only thing you have that belonged to your mother's family. You told me you were never going to part with it."

"That was then. This is now," Hope said, thinking even as the words came out of her mouth that those six short words had to be the understatement of the decade. Everything – everything – had changed the day David had gone for a joy ride in his trusty old Coupe de Ville and come home in a casket.

She grabbed the next drawer down and pulled it free. "It's all cleaned out and ready to go. You can take the drawers and come back for the chest later."

"Call the bank and talk to Billy if you need money," Sharon said. "Construction loans are supposed to cover your expenses until you start generating income."

"My loan is for business expenses," Hope said. "Maybe I want some new clothes. Maybe I've decided to get away from here and spend the winter someplace warm. Maybe I'd like to go on a cruise."

"Yeah, right," Sharon said, picking up the drawer and sliding it back into its slot.

Hope grabbed the brass pull and yanked it out again. Sharon could have been a great ice fisherman if she'd been so inclined. Her technique was flawless. First, she bored a little hole through the ice. Then she dropped her line, dangled the bait, and kept fishing for answers until you bit.

Why Hope had ever thought she could keep her business to herself in this town was beyond her. "Billy notified me yesterday that as far as the bank is concerned, construction came to a halt when the Justinen Brothers moved their trailer into town and started pouring the foundation for the Hansen's new house. Which means my first loan payment is due. Now."

"The little weasel. He knows very well you can't open until spring."

"Everybody knowing everything around here is half the problem." Hope slid out another drawer.

"I thought the Justinens were going to come back and do your kitchen in March."

"They still are, assuming I can get things worked out with the bank." Hope snatched a dust rag and ran it over the drawer's back and sides. The rich mahogany was as butter smooth as the day it had been built. "Which puts me between a rock and a hard place. The health department won't let me reopen until the kitchen meets code."

"Billy's up to something." Sharon grabbed the top drawer again. "We may have been divorced for twenty years, but I still know how his mind works."

"There are some things you just never forget," Hope said.

"Maybe he has a buyer." Sharon still had a vice grip on the drawer. "It would explain why he's so eager to see you default on your loan. Just think of the money he'd pocket if he foreclosed, then found someone with money enough to pay market value for this much lake-front property."

"There were two men out on the lake in a boat earlier today."

"In this wind?" Sharon said.

"The wind didn't come up until about ten. Still..." She went on to tell Sharon about her efforts to rescue them. "I couldn't see them all that well, but the one that was driving was all dressed up. It's too late for tourists and the only people who aren't at work in the middle of the day are retirees. This guy looked more like a business man than a boater. And he was too young to be retired."

"Don't underestimate Billy," Sharon said, forgetting the drawer. "The man thinks he's so high and mighty that he can do whatever he wants and get away with it."

"Yeah, well, thank goodness Billy only thinks he's the one controlling my future." *Please Lord. Please send me a banker who will take a chance on me.*

"I know God is looking at the big picture as far as your future," Sharon said. "But Billy can make your life pretty miserable in the here and now if he wants to. Maybe if you talked to Rose..."

Her relationship with the bank had been excellent until Rose's son, Billy, took over. Billy's actions had been totally contrary to the way his mother had always treated her. "I tried. The head teller said Mrs. Bjorklund has stepped down as president and moved into the nursing home."

"When did that happen?" Sharon almost dropped the drawer.

"No idea," Hope reclaimed possession of the drawer. "I also telephoned banks in Hibbing, Ely, and Virginia, but no one seems interested in talking to me. Which, sadly, makes sense. Billy's father loaned David's parents the money to open the Lodge forty years ago. Everyone at the local bank knows how hard working and motivated I am, and how popular the resort was – will be – once I reopen. If the Bjorklunds won't trust me with another few thousand dollars, why would someone in a big city where I'm completely unknown take such a risk?"

"There's got to be some other way to raise the money," Sharon said, not seeming to notice that Hope was halfway to the door. "Finding a job this time of year is going to be next to impossible with half the places in town closed for the winter."

"The nursing home is always looking for more help."

"The roads are so iffy this time of year that you'd have to rent a place in town to make sure you could make it in for your shift," Sharon said.

"With the wages they pay, I wouldn't even earn enough to cover the cost of an efficiency apartment." Hope took another drawer and carried it to the door.

"Maybe God's trying to tell you something here," Sharon said. "Like maybe it's time to call it quits."

"I can't believe you'd say that." She could see Sharon diving for the drawer at the precise moment she lunged for the keys to the Hyundai. Pain sliced through her finger. She yanked her hand back like she'd been bit. A sliver.

"I know this place means everything to you, Hope."

Right. Hope didn't expect Billy Bjorklund to understand why she felt compelled to keep Rainbow Lake Lodge – that she hadn't given David the son he'd wanted, or the Andersons the namesake they'd longed for – that keeping Rainbow Lake Lodge open was the only way she knew to honor the man she loved. But Sharon... Sharon, of all people, should have known.

She steeled her voice and her resolve. "How much do you think you can get for the armoire?"

Sharon eyed the vaulted beams and floor-to-ceiling windows. "If you're lucky, enough to cover your next utility bill."

Yeah, well, she'd worry about the next one as soon as she figured out a way to pay the last two.

Hope turned away before Sharon could see how embarrassed she was. Getting the disconnect notice was the first clue she'd had that something was wrong. The bank was supposed to have advanced her enough to cover all her utility bills.

Sharon slid the bottom drawer back into the armoire and went to retrieve another. "Sweetie, I don't want to see it happen any more than you do, but you may have to sell this place. Getting the lodge renovated is only half the battle. Operating costs are astronomical between insurance, electricity, and ongoing maintenance, even at my little antique shop. And you're going to need employees. It took the Andersons, you and David, and at least four part-time people to run this place in its heyday."

"I'm well aware—"

"You obviously wouldn't be borrowing from the bank unless David's life insurance money was gone," Sharon slapped another drawer into the frame of the armoire with a resounding clunk. "Without the support of the bank, you're at a dead end."

"Thanks for the vote of confidence."

"I am sorry. But I really think it's time you let go of the past and start looking ahead. This place would fetch a pretty penny with all the work you and David have already done. And when that happens, you're going to wish you still had your Grandma's armoire."

That was when Hope saw the envelope taped to the back of the last drawer. Four little words – For a rainy day – scribbled in David's still-familiar scrawl. She tore the envelope loose.

"Hope?"

One hundred, two hundred, three, four ... a thousand dollars in cash. *Oh, David!* It was so like him to keep looking after her, to go from being her knight in shining armor to her guardian angel.

Sharon's eyes darted from an old oil painting on the far wall to the Oriental rug under their feet. She got up, picked up a music box sitting on the bookshelf and opened the lid. "So where else haven't you dusted in the last two years?"

"David was always squirreling away tip money." The thought of David tucking the money away for safekeeping, never dreaming that he wouldn't be there to take it out and put it to use, was enough to break her heart all over again.

"So the armoire stays."

Hope stared wistfully at the heirloom and thought about how

much she'd already lost. "No. That part of my life is history. If I'm going to make it through the winter, I'll need to pay the bank what I can as a good-faith promise. The rest will go to the utility company. A thousand dollars helps, but ultimately, it's a tiny little drop in a very deep bucket."

"What then?"

"Talk to Billy again. Try to renegotiate my loan. Sell off anything I can't live without. Pray for another miracle."

"You're sure?"

"They're estimating fifty thousand for remodeling the kitchen and buying the new stainless steel equipment I need to install."

"You've got more guts than I do," Sharon said, giving up.

"Please try and get as much for it as you can – without taking too long." There – she'd swallowed what she had left of her pride and survived.

"Speaking of..." Sharon looked out the window at the lake. "I know we were going to take the boat out of the water today, but I'm afraid if I don't go now, I'll get stranded out here. The revised forecast sounds horrible."

Thank God for the weather – safe, impersonal topic that it was. "I haven't had the radio on."

"Yesterday's storm hit Lake Superior, stalled, and is now swirling back in our direction. And there's a Canadian Clipper coming through that's going to drop the temperature by thirty degrees." Sharon tightened her jacket.

"That explains the wind." Hope picked up a drawer and headed toward the door. Lord, what was she going to do? Fuel oil and electricity were at all-time highs.

She followed Sharon to her Hyundai and watched as she beeped the car door open. After David died, she'd started locking the doors to the lodge at night, but it had never even occurred to her to lock her car doors.

Sharon lifted her hatchback and Hope slid the drawer she was holding into the back as tenderly as she could.

This was it then. The armoire was lost. Try as she may to sugarcoat her situation, the truth had a way of slinking in and snapping your dreams like a tree branch weighted down with too much ice.

Sharon gave an anxious look to the sky. "I'll be back for the rest tomorrow if the weather holds. If not, I'll see you soon. It's supposed to be warm again next week. We can get the boat out of the water then."

She watched from the door as Sharon wove her way down the driveway. She was starting to feel like the ball in a foosball game, dodging this, dodging that, while everyone tried to kick her in the direction they thought she should go. Her only prayer was that Billy wouldn't be able to follow through on his threat to foreclose until spring. But even then...

Chapter 5

Tommy Love tilted the rear view mirror so he could see himself, swept a loose strand of mostly blond hair away from his temples, and put both hands back on the steering wheel just in time to round a curve. He'd bought the Porsche new in 1983 at the tender age of twenty to celebrate his first platinum record. The old girl might be a little over the hill as cars went, but her ride was still as smooth as silk - even doing eighty-five.

He slowed and glanced at the bright colors dotting the side of the road for just a second before he put the pedal to the floor again. The birch trees were an amazing shade of gold. The sugar maples were a faded red - well past their prime, but still prettier than anything he'd seen since he was a kid.

He glanced in the mirror again. His eyes had always been his best feature – probably still were. "Eyes that make women melt", *Rolling Stone* magazine had said about a millennium ago. Stupid gray hairs. He'd have to buy more Just For Men as soon as he got out of Embarrass.

Tommy flicked on the radio. Nothing but static. There were all kinds of dead zones out in the boonies. He had a couple of CDs in his bag, but the Porsche only had a cassette tape player. He sighed. Knowing he was two decades older than a car that was considered "vintage" did nothing for his ego, but he wasn't ready to concede defeat just yet. He spun around a corner and narrowly dodged a pair of white-tailed deer bounding across the road. Like his car, he was just beginning to hit his stride.

A wave of excitement washed over him as he urged the car to go even faster. By this time next year, his dream house would be built, and he'd be on the lake in time to see every last leaf turning. If what Billy said was correct, he'd be able to view the whole spectacular show from his deck.

He flipped his cell phone open, checked his bars and pushed a button to connect him to his attorney / agent / accountant, using his right arm to steer the car over a hill and around a curve that would have been lazy if he hadn't been going so fast.

"Jack?" He started to talk without waiting for an answer.

"Tom? Come again. You're breaking up."

He repeated his directions to sell 500 shares of stock twice. He wanted to have cash at the ready in case Billy called about the resort.

"Tom? I'm only getting about every sixth word. Can you..."

His phone made an unfamiliar chirp and he glanced down long enough to see that the call had been dropped. So being tucked away from the world had its drawbacks. Once he closed on his property, he might have to build his own cell phone tower.

He glanced up at the sky. The sun had slipped behind a dark bank of clouds, but the sky looked clear in the west. If he delayed flying out until the squall passed, he'd have a smoother time heading south. Why have your own plane if you didn't use it to indulge your whims once in a while?

He gave a quick thought to Billy. He had promised him he'd stay away from the Lodge, but then, he doubted Billy had been exactly honest about a few things, either. He looked at the sky again and decided he needed to do this one way or the other – to set his conscience at ease if nothing else. If the Anderson woman was as in-over-her-head as Billy claimed – if the lodge truly was irredeemable – he'd be able to confirm that with a quick perusal of the property.

He preferred not to have to speak to Hope Anderson, especially now that it was very likely she would recognize him from the debacle on the lake. If worse came to worse and he ran into her, he'd figure out something. He put Hope Anderson and her rainbow-colored cabins out of his mind and thought about the way the water looked lapping on the sandy shoreline of his property-to-be.

He veered away from the turnoff to the Ely airport and headed south toward Rainbow Lake Lodge. He and Billy had flown over the lake as many times as they could without arousing suspicion, but the land was so heavily forested that he still hadn't been able to get a true feel for the breadth and width of the place. Out of respect to Billy, he didn't want to alert Hope Anderson that something was in the wind until Billy had done what he needed to do down at the bank, but he really wanted to have an up-close and personal look at the place before he left town.

His tires squealed as he rounded another corner. The road ahead was wet – the forecast he'd heard last night had said nothing about showers. The sliver of sunshine peeking out from between the clouds twinkled and winked at him as if to say "not to worry". Which seemed very fitting – for the first time in a long while everything finally felt right with the world.

A splattering of florescent red maple leaves against a shimmer of yellow and a smoky green fir caught his eye. It had taken him eight homes in six states to realize it, but his heart was - had always been – in northern Minnesota.

He wanted this so badly he could taste it. He'd made a lot of money living in Nashville, Santa Fe, and L.A, but now it was time to come home. He hadn't been able to write for years – in his heart, he believed that this place was the key to unlocking his creativity. Was it so wrong to want one last big hit? To be somebody to someone? Well, a few million someones if the song made Billboard's Top Ten list. He needed this – one last song – a song that would fix his name in the hearts of a new generation.

He tried the radio again, just in case, hoping to hear an updated weather report. He twisted the knob, got a weak signal, turned up the volume and tried to make out what the announcer was saying. *Stupid static.* He was really starting to notice how negatively background noise affected his ability to hear. He was nearing fifty and fading as fast as the last few leaves clinging to the maple trees. That's why he was so determined to make this work. A new song would generate one last blaze of glory; prove that he'd done his very best with the gifts God had blessed him with. It just wasn't in his nature to go out on a low note.

He flicked on the defroster and squinted through the windshield. The windows appeared to be fogging up. Either that, or... What was happening? He'd checked weather.com on his wireless laptop several times in the last twenty-four hours and no one had mentioned precipitation.

The little wisps of moisture that had peppered the windshield seconds before became a thick slathering of syrupy sleet faster than he could flick the radio back on.

The speakers cackled incoherently.

He slowed his speed a little. Not too much. He needed to get back to civilization, and fast, before the roads became impassable. He'd grown up in Embarrass. He knew how to drive on slippery roads. But he didn't want to take chances in his Porsche.

He tried to relax. The dented, rusty old pick-up he'd driven as a teenager would have handled ice a lot better than the Porsche. With the wages three generations of Lubinski's had earned mining iron ore, he'd been lucky to have the old beast. Most weeks, they wouldn't even have had food on the table if it hadn't been for what he and his Dad had brought in hunting and fishing. They'd fished out of a squatter's shack his dad had built on the edge of a pathetically shallow waterway the locals called Little Leech Lake. Nobody ever bothered to chase them away because nobody else wanted to be there.

The memories only served to make him feel more elated about finding a piece of land where he could build his dream house. Buying a chunk of Northern Minnesota was all but impossible these days. Most people who had cabins, his friend, Billy included, had inherited them from their relatives. The National Forest Service or the state owned what wasn't already in the hands of third or fourth generation descendants.

The few lots that did come on the market were usually about twenty feet wide – fine if you were into being friendly with your neighbors. Tommy liked people just fine, but after living in the limelight for three decades, he also knew the importance of a little privacy. Okay – a lot of privacy. Seclusion even. Being around hordes of clamoring fans was fine as long as you knew you had a quiet place, far, far away from the racket to go to afterwards.

He leaned forward and slowed his rate of speed a little further. It was getting harder and harder to see. The windshield wipers weren't making a dent against the onslaught of the molten mixture of rain and ice slathering his car.

Memories of his father rumbled through his brain. If he'd listened to his old man when his first song hit the airwaves, he'd have invested in some land back in the eighties, when lakefront property in northern Minnesota had still been cheap. But all he'd cared then about was fast cars, faster women, and where his next case of beer was coming from. That, and getting far, far away from Embarrass, Minnesota.

Was that the turnoff? He slammed on the brakes and fishtailed to the left, afraid he'd missed the turn.

He peered out the window and tried to get his bearings. He hadn't seen the road sign, but then he hadn't seen much of anything since the blasted sleet had started coming down.

He clutched the steering wheel a little tighter and kept driving. He usually had good instincts about space and distance ratios, but creeping along so slowly had confused him.

He tried to relax his shoulders and hold the wheel as steadily as he could with one hand and flicked open the case of his cell phone with the other. He needed to let someone know where he was - just in case... Zero bars. He rounded another curve and glanced down at his phone. One bar – still not enough oomph to connect. All the more reason to keep his foot slow and steady and keep this baby on the road. If the sleet kept coming down the way it was for long, it could be hours, even days before anyone else ventured along this road. Assuming he was where he thought he was.

Panic clutched at his stomach. He should have told Jack where he was going. Billy would assume he'd flown out on schedule. He'd left his BMW at the airport in Minneapolis instead of arranging for a limo because he hadn't known when he was coming back. His staff would eventually wonder why they hadn't heard from him, but he'd always been erratic about checking in.

He wiped his concerns from the forefront of his brain about as effectively as his wipers were ridding the slick, thick coating of ice from his windshield, and tried to focus on driving. All he could think about was Hope Anderson.

His last thought before he missed the curve, slid off the road, and landed in a ditch half-full of water was that if Hope Anderson had any sense at all, she'd take his money, run, and live happily ever after... somewhere else.

Chapter 6

Hope pulled the curtain to one side and peered out the window. Her view of the driveway was all but blocked by trees – slender birches flirting with the wind, their shiny, golden tresses shimmering in the sunlight, and, closer to the lake, firs, swaying to the beat of the breeze like ladies in rich, lace-trimmed, green hoop skirts waiting at a ball. Until David had died, she'd thought Rainbow Lake Lodge was the most romantic place on earth.

Yesterday's winds had finally died down, but the forest was still buzzing with energy. It had sleeted late in the afternoon the day before and everything was coated with a thick layer of ice. It was too early in the season to be severely cold, but it had been as cold as it needed to be to turn rain to ice – and with it, a lovely Indian summer to winter.

The temperatures had dropped even further overnight, turning the last raindrops of the year from syrupy thick sleet to fluffy, white snow. It would have been mess enough without Superior's legendary winds whipping themselves to a fury.

She'd hardly slept all night what with worrying about David's boat still being in the water, flickering lights, and branches made stiff and icy by the sleet screeching eerily against her window. If the wind kept blowing, it was only a matter of time before the electrical wires that ran from telephone pole to telephone pole started snapping like overcooked peanut brittle from the weight of the ice. She was lucky the power hadn't already gone out.

She'd fretted about the ramifications of a potential power outage through much of the long, sleepless night. No danger of starving – she had a freezer full of meat. She'd stocked up, knowing there would be times this winter she wouldn't be able to get to town. The meat would stay solid for a day or two if she didn't open the freezer door, but any longer than that, and she'd lose hundreds of dollars worth of food. Her car might act as a temporary, bear-proof refrigerator, but it wasn't cold enough outside for her auto to do double duty as a freezer.

Stewing about things didn't get the work done. Her hands had been tied until the sun made its appearance, but now that it was up, she had tasks to attend to. She'd showered while it was still dark outside so her hair would have time to dry before she went out into the wind, not wanting the increasingly frequent power surges to fry her hairdryer. She'd filled every kettle, pitcher and bowl in the house with water while she waited. Once the electricity went, she would have no pump.

She looked back at the inviting haven of her bed, piled high with homemade quilts and wool blankets that her mother-in-law had kept in the cedar chests for decades so the moths wouldn't get at them, and turned to wrap herself up in sweater, coat, hat and mittens.

The sooner she got more firewood inside the house to dry off, and went out to fetch the mail she hadn't got yesterday afternoon because she hadn't wanted to go out in the freezing rain, the greater the likelihood that she'd still have heat to dry her and the firewood off when she came back inside.

She said a silent prayer that the new battery she'd ordered for the generator had come in yesterday's mail. Once the power went, it could be off for days, depending on how many wires snapped and how cold it was. The mailman definitely wouldn't be around again until the ice thawed, and from what the weatherman said, that could be a few, very long, very dark, cold days from now. She hadn't realized the old battery was bad until last week, when she'd tried to start it for a test run, just like David had taught her.

She edged the front door open, pulled her scarf around her neck a little tighter to ward off the chill, and stepped gingerly onto the front step.

Her feet flew out from under her and her tailbone hit the ground with a resounding clunk. "Ouch!" The word echoed through the forest and back again, as if chiding her for her foolishness in thinking she could make it through a north woods winter all alone. Even the birds seemed to agree; or were they simply scolding her for disrupting the peace?

Okay, so this was going to be more difficult than she had thought. She crept over to the sandbox. The swing set glimmered in its shiny coat of ice while she dug down through the powdery snow using an old beach pail and shovel that had probably been David's. The sandbox was frozen solid. If she'd had a pick ax and muscles, she might have been able to chip enough loose to sprinkle around the yard.

Standing gingerly, she trudged back through the footprints she'd made earlier. The snow was not the problem – the ice underneath was. Once she got on the gravel driveway, she hoped there would be enough bits of crushed rock poking through to make for a more solid footing. The driveway was almost a mile of twisting, turning path, winding its way through the forest. But she needed that battery. Assuming it was even there.

She quickened her step when she reached the gravel, hugging the side of the road where the frozen spikes of grass gave her the extra traction she needed to stay upright, and made it to the end of the driveway with only two more spills. If the wind hadn't been slapping the icy tree branches together with the force of a turbo fan, or if she had been naive enough to forget the high wires overhead were doing the same stiff, unnatural dance, she might have thought the winter wonderland that the storm had created beautiful.

The main road was blacktop, and couldn't have been more slippery if it had been purposely buffed for a Minnesota Wild hockey exhibition. The straightaway wasn't sheltered like her densely forested driveway, and wind had blown the road clear of most of the snow, leaving behind a frosty glaze that made the ice even more treacherous. She slipped and slid her way across the road without falling down. Barely.

That was when she heard the noise of an engine turning over. It sounded like it was somewhere to her right, but there was nothing in sight. The hum of what had sounded like a vehicle starting was all but drowned out by the whistle of the wind and the cackle of two high wires sparking as the wind buffeted them together. She looked at the mailbox, convinced herself she was dreaming, and pulled down the lid.

A few letters fluttered dismally as the wind invaded their cloistered hideaway. There were no packages. No battery. Which meant no generator. It was so discouraging that if the mailbox had been big enough for her, she would have crawled in, curled up in a ball, and waited out the storm away from the wind.

The wind stopped blowing on cue, almost as if to catch its breath before the next big gale. For a few seconds, her whole little world was absolutely, could-have-heard-a-pin-drop quiet.

That was when she heard the noise again. Not of an engine turning over, but the steady, unmistakable sound of an engine idling. A big engine, if her ears weren't playing tricks on her. A powerful engine. The noise ricocheted back and forth in her head and her vulnerability washed over her anew.

If David were alive, she wouldn't have walked out to the mailbox all by herself in such dangerous weather in the first place. He would gladly have gone himself, done it for her, insisted she stay safe and sound in the lodge.

As if to make her point, two brittle, ice-coated power lines slapped together as the wind resumed it's huffing, sending a shower of sparks down to the ground just inches from her feet.

David was dead. She was miles from the nearest neighbor. Someone was in a truck of some sort, somewhere close by. She looked around and saw nothing. They had to be in the ditch. Her stomach tightened and fear's fingers tickled her spine. There were many warm-hearted, do-anything-for-you-including-give-you-the-clothes-off-their-backs kind of folk that lived in the north woods. There were also loonies, people who liked living miles from everyone and everything for a reason.

She couldn't leave whoever was in the ditch stranded. Who knew how many days it would be before the roads were safe for rescue vehicles? There could be children in the car. They could be hurt, hungry, cold, or all three.

She thought of the thousand dollars cash she had left in an envelope on the kitchen table back at the lodge. She had to hope that whoever was in the ditch was someone she could trust. She squared her shoulders and walked toward the frustrated whir of the vehicle's engine.

Chapter 7

Tommy revved the engine just long enough to make sure the battery was charging, broke open his last package of ketchup, stretched back in his bucket seat and wondered how long he'd slept – long enough to stiffen up and half-freeze to death if his sore hips and chattering teeth were any indication.

Not a good situation. Old ketchup wasn't exactly what his personal trainer would have called a well-balanced meal. Nor was his car seat anywhere close to the king sized, Swedish memory-foam mattress he was used to. But he'd stayed dry and made it through the night – that was the important thing. He held his fingers in front of the heater vent and thanked God there was still enough gas to warm him up one last time.

He slipped out his cell phone to check the time. Great. The battery was dead. Not that it mattered much when the bars were at zero. But he'd hoped that this morning, when he set out walking, that if he didn't find a house first, that he'd find some magic spot where he would have reception strong enough to make a call. He didn't know exactly where he was, but he figured he was still somewhere in the vicinity of Rainbow Lake. Around here, one curve in the road could make all the difference.

That was when he heard the shuffling noise outside the car. He'd listened to the sounds of the sleet pelting the car, the howl of the wind, the utter stillness of fresh snow falling, falling, and still falling as the night had droned on. This sound was entirely different. There was someone, or something, outside the car.

He sat up a little straighter and tried to scrape away the frost and fog that had accumulated on the inside of the window. First choice was a hot babe with a big SUV – one with studs or chains on the tires. Last choice was a bear. Next to last was a bull moose. In between were all kinds of possibilities. He'd take any option that included a warm fire, a hot shower, a cozy blanket, and if he was lucky, some hot chocolate.

"Anybody in there?" a voice called out.

Found. "I'm right here!" he said, rolling down the window and looking up at Hope Anderson in a ski parka trimmed in fur.

Great. Just great.

She smiled hesitantly, tucked a stray hair into the rainbow-colored scarf wrapped around her thick, auburn hair, and did a double take. Her face went from the slight side of fear to curiosity, then awe. A look he knew very well.

"Sorry. I didn't mean to stare." She looked away. "Are you okay?"

"Cold and hungry. I'd give anything for a heated bathroom."

"If you can get the door open, you can step on that rock," she said, pointing down past the edge of the car.

"It's dry in here," he said, answering one of the questions in her eyes. "But I knew the car was sitting in some water and I didn't think it was smart to get wet last night, seeing as I was probably going to be stuck in the car until morning."

He leaned halfway out the window and saw a boulder sticking up from the ice-crusted pool of water that filled the bottom third of the ditch. He looked up – and caught her scoping out the balding spot on the top of his head.

The look of adoration he'd seen on her face a few minutes ago faded to... what? Relief? Disappointment? He couldn't tell.

"You're the man from the boat," she said. "No wonder you looked familiar. For a second there I thought you were Tommy Love."

Crap. "Yah. Um. Thanks again. I'd probably be an ice cube by now if you hadn't heard me yelling."

"Not to alarm you, but you look about as cold as you did the first time I rescued you. If you can get out of there, you can warm up at the lodge." She gave him another look. "You really do look like Tommy Love - the picture that's on the front of European Adventure..."

The gig was up. "Yeah. They can digitally remix my music until it's better than ever, but they can't find a way to make me look like I'm twenty-five again," he said, reaching around to grab his guitar, then his suitcase, before he climbed out of his seat, balanced his foot on the edge of the running board, and hopped on to the large rock she'd pointed out a minute ago.

Ouch. "Tom Lovinski," he said, trying not to wince even though he was cold and stiff and his hip was throbbing. She'd seen the bald spot – no sense letting on that he was also evidently no longer spry enough to be hopping on hard surfaces.

"Tommy Love is your stage name," she said, rather than asked, grinning as she crouched down and took his guitar.

"Yup," he said, feeling guilty that he hadn't told her his real name. It wasn't really lying – after four decades of calling, even thinking of himself as Tommy Lovinski, and usually Tommy Love, Lubinski just never occurred to him.

She had one of those open, honest faces that made him feel immediately guilty. Not that he wanted to lie to her - or anybody else - but he was treading on thin ice here, trying to be above board yet remain loyal to his oldest friend in the world. Unless Ms. Anderson was totally not the curious type, there'd be no getting around having to tell a few half-truths.

His collective insides groaned. Sweet as it was of her to come along and rescue him from his snow bank, he had the feeling she'd more likely be his damnation that his salvation. "Your husband doesn't by chance own a tractor, does he, ah...?" She flinched and he hated himself for even saying the words, but he could hardly let on that he knew who she was or that she was a widow.

"Hope Anderson." She smiled, leaned forward, and stretched her mittened hand toward his. "I have a small tractor, but it hasn't run for over two years."

He took her hand, shook it slowly, and attempted to size up the competition. Unfortunately, in addition to having that childlike, hard-to-lie-to quality about her that he found so equally distasteful and intriguing, she seemed pretty nice. Unfortunately, because she had the one thing he wanted most, they were doomed to be enemies instead of friends.

"It's a good thing you missed the rock when you drove into the ditch or you'd be paying for a wrecker instead of a quick tow," she said, smiling again.

So she was a knockout. That didn't qualify her to run a resort all by herself, or mean that she wouldn't get along perfectly fine taking care of demented old people at the Embarrass Care Center.

"It all happened pretty quickly. From what I can tell, I glided in gently," he said, feeling a momentary urge to take advantage of a situation of which she knew little and he had insider knowledge. "If I can use your phone, I'll call someone to pull her out of the ditch. I'm supposed to be in Duluth catching a hop to Minneapolis, then on a flight to Nashville for a rehearsal."

Her smile said she was the one with insider knowledge. "You can try," she said. "The lodge is down the road a bit."

She looked down at his shoes. All six hundred dollars worth of them – smooth Italian leather uppers and bottoms, great for twirling around a polished wood dance floor, comfortable as a chamois skin, the worst possible thing in the whole world, Italy included, for walking on ice. He'd gotten them near the Pont du Vecchio on a trip to Florence last spring. She wasn't impressed. She thought he was a putz. Ironic, since he was perfectly at home here and she was so obviously out of her element.

"It won't be quite so bad when we get to the gravel."

He lifted his suitcase chest high, handed it to her, and eyed a handful of scraggly, roadside weeds that looked sturdier than they were because of the half-inch of ice coating them. Grabbing a handful, he tried to hoist himself up out of the ditch. And slid backwards. Three times.

"It's wicked stuff," she said, trying to hide a laugh. "Here. I can help if I set these down." She laid his suitcase on the snow-covered ground and perched his precious guitar on top of it.

So she was gorgeous and thoughtful. That didn't mean she could run Rainbow Lake Lodge all by herself.

She took off her mittens and dug the heels of her boots into the gravel at the shoulder. "Let me give you a hand."

"I'm fine," he said. And he was, once she'd helped him out. The woman had a strong grip – he'd give her that.

"What brings you to Rainbow Lake?" Hope asked as they headed into the woods, toward the lodge he was going to bulldoze.

"Um... I had a gig at the Indian Casino at Fortune Bay the night before last," he said, not wanting to say too much. "I have a small plane that I use when I'm in Minnesota. I was on my way to the airport."

She looked over her shoulder at the Porsche as if realizing that his car was pointed in exactly the opposite direction that it would have been had he been telling the truth.

"I must have taken a wrong turn," Tommy said, stopping to shift his weight as he skated along on the icy road. His guitar was lighter than his suitcase and he felt totally unbalanced. "I couldn't see a thing with that sleet coming down."

"I was just thinking that you're mighty fortunate that you weren't in the air when this weather started up. Or it could have been your plane that crashed instead of your car. In a lake instead of a ditch."

He looked her in the eye for the first time and nodded.

"I learned a long time ago that God has ways of getting us where he wants us to be," she said. "Usually at the precise moment he needs us to be there."

He assimilated her words and chose not to respond. What he wanted to say was, if you really believe this, how do you make sense of the fact that a drunk driver just happened to come around a blind curve on the wrong side of the centerline at the exact moment your husband was coming upon the same curve from the opposite direction? He wanted to ask it, but how could he, when he wasn't supposed to know her, or that her husband was dead?

"Is your friend okay?" she asked.

"Fine, just as soon as we got off the water."

"Good," she said, her facial expression practically shouting that she didn't quite believe him.

"I grew up in Embarrass, you know," he said, not knowing whether he should just keep his mouth shut or try to distract her from asking him point blank who was in the boat with him and what the hell they'd been doing snooping around her property.

"I think David did mention it now that I think about it. I didn't grow up around here, so I'm a bit clueless when it comes to who went to school with whom and that sort of thing."

"Then I guess I could ask you the same question," he said, feeling safe, for the moment anyway. "About what brought you to Rainbow Lake."

"I'm renovating a lodge and a cluster of cabins that's been in my late husband's family for almost half a century", she said, not mincing any words. "I hope to be ready to reopen on Memorial Day weekend, but there have been a few glitches and things aren't moving along quite as quickly as I'd hoped."

"They never do," Tommy said, trying to convince himself that he wasn't the jerk he felt like. She needed to sell this place – it was what was best for her. Everyone knew it except for her. Besides, it wasn't as though he had just randomly decided he had to have her land. Billy had made it clear that Hope was going to lose the property regardless of the fact that Tommy was in the picture. Somebody was going to buy the place. Why shouldn't it be him?

He'd nearly convinced himself he was right when they turned a corner and he saw the lodge poking through the trees off in the distance, looking as big and grand as the Emerald City at the end of the yellow brick road.

Maybe it was the snow, or the fact that he was chilled to the bone. Maybe it was the way Hope kept referring to the lodge with such love in her voice – whatever, he was mesmerized at first sight. Until that moment, he'd only seen the roof and the top few feet of the exterior that had been visible from the lake. The plane had revealed even less because of the dense ground cover and tall trees. He'd really had no concept of what the place was like. So when the rough hewn timbers and river rocks and old green mortar started to appear through the thick veil of lacy snowflakes falling from the sky, he felt like he was on the inside of some kind of pretty little snow globe, walking toward the fairy-tale-like building in the center.

Get a grip, he told himself. *Stay cool. Be objective.*

"This is it," she said. "'Home Sweet Home.'"

Don't let her get to you. It wasn't as though he was going to be evicting her and her six children. She was young. She had options – or would have, when Billy convinced her she needed to relinquish the land and Tommy paid her more than it was worth.

Who was he kidding? Not only was he inside the snow globe, some maniacal kid was shaking it as hard as he could. He was so shook up he could barely swallow.

"Cool," he said, thinking she would expect some kind of comment from him. He looked up at the impressive facade and gulped. No way could he bulldoze the place. It was the most masculine piece of architecture he'd ever seen. Yet it had a sort of magical, romantic quality about it that made him want to go inside, cozy up to the fire, and never come out.

"Were you ever here as a kid? A lot of locals used to come out for dinner," Hope said in a voice so golden sweet and sincere that he couldn't help but like her.

"Not that I remember. My parents were more ten-cent-hamburger kind of folks." But he felt like he had seen the place, or someplace like it – maybe on a postcard one of his friends had brought back from their family's summer vacation. The postcards they'd brought back from Yellowstone, Yosemite, and Sequoia National Parks year after year for show-and-tell had epitomized everything he was and had ever missed out on because his family was poor.

"I'll never forget the first time David brought me up here," she said.

No kidding. They were close enough now that the massive building filled his whole frame of reference. He was embraced with a sense of well-being so profound it was like coming home. Except that home was a rickety old trailer house in a treeless lot on the edge of Miller's Swamp.

"I just assumed everybody who grew up around here had seen the place at one time or another," she said. "The Andersons used to host hay rides and horse-drawn sleigh rides for the church youth group every year."

"We went hunting on Bear Island one time. I think I was twelve, maybe thirteen. I suppose maybe I saw the Lodge from a distance." He hadn't stayed here, that was for sure. The Lubinskis weren't resort-going folks. Could his dad have delivered something to the lodge, applied for a second job, or come to see about something? It was the only way he could explain the effect the old building had on him. And that was just the outside. He was a goner before she'd even opened the door.

"You can leave your shoes on the rug by the door," she was saying.

By the time he saw the inside, he'd already decided that he was going to find some way to turn the lodge into his dream home. As soon as he got back to civilization, he'd contact the architect he'd hired to draw up the plans and tell him he'd had a change of heart.

He shed his shoes, followed her into a kind of vestibule, and looked around, silently admiring the honeyed oak floors. They'd have to be re-sanded, but the look was perfect. He could gut the place and start out fresh. Old on the outside; completely new on the inside. The best of both worlds.

That was when he rounded one of the thick support poles, a rough-barked tree trunk that was aged to a rich, deep amber color, and saw the mural. The painting formed a panoramic view that encompassed a good quarter of the room. Eagles, bears, raccoons, bluffs, an Indian encampment and the sparkling waters for which Rainbow Lake was famous were all depicted with amazing clarity. And of course, there was the rainbow itself, arcing across the wall over the lake where the ceiling rose to a peak. It had the look of an antique linen postcard, the rich colors of an ornate rococo cathedral, the feel of an old friend he hadn't seen in a long while but knew intimately.

His silence was probably making her wonder, but he didn't dare speak for fear he'd reveal by some slip of the tongue that this place was far more to him than the place where she lived. For now.

Stay cool. Impossible. Directly across the wall from the painting was a floor-to-ceiling bank of windows that showcased the real lake like a gem in a glass case. Each windowpane was encased in a frame made of slender birch trunks, made not of resin, but real birch bark that was unraveling horizontal strips of white. The lodge was just high enough to see over the shiny, sparkling in the sunlight, snow dusty treetops, to look out over the lake and the sky, which stretched for miles into the distance. His heart stood still. The view was just like he'd imagined, except that now, he wasn't dreaming.

Hope cleared her throat behind him, momentarily shattering his reverie. This was a real place, not a dream, set in real time – real time occupied with a real, flesh and blood woman.

He looked at Hope and didn't know what to say. Why hadn't Billy said anything about how magnificent the lodge was? Tommy had talked to Billy for hours, babbling on and on about his plans to bulldoze the place. You'd think...

A bald eagle, head down, wings outstretched, talons poised to pluck, soared from one corner of the room in all its stuffed glory. A black bear who had at least two feet on Tommy stood beside the entrance of what looked to be a dining room.

"I hope the taxidermy doesn't offend you," Hope said. "Stuffing animals was perfectly acceptable in the twenties. I thought about donating them to a museum, but I've grown sort of attached to them in a strange sort of way. Besides, I figure since they're already dead, people may as well enjoy them."

He wandered deeper into the lodge, past the bear, to a large ballroom with an inlaid dance floor off to one side. A blackboard with a delicious-sounding menu chalked in an old-looking script still lined one wall. "Almond Crusted Walleye," he read aloud. "Your handwriting?"

"My mother-in-law's. Grace had already closed the restaurant by the time we moved up here, but after she died, I couldn't bear to erase it."

"Looks like one of those French Bistro signs they sell at Macy's," he said.

"That's me." She laughed. "Inadvertently in vogue."

But he could see that wasn't the case at all. Everything in the place was old and worn – it had to be her touch that made it all come together so magically.

She moved past him to the far side of the dining room and motioned to a door. "You're welcome to use the phone in the kitchen if you'd like, but I'm sure the highway patrols have pulled the wreckers off the roads until the snow stops and the wind quits blowing. My car is in the shed out back, but my tires are worn practically smooth, so unless you want both of us to end up in the ditch, I would recommend you stay here until the storm blows itself out."

"Do you mind if I plug in my cell phone?"

"No problem." She stepped through the door and indicated he should follow. "This is the old guest quarters for the restaurant workers who stayed here over the summer. You can bunk here if you don't mind sleeping on a twin size bed."

"No offense to my car, but I'd take the sofa if it meant I could stretch my legs out and lie flat."

She smiled again. "Sorry it isn't fancier. I spent the summer working outside, re-chinking logs, polishing canoes, and painting the cabins, knowing I wouldn't be able to work on them this winter. The next job was to winterize this place and get the new furnace in, then to put in a new commercial kitchen. I had hoped that by staying out here this winter that I could have the inside of the lodge more or less refurbished by spring. I have a lot of sewing to do, too – curtains, pillows, and bed skirts, a few more quilts for the cabins."

"Sounds like you have a lot of talents," he said, thinking that she would have no trouble getting a job if she knew how to do all that. The lights flickered eerily, and he let his eyes rest on her for a second. "Being holed up in a cozy place like this, doing something you enjoy – something worthwhile," he said, almost envying her, "sounds pretty perfect."

The second the words were out of his mouth, he wanted to kick himself. How could it be perfect when the man she'd planned on cozying up with was dead? Of course he didn't envy her that. But the rest... She had determination. She was motivated. She had a plan. The only thing she lacked was the money to fund her dream.

He had plenty of money... and he knew what he wanted. He'd planned to start writing again for as long as he could remember. For over two decades, he'd been saying it was time to reinvent himself, tap into his old fan base and take a stab at making a name for himself amongst the new generation.

His motivation and determination couldn't hold a candle to Hope Anderson's. Babies had grown into college graduates while he'd been talking about writing a new song. He'd lost out on a whole generation. *How sad was that?*

She handed him a towel. "You can use this to wipe off your suitcase. I hope I didn't ruin the leather, but I figured better it than your guitar."

"You did what you had to do," Tommy said, thinking of all she'd overcome, all she'd accomplished in the past two years and feeling downright ashamed. The only obstacles in his path were too much money, too much freedom, and too much time to think. He was good at talking, planning, and dreaming, but even though he had enough money to do whatever he wanted to do, wherever in the world he wanted to do it, he'd accomplished next to nothing. Instead, he'd let his life drift by, year after year after year.

Hope went to find him some yogurt and make him a hot ham and cheese sandwich. When he'd freshened up, he walked back to the main room. He looked at the faded sofa in front of the fireplace, the rough-hewn table in front of the window. People thought he had everything a man could want. The reality was he had nothing. Nothing except a very tarnished, extremely dusty, tired old thing called fortune and fame. Even that was fading fast.

"Make yourself at home," she called out from the next room. "I've been trying to get things ready in case the power goes out. I didn't know I was going to have company." Her laughter tinkled out from the kitchen, sweet, unsuspecting.

The lights went out for half a second and blinked on again. He started to get angry. It wasn't Hope's fault that he'd taken so long to get where he wanted to be in life, but why now, when he'd finally decided what he wanted and found the perfect place to make the dream happen, did she have to get in the way? It wasn't his fault her husband had died. It wasn't his fault she'd gone over budget on her renovations. It wasn't his fault her string of bad luck had turned the bank sour. It wasn't his fault she didn't have the good sense to give up and move on.

The time was clearly right – for both of them. Her, to move on. Him, to move in.

The lights flickered one last time and finally gave up the ghost. Neither of them said a thing while they waited for the lights to come back on.

"I was afraid this would happen." She finally broke the silence.

The temperature in the room couldn't have dropped that quickly, but he was suddenly cold. "Shouldn't we call the power company?"

"The phone lines are probably down, too," she said. "And they don't work without juice, just like most everything else in the house. I never should have gotten rid of that old rotary."

For a second, she seemed irritatingly unconcerned. Then she swung into high gear. "Mrs. Walsenberg has cell phone reception down at her place. She always calls. Not that this will be any surprise to the power company. You learn to expect it when the wind blows. Our forests may be lovely, but tree branches, ice, and wires strung on telephone poles are not a good mix."

"They have something against underground cables in this part of the world?" he said, realizing what an idiot he must sound like as soon as the words escaped his lips.

"They buried a cable under the lake to get power to some rich folks building a summer home on the far side of the lake almost fifty years ago. Unfortunately, the water, and I'm sure the weather, have taken their toll on technology that probably wasn't the greatest to start with."

"Time to be replaced," he said.

"Nobody who lives on the lake now is evidently rich enough to want to spring for replacement costs, so the utilities aren't the most reliable. We like our solitude up north, but the flip side is that you have to expect a little honest to goodness isolation at times."

"I never thought of it that way," he said, thinking about the allure seclusion held when you lived in a city of half a million people, and how different it felt when it was imposed on you against your will at an inopportune time.

"My closest neighbor is three miles by car," she said, walking to the door and pulling on her snow boots. "Once the lake freezes, it shaves seven miles off the trip to town, and I can get to my neighbors houses like that."

She reached for her parka. He followed suit. "They drive on the ice?" He didn't remember that, but then, why would anybody have wanted to drive on Miller's Swamp?

"I thought they were insane when I first started coming up here. Then one Christmas David and I looked out over the lake, and there was a snowplow, clearing away the fresh snow from the strip where people had been driving, like it was a real road. If it will hold a snowplow, it'll hold my little Subaru."

She pulled her fur-rimmed hood around her face and reached for the doorknob. He didn't know exactly what she had in mind, but he figured he should be helpful. As helpful as he could be in smooth-soled, Italian leather shoes.

"I was planning to start hauling in firewood after I'd gotten the mail," she said, on her way out the door. He followed. "The generator won't start, and the battery I ordered didn't come like I'd hoped, which means we need to get some firewood inside and get a fire going before the temperature drops. Once the sun goes down, it will really plunge."

"I remember." He shivered, buttoned his jacket around his neck and stepped out into a swirl of wet, heavy snow. He was beginning to catch the sense of urgency she must be feeling.

She looked over her shoulder and sighed. "Nice shoes, but they're going to be fairly worthless in this kind of weather. Plus, you're going to wreck them unless we find you something else to wear." Her eyes stopped their merry dance and stilled. "There's a pair of men's Red Wing work boots in the closet that will probably do, unless your feet are bigger than a size twelve."

They were, but pinched toes seemed better than landing on his rump every two minutes. He nodded. She stepped back in the house and opened the coat closet.

A second later, she pulled out a pair of barely worn work boots with tall ankles and lace up fronts that had to have belonged to her husband. Not the sort of thing you'd bury someone in, yet too good to throw away. He wondered if her closets were still full of his things – if she'd found the heart to throw anything that had been his, or if the boots were one of a few precious things she'd saved to remember him by. Her hand trembled ever so slightly as she handed them to him.

Man, he felt uncomfortable. He almost blurted out *I should know better than to try and fill these shoes*, or *No doubt these will be hard shoes to fill*, or something equally stupid. Thank goodness he managed to keep his mouth shut.

"Sorry to have kept you from your work for so long," he said, squeezing his thick, microfiber socks into the boots and crouching down to lace the strings.

"Are you kidding? I don't mind admitting that I'm more than a little happy not to be stranded out here all alone."

That was when he realized he'd been so intent on seeing the lodge that he hadn't even remembered to try to phone for a wrecker. Hope opened the door again and a blast of wind gusted snow all the way into the entryway. For the first time, it finally sunk in that he – they – really were stranded.

There was going to be no wrecker, no rescue, until the storm had had its fill.

Chapter 8

Hope hunched her shoulders against the wind and dropped another armful of firewood onto the growing pile propped against the east wall of the front porch.

How could she have let herself get into this predicament? She'd intended to be ready for winter by the end of September. It wasn't normal for winter to come so early, but it wasn't unheard of either. Looking back, it had been ridiculous to think that she could get the old tractor or the generator started, but she'd been so determined to save money by doing everything herself that she'd overlooked all the signs that she was falling more behind with every day that passed.

She should have had her boat out of the water two weeks ago. Of course, it was a good thing she hadn't since she'd needed it the day before. But right now, at this moment, it was down there freezing. What if there weren't any more warm days? She'd known her tires were practically bare and would be worthless when it came to driving on icy roads. She'd intended to get new ones as soon as the bank approved the extra funding she'd requested. Yeah. Right.

Having to carry in wood in the middle of a blizzard was the final insult. She'd meant to restack the woodpile on the porch ever since Ralph Johnson had dropped off the logs. She'd known she needed the extra insulation on the outside of the stone walls to help keep the inside warm without running up a huge heat bill. She'd also known it would be much easier carrying the wood on a warm day than it would be over frozen terrain, in freezing cold temperatures.

She just hadn't expected winter to come quite so soon. She turned on the path she and Tommy Love had carved through the snow and met him coming from the opposite direction.

"Sorry to have to drag you out in this weather," she said.

"Better now than later. It's getting colder by the minute." Tommy nodded and smiled as they slowed to inch past each other. "At least when we're done, we'll have a fire to warm us up."

She should have been cold, too. Should have been freezing. This was the first cold spell of the season. She wasn't used to it any more than he was. So why did she feel like she was warm all over and positively glowing heat, looking up at Tommy's wide shoulders and sun-bleached blond hair and reveling in the crinkles at the corners of his baby blue eyes?

He reached out and steadied her, her arms cocooned inside his, still wrapped around the stack of logs she was carrying.

"Be careful," he said. "We don't want you toppling into a snow bank."

She nodded like some dazed, star-struck teenager and tried to ignore the sensations she felt as they attempted to slip gracefully by one another on the narrow trail. Of course the man affected her. This was "The Great Tommy Love." She and every other woman who had come of age in the eighties and nineties had been primed to melt when they saw those long, graceful fingers strumming the strings of his guitar.

She looked up, compelled by some fool-hardy, schoolgirl passion she felt powerless to control, and felt her body-temperature rise another two degrees as they rubbed against each other, hip to hip, and finally finished their brief dance. Tommy Love was double trouble waiting to happen – six-feet something of rock-star charm and drop-dead gorgeous all rolled into one.

Tommy released her shoulders and passed down the trail to get more wood. She hurried in the opposite direction to drop off her load and get more. The drifts crisscrossing the driveway in sculptured patterns had quadrupled in size in the short time they'd been outside. What would she have done without his help? It was almost as though God had sent him, knowing that she was tired, discouraged, and in need of reinforcement, both physically and emotionally. Why else would Tommy have made a wrong turn and ended up practically on her doorstep? God was obviously watching over her, just as He always did.

"If you'd like, I can take the next few loads inside so we can try to get a fire going," Tommy said from a few feet down the trail, a distance that should have been safe.

Which didn't explain why her heart was dancing in her chest. "That would be great," she said, turning toward him. "We're down far enough that these bundles should be fairly dry." As dry as they could be when it was still practically pouring wet, heavy snow.

"I'm on it," he said, limping back toward the pile.

"I'll make one more trip and then I'll be in to fix us some dinner," she said.

He was getting blisters from David's boots. She turned to watch as he bent over, crouched, and cradled piece after piece of firewood into his waiting arms.

Big mistake. Even her cheeks were flushed.

Appreciation. That's what it was. He'd been such a regular guy, and so amazingly helpful – who wouldn't be impressed? No wonder she was having trouble separating reality from fantasy. He was a star, probably used to having a concierge to serve his every need. This had to be a first for him.

She uncurled one finger, reached for the screen door, pulled it open and caught it with her knee. Yeah, well, this was a new experience for her, too – the first, hopefully last time she'd have to put a guest to work doing hard manual labor.

She set her logs down beside the fireplace and turned to head back to the woodpile for one last armful. Tommy had been an angel. They'd been at it for over three hours without anything to eat or drink.

They. Tommy Love hadn't even been at the lodge for half a day, and she was already thinking in terms of we, they, and us. It had taken her over a year to break the habit. She'd slipped back into it so reflexively it was as though she'd never stopped, as though David had never died.

It had been hard enough seeing him in David's boots. She could not – would not – get lost in the land of make-believe she'd been drifting toward all summer. Whether God wanted her to remarry and have a family, or spend the rest of her life alone, daydreaming about what might have been if David hadn't died – or even what might happen someday – was a futile waste of time.

"You must be hungry again," she called out as they passed each other on the path one more time, remembering the empty ketchup packets she'd seen on the seat beside him in his car. She dumped the wood on the porch, and tried to think of something simple but elegant she could cook over the fire. She came up blank. She'd been alone way too long. If she were by herself, she'd happily have eaten peanut butter right out of the jar.

"Don't feel like you have to make anything fancy," Tommy said. "I'd be happy with a peanut butter sandwich."

Chapter 9

Tommy leaned his face over the steaming mug of hot chocolate grasped in his hands and wondered if his toes would ever feel warm again. Without his cell phone, he had no idea how much time had gone by, but it was dark, he'd been fed, and Hope and he were finally relaxing, sitting in front of a roaring fire wrapped in assorted blankets and quilts on a loveseat that looked like it had been recovered several times and would soon need it again.

Hope had fixed a simple dinner of hamburger, carrots and potatoes wrapped in foil packets that she'd cooked on an oven rack propped on four rocks in the massive fireplace. They'd covered her history, then his, in nutshell versions, after which he'd grown quiet. Starved as she seemed to hear the sound of her own voice, his reticence to talk had seemed to suit her fine, and she chattered on about this and that, from her favorite Tommy Love hits to life alone at Rainbow Lake Lodge.

"I suppose I should be embarrassed," she said. "Gushing on about all this stuff to a complete stranger."

"People always say they feel like they know me," Tommy said, feeling about an inch tall, knowing what he knew. "Because of my music."

"You don't know how nice it is to have someone to talk to," she said, wiping off the hearth and stacking the dishes to take back to the kitchen. "David and I talked about everything. Since he died... I've got friends, but it's a small town, and there are some things you just don't want everyone knowing."

He felt like a jerk all right. But even that didn't deter him from his resolve. Seeing the lodge, the land, the beautiful view of the lake up close, had only intensified his goals.

"I figure I'm safe talking to you - I mean, I know you're from here originally, but you don't live here, and you are on your way out of town," she said, smiling. "Who are you going to tell?"

She trusted him – enough to confide in him. Guilt. Massive guilt. He got up, shed his blanket and went to the phone. Still dead. The phone lines had evidently snapped right along with the power lines.

"One year when David and I came up for Christmas there was an ice storm," Hope said. "Telephone poles all over the area cracked in two from the weight of the icy lines and fell down. It created total havoc for months afterwards."

Just his luck. He sighed and went back to the fire. The last thing he wanted to do was to spend an evening listening to Hope Anderson talk about what Rainbow Lake Lodge meant to her. But every time he managed to get the subject steered in a different direction, she deftly maneuvered the conversation right back where it started. Rainbow Lake Lodge.

"It must get discouraging at times," he said after listening to the brief description of the various ups and downs she'd faced since her husband died. "The work load has to be overwhelming. I know how exhausting bookwork and decision-making can be when you're trying to do it all by yourself. A friend of mine owns his own business; works three times as hard as any employee, and never gets paid. He tells himself he's building up equity, but I don't think he could sell the place if he tried. Nobody but him would be willing to work eighteen hours a day seven days a week to keep the place going. If you ask me, it sounds downright demoralizing."

He hadn't experienced a shortage of cash in years and, because he had two staff members at his beck and call, he didn't have a clue what it was like to work that hard, day after day after day. But he did have a good imagination, and in this case, it could pay to be empathetic.

"Before David died, we worked on things together, and everything seemed to get done so quickly. Now..." She sighed.

Guilt. Waves of it. He wasn't exactly proud of the fact he had Hope Anderson eating out of his hand, but he sure as heck wasn't going to stop now, when everything was going so nicely.

"I admire you for everything you've accomplished," he said in the voice he reserved for those hushed moments in a song when you could bring an audience to their knees with a word. "But sometimes it really is best to cut your losses and get out while you can."

She reached for a tissue and wiped her eyes. "If there weren't so much history wrapped up in these walls, I'd be tempted. But when I think of the way David's mom and dad happened to buy the place, and why, I know I have to do whatever it takes to make sure Rainbow Lake Lodge stays open."

"I've also learned, the hard way," he said, keeping his voice low but hard, "that when it comes to business, you have to make decisions with your head instead of your heart. Sentimental attachments have no place in the business world. Not knowing when to move on is one of the main reasons people go bankrupt." There. That should do the trick. He so did not want to know when, why or how David's parents had come to buy the lodge.

"They stayed here on their honeymoon, in a cabin called Daisy that's on a little peninsula that juts out into the lake," Hope said, seeming to miss the point entirely. "It's very romantic – surrounded by water on three sides. The lake is so close you can hear the waves lapping on the shore. David was conceived there."

Great, Tommy thought. The poor guy probably would have been named Daisy if he'd been a girl.

"You can probably guess the rest," Hope said. "They loved the place so much that they came back every year on their anniversary for five years, and then, when they called to reserve their cabin for their sixth, they found out the resort had closed. They were so heartbroken, they started making inquiries, ended up buying the place, and eventually quit their jobs and moved up north to reopen and run the resort."

"So David basically grew up at Rainbow Lake Lodge," Tommy said, not wanting to hear any more of the heart-rending details. Hope Anderson seemed like a very nice lady, and he had the utmost respect for her, but he refused to be sucked into her syrupy sentimentality. He had no reason to feel guilty. Besides, he didn't have to bulldoze all the cabins. Daisy was probably the cabin he'd wanted to get a closer look at earlier – the one and only cabin that hadn't been painted some sappy color of the rainbow. The old girl would make a good boathouse, maybe even a cabaña where he could store a handful of swimsuits for people to change into when they were visiting. If it had a shower, it would be perfect. If not, he could add one.

Come to think of it, having a bed down by the lake wasn't a bad idea either. There were bound to be times when he and whomever he was seeing might like to have the option of getting cozy on the beach. From what he'd seen from the boat, it looked like a long, steep walk from the dock back to the house, and he was a firm believer that when the mood hit, you should be ready.

"I couldn't believe how many of the kids who used to spend their vacations here came to David's funeral," she said. "The ones who came summer after summer were like one big family."

He reminded himself that once he had bought the place, Hope Anderson would be a very wealthy woman, able to buy another business, or do whatever she wanted to do.

"Have you thought about putting together a business plan?" He heard something that sounded amazingly like his voice – except it couldn't have been him, because he was trying to talk her into selling the place. "Detail exactly what your expenses are now, and estimate what they'll be when you're up and running?"

When she's up and running? He chided himself mentally. *It's never gonna happen. Stop it! You're just getting her hopes up.* "When you're done with your business plan, you should make a chart showing your projected income," the strange voice that was his, but not his, said.

"My banker has already seen the books from the last forty plus years," she said. "Typing it and putting it in a neat plastic folder isn't going to change anything."

"You said your in-laws weren't wealthy people," he said, "and that there were months / years when they really struggled to pay the bills."

"They loved what they did," she said, sounding stubborn. "They brought peace and rest and happiness to the lives of countless people. They raised a son here – a good man. That's certainly success by my definition."

"That's all very nice," he said. "But you can't expect bankers to come clamoring to finance a place that makes a subsistence level income. They don't want to *hope* you can pay the bills each month. They want proof – or as close as you can come – that this place is going to generate enough money to pay back their loan, and maintain the property, which by the way, they essentially own until you pay them back."

"I've always honored my commitments," she said, looking so sweet and huffy and determined that for a second he was tempted to confess all and beg her to forgive him.

He thought about the hip hop mega hit he was going to write from the deck of Rainbow Lake Lodge, the song that would make him a legend that would live on for at least one more generation, and steeled his heart. "In this business, any business, you've got to have a lot more than good intentions and a kind heart," he said, intending to be brutally honest.

And then his helpful, brotherly alter ego took over again. "You've got to be able to sell yourself and your ideas," he heard himself saying. "Convincingly, dynamically, positively. Guarantee them you're going to succeed. Tell them that you're going to exceed their wildest expectations, then back it up with some good old fashioned black and white facts and figures." He stopped cold. He was doing it again. *What was wrong with him?* The last thing he wanted to be to her was a mentor.

Thankfully, she didn't seem impressed enough by what he'd said to change her mind about the way she'd been approaching things. "I know," he said, lowering his voice from enthusiastic to cynical and going back to the plan. "The Andersons ran a solid business for forty years without computer-generated graphs, spreadsheets, and power point presentations. If it was good enough for them, it's good enough for you."

"Now you can read my mind?" Her voice dripped sarcasm.

"Okay," he said, backing down a little. "Let's talk about your business model, all the things that have changed in the last forty years, and how the two affect one another."

"Everything has changed. I know that. That's why I'm updating the cabins. That's why I'm renovating the lodge. That's why the state is requiring me to put in a new kitchen. That's why I've had to work so hard – "

"And you've done a beautiful job. But I'm not talking about decorating." He hated being so harsh, but she needed to hear this. If he knew anything about her, and he thought he did, her friends were way too nice to be brutally candid with her. "First of all, you keep talking about how *they* did things. Your in-laws. Well, I hate to be the one to point it out, but there were three of them – father, mother, son. Four after you come into picture and started coming up summers. All working hard, long hours for no salary.

"I know. They did it because they loved the place," he said, waving away her objections. "But the fact is, there's only one of you. One person can't possibly do the work the four of you did. You're going to have to hire help. That's going to cost you..." He did some quick calculations in his head. "...in the ballpark of fifty grand a summer. That's assuming you can find seasonal help. You'll very probably have to hire at least one full time person who can help get things ready in the spring, shut things down in the fall," he said, hoping she saw the futility in the picture he'd just painted.

Her face fell, and she nodded, as though what he was saying was finally sinking in.

"So you've got to extend the season as long as you can to maximize your profit," the subversive mentor said, encouraging her again. *This was insane.* "The fifty grand could easily double if you hire just one person year-round," he added. "Assuming you want someone high caliber, someone you can trust."

She nodded glumly. "Is that it?"

"That's just the beginning. Let's talk about how your client base has changed in the last, say twenty years."

"Thanks. For limiting it to twenty I mean."

"Sure." He smiled, ignoring her cynicism. "Families are history. Single parents and every sort of blended family known to man outnumber traditional ones by some astronomical figure I can't quote but know to be high. The families who used to come here are grown up, retired, and living an entirely different lifestyle than they did back in the good old days."

"So I'll cater to new families," she said. "There are a lot of people who'd love to come to a place like this."

"Sure, if it doesn't cost them anything," Tommy said. "The family of the new millennium can't afford to spend their summers at a resort on a lake. They're mortgaged to the hilt, and they both have to work to make ends meet, which means they have to hire a nanny or pay for daycare all summer long when the kids are out of school. Bottom line, they're broke. Plus, Mom and Dad have both been laid off six times in the last ten years, so they work at jobs where they have no seniority and only get one week of vacation a year. The chances that they can both get away in the same week are next to nil."

Her jaw dropped.

"You have to admit I have a point," he said. "Besides, the few families who are wealthy enough for an old-fashioned summer resort experience are going to a Dude Ranch outside Aspen. Or is it Telluride that's hot this year?" He laughed at his own joke. She didn't seem amused.

"Thanks," she said. "That's so encouraging. Someday I'll look back on this moment, remember you fondly, and tell my friends that I once had a dream..."

Tommy sucked in his breath and didn't say a word. He had her right where he wanted her. *Didn't he?* And he hadn't taken advantage. Not really. He was just speaking the truth. "It's good to have a dream, but there are also times when you have to adjust your plans to fit reality."

"That's funny," she said, glaring at him. "Maybe your reality is so picture perfect that you don't need dreams to get you through the day, but we mortals are entitled to a little hope."

"Imagining wonderful scenarios is one thing," he said, his voice just as prickly as hers. "I just hate the thought of seeing someone as beautiful and talented as you are spending their whole life trying to recreate something that doesn't exist anymore."

His own words hit the wall and boomeranged back at him like a torpedo locked on a target. Who was he kidding? He could write all the songs in the world, sing his heart out in every small venue between here and L.A. and he'd never rediscover the old glory days when Tommy Love and the Love Notes were the biggest thing since color television. The world was a different place. It wasn't going to happen.

"Sometimes you have to quit while you're ahead," he said quietly, the oomph gone from his voice. *Sometimes you have to admit that you're a dried up old prune who doesn't impress anyone anymore, a washed-up has-been who isn't worth his weight in fool's gold.*

"And sometimes you have to keep fighting," she countered. "Give it everything you've got. Go for the gold."

The fire sputtered and popped as the last big log fizzled and dissolved into a mass of glowing embers.

"I'll stoke the fire," he said, so cozy in his blanket and the slippers she'd loaned him that he didn't want to move.

"That's okay," she said, standing. "I'm the hostess. You're the guest. I really should start treating you like one."

She looked as deflated as he felt. Not only was he lacking in whatever magic ingredient it took to see his own dream to fruition; he had robbed her of the only thing in the world she still had left. Hope.

Sherrie Hansen

Chapter 10

An hour later, after they'd stoked the fire and brought in some snow to melt to flush the toilet so they could conserve what water they had for drinking, they were back in front of the fire. No checking e-mail, no computer games, no surfing the net. He could have played his guitar, but had no desire – it was kind of novel, getting to know someone from the perspective of Tommy Lubinski, the man, instead of Tommy Love, the musician.

He rubbed the satiny edge of a blanket and stared into the flames. "I understand your business goals and why you want to achieve them. I may not agree with them, but I understand." No sense trying to be coy at this stage of the game. She knew exactly how he felt. He could see it in her big, distrusting eyes. "What we haven't talked about is your personal goals – where you hope to see yourself five, ten, thirty years from now."

Her face lit up a little while he waited for her to speak. If you asked him, she didn't have anything to be all that cheery about, but she was obviously an optimist. Oh, well. Whatever made her chocolate swirl.

"I've always wanted to be a mother," she said. "It still – well, David and I had been trying. For a few weeks after he died, I thought, well," she said, looking embarrassed, "I thought maybe I was pregnant. But the doctor said it was just my body reacting to the stress and shock of what happened."

Great. Tommy tried to cop a look at her face without meeting her eyes, which for some reason, he couldn't handle right then. She was definitely younger than he was, hopefully by about ten years if she really wanted kids. But by the looks of things, if she was going to have them, she needed to get on it right away.

He didn't want to be cruel, but he didn't know how else to say it. "Okay. So you've got this dream. And I'm not saying there's anything wrong with wanting to have kids. It's a nice dream. But it's not something you can do on your own – I mean, assuming you're planning on doing things the traditional way. And not to get personal, but it's a dream with a time limit."

"I'll be thirty-nine on February twenty-eighth," she said, her chin lifting a notch. "My doctor assures me that everything is still in good working order. Most importantly, I've got lots of energy. And – I feel good."

"I feel good," he started to sing. "I knew that I would now." He stopped and laughed. "But you're thinking James Brown. Tommy Love is in the house."

"You corn ball," she said. "The point is, I'm perfectly capable of bearing children."

"Now." he said. "No offense, but at your age, you'd better not be dawdling around for too long. And speaking as someone who's been thinking about meeting the right woman and having kids for the last two or three decades, I'm here to tell you that finding the perfect candidate is not an easy job."

She didn't say a word, but there was something – disgust? – written all over her face. "Candidate?"

"I said it's a very valid dream," he said. "I'm just worried... I mean, you're going to meet the father of these children you want to have at a resort for families, or if you take my suggestion, a romantic retreat for couples?"

"Maybe one of the families will bring along their kids' uncle."

"Yeah. That's likely."

She rolled her eyes. "So the odds are against me. All it takes is one."

"One who happens to be at the right place at the right time. And unless you're not planning on being picky, one who meets your criterion. I mean, even if he does show up by some fluke of chance, he's going to come with his own wish list. Nice as you are, it's really next to impossible – "

"So it's a long shot," she said. "Sometimes you just have to have a little faith."

It was hard to argue with that, but being as he had come this far, he had to try. "So you're telling me that the reason I haven't found the woman of my dreams is that I don't have enough faith?"

"I don't know if you have any," she said, turning downright feisty on him. "Have you prayed about this woman you say you'd like to meet? Have you been open to what God is trying to show you, or willing to set aside your own criterion and trust His judgment?"

Ouch. "Personally speaking, I always figured the Big Guy had enough on his plate without having to worry about who might be a good mother for my children and how to get us together. But if you want to persist in thinking He's some sort of cosmic matchmaker, then –"

"I do," she said.

"Fine." He glared back at her. Man. She was so stubborn you'd have to be God Almighty to get her to take a little advice. Hopeless.

Was it his imagination, or was it getting colder? He shifted under his blanket and yawned. "I've always been able to fall asleep sitting at my desk chair, so when I was in the car I figured, what the hey, I can sleep sitting up. But after last night, I'd say sleeping in an upright position is vastly overrated. In fact, that bed you mentioned earlier is sounding pretty good about now."

"That was before the power went out," she said, not looking happy.

"I'm not afraid of the dark," he quipped. "The whole point of sleeping is to –"

"You can sleep anywhere you want to if you don't mind freezing to death." She sounded like she was still mad at him.

Realization dawned fresh. They were both going to be sleeping right here in front of the fireplace. "I hope you don't snore," he said, feeling as catty as she sounded.

"One of us will have to stoke the fire every few hours. Between the stone walls, the high ceilings and the big windows in this room, it's as drafty as an old barn."

"If we move that ottoman over in front of the loveseat, I'll almost be able to stretch out my legs," he said.

She looked as uncomfortable as he felt, and for that, he was truly sorry. "We'll be a lot warmer if we get under the same blanket."

She didn't look convinced.

"I know what you're thinking." He tried again. "And I agree that what I'm proposing is a little risqué. It's going to be hard for you not to get carried away." Good. She had that adorable insulted look on her face again. She was way too easy to play. "I'm telling you right now, that if you try to cop a feel, even one, that you're going to be out in the cold, no second chances."

"I'll try to control myself," she snipped, disgust dripping from her voice.

"It's the way it has to be," he said, trying to keep a straight face.

"It's going to be hard, but if I muster every last drop of restraint I possess, I suppose I can handle it."

"That a girl," he drawled, slipping back to Nashville-ese.

"I'm going to find a few more quilts," she said.

"Anything else I can do to help?" he asked, trying so hard to look penitent that she started to laugh.

"That depends. Do you mean other than, or in addition to dashing my hopes and making mincemeat out of my dreams?"

"It's all in the perspective, darlin'. You could be thanking me some day."

Some day very soon.

Chapter 11

He awoke – maybe half-awoke was a better word – to the scent of peaches. Fresh, juicy ripe peaches warmed by the sun. And vanilla ice cream. Cool, slippery, cold, made in Grandpa Lubinski's ice cream maker. Homemade. Like nothing you'd ever find at the grocery store. The real deal.

He snuggled into the soft spot at the nape of her neck and threaded his fingers through the silky layers of her hair until he found her cheek. Hope.

Hope.

"Are you awake?" she said, her voice as satiny smooth as her hair.

He jerked away from her like he'd been shocked with a jolt of pure energy.

Her hair was mussed, probably from his fingers. She wore the drowsy, rumpled look well. Too well. He leaped out from under the covers.

"I'll get the fire going." Thank God he'd opted to sleep in his heavy denim jeans and not the flimsy pair of sweat pants she'd offered him.

"Aren't you cold?" she said, still half asleep, her voice sultry with drowsiness.

"One of us has to be. Might as well be me," he said.

"It's my lodge," she said.

Not for long.

"You've done enough already," he said gruffly. "Go back to sleep."

It was later that morning when he realized their supply of drinking water was almost gone, and that there would be no more until there was electricity to run the pump. That was reason enough to have a look at the generator. The hundreds of dollars worth of meat thawing in the not-so-freezing-cold-freezer was an extra impetus to say the least. Hope didn't have that kind of money to spare. He had to help if he could.

"Are you sure the battery is bad?" he asked, lacing up David's boots one more time. "It could be the starter, or the battery cable."

"I think I would have noticed if the battery cable was missing."

Man, she was cute when she was huffy.

"No one said anything about missing," he said. "It could be corroded."

"So if this cable is ruined, the generator might not work even when the new battery comes?"

Her face was so readable. She looked like a kid when she was dreaming, but ten years older than her age when she was talking about anything that cost money.

"So you might not even need a new battery," he said.

"But I'll need a new battery cable."

"Not if we clean it up and reconnect it," he said, feeling more useful and capable and manly than he did when there were a thousand women screaming his name at the foot of a stage.

"Will you show me how?" she said, her eyebrows worrying their way to his heart. "David was so good at... I mean, I never thought I would have to do anything like this... David always took care of these kinds of things."

David. The man might be dead, but the mere mention of his name was like the sharp tip of a pin against a bubble.

"Sure thing." He held the door open for her and took her mittened hand in his to steady her in case she started to fall. "By the time I'm finished with you, you'll be an old pro."

"How did you learn to fix engines?" she asked, inadvertently stoking his ego into a little bit more of a tizzy.

"I haven't always been a rock star," he said, his conscience pricking him right where his toes were crammed into David's too tight boots.

Fine. Strictly speaking, he'd never been a rock star. James Taylor was more his speed. But he could hardly say, 'folk star'. Hmm... *Legendary folk musician* might work.

He spent the next hour regaling her with stories of Nashville, Los Angeles, the Grammy's, Vince and Amy, REO Speedwagon and George Strait while they stripped the battery cable of every last bit of corrosion.

She made him feel like some sort of super hero for fixing the silly thing. Between his frequently muttered, "Aw, shucks," and the oft repeated "Really, it's not that big of a deal," he decided it was vastly better being her hero than a lonely old superstar.

The afternoon went by in a blur. The generator was working, but it wasn't powerful enough to operate Hope's furnace, or more than one motor or appliance at a time. Plus, Hope had limited amounts of gas. When it was gone, it wouldn't matter how good he was at fixing generators. The thing would be useless unless he figured out how to manufacture ethanol.

They plugged in the pump first, then the hot water heater. Showering in the slightly rusty, beginning to mildew, rickety old shower stall in a fifty-five degree above zero temperature room was still a far stretch from the luxurious double shower he was used to, but he was thankful for the warm water. After they'd each showered, they alternated plugged in each of the freezers just long enough to lower the temperatures to acceptable standards, then plugged in the pump again and drew more water for drinking and a sponge bath in the morning in case the generator had run out of gas by then.

By the time they'd done all that and roughed up the still icy sidewalks and paths so they could haul in more firewood without fear of breaking their necks, the sun was starting to set again. They were both exhausted.

"Do you think there's any chance they've plowed and sanded the roads yet?" He didn't have enough energy to make the near mile long trek down Hope's driveway unless the odds were pretty good.

"I'm so sorry," she said, looking as though she'd come to accept his presence so thoroughly that she'd forgotten his car was in the ditch – or that he'd be leaving as soon as he could get it out. "I've been so focused on taking care of everything that needs to be done around here that I almost forgot about you." She blushed.

"Yeah." He grinned. "Pretty selfish of you, putting basic, survival-mode needs ahead of important things like my Porsche."

She laughed and collapsed into the nearest chair, snowy boots and all.

"Hey," he said, pretending to be offended. "If I'd known you were going to take that attitude..."

"Are you as tired as I am?" she asked.

"I think more, if that's possible. Lifting, hauling, bending, crouching – I'm embarrassed to admit that I'm using muscles I haven't exercised in over two decades."

"You'll be sore tomorrow," she said. "Especially after another night on our loveseat."

She froze, and the "our" she'd uttered hung in the air like a dreaded, dangling participle.

"Lumpy as our make-shift bed was, I slept very soundly last night." He met her eyes, and wondered if she was thinking about how they'd snuggled under the covers.

"Me, too," she said.

Chapter 12

Hope could tell Tommy was tense by the way he kept pacing the floor and poking at the fire even when it didn't need tending.

She understood, even kind of envied, the fact that Tommy had someone who cared where he was, even if they were only paid employees. She was very sympathetic to his desire to let his agent and his business manager know where he was and that he was okay. She was very thankful Tommy had fixed her generator and helped her isolate which breaker controlled which electrical outlets. But as far as going to all that effort so he could recharge his cell phone so he could use it to initiate a rescue effort – well, she was doubtful his phone would work even once it was charged, that was all.

Tommy was optimistic that if they could just get it recharged, he could make a connection at some point. That was understandable. What was bothering her was that he seemed so horribly urgent about it. He didn't have to be so all-fired desperate to get away from her, did he?

Not that she cared about his personal state of mind. He was no one to her except in the sense that he was The Great Tommy Love, and that he could have sent a lot of business her way if he'd been as charmed by Rainbow Lake Lodge as she'd hoped.

The whole premise of her business was that Rainbow Lake was a place where people could escape the hustle bustle of their hectic lives and relax, find peace, and enjoy a bit of contentment, even if it was short-lived. She looked over at Tommy, who was fussing with the fire – again. Granted, the two days Tommy Love had spent at the lodge hadn't been relaxing by any stretch of the imagination, but they hadn't been that awful, at least, not by her estimation. She'd enjoyed his company. She'd had fun. Tommy looked about as peaceful and content as a rodeo bull before the chute was unlocked.

She wanted to believe that the romance that was Rainbow Lake Lodge had influenced Tommy Love the same way it had affected her. Not that she thought she'd ever see him again once his Porsche was out of the ditch and he went roaring away in his airplane. She'd simply wanted to believe that Tommy Love had found her company as stimulating as she had his.

"You know," she said. "You should come up here again next summer, rent a cabin, stay for a month, and see what happens. There's something very special about this place. I really think you'd be able to relax if you came up and stayed for awhile."

"I'm plenty relaxed." He looked like a tiger about to pounce.

The fact that Tommy seemed immune to the Lodge's charm was very disappointing. Having Tommy at the Lodge had made her feel more relaxed – more cared for, safer, happier – than she had since David died. Yet he was obviously untouched by her.

Traitorous emotions. Maybe it was because Tommy had turned out to be such a good listener. It had helped to talk things out with him – just the way she and David used to – hashing out their problems, dissecting their options, weighing the pros and cons.

Tommy Love had been just what she needed. She smiled dreamily and tried to wipe the shiny-eyed, passion-oozing look from her face. The guy had grown on her. Not Tommy Love, although she'd always adored him in a Teen Idol sort of way. No, the one she liked was Tommy Lovinski, regular guy. Thomas Lovinski, generator-fixing, motor-oil-under-his-fingernails guy.

"I wouldn't be surprised if you were inspired to write again," she said, surprised at how timid her voice sounded. *What was her problem?* Tommy hadn't minced any words when he told her what he perceived to be the answer to her dilemma. "I mean, if you came back up here and stayed the summer."

She cleared her throat and started again, louder, more confidently. "Forget one last big hit. You lectured me about the baby boomers – there are millions of us out there who love and remember every word of every song you wrote. And although we apparently don't have the time or money to spend our summers at resorts any longer, we buy all kinds of CDs so we can listen to our favorite tunes as we race from our jobs to our day care providers, the gym, and whatever other adventures we're inclined to pursue."

This time, she ignored his protests and steamrolled over him as if he were a rag doll. "I'm serious, Tommy. If you released another album – CD – it would top the charts faster than Apollo made it to the moon. If the adults like it, their kids will hear it, and..." She sputtered from talking too fast, sucking in too much wind. "It could launch a whole new career for you. There'd be an American tour, a European tour, probably even a book deal."

So why was she talking about tours? Tommy already had more than enough reason to want to get out of town fast. Why was she trying to give him one more reason to leave? She'd lost her mind. Just a few minutes ago, she'd been wishing he would give up his dream of being a refitted rock star and retire, settle down somewhere nearby, be a part of her life. She hadn't felt this flicker of excitement since she couldn't even remember when, if she'd ever felt precisely as she did at this moment. And now, here she was, pushing him out the door and back to Nashville or L.A. or wherever it was people made records. CDs.

"If I had a place where I could escape the rat race in the city and all the people who want a piece of me and just write, I'd have a new hit recorded in no time." Tommy stood up, looking... *What was it? Guilty?* That, she didn't get. What did he have to feel guilty about? He started to pace. Again. He was driving her crazy.

"So if I did come up here and stay for a month or two" he said, while she tried not to look like her heart was lurching erratically inside her chest. "Where would you suggest I stay?"

"I wish I could take you on a walking tour." She glanced out the window at the hostile winter landscape. "The cabins are painted in the colors of the rainbow, which is kind of a no-brainer. The unique thing is, they're each named after a woman – Rose is, well, rose colored. Lily is painted peach, and Daisy has a yellow door, shutters and window box. Fern is a lovely spring green, Ivy, more of a deep forest green, Bluebell is, obviously, blue. And Violet is the most divine shade of purple. Which leaves Petunia – she's a deep raspberry right now, but I might change her dress, I mean, her color, this spring, if the mood hits me. Petunias come in so many pretty colors. Oh. I almost forgot Jasmine – she's a pale shade of pink." She smiled. "She's my favorite." No need to reveal her reasons.

"You make it sound like they're real. You'd think they each have their own personality."

"They do. I wish I could show you! I may not be the best at playing the numbers game or coming up with effective marketing strategies, but I've been told I have a gift for making a house, or a cabin, or a lodge, a home. David used to say I was an artist."

Tommy looked at her long and hard until she could feel herself blushing.

"My first thought is that if you really think of these cabins as ladies, then it might be dangerous to unleash a single man on any of them. How do you know you can trust me with this Jasmine?" He laughed, but in a kind way.

"I trust you," she said. The room was silent except for the crackling of the fire.

He stood, joined her on the loveseat, and took her hand in his. "It feels very wrong to hear you talking about your art in the past tense. I know David is dead, but you can't let yourself die with him. Especially not the part of you that's creative."

She felt her chin trembling. She'd lost at least one very real aspect of her ability to create when David had died – the part that needed a sperm to fertilize an egg. Since then, she'd struggled day and night to keep the artistic part of her soul alive. David had been her inspiration. She'd poured what she'd felt for him into the cabins, the lodge, the things they'd both loved so very much. Everything she'd done was a tribute to him.

But none of it, nothing in this world, could bring him back. David was gone. He'd been gone so long that his image was starting to fade from her mind. When she lay in bed and thought of him at night, she could barely envision how he'd looked. His scent had long since faded from the pajamas he'd worn when it was cold, the suit coat he'd saved for special occasions, even the blue plaid flannel shirt he'd practically lived in.

Lived. Much as she'd loved him, David was past tense. A person could only live in the realm of what used to be for so long. She suspected a part of her would grieve for David for the rest of her life, but still, she knew it was time to move on. Did that mean leaving the lodge?

She lifted her chin defiantly. "We were talking about you. Your art. Why you can't write. I may not... I mean... I know I haven't... but at least I have an excuse," she said lamely.

"We all have excuses, darlin'," he drawled, sounding way more Nashville than Northern.

"So what are yours, Mr. So-busy-taking-the-specks-out-of other-peoples-eyes-that-they-can't-see-the-log-in-their-own?" she taunted him. Tommy Love was way too easy to tease. "Somebody or something must inspire you. Whoever, or whatever she or it is, you should go to her. Let your soul be unlocked."

"I've tried," he said, not looking amused in the slightest. "There's no one."

"So there was no real Jenny behind *Jenny's Song?*" she asked. "I thought I remembered reading something about that song once upon a time..."

He stood and started to pace again. "There's a Jenny. It didn't end well. I've known plenty of women since then, but I've never loved any of them enough to write a song about them." His face looked so tortured that she had to believe he was being truthful. "I've lived in six different houses in the past five years. I've played in honkytonks, clubs, and county fairs in all but two states. Everywhere I go, I look for her, it, some place that will make me feel like I'm at home. All those women, all those places, every thing that I have, and I've never even come close until..."

"Until what?" she asked quietly.

His silence hung between them, as thick and impenetrable as the stone walls surrounding them.

"If I can borrow David's boots again, I'd like to go for a walk." The look in his eyes said he knew he could never fill those shoes. Wouldn't even try.

A jolt of realization raced through her veins. He felt it! He really did! The magic of Rainbow Lake Lodge had touched The Great Tommy Love.

She met and held his eyes, eyes filled with admiration, passion, love, eyes that said, "This is impossible. I'd be a fool to even try." Eyes that said, "Don't even think about it." Eyes that said, "Tommy Love doesn't do foolish."

She said nothing as he laced the heavy boots and bundled up in his coat and her scarf.

So she hadn't been dreaming. She'd felt him, just before dawn. She'd been half-asleep, but she'd known he was snuggling with her, cuddled up to her. Thinking back on it now, it wasn't upsetting that he had been in such an intimate pose – just the opposite. The reason snuggling with Tommy Love was so unsettling was because it had felt so... perfect. Right. Meant to be. As though they'd been in love forever.

The door slammed shut behind Tommy Love. *Get a grip*, she told herself. Of course it had felt good to feel a man's body next to hers. It had been way too long since she'd felt the strong, protective touch of a man in her bed – or on her sofa. That didn't mean she had feelings for Tommy. It meant she had a good case of skin hunger. Skin starvation was probably an even better description. People who were starving were not known to be discriminating. Give a starving man a meal, and he wouldn't ask if it was God or the devil who'd prepared it.

Where Tommy went in the moonlight and how long he stayed away, she had no idea. All she knew was how lonely it seemed without him.

When she had stood as much quiet and aloneness as she could, she re-stoked the fire and climbed under the covers by herself. All in all, it seemed easier to close her eyes and pretend she was already asleep than to take the risk that Tommy might look into her eyes and know that she wanted him to cuddle her again.

Sherrie Hansen

Chapter 13

She must have been half-awake, because she vaguely realized that she was dreaming – which made being caught in the middle of a tornado no less terrifying. She swirled around and around, dodging this way and that to avoid the chunks of wood, rocks, trees, cows, chickens and pigs that were circling inside a cloud of debris so big that it stretched as far as she could see.

The tornado's roar was just as deafening as she'd always heard. Louder than any train, it pierced the quiet reverie of the lake with rumbles so deep and earth shattering that they shook the windowpanes in their frames.

In the middle of the chaos, someone started pounding on the door, which made no sense, given she was aloft at several hundred feet.

Tommy bolted out of bed and a whoosh of cold, dry air rushed in to replace the warm, moist, summertime temperatures of her dream.

"I was dreaming," Tommy said, clearly disoriented. "I was trapped inside a snow globe, and someone was shaking it as hard as they could. They wanted it to snow."

The pounding continued and grew louder, if that was possible. An engine revved, and she watched as Tommy headed for the door, mumbling about the cold. If the tip of her nose was any indication, the temperatures must have dropped even further overnight.

They'd both been sleeping so soundly that the fire had gone out. She was still trying to decide if she should stay in bed until Tommy had stoked the fire, and more importantly, if the knocking and the engine were part of her dream, or if she really was awake.

Tommy grabbed the doorknob and wrenched the door open.

A uniformed sheriff and two deputies stood with their badges extended. Her heart lurched. Was something wrong? Had somebody died? When David…

And then she thought, what more could be wrong than the things that already were? Everyone she loved was already dead.

The sheriff said, "Tommy Love?", like he didn't know what

Tommy looked like. His two deputies scanned the room until their eyes reached her – in bed. One bed, rumpled covers, her in it.

Tommy extended his hand to the front man and said, "Yes," while the other two gaped at her, assuming the obvious, except that she wasn't some nymphomaniac groupie, or even a wanton divorcee, and her reputation should speak for itself. How dare they think that she would...

She pulled the covers around her neck, wanting to crawl beneath the blanket and hide her shame, until she remembered she had nothing to be ashamed about, unless it was the dream she'd had right before the one with the tornado. Which had been a lot nicer – she hadn't been swirling around in a debris cloud, she'd been skinny-dipping with Tommy Love.

She blushed, and realized that her behavior was just making her look guiltier, which she couldn't be, since she wasn't.

She could just imagine the rumors that would fly once word got out that Tommy Love had been stranded at the lodge. She flung the quilt off the bed and went to join Tommy at the door, trying to do what damage control she could. *You can get your minds out of the gutter, you decrepit old busybodies. As you can see, I'm fully dressed* – which, of course, didn't prove anything except that it was too cold to sleep in anything less.

"A snowmobiler saw your car in the ditch and called in your license plate," the one in the sheriff's uniform, whose name she thought was Alvin Turppa, said briskly. "Your agent and your business manager have been calling the emergency response team practically every hour since they realized you never made it to Minneapolis."

A deputy, who she thought might be Doris Hakala's son, cackled into a short-wave radio.

"I'm fine," Tommy said, putting his arm around her waist and pulling her to him like he was playing to a mob of reporters. "Hope found me the morning after I went in the ditch. She's taken real good care of me."

He hadn't winked, had he? Stupid, stupid man. She watched as three knowing grins spread across the men's faces.

"Alvin Turppa," the sheriff said, extending his hand to her, then Tommy.

"Mr. Lovinski carried in load after load of firewood, fixed the generator, and shoveled so much snow that all he could do by the time

I got done 'taking care of him' was to collapse in front of the fireplace and sleep," she said, trying to sound stilted and formal and cold, which wasn't hard. It was freezing.

The men laughed but looked unconvinced of her virtue.

"We're just glad he made it to shelter," the tallest one said. "I know several people from Embarrass who've had run-ins with hypothermia and have the missing toes and fingers to prove it. We were afraid someone who's gotten used to living in the south might not fare so well in this cold."

"I'm fine, Tommy said again. "I've sorry to have caused anyone concern, sorry to have dragged you guys out of your beds and into the storm."

"It's a beautiful day out there. The clouds lifted overnight, there was a beautiful sunrise, and the temperature's up enough that this dang blasted ice should start melting anytime now. The roads aren't quite good enough to send the wrecker for your car, but if you don't mind hitching a ride on a snowmobile we'd be happy to take you back to town."

"Great." Tommy's voice was a mixture of relief and regret. "I'll grab my bag and be ready to go in five minutes. Come on, Hope," he said. "It won't take you long to pack a few things, will it?"

"I'm not going anywhere," she said, looking at him as though he'd lost his mind.

"I can't leave you here alone," he said, looking back at her just as incredulously.

"This is my home," she said. "I live here. Alone."

"But you have no heat. No telephone. And your driveway's not plowed yet. It could be weeks before – "

"Days, maybe," the sheriff said. "It'll thaw pretty quickly once the warm front they're predicting moves through. The telephone and utility crews are already out. They started close to town but they'll work their way out here soon enough."

Tommy looked at her and shook his head. "This really isn't any place for a woman to be..."

The man might have limited mental faculties, but he at least had the sense to stop when he saw the look she gave him.

"Could I see you in the kitchen for a moment?" he said, gripping her arm and steering her gently but firmly toward the other room. "Gentlemen, I'm sure you don't mind giving us a minute, do you?"

"Course not," the probable Hakala boy said politely.

She allowed herself to be steered halfway to the kitchen before she spoke. "Do you know what they're thinking right now?" she said, gritting her teeth.

"Probably that I care about you," he started to say. Then, "Oh."

"We just need a second," she said, turning to wave at the deputies and smiling as though she had nothing to be ashamed of, which she didn't. She turned back to Tommy and spoke in a stage whisper. "So say what you have to say and then help me restore my virtue with Barney Fife and his deputies over there so four counties of Northern Minnesotans don't think we slept together."

"But we did," he said.

"Key word being slept," she said. "Which is open to a lot of different interpretations on the grapevine."

"Who cares what they think?" he said, while she thought he'd been away from his hometown for far too long if he had forgotten what it was like to be the topic of gossip – untrue gossip at that.

"No one, if they're right. But I'll be darned if I'm going to have everyone thinking I had sex with you when all I got was snoring," she said, her feistiness inadvertently camouflaging her panic at the thought of him leaving.

"You never said you wanted sex. If you had said you wanted sex..." He looked at her like he was seeing her, really seeing her, for the first time.

"I didn't want sex," she said, feeling her cheeks on fire. "I mean, I did. Do. Generally speaking, I mean. When I'm married again. Which can't come too soon when it comes to that part." She gulped. "But not right now." She dared raise her eyelashes for a nanosecond. Man, the look he was giving her. "Sex, I mean." And then, "You're confusing the issue."

"Which I've forgotten entirely," he admitted.

"You're the one who asked to see me in the kitchen," she said.

"Oh. Yeah," he said, looking dazed for just a second before the hardheaded, stubborn look she'd already learned to recognize regained control of his features. "I'm not sure if the lame-brained idea of spending the winter out here all by yourself was born out of financial desperation or just plain stubbornness," he said, ignoring her huffs. "Have you stopped to think what could happen if you stumbled on the ice, hurt yourself, and couldn't get back to the house? Or any number of things that could happen once winter really sets in? The snow will be three feet deep and the wind chill will be sixty below zero, and you'll be out here alone with a stone-aged electrical grid that goes out every time the wind blows. No one will be here to cover your back. It's insane. I can't let you stay here."

"You have no say in the matter," she said, alternately feeling mad that he was being so presumptuous, and touched that he cared.

He looked at her sadly. "No, I guess I don't. That doesn't mean you shouldn't take my advice."

"My resolve is the only thing that's gotten me this far," she said, starting to wonder if any of this was worth it, if her toughness had any point. If Billy Bjorklund had his way, foreclosed, and had her ousted by spring, would it have been worth risking her health and well being only to face an eviction notice just when the warm temperatures returned and the flowers started to bloom? She thought about the wildflowers, and the ferns that grew around the shaded cabin named Fern, and the rose bush she'd planted beside Rose's front door, and the bluebells that bloomed every spring in the woods behind Bluebell and thought, yes, it probably was. She just had to have faith that Billy's heart would thaw before spring.

"Just come into town until we can find someone to plow your driveway and get the phone hooked up again," he said, gently this time.

"You know, if any one of the people who are so determined to get me out of this place would offer to help instead of working against me, I might have a chance," she said, knowing she sounded desperate. Which she was very close to being.

"Is that a proposal?"

"It's a proposition," she said, figuring, what the heck. "I truly believe that getting away from whatever kind of lifestyle you live and coming to live here at the lake would be the best thing you could do for yourself and your, um, present career slump. I mean, I know you think being where the action is is the right way to get back on track, but you've tried that for over two decades, and it hasn't worked. If you want something to change, you have to do something different."

"So what are you proposing?"

"Propositioning," she said.

He grinned. "I like it when women proposition me."

"Fine," she said. "Here's my proposal. I give you free room and board. You can have the whole west wing this winter."

"Great," he said. "The luxurious, bunk-bed-lined servant's quarters. A personal dream come true."

She ignored him. "And your choice of the cottages this summer, probably Petunia, because you're petulant and she's the most secluded."

He rolled his eyes.

"In return, you help me with anything that needs a man's touch. The rest of the time, you'd be free to write – lyrics, music, your memoirs – whatever excites you. I'm sure my customers would love to listen to your songs while they're eating dinner at the lodge. They can be guinea pigs," she said, plotting as she went. "We can have them fill out comment cards so you know which of your new songs resonates with the greatest number of people."

He stared at her like she was an alien life form. "People drive hundreds of miles and pay a hundred bucks a ticket to hear me in concert."

"Good. Then I can charge more for dinner on the nights you're playing. It will help offset the rent I'm going to lose on Petunia."

"You're crazy if you think – "

"What?" she said. "That The Great Tommy Love would lover himself to my level? I mean lower. Lower himself to my level."

Thank God he had the sense not to laugh.

She took a deep breath. She'd said her piece, made a complete and utter fool of herself.

"I can't," he said. "I'd love to have a place like this on a lake, but you have to know I can't – "

"You're The Great Tommy Love. You can do whatever you want to."

"You don't understand what it's like to be a – "

"A what? A superstar? No, I don't. I don't even know what it's like to be a man. But I do know that if you want something to change, you have to do something different."

"So you said."

"It bears repeating." She looked at him sadly for a moment, then peeked around the corner. "Sorry we're taking so long."

She turned back to face Tommy. She'd said all she had to say. It was obvious...

That was when The Great Tommy Love took her in his arms and

hugged her for what seemed like a very long time. Which was right before he lifted her face to meet his and kissed her, which of course, shut her up good, which was probably what he had planned all along. At least that's what she told herself to beat off the waves of whatever it was that was making her insides hum with excitement.

He said nothing when he finally ended the kiss. He took her hand in his with what seemed like reluctance, at least to her, and led her back to the great hall – mussed hair, bleary eyes, puffy lips and all.

Tommy walked over to their makeshift bed, reached down, found his Italian leather shoes and grabbed his overnight bag and guitar. "She's staying. Would one of you mind getting the fire going again?" The Hakala boy hurried to the fireplace and started piling logs and kindling on the embers in the grates. Tommy nodded at the sheriff before turning back to her.

"Are you sure you won't come with me?"

"I have no place to stay in town." And no money, she thought sadly, thinking of the thousand dollars David had hidden in the armoire – money she hoped would forestall the foreclosure long enough that she could come up with a plan to make things work. She wondered what David would want her to do with it and suddenly didn't care. David would probably agree with Tommy. She could almost hear him, insisting she should go into town, spend the money on a B&B, take care of herself. "I really can't," she said.

"Sure, you can," Tommy said, cannily sensing her weakness. There's plenty of room at..."

She wasn't glaring at him, so she wasn't sure why he'd stopped talking.

"Billy said to tell you he hasn't even changed the sheets in the guest room, so you'd better get your butt back there and pronto. Nice place," the sheriff said. "Although it sounds like the room service stinks."

"Billy Bjorklund?" Hope asked.

Tommy's face blanched.

She couldn't believe it. "You know Billy Bjorklund?"

Nothing.

"You probably own the bank," she said accusingly.

"We were friends in high school. We get together once in awhile."

"You've been staying with Billy Bjorklund, and you expect me to believe it's a coincidence that you showed up on my door spouting all this stuff about having to make business decisions with my head instead of my heart?"

"Maybe at first," he said, not even trying to excuse his behavior. "Once I got to know you, I tried to give you advice on how to make a success of the place. Because I cared."

"Which you know is a moot point seeing as your friend Billy is going to force me into bankruptcy when he forecloses on my loan."

"Which was inevitable anyway, seeing as you're too stubborn to take my or anyone else's advice, and too bullheaded to admit you can't run this place by yourself."

She could feel her face go icy cold, then raging hot, as her fury took control of her body. "Get him out of here," she said to no one in particular. Her voice sounded like a stranger's. Emotionless. Empty. Disillusioned. Heartbroken. Horrible.

"You act like I've done something terrible," he said.

"I trusted you. I confided in you."

"You never mentioned the words foreclosure or bankruptcy once in all the times we talked," he said. "You didn't trust me enough to confide in me about that."

"Yet, for some reason, you don't seem surprised that Billy's planning to rob me of my land," she said, in as triumphant a voice as she could master.

Three pairs of eyes switched from her, to him, and back to her again.

"Sorry, people, but the show's over," she said. "Tommy Love is leaving the premises."

Sheriff Turppa tipped his hat and nodded appreciatively, as though he were thinking this had been a whole lot more entertaining than the summer theatre his mother made him attend in Embarrass.

Tommy handed his overnight bag and his precious guitar to one of the deputies, bent down to put on his Italian leather shoes, stood, squared his shoulders, and walked out the door without saying another word.

She watched from the front door as he slung his leg over the seat of the snowmobile, settled in behind his rescuer, and disappeared down the winding road that led to Billy Bjorklund's house.

Chapter 14

Billy's face was a livid maze of cracks and fissures. "You admitted we're friends? You told her you knew about the foreclosure?"

"I didn't know about the foreclosure. I assumed we were trying to get her to sell because foreclosure was an imminent probability if she didn't. And I didn't admit anything. She figured it out the second the sheriff said your name," Tommy said, his anger leaking through the edges of his soothing Nashville voice like an oil pan with a blown gasket. "Trust me. Lying about it would have made it worse."

"I did trust you. I trusted you to drive to the airport, get in your airplane, fly your butt back to Nashville, and stay away from Rainbow Lake Lodge until the foreclosure was complete and the land belonged to the bank," Billy said, the veins in his neck throbbing. "I trusted you not to do anything stupid between now and then. One simple thing. That's all I asked. One simple thing."

"I just wanted to drive by the place. I didn't know we were going to have sleet," Tommy said, remembering what Hope had said when she found him the morning after the storm. "Actually, the whole thing is probably a blessing in disguise. Just think what could have happened if I'd been up in my plane when the storm hit. I'd probably have ended up at the bottom of some lake instead of being stuck in a ditch."

"So you got stranded and Hope Anderson rescued you," Billy said, oozing disgust. "You didn't have to talk to her."

"What did you expect me to do? State my name, rank and serial number and refuse to talk until I was rescued?"

"You didn't have to tell her you knew me." Billy ran his fingers through his hair and balled them into a fist. "Do you know what this means?"

"I can only imagine."

"I could be accused of conflict of interest. I could be charged with violating every ethical code the Board of Realtors and the Banker's Association adhere to," Billy said, moaning pathetically.

Tommy figured the moaning had more to do with the money Billy was going to lose than with guilt over what he'd been about to do, but he didn't voice his opinion.

"Dang blasted sheriff and his big mouth," Billy said. "What are we supposed to do now?"

"I won't buy the place," Tommy said, unwrapping the sweater that he'd tied around his neck. "I mean, I want the place like the devil, and having seen it up close, I'm even more convinced it's the perfect place for me. But if my living there is going to jeopardize your career or hurt Hope..."

"Hurt Hope?" Billy asked incredulously. "Since when are we worried about hurting Hope?"

"Maybe since she saved my life?" Tommy said, unbuttoning his coat.

"Like crap she did. It never even got below zero, you pansy," Billy said. "You said you had a full tank of gas and over two dozen ketchup packets in your car. If you had stayed with the Porsche, the snowmobiler who drove by the afternoon after the storm would have had you back to town and on your way a whole day earlier."

And he never would have met Hope Anderson. Billy would have proceeded with the foreclosure, he would have bought Rainbow Lake Lodge, probably hired someone to bulldoze the main building and all the girls – Rose, Lily, Daisy, Fern, Ivy, Bluebell, Violet, Petunia and Jasmine – before he even got a look at the place. He would have built his dream house exactly per the plans he'd had his architect draw up, moved in, and lived happily ever after.

"So what was I supposed to do when the merry widow came waltzing by?" Tommy said. "Say no to a hot shower, a tasty meal, and a comfortable bed and tell her I and my ketchup packets preferred to wait out the blizzard in my car?"

He never even would have met Hope Anderson. He wouldn't have been there to help her haul in firewood, get her generator going, or keep the fire stoked. Yes, he probably would have made it just fine. So, probably, would have Hope.

What was it she had said? Something about God having ways of getting us where he wants us to be, if he remembered right.

"She got to you," Billy muttered. "I've known you for over forty years, and two lousy days is all it takes for her to worm her way under your skin. Conniving little – "

"I won't have you talking about her that way," Tommy said, surprising even himself when the voice that came out of his mouth sounded supercharged with testosterone.

"Oh, man." Billy sounded like he was going to be ill. "Please tell me she just got under your skin and not into your heart."

"I'm just worried about her," Tommy said. "She's out there all alone with no power, no telephone, and very little gas." The left side of his brain clicked into problem solving mode.

"Sounds like just the thing she needs to help her realize that she's in over her head," Billy said. "Too bad it didn't get a little colder – she would have been back in the bank with her tail between her legs, begging me to take the place and put her out of her misery."

And I might have been a six-foot, six-inch ice cube, Tommy thought. "I know you have goals," he said, racking his brain to think of a way to get through to Billy. "But you can't go around stomping on other people to get what you want. Not in a town the size of Embarrass. The people in this town look up to you. You're a Bjorklund. Going after a nice lady like Hope, a recent widow whose husband's family was well-known and well-liked, is not going to win you the trust of the people in this town."

"You're starting to sound like my mother. Or my father."

"Yah, well, I can imagine a lot of things a whole lot worse than being like your parents," Tommy said, stripping off the heavy sweater Hope had given him to put on over his shirt.

"Et tu, Brutus?" Billy said.

"Your dad was a great guy," Tommy said.

"Remember when I beat up Nate Kangas?" Billy said.

"Vaguely," Tommy said. "Not exactly one of my most cherished grade school memories."

"Nate Kangas told me that his dad had been in the bank talking to my dad. The jerk told my dad some sob story about his little sister being sick."

"Didn't Nate's dad end up in prison?"

"A couple years after this happened," Billy said. "He would have gone a lot sooner if my father had had the nerve to press charges like he should have."

Tommy was silent.

"My dad didn't even check it out. He just handed Kangas the money and waved as the jerk went skipping out of the bank."

"Nate's little sister wasn't sick?" Tommy said, letting the warmth from the furnace vent sink into his bones.

"The whole thing was a crock."

"There will always be people like Mr. Kangas."

"Nate called my father a wuss," Billy said. "I was in the process of making him eat his words when my Dad showed up. I tried to tell my dad what was what, but he wouldn't listen."

"He probably already knew."

"He grounded me." Billy slammed his fist into his pocket. "He said beating up Nate was unacceptable even if he deserved it."

"He probably knew Kangas was lying from the start," Tommy said.

Billy scowled. "So now you understand why I want to run things differently now that I'm in control."

"You're forcing Hope Anderson off her property because Nate laughed at you in third grade?"

"No," Billy said, turning red. "Because I don't want to be known as a wuss."

"That's the last word that comes to my mind when I remember your dad," Tommy said.

"All I want is a little respect," Billy said, squaring his shoulders like a bull about to charge. "Everybody else in the world gets paid for what they do. Is there anything wrong with me wanting to make a little money?"

"Not a thing," Tommy said, thinking that Billy's dad had always seemed to have plenty of money despite the fact that he'd been generous.

His toes started to itch inside his shoes as heat permeated his body. The better the heat felt, the more guilty he felt thinking about Hope, trapped inside a house whose only warm spot was under a blanket in front of the fireplace.

"I can't stop thinking about Hope," Tommy said.

"She'll be fine. She'll be thanking me before you know it. Finding a new job in a new place, meeting somebody else and getting on with her life is the best thing that could happen to her."

"Not that way. Not someday. Now." He started to move and slipped on a puddle of water from the snow that had melted off his shoes. "If the sheriff's snowmobile could get out to Hope's place to rescue me, then they or I can get back there with enough gas to keep her generator running," Tommy said, grabbing David Anderson's sweater and pulling it back over his head.

"Now I know you've lost it," Billy said.

He reached for his coat. "Do you have some boots I could wear?" Tommy said. "These shoes really aren't made for snow."

Chapter 15

Tommy finished strapping three five-gallon containers of gas to the back of the snowmobile and nodded at the sheriff.

"You're going to stay as close to me as a rat caught on a sticky pad," Sheriff Turppa said for the third time since they started loading the gasoline. "Is that understood?"

"Perfectly," Tommy said.

"The trails aren't marked or groomed yet," Turppa said. "There are barbed wire fences, posts, stumps, utility boxes, marshes, sink holes and every other kind of obstacle between here and there. It's a regular mine field."

"I'll stay right behind you," Tommy reassured him.

"You already appear to have lost your head over this woman. You do exactly what I say or you could lose it, literally."

Tommy shuddered. "I get it."

"Let's get going or we won't be back before dark." Alvin climbed on his snowmobile in front of the gas containers he was carrying. "I know you'd probably like to have an excuse to spend another night with the pretty lady, but my mother will have my head if I get stranded out there."

Tommy laughed, thinking there seemed to be a lot of ways a man could lose his head around the so-called fair sex. "Three of us might be a bit of a crowd for what I had in mind."

"You're assuming she's even going to let you in the door," said Alvin. "She might be happy to see me and the gasoline, but from the sound of things this morning, you might not get such a warm welcome."

The sheriff started his machine and revved the throttle. Tommy followed suit. That was it for the sheriff's witty repartee – there would be no further conversation until they reached Rainbow Lake Lodge.

* * *

Hope pulled up the covers on the makeshift bed she'd shared with Tommy Love, unfolded a wool blanket, and spread it on top of the quilts they'd slept under for the past two nights. She repeated the exercise two more times, smoothing each blanket over the others.

She was as mad as all get out at him. But she was going to miss his body heat. It was going to be colder than Siberia without him.

She'd restarted the fire and hauled in enough firewood to make it through another night as soon as Tommy and his posse had left her alone. Still, her insulated little bubble had been burst. Without him, she couldn't seem to get warm.

She pulled aside the fireplace screen and added another couple of logs to the fire. She wasn't surprised that Tommy Love had turned down her proposition. The advantages had been embarrassingly stacked in her favor. She needed him, someone, anyone, to help her out – without money to hire someone, her options were extremely limited. Tommy did not need her. Tommy had money. Tommy had Jeeves and Hortence to take care of him.

A glowing, well-charred log on the bottom of the fire collapsed under the weight of the new wood she'd just added, emitting a poof of soot and sparks.

Who had she been trying to kid? She honestly believed Tommy would be able to compose beautiful songs if he had a place like the lodge to retreat to, but as far as the arrangement she'd proposed – there was a big difference between a husband and a wife working together as a team to accomplish their mutual goals, and one perfectly sane person taking pity on an insanely stubborn loser who didn't have enough sense to call it quits and sell out to the highest bidder. Assuming there would be any, since, according to Tommy, she would have to be able to prove the lodge was financially solvent before anyone would want to finance or buy the place.

She shivered and pulled both sweaters around her as tightly as she could.

Desperate to be warm again, she went to the bed, lifted back the heavy layers of quilts and comforters, and crawled under the covers.

"Please, God," she whispered. "I'm so cold. So tired. I don't know what to do or think. Please, show me what you would have me to do."

She wasn't sure how long she'd been dozing when she awoke to the sound of someone pounding on the door again. For a second, she'd thought she'd slept right through the night, but in contrast to her dismal spirits, the fire was crackling merrily. She couldn't have been asleep for too long.

She sighed. She had no clue what time it was – the clock in her bedroom was battery operated, but she hadn't bothered to bring it into the great room where the fireplace was. They'd been using Tommy's wristwatch as a clock, but of course, he'd taken it with him when he left.

The pounding resumed. Had Tommy forgotten something? Changed his mind? Whoever it was must have come on a snowmobile or hiked in on snowshoes. Her heartbeat quickened as she climbed from the bed, found a comb and went to the door, trying her best to look nonchalant and unworried in case it was Tommy.

She tugged on the doorknob, put a cheery smile on her face and prepared to greet him in the royal fashion he was no doubt accustomed to. She flung open the door. "Uh?" she said stupidly, looking out at a man who was the antithesis of Tommy Love in every conceivable way. A pair of wary eyes stared out at her from a dark, swarthy, unkempt face. A scar over the man's left eyebrow twitched nervously.

"Everything all right in here, ma'am?" the man said, not bothering to introduce himself, which she could only suppose was standard practice among the fugitives, drifters and escaped convicts of which he looked to be.

"I'm fine," she said, hoping she was right, and thinking everything had been until he had shown up. Well, kind of. She could see a snowmobile parked a hundred yards or so down the driveway, which explained why she hadn't awakened until he pounded on the door.

"There's a car in the ditch out at the end of your road," he said, his voice gravelly, like he hadn't talked to anyone yet that day. Which she could certainly relate to. Some days, when she answered the phone, her voice sounded that way as late as noon, unless she'd remembered to clear her throat, say her prayers out load, or sing along with one of her favorite CDs.

That didn't mean she wasn't afraid.

"I'll be right there, Dad," she said, thinking that if this man was from anywhere around Embarrass, he probably knew that her husband was dead and that she was alone. Few people knew her parents had both passed away soon after she'd married Tommy. *David.* Good grief, what was wrong with her?

"Can I help you with something?" she said, when he didn't say something, or leave, which was definitely her first choice of scenarios.

"I radioed in the license of the car in the ditch earlier this morning. Wanted to make sure everything was okay," he said, his creepy eyes scanning the room behind her. "You being all alone."

C'mon, house, she prayed silently. Make a noise – a rattle, a creak, an echo – anything that could be another person. The floors, beams, furnace and hot water heaters were a regular chorus of snaps, crackles and pops when she was alone. Silence.

"Thankfully the storm hit when I had company," she said, ignoring the fact that without electricity, the house was so quiet that you could have heard a pin drop. "Be with you in a second, Dad," she called out. "There's a man at the door, checking to see if Tommy was alright. He saw the car in the ditch," she said loudly, looking over her shoulder like she expected her invisible guest to appear at any moment.

"He must be in the bathroom," she said, noticing for the first time that the man was very muscular. What she had thought were camouflaged hunting clothes were actually army fatigues. "And we're all just fine. But thanks for stopping by. Have a safe trip home."

She started to close the door.

He put his hand out to stop her.

The familiar roar of snowmobiles filled the air and reverberated through the forest so loudly the pine trees near the driveway shuddered off their coats of snow in a poof of white.

The men were so bundled up that she couldn't be sure who they were, but the machines looked like the same ones that had been there earlier.

Stranger Danger tipped his hat and beat a path to his snowmobile, which, unfortunately, had been parked underneath one of the formerly snow-covered trees.

The rider of the first snowmobile saluted Stranger Danger, swooshed up to the porch in a cloud of white, cut his engine, and leaped off his machine. "What was Dirk Westola doing here?" the sheriff's familiar voice said, his body language indicating that he thought less and less of her the more he learned about the company she kept.

"I certainly didn't invite him over, if that's what you're thinking," she said, as the second snowmobile rider, none other than Tommy

Love, hopped off his machine.

"Where did that slime ball come from and what was he doing here?" Tommy said, his roar loud enough to do a voiceover over Dirk's snowmobile.

She rolled her eyes. "Like it's any of your concern."

"It's mine," the sheriff said. "Guy's a survivalist. Used to live in some compound in Wyoming before all the movie stars started to buy ranches up there. Got too crowded for him," Sheriff Turppa said.

"Is he as dangerous as he looks?" Tommy said.

"His house is probably the safest place in ten counties if they ever unleash a nuke," the sheriff said, taking off his facemask. "Guy literally buried the old Johnson cabin in dirt – and who knows what else. His version of an earth house."

"Whacko," Tommy said. "There's no such thing as a safe whacko."

"Is there a reason for your visit?" she asked, still holding the door half-open. "Because I'm getting cold, and I should restock the fire, unplug the refrigerator, and plug in the freezer."

"We brought gas for the generator," Tommy said.

"Thank you," she said. Tommy was the one who knew that the gas she had in the generator was the last of her supply, not the sheriff. But looking at the sheriff was easier than looking at Tommy.

"I found someone to plow your driveway," Tommy said. "His name is Hal Smith, and he lives on the other side of the lake, which will be a little bit of a pain until the lake freezes. He does two other places over this way, so he'll take care of you one way or the other."

"Thanks," she said. "I know who Hal is. My friend Sharon told me he'd retired."

"He had," Tommy said, watching her closely. "I talked to my agent when we got back to town. He got me out of a gig I had booked for the week before Christmas."

"Why did he do that?" she asked, trying not to sound too cynical and heartless; one, because the sheriff was listening to every word, and two, because Tommy had just brought her gas.

"Because you need help," Tommy said. "I'm filming a live Christmas Special at the Lodge in Yellowstone on Christmas Eve, so I'll only have six days, but I can get a lot accomplished in that time, especially if you can get a list made and some materials rounded up so we can really go to town while I'm here."

She frowned. "I never asked for your help."

"You most certainly did," Tommy said.

"I put a proposition on the table that would have benefited both of us. You turned me down."

"I'm trying to renegotiate the terms," Tommy said. "If you'd stop being so stubborn – "

"A million things could happen between now and Christmas," she said. "You said it yourself. I appreciate what you're trying to do, but I think we both know that there are a lot of things around here that need to be taken care of on a regular basis, and I'm afraid one mid-winter visit just isn't going to do it. I should have realized it a long time ago and made other arrangements. But as you also know, I've been a little tight on funds."

"I could do it," Alvin Turppa said, taking off his cap and gloves.

"What?" Tommy said.

"My day off is Monday," the sheriff said. "I could be here at daybreak and work until dusk, take care of any maintenance work that needs to be done outside, and start on some simple remodeling jobs on the inside. If you're agreeable."

"I appreciate the offer. I really do," she said. "But I have no way to pay you."

"My mother's pushing eighty-five and doesn't like to cook anymore. TV dinners get awfully old. If you cook me a good, homemade breakfast, dinner and supper every time I come to work, maybe a little extra to take home to Mother when I leave, it would be plenty reward enough for me."

"I could do that," she said, thinking of the freezer full of meat and feeling hopeful for the first time since she'd found the thousand dollars cash Tommy – no, David – had hidden away. "It doesn't seem like much payment for doing a lot of grunge work outside in the cold." For the first time, she noticed Tommy's face, which did not look happy, which it should have, since Alvin's gesture effectively let him off the hook. Which meant Tommy wouldn't have to worry about her any more.

"I'm sure we can come up with some other favors to exchange if the situation doesn't seem equitable," Alvin said, smiling for the first time. "I see you have a sewing machine."

He nodded at the sewing table she'd set up by the window before the power had gone out, intending to work on the quilts she was making for the cabins.

"It seems like I've always got buttons falling off or socks that need mending," Alvin said.

"Let me guess," Tommy said. "Mother can't see well enough to sew anymore."

"Exactly," said Alvin.

"Can I see you in the kitchen for a moment, dear?" Tommy looked at her so pointedly she could almost feel the poke.

"I can't imagine what you have to say that can't be said in front of Alvin," she said sweetly, ignoring him and smiling at Alvin. He was the sheriff after all. If you couldn't trust the sheriff, who could you?

She looked at Alvin, and thought about Tommy's kiss. As professions went as a whole, it made a lot more sense to trust a sheriff than it did a rock star. And Alvin didn't look like he wanted anything more than sewing and cooking. Alvin was well known and respected in the community. Not in a big shot, Billy Bjorklund The Banker kind of way, but in a down-home, good old boy manner. He wasn't scary like Stranger Danger or a loose cannon like Tommy Love. She didn't get the feeling that she had anything to fear from Alvin Turppa.

She turned to look at Tommy just as he took her arm and started steering her into the kitchen. Ah – the scene of the crime. Not that kissing was a crime. Kissing could mean many things – a kiss could be a beginning; a kiss could be goodbye. A kiss could mean everything; it could mean nothing. A kiss could have a thousand words wrapped up in it, like a present waiting to be opened; a kiss could be perfunctory – crisp and polite – and that's all.

If that had been all Tommy Love's kiss was – a hey, babe, we've been through a lot these last couples of days, and well, it's been real – it would have been fine. And maybe that's all it had been to him. But to her... She thought back on the way she'd felt in his arms, with his lips on her. Sadly, she'd liked it. Entirely too much. That made Tommy Love way, way more dangerous than Alvin, probably more dangerous than Dirk the Survivalist.

"I don't understand why you're being so stubborn," Tommy said in a stage whisper. "If we're going to have a relationship, we're going to have to decide who gets to be the stubborn one, and who gets to be the one who gives in and smoothes everything over. In my opinion, you have a real gift for the latter."

"Which means you get to be the stubborn, unreasonable one?"

Yeah, right, Hope thought. "The last thing you need is free reign to indulge in your most irritating behavior."

Calm down, she told herself, feeling the flush that was racing through her. Even when Tommy was being polite, she could feel the wild streak that lurked under his polished, gentlemanly demeanor. If he stayed, or even returned, it would come out, probably sooner than later, if his present forwardness was any indication. She did not need wild. Not now, after two years with no male companionship. Who knew what she might do?

She looked over her shoulder at Alvin. Tame and unthreatening as a twenty-year-old cat. From what she knew, he'd never been married. He'd lived with his mother for maybe fifty, fifty-five years if the gray hair at his temples and in his beard was any indication. What or who could be more harmless?

"Do not spoil things with Alvin," she said when they got to the kitchen. "He's here. You're not. I've been praying that God would send someone to help me out of my dilemma, and it's obvious he sent Alvin."

"How do you know he didn't send me?" Tommy said.

"Oh, I think he did," Hope said. "You're like John the Baptist, pointing the way for the Savior, or at least, your car was. If you hadn't gone in the ditch, if your manager hadn't called the sheriff's office, Alvin never would have come looking for you. He never would have known I needed help."

"So, you're saying Alvin here is the real thing, and I'm a half-naked, loin-cloth wearing, bug-eating wild man who's headed for beheadment? No pun intended."

"If the shoe fits," she said, noticing his boots. "You've been shopping."

"They're Billy's," he said.

"Figures," she said, thinking he'd sunk about as low as he could go in the few hours it had taken him to step out of David's boots and into Billy Bjorklund's.

"Just be careful," he said. "Alvin may think all he wants is some good food and a needle and thread, but unless the man has an old war injury I don't know about, he's going to start liking your food, appreciating your talents, and enjoying your pretty smile. And then, he's going to want more."

"Don't be silly," she said.

And then he kissed her. Deeply. Tenderly. As softly as a whisper.

Not wild and bug-juicy at all. And then they were cheek to cheek, just standing there, drawing warmth and strength and joy from each other, and evoking feelings that were at the same time indescribable and wonderful and terrifying.

"Hope?"

"Yes?" she whispered.

"Please don't ask me what this means."

"I wasn't going to."

"Yes, you were," he said, his lips moving against her hair.

"Okay, I was."

"I don't know," he said.

"Me neither," she said.

"You could come and cook for me in Nashville. And mend the holes in my pockets."

"And your socks?" she said.

"No," he said sadly. "My housekeeper throws them away and buys me new ones as soon as the toes even start to get thin."

"Oh."

"It's awful," he said. "I just get them broken in, all soft and comfy like socks should be, and then they disappear."

"I'm so sorry," she said, trying not to giggle.

"She doesn't even let me say good-bye. Gone. Just like that."

"Will you be serious?" she said.

"I am."

"About your socks, or about Nashville?" she said.

He didn't say a word.

"That's okay," she said. "I could never... I mean, I really couldn't."

"Wouldn't," he said. A board creaked somewhere to her left. A rafter let out a snap as it constricted against the warm air replacing the cold. And suddenly, the lights came on, and the entire lodge started to buzz, sing, whisper in relief.

"This is where your heart is," he said.

"Yes," she said.

"Then I wish you all the best."

"I'll be listening for your new song. I know I'm not your target demographic, but I'm sure it will be wonderful."

"I appreciate that." He kissed her on the cheek and walked out the door.

Chapter 16

It had been four weeks since Tommy Love had bopped in – and out – of her life. Hope rethreaded the needle of her sewing machine with yellow thread, bent her head over the cluster of daisies she was appliquéing, and tried to put Tommy Love out of her mind. She was halfway around the first petal but no closer to forgetting him when the doorbell rang.

"Alvin?" she said, finding the sheriff on the other side of the door.

The sheriff shifted his feet nervously. It wasn't a Monday. It was a Wednesday, and Alvin worked on Wednesdays. Not a good sign.

"I'm sorry to say I'm here on official business," he said.

"What on earth?" she said, wondering who had died now, or what she possibly could have done that could be construed as illegal.

"You should have told us you were in trouble before it got this far, Hope. We could have had a benefit," Alvin said.

"A benefit?" *What was going on?* A chill washed over her and in an instant, she felt ten years older than her age. "This doesn't have something to do with Billy Bjorklund, does it?"

"We raised two thousand dollars at the soup supper we had for the Johnson boy who came down with leukemia and the Lutherans matched that with funds from Thrivent."

"I'm not sick," Hope said, which in about thirty seconds was going to be a lie. "Tell me."

"I'm required to serve you with this notice of foreclosure according to the laws of the State of Minnesota," Alvin said, gulping like a nervous teenager.

It didn't take much to fluster Alvin. Hope, on the other hand, was normally very cool under pressure.

"What?" she said stupidly, feeling the heat spread across her cheeks until she could only assume they were as red as Alvin's. Shock, disbelief, then anger washed over her. "Let me see it, please."

He handed her the paper. "I'm so sorry," he said, like she was a loser with a terminal case of pathetic.

"I gave the bank eight hundred dollars less than a month ago," she said. "I knew Billy intended to do this, but I took in eight hundred dollars. That should have been more than enough to... We shook on it."

Alvin shrugged. "It's common knowledge around these parts that Billy's handshake isn't worth much."

"I hate common knowledge. People talk about stupid, trivial things from sunup to sundown, but they don't bother to mention the things you really, truly need to know because it's common knowledge."

"They assume you already know. Everybody around here knows that—"

"Well, I didn't," she said, reminding herself that this wasn't Alvin's fault, that he was on her side, that she shouldn't kill the messenger.

"I know a good attorney in Ely," Alvin said. "He's butted heads with Billy before."

"If I had the money for an attorney..."

"He'll probably talk to you for nothing," Alvin said. "If for no other reason than the fact Billy's involved."

"I really thought..." She was going to say that she had been foolish enough to think that Billy would treat her right because of Tommy. She hadn't given a second thought to handing over her eight hundred dollars to Billy. Tommy had just been rescued and she'd felt so full of herself, so infallible, so hopeful. She'd been such an idiot.

You can trust me, a voice whispered inside her head.

Oh, Lord. She'd gone from anger to blame to bemoaning her fate without once thinking about Him.

"Thanks, Alvin. If you think the attorney will do a preliminary meeting gratis, I'd be happy to see him." Her mind whirled with possible scenarios like a bingo machine tossing around numbers. And then she grasped at the only straw she had left. "If you can put me in touch with whoever it is that organizes local fund raisers in Embarrass, I think I'd like to have a quilt auction."

"Quilts take time to make," Alvin said. "Soup suppers are quick and easy."

"I don't want charity," she said. "There are all kinds of people out there who have far less than I do. It wouldn't be right. And I have a lot of quilts. I've got more than a dozen that were made by my mother and grandmother that should bring a lot of money, and several I've made myself."

"Kind of like Scarlett using the drapes to save Tara," Alvin said.

"I was going to put them in the cabins this summer, but there's no reason to hang onto them if I'm not going to have cabins to use them in."

"But if you sell them to raise money, you'll have cabins, but no quilts."

"I can make more quilts, Alvin. There will never be another Rainbow Lake Lodge."

It was well after midnight when she finally climbed into bed and tried to go to sleep, tried being the operative word.

She tried to pray – to give her anxiety to the Lord – but found no peace. If her Nanny DeLacouer had still been alive, she would have said that this was one of those times when she needed to use the mind the good Lord gave her and get to work.

She was just about to drift off to sleep when something Sharon had said weeks earlier started niggling around in her subconscious.

She lay in the darkness, heart pounding, and finally put two and two together. Tommy Love was Billy's buyer. Tommy Love wanted Rainbow Lake Lodge. It all made perfect, undeniable, horrific sense. *Just happened to be out on Rainbow Lake in a boat on a cold day in October – yeah, right. Wandered off course because of the sleet – yeah, right.* The jerk had been coming out to look over the parcel of land he planned to acquire when he slid in the ditch.

Why hadn't she seen it before? What a fool she was – Billy and Tommy were probably laughing their guts out over her stupid, trusting, naïve nature even now. She'd even let him kiss her. Twice. The first kiss she'd shared with anyone except David since she'd met him twenty-four years ago, and she'd wasted it a piece of slime who wouldn't have looked at her in the first place except that she happened to have what he wanted. *Make nice to the poor widow so she doesn't put up a fight when we try to steal her property.* She could almost hear them talking about her.

She pulled on the quilt, clenched it around her shoulders and tried to stop shivering. Billy Bjorklund was trying to take Rainbow Lake Lodge away from her so Tommy Love could move in. And they'd already won round one. They'd stolen her peace of mind. When her parents had died, she'd had David and the Andersons to see her through. When David's parents had died, they'd still had each other. When David had died, she'd lost not only a husband, but any chance she'd had of having a family of her own. But through it all, she'd still had Rainbow Lake Lodge. If she lost the Lodge, she'd have nothing. No one.

Except me, a still, quiet voice whispered to her heart. *I've been there with you, through it all. I'll be beside you forever.*

Her trembling ceased and she released her death grip on her quilt. *Oh, Lord.* How quick she was to discount the One who could meet all her needs. No matter what was taken from her, she would always have her faith.

Chapter 17

Whitecap after rolling whitecap broke the teal blue horizon of the Pacific panorama spread out in front of Tommy Love. If this wasn't inspiration, he didn't know what was.

He shoved the image of Hope's smile that he carried in the billfold in his mind to the back of his brain. He'd given his dream of moving back to Minnesota a fair shot, but it just hadn't worked out. Even before he'd thought about going back to Embarrass, he'd had it with Nashville's old history, old money, old songs, old news.

Everything about California was new, from the newly constructed mansions lining the hillsides facing the ocean to the punk, pink hairstyles, shiny new cars, and newly made millionaires visible on every corner. California dreaming. California was what he'd needed all along – he just hadn't known it.

He watched as a surfer caught a wave and glided back to shore. The beach was dotted with surfers in wet suits like a baked potato sprinkled with pepper.

He'd been a fool to think that he could find what he was looking for in Embarrass. He should have realized that you can't go back. Nor did he want to regress. He was trying to reinvent himself, wasn't he? Capture the fancy of a new generation. Preserve his fading, practically non-existent popularity for all time. Start out fresh. Explore new worlds. Go where no Lubinski had ever gone. California was a perfect fit.

He tore his eyes from the mesmerizing beat of the waves and looked to the right, then the left, where the walls of the beach houses on either side of the deck of the place he'd rented rose in parallel symmetry.

Granted, he'd never have the privacy or the seclusion he would have had if he'd booted Hope out of the Lodge and made Rainbow Lake his private abode. But here, he didn't need it. First off, people weren't nosy like they were in Minnesota. No one cared. He'd laid in bed that very morning listening to his new neighbors argue about where and how to spend their next vacation. Their conversation had morphed into a list of accusations which included multiple indiscretions and affairs on the part of both the husband and the wife, assuming they were married in the first place, and ended with noisy make-up sex. And the best part was, he hadn't even cared. He didn't know the people from Adam except that they pulled out of their garage once or twice a day in a white BMW convertible.

Californians were so desensitized by movie stars and business moguls that no one was likely to look twice at an aging rock star – unless he hired a publicist to make sure he was in the limelight, and then, the possibilities were as infinite as the stars on Hollywood Boulevard.

His mind drifted back to Hope, and for a moment, he let himself wonder how she was faring.

Sure, a part of him longed for lazy afternoons on Rainbow Lake, quiet evenings at the Lodge eating Almond Crusted Walleye and homemade apple pie, nights... He sighed... nights tucked under a handmade quilt strew with violets or roses, even petulant petunias. He wasn't picky as long as Hope was under the covers.

He stood and paced the length of the deck.

Bottom line, if he'd stayed in Embarrass, he'd have probably ended up married to Hope Anderson, singing oldies but goodies for a bunch of snot-nosed kids and their mommies and daddies at Rainbow Lake Lodge, and writing Christmas anthems for the church choir in Embarrass. The Flying Finn would finally have had something noteworthy to write about in their monthly newsletter and all would have been well... and boring as hell.

His blood surged through his veins like molten lava as he fought back the protective instincts he felt for Hope. *Fine.* So he wanted Hope Anderson, wanted to sit on the deck at Rainbow Lake Lodge and write songs about hope, joy, peace, and love.

What he wanted even more was a new hit single. Hope wasn't the only one motivated by her need to preserve a legacy. He'd worked hard to make good on the talent God had given him – but unless he kept working, it would all be for naught. Hope deserved a chance to make her dream come true. Well, so did he.

He turned his back on his rental cottage and tried to let the sound of the surf soothe his hurts. What he really needed was a twenty-something girlfriend. Think old, and you were old. If he thought young, went to the right clubs, partied with the right people, caught the attention of a few influential folks, he'd have a new record contract in no time. The Tommy Love legacy would live on... and on... and on.

He flipped open his cell phone and checked his messages. Unfortunately, one thing the central coast did have in common with northern Minnesota was crappy cell phone reception. Thankfully, he wasn't likely to be sliding into any ditches during ice storms while he was in sunny California.

He opened his laptop and scanned his emails next, most of them from the secretary at his answering service. Vince wanted him to do background vocals on his new CD, JT needed to know the name of the bass guitarist he'd used on his last album (which told you exactly how long ago that had been). His agent was trying to negotiate a deal for Tommy to open for Barry Manilow on his upcoming "Remember When" Tour.

He quickly typed a reply to his agent stipulating that he would do no more concert appearances where he was required to do nothing but oldies. Not that playing his new music for a bunch of Barry Manilow fans would be a huge help, but it was always possible that someone might bring a kid along to hear the music the parent had loved as a teenager, or that a disc jockey or producer might be in the audience. That aside, it was a matter of principal. He knew his old hits would always follow him around. That was fine as long as he was also allowed to give people a glimpse of the new, improved Tommy Love.

He made some notes while his thoughts were fresh in his mind. He hadn't been on tour in so long that he would have to reassemble a band. The instrumentalists would have to be able to play his old stuff and the new. He made a note to talk to his agent about a drummer he'd heard the week before in a club in San Luis Obispo, a guitarist who'd played for Brittney Spears on her second tour, and a bass player who'd wowed the crowds at the Telluride Bluegrass Festival a couple of years back.

Hmmm... He'd heard a banjo player named Bela Fleck perform at the same festival. The guy had gone from traditional bluegrass to a new genre that he called fusion – a little bit of bluegrass mixed with hard rock, blues, and classical. Tommy's goal wasn't to invent his own style of music like Bela had, but he suspected the banjo player could give him a few clues on how to convince your old fans to stay with you through the transition – better yet, how to capture the hearts of a new genre of listeners.

He made some more notes on his computer. The fresh, sea air was already working wonders. He hadn't thought of any of this stuff back in stodgy, old, everything-always-stays-the-same Embarrass. California was obviously exactly what he'd needed to get the old juices going. Much as he'd always loved the north woods, California was going to work out much better than Rainbow Lake would have in any number of ways, including being closer to Leno when his new song started to climb the charts and his phone started to ring.

And talk about inspiration. How many songs could a bunch of white birch and green pines trees inspire? He'd been a fool to think he could write in such a homogenous environment. He looked out, albeit straight out, at the panoply of ocean, flowers, rooftops, trees, colors, and sky. Even the cars flying by on the relatively straight section of Highway One between him and the ocean were stimulating in their own way. The whole place was a microcosm of society – its ills, its woes, its beauty, its opulence, and its deficiencies. Which is exactly what he wanted his song to be about. Rainbow, shmainbow. Been there, done that. The only stars he knew who'd made it big because of a rainbow connection were Kermit the Frog and Judy Garland. Enough said. He was all about California now. Upscale. With it. Cutting edge. Down and dirty. Happening.

With a chuckle, he acknowledged the irony of his own antiquated vocabulary and flipped from his email to a search engine where he could look for a dictionary of modern slang. He'd give Vince a call after he'd written another line or two of the Loveman's new hit.

Which reminded him – the Love Notes may have worked back in 1984, but they would never do for the new millennium. He opened another Word file and started to toy with names that would be related but unique. He played with Tommy Love and the e Males, Tommy Love and the Diss Chords, and Tommy Love and the Quarter Notes – all lacking in pizzazz, but he had to start somewhere.

An hour later, he was still staring at his computer screen, trying to think of a word that rhymed with junk. Trunk, bunk, clunk, drunk. He rapped his fingers against the desk. Thunk. No. Still not right. He needed something upbeat. Thunk described his life. A big, empty zero. A waste. A major disappointment. Unless he wanted his new song to be a flop, he had to start thinking differently. Young. With it. Hip. Which once again proved how out of it he was. Think chick-lit in music form, he told himself. Phat. Punk. Punk! That was it.

He settled back in his chair and tried to work out the rest of the chorus. A coastal robin (he had no idea why people called the deer, birds and rodents who lived along the coast coastal deer, birds, and rats – they looked like regular old animals and fowl to him), chirped saucily from the branch of some sort of redwood tree he didn't yet know the name of. He ignored the sound and started to type.

Hope for every tomorrow.
Sunshine and joy after rain.

He pressed delete and erased the words. Cute and sweet was not going to endear his work to a new generation. Thinking about Hope Anderson was not going to help him acclimate to California. He flipped back into his email so he could fire off a memo to his realtor. He ended the note with "Soon is not soon enough."

Chapter 18

Stan Paulsen's office didn't look anything like Hope had expected. The chairs were glorified folding chairs for which the word glorified was way too nice. His desk might have qualified for retro except that retro implied a standard of workmanship associated with the fifties, when things were built better than they were nowadays. His old, decrepit desk wasn't. She hadn't expected *L.A. Law*, but she'd been told Mr. Paulsen was a hotshot lawyer and the rumpled, disheveled man before her did not jive with her preconceived notions.

"Stan Paulsen," he said, looking at some papers instead of her. "Please have a seat."

It was common knowledge, what attorneys were supposed to be like. Evidently no one had told Stan Paulson that he was supposed to look pressed and starched, that attorneys were supposed to have plush leather arm chairs and huge, solid cherry desks and a conference room with the door left ajar so you could see the cavernous, boat-shaped table as you walked past the receptionist, which Stan didn't have either.

Obviously, no one had told him what he was supposed to have done with his office. They'd all assumed he knew. Maybe that's what made her feel the first stirrings of an odd sort of kinship with Stan Paulsen.

"I'm not sure what Alvin told you when he called," she said, wondering if it was okay to start, or if she was supposed to not speak until she was spoken to.

"He mentioned Billy Bjorklund," Stan said, ruffling through some papers.

"Yes," she said, feeling like she was taking him away from business much more important than she.

Stan leaned back in his chair and looked her square in the eye. "Why don't you tell me what brings you here today?"

"I own a resort called Rainbow Lake Lodge. My husband and I inherited it from his parents when they passed away," she said in a rush of words, not wanting to take up time she wasn't paying for.

"When my husband died, I used the insurance money I received to continue the renovations we'd begun on the guest cabins and the dock. Then the building inspector came and told me that the existing kitchen at the Lodge would no longer be grandfathered because I had closed the Lodge and would be reopening under new ownership. When I learned that I would have to bring the kitchen up to code before I reopened, I made an appointment to see Rose Bjorklund at Embarrass National Bank and applied for a construction loan that would enable me to finish the work I'd begun, put in a commercial kitchen and reopen the resort for the upcoming season."

Stan stopped taking notes and looked up at her. "And the terms of the loan?"

"The maximum amount I was allowed to borrow was a hundred thousand dollars, and the money was loaned on an as needed basis as I submitted bills."

"Standard terms for a construction loan," he said. "Payments deferred until the work was completed?"

"Yes," she said. "Which is part of the problem."

"In what way?"

"The construction crew worked all summer to finish the repairs on the cabins, which they did in late September. I had hoped to have the lodge done by then as well, but everything took longer than I thought it was going to, and they had to wait for some of the materials to come in."

"Also more or less standard for the construction business. What contractor did you use?"

"Kevin Justinen and Sons."

"They have an excellent reputation."

"I've been very happy with them," she said. "When it became apparent that they weren't going to be done by winter, Kevin asked if he could come back and finish the work early next spring. My place is too hard to get to in the winter, and he had already committed to another job in town that he was supposed to start in October. He could have gotten the kitchen torn apart before he left, but I preferred not to live with the mess over the winter if I didn't have to. Kevin promised to be back on March first, and to have everything completed by Memorial Day weekend when the Lodge always opens."

"Sounds fair enough. So when did the trouble start?"

"When Billy notified me that the loan was closed and that

payments were to begin immediately."

"Had you reached the loan limit?"

"No. Not even close. Although I probably would have before the kitchen was done." She squeezed her hands together. "Everything keeps going up – lumber, copper, utilities. Kevin warned me we would likely be over the budget if the current building trends continued."

"But construction had stopped?"

"Only temporarily. And Billy knew I had no way to start loan payments until May when the Lodge reopened."

"My understanding is that Rose Bjorklund has retired and is no longer actively involved in the bank. Is that correct?"

"To the best of my knowledge, yes."

"What did you do when you received the notice that you had to begin making payments immediately?" Stan asked, scribbling furiously.

"I didn't know what to do. I fretted. I prayed. That's when I found a thousand dollars in cash taped to the back of a drawer in my Grandma's armoire. I took what I could in to Billy as a good faith payment. I told him it was all I could do until June, and we shook hands. I assumed that would be the end of it. Then the foreclosure notice arrived."

"Alvin mentioned that you have a theory as to why Billy was so quick to foreclose."

"Yes." Hope swallowed hard. It all sounded so petty when she said it out loud. They were supposed to be adults, not a couple of grade school, hair-pulling girls fighting over noon recess.

"I believe that Tommy Love told Billy he wanted to purchase a property like mine. Billy has always made it clear that he thought I should move into town and give up trying to run the Lodge by myself. My theory is that when Billy realized he had a buyer with cash in hand, he decided to speed things along so he could sell the Lodge to his friend, Tommy Love."

"Sounds like a plausible theory, knowing Billy. His commission would be motivation enough, even if he wasn't friends with Tommy Love." Stan Paulsen looked at her over the rim of his glasses. "I'm assuming you have some proof."

"No," she said, knowing she was probably blushing. "Idle accusations all."

Stan leaned back in his chair and stroked his chin, looking relaxed except for his eyes, which bored into her as if he could see her very soul. "Alvin mentioned you formulated your theory after Tommy Love was stranded at the Lodge during the ice storm. Any chance Love will corroborate your theory?"

She could feel her cheeks going from warm pink to red hot. "I don't know. I like to think he'd be honest if I confronted him, but I have to assume his loyalties would be with Billy."

"If the two of you bonded on some level while you were stranded at the Lodge, he may not be so ready to stand by and watch Billy throw you off the property as he was when the plot was first hatched. Assuming he has a heart."

"I think Tommy is a pretty decent man," she said.

"With bad taste in friends," Stan said, closing his notebook. "Honor among thieves. It could hurt us."

"Can you help me?" Hope said.

"We can sue Billy for unethical conduct and report him to the Banker's Association and the Board of Realtors. If Billy had a reputation to maintain, that alone could be threat enough to get him to back down. But Billy has no conscience, and everybody already knows he's a weasel, so without proof, I don't think that will faze him."

"And the bank or the other realtors wouldn't take disciplinary action?"

"Not without proof," Stan said.

She hesitated, and Stan was patient enough to allow her a few seconds of quiet.

She wasn't looking for an excuse to call Tommy Love. Really. She wasn't.

Stan cleared his throat. "If you have a number where Tommy Love can be reached, I'd be happy to call him. I'm assuming he has an unlisted number, or at the very least, a service to screen his calls."

Stan's offer was tempting – isn't that what people paid attorneys for? To do their dirty work? But she wasn't paying Stan Paulsen, and more importantly, deep inside, it felt like something she needed to do.

"I'll do it," she heard herself say. "I'll call him." If she could. For the first time, she felt the difference in their stations in life. She, after all, was a nobody, and he, a star.

Stan reached for a file.

"So everything hinges on Tommy Love," Hope said.

"In a word, yes."

Chapter 19

Tommy Love was happy that he had a blond bombshell who was stacked to the max for a realtor for a variety of reasons, but mostly because her scantily clad body and bleached hair rendered her as unlike Hope Anderson in mannerism and attire as a woman could be. Unfortunately, at the moment, he was very close to firing Buffy Morganstern, despite her multiple assets.

"It's not the house," he said patiently. "It's the noise. It's too close to One – the traffic sounds like it's coming from the living room."

"I really think what you're hearing is the ocean," Buffy said. "Scientific studies have shown that the sound of waves crashing on the rocks is so similar to the sound of cars driving on the highway that the two are virtually indistinguishable."

"Yeah, right," he said.

"Really," she said.

"Well, then," Tommy said. "The way the waves crash against the rocks at this particular location is too noisy for my taste."

"If you don't like the ocean, we should drive up toward Paso Robles and see the vineyard I told you about last week," Buffy said.

"I like the ocean," Tommy said. "Maybe a section of beach that doesn't have such a rocky shoreline wouldn't be so noisy." With a house that doesn't back up to the interstate, he wanted to add.

"The house at the vineyard is set in the middle of one hundred twenty acres," Buffy said. "It's fifteen miles from the nearest highway, and four miles from the nearest neighbor. A lot of movie stars are buying vineyards when they retire," Buffy said, not knowing it was exactly what he didn't want to hear.

"I'm not retiring," he said. "I'm here to get a fresh start."

"Okay," she said, sounding patronizing. "So how about we look at the house on the north side of Morro Bay?"

Tommy let Buffy drive to the next property, and the next, and the next, although it was clear they were on a hopeless mission.

He lowered his head against the wind. It seemed to have come from nowhere.

"The ocean has a very serene sound from the deck of this home," Buffy said, her voice so full of hope that he wanted to scream. "I can barely hear the ocean at all. The waves are like little baby bear laps, lulling you to sleep."

She was right about the ocean. He could barely hear the surf – the wind was so incredibly loud that everything else was muted in comparison. He looked at Buffy's moving lips and tried to pop his ears, but the dull roar of the wind was still there, muffling, whistling, irritating him like a dripping faucet or a woman with a whiny voice.

"I think I've seen enough," he said, not bothering to go into detail. Buffy Baby just didn't get it – or him.

Because he wanted to be polite, he let Buffy show him three more houses before he called it quits – one with a cactus garden for a yard, one with termite damage, and the last with three kids and four hyperactive dogs frolicking on a deck that was six inches from the house they were touring. If he'd wanted that kind of togetherness, he could have stayed and done the gig at Rainbow Lake Lodge.

He looked away from the dry, baked, golden-colored sand, rock and dirt mixture under his feet as they climbed into Buffy's car and finally admitted the truth. He'd been at the beach for a month and he hated it. Every dry, hard, drop of it. He'd had it up to here with rocky shorelines and the way the ocean kept eating away at it, relentlessly, night and day. He'd had it with waves that never stopped, gritty, abrasive, insinuating sand, salt water that dried your skin and burned your throat, and shallow, materialistic people who didn't care who he was or what he did. What he wanted – had always wanted – was quiet, blue, lake water that soothed and slipped over you like satin and lapped the shore in lazy, peaceful sips. He wanted green, full-of-life firs and pines, white-barked birch trees, soft, mossy dirt covered with pine needles, and nosy neighbors who knew everything about you – well, not really, but he was willing to put up with them to have the rest.

As if on cue, they drove past a grove of eucalyptus trees, their bark hanging in tattered shreds like excess skin on a dying man. Other trees were covered with so much Spanish moss that the life had literally been squeezed out of them. A pair of buzzards circled overhead, their vast wings casting ominous shadows over the already dead terrain below.

"Let's skip the rest of the properties for now," he said. "I need to mull things over."

But he didn't. He already knew. He wanted Rainbow Lake Lodge. He wanted to be Embarrassed. He wanted to go home.

"Sure," Buffy said. "I'm free on Wednesday afternoon if you'd like to get together then. Most of the houses we're looking at are vacant and on lock boxes, so I won't have to rearrange things with any owners."

"Great," Tommy said. "I don't want to cause any trouble."

"Wait," Buffy said, rechecking her list while they sat at a stoplight waiting to get back on One. "I forgot about the house on Rainbow Bay. We're supposed to be there between four and six."

Rainbow Bay? Tommy looked out the window and up at whatever square of sky happened to be framed by the opening. *What was God trying to pull now?* Just a second ago, he'd been ready to move back to Minnesota, marry Hope Anderson and join the church choir. If God were as buddy-buddy with Hope Anderson as it seemed, then you'd think that would be that – end of story.

He looked up again. He knew he could be thick-headed sometimes. *Okay. Stubborn.* He snuck another glance at the sky. *Okay! Obstinate might be a better word. But mulish? I thought you liked mules?* He asked God silently. *You trusted your son and Mary to ride the back of one, didn't you?*

That's my point, God seemed to be saying. *I can use you even when you're acting like an ass – if you'll let me.*

Oh, I'll let you, Tommy conceded. He might be mulish, but he wasn't stupid. Arguing with God was never the smart thing to do. He'd been guilty of temporarily forgetting that God wanted a say in how he lived his life and doing his own thing at times, but he drew the line at downright arguing. What was the point? You weren't going to win.

So he might as well play along. He had no inkling what God was trying to tell him, but somehow, he felt sure he was about to find out.

Buffy glanced at her watch. "The house on Rainbow Bay is still occupied, so I had to schedule something that was convenient for the family. We had a really hard time finding something that would work. They have little children and a newborn and between doctor's appointments and naps and feeding schedules... If you don't mind, it would be nice if we could see it before we quit for the day."

"Sure," Tommy said nonchalantly, as if he hadn't just gotten a nod from God Almighty. "Let's take a look."

It turned out that Rainbow Bay was six or so miles north of Cayucos, between a little town called Harmony that had a population of eighteen, and Green Valley Road, the main highway to Paso Robles.

Whoever had named the places had obviously had a sense of humor.

"If this place is so perfect, why are the owners trying to sell?" Tommy said. And why didn't you bring me here first, he thought, grumbling to himself about realtor strategies that involved showing the prospective buyer dozens of places that were totally wrong for them until you broke their spirit, only to show them one last place that was perfect for them at the very moment they reached the desperate, I'll-buy-the-first-place-that's-halfway-decent point. If Buffy was smart enough to figure out such strategies, which he wasn't entirely sure of, she'd certainly played him like a fiddle.

Or maybe he should be giving God credit where credit was due. When it came down to it, the theory that God could work through Buffy was more plausible that the one about Buffy being smart.

"They don't want to sell," Buffy said. "The wife is a children's author and illustrator, and loves it here. But her husband's company transferred him to San Francisco, and houses are so expensive up there that they really can't afford to own places in both areas."

"Couldn't he rent an apartment and commute on weekends?"

"From what I understand, they talked about it, but neither of them is willing to have an arrangement that would mean he wouldn't get to be home with the children every night."

"Oh," Tommy said.

"So they compromised," Buffy said, implying he could learn something from their example.

"Okay," Tommy said. "When are they going to be out?"

"It was just listed earlier this week – I almost didn't bring you up here. I know you want to move into something immediately, and the Fisher's can't be out for a month."

The outcropping of land the house was built on was set far enough back from the highway that traffic noise wouldn't be a problem. "Doesn't hurt to take a look," Tommy said.

And it didn't. Hurt at all. Rainbow Bay was too small a bay to be listed on the map, but he found out immediately why the locals had named it such – the house was built on the top of a cliff. The water crashing on the rocks at the bottom of the bay created a mist that more or less resulted in a permanent rainbow whenever the sun was out.

The novel thing was, the beach was far enough from the house and the walls of the cliffs juxtaposed just so that the sound of the breakers was amazingly quiet. That was at high tide. At low tide, the waves receded to expose a tidy square of absolutely private, inaccessible-to-anyone-else-except-by-boat, sandy beach with the most amazing rocks he'd ever seen. That, judging from the collection the current owners had amassed, and photos they'd taken at high and low tides.

The fact that Mrs. Fisher had painted murals on several walls throughout the house and decorated each of the rooms in keeping with the theme of one of her favorite children's books was the icing on the cake. The *Amelia Bedelia* room was inexplicably his favorite. Handbags, hats and quirky dresses Mrs. Fisher had collected from area thrift shops and second hand stores shouldn't have been his thing, but the room had such a homey feel that he couldn't help himself.

"I'll take it," he said, the shock on Buffy's face mirroring his own. "We should get the paperwork started immediately. I can't imagine this place will be on the market for long."

"Don't you even want to know what the asking price is?

As it turned out, he really didn't. But it was doable, and that was the important thing. He'd have to sell some serious stock and get the new song done like yesterday so the thing could be produced and start raking in the bucks, but he could do it. He could do it!

The one big catch was, he was going to have to talk to Billy. Buying the house on Rainbow Bay was going to stretch him to the limit financially. If Rainbow Lake Lodge did come on the market at some point, which he really hoped it didn't, buying it was out of the question now that he'd committed to California.

Much as Tommy hated going back on his word – ever – in a way, this was the out he'd been looking for. Being involved in Billy's plot in any way, shape or form had been so distasteful to him since he'd met Hope that he could barely stomach thinking about it. Staying in California permanently was the perfect excuse to wash his hands of the whole mess.

At least he wouldn't be the one to dash Hope Anderson's dreams. In fact, he need never see her again.

Not that he wouldn't love to. His thoughts wandered to her thick, auburn hair, her smile, the dimples at the sides of her cheeks, and the hopefulness, however naïve, that made her Hope. If he'd met her in a different place, under different circumstances, they might have been able to forge a life together.

That was assuming she was over losing David. She was still so much in love with him that it hurt to watch.

Even then, their chances would be next to nil. He and Hope Anderson were very different, and in ways that really mattered. She longed to be surrounded by people – customers and kids and co-workers and friends – the more the merrier. He wanted a place where he could enjoy a little privacy, a quiet, peaceful home where he could write uninterrupted, a secluded retreat where he would be free to create.

Much as he cared about her, much as he wished he could spend more time with her and see where things went, it would be more caring to simply walk away than to lead her on.

He dialed Billy's cell phone number as soon as he reached his rental house, using the cordless so he could flip on lights & open doors as he went. He'd fretted that there weren't any screens when he'd first reached the shore, worried that a coastal mouse or coastal fly might sneak in when he wasn't watching. He hadn't seen a single fly, say nothing about the pesky mosquitoes Minnesota had millions of, since he'd been here. As for the coastal mice, if they existed, he'd deduced they all stayed out because there was no reason for them to come in.

The House on Rainbow Bay was going to be perfect for him.

It was two hours later in Minnesota than it was in California, so he dialed Billy's home number, assuming Billy would be home from the bank unless it happened to be his night to bowl.

"Hey, bro," Billy answered. "You find a beach babe yet?"

"No, but I found a house that has my name written all over it," Tommy said, hesitating, hoping Billy would get the point.

"Perfecto," Billy said. "California in the winter, Minnesota in the summer. If I was retired and didn't have to be at work every day, that's the way I'd do it."

"I'm not retiring," Tommy said. "I'm starting out fresh. I'm reinventing myself."

"You know what they say about the wheel," Billy said.

"I know what they say," Tommy said. "I also know that wheels used to be flat and made of steel, and that now they're round and made of rubber."

"Still wheels," Billy said.

"Wheels, yes, but of a whole different variety. Better than they were."

"I like your old music," Billy said. "Make some more of the same and your old fans will clamor to buy it."

"Hopefully, they, and a few million new fans will both buy my new song," Tommy said.

"Have you been able to write it yet?" Billy said.

"It's coming along," Tommy said.

"That's what I'm saying, man," Billy said.

Tommy swallowed his rebuttal, which wasn't hard, because there wasn't much he could say. The only song he had even halfway written was *Hope for Every Tomorrow*. Which he was so not going to finish.

"I'm calling about Rainbow Lake Lodge, Billy," he said, dreading his friend's reaction.

"Oh, yeah," Billy said. "Sorry I haven't been keeping you filled in on all the nitty-gritty, but I figured after meeting Hope, you probably preferred not to know all the gory details."

"There are gory details?" He had hoped things would have resolved themselves by now – one way or the other. If Billy knew he wasn't interested in buying the property, maybe he would be more motivated to strike some sort of workable agreement with Hope.

"Here's the thing," Tommy said, clearing his throat. "Now that I've found a place in California, I'm no longer interested in buying Rainbow Lake Lodge."

"You're kidding," Billy said.

"Not at all," Tommy said.

"I knew this would happen," Billy said. "This is because of Hope, isn't it?"

"No," Tommy said. "It's because of me. I don't have enough money to buy both places. Do you have any idea what real estate goes for in California these days?"

Billy was silent for a second. "Screw you, Lubinski."

"I'm sorry, Billy. Sorry I ever got mixed up in this mess. I'm sure you don't care what I have to say, but I really think you should find a way to help Hope keep the lodge instead of taking it from her."

"You just don't get it, do you, Lubinski?" Billy said. "When I declared my intent to start foreclosure proceedings, no one knew that you were interested in buying the place. If they had, I would have been accused of unethical practices. That's why I told you to stay away from the lake."

"I never told Hope anything. If she figured it out, it was all on her own," Tommy said. "Which should tell you you're dealing with someone smart enough to win this little game."

"It wasn't a game when you wanted in on the action," Billy said. "And I can't go back now even if I wanted to. Do you know how suspicious it would look if I halted the foreclosure proceedings at the same time you decided not to buy the place? May as well announce my underhanded dealings to the press, lock me up and throw away the key."

"Isn't there anything we can do?" Tommy asked.

"Not unless you're prepared to back out on the California deal and go with the plan we agreed on."

"Sorry, pal. I just don't think I could be happy there after what happened."

"For awhile, I thought maybe you and Hope... " Billy's words trailed off mid-sentence.

"Different dreams," Tommy said.

"Missed your chance anyway," Billy said.

"Oh, really?"

"The sheriff has made his move and is circling for the kill."

"Alvin?"

"Strangely enough, I think it was you breaking the ice that opened the door for Alvin to move in," Billy said.

"He's moved in?"

"Not that I know of. But from what everyone says..." Billy laughed.

"Well, I guess you're not the one to pass along a greeting on my behalf," Tommy said.

"Afraid not," Billy said.

Tommy looked out at the ocean and steeled his heart. He was going to finish his new song and move on. It was what he'd wanted for years. A couple of kisses didn't change that. He had an opportunity to start over, and he was going to take it, Hope or no Hope.

Chapter 20

Hope pinned two squares of calico together – one, lavender, and one, violet – then checked to make sure she had the pieces right side up before adding one of pale yellow and two of green. Speed quilting was hardly the way she liked to do her sewing – the pace she'd set for herself was so frenzied that she might as well be sewing underwear in some sweat shop in Taiwan. But she had no choice if she was going to be ready for the auction.

"How does this look, Hope?" Sharon stood in front of the windows that looked out to the lake holding a poster. "It's all on the computer, so if you want me to change anything, I can."

"I just hope we have a good turn-out. I'm worried that the week before Christmas will be such a busy time that no one will come. Of course, if we have another blizzard, it won't matter."

"Stop," Sharon said. "You've got enough to worry about without adding *what-ifs* to the list."

"Thanks. That's very comforting. I think," Hope said.

Molly, a friend from church who'd come out to help cut fabric, said, "December is a great time for an auction. People will probably buy all kinds of last minute Christmas gifts."

"A lot of people get money for Christmas – what better way to treat themselves than to splurge on something beautiful like a quilt?" Sharon added.

"And anyone who can't afford a quilt will still be able to bid on the pies," Molly said. "Last I heard, the ladies from church had commitments for over a hundred pies. If they sell for ten dollars each, that's over a thousand dollars right there."

"At Harley Peterson's benefit last spring, Marge Yoder's sour cream raisin pie went for twenty-five," Sharon said, inserting a new color cartridge in Hope's printer.

"I didn't want anyone to feel obligated to donate anything," Hope said, feeling even more uncomfortable than she had a minute ago.

"Posh," Molly said. "This is Minnesota. You can't have a sale without food."

"But it's also Embarrass, and this is embarrassing," Hope said. "The middle school youth are going to keep the money from the cake walk and the sloppy joes to buy new football jerseys for the Nighthawks, correct? I don't want to hear anything about them taking a vote after the fact and deciding to donate the money to save the lodge. I meant what I said about charity."

"I told everyone how you feel," Sharon said. "But you have to realize that people care about you. They knew and loved David from the time he was a baby. And they haven't forgotten all the church hayrides and wiener roasts and canoeing parties the Andersons held out here over the years. If they decide to share what they have, it's because they want to."

"You can't let your pride stand in the way of the joy they'll get from giving," Molly said, setting down the periwinkle calico she was cutting long enough to give Hope a hug.

"If it makes you feel better, you can pass along the favor once you get back on your feet," Sharon said.

"You guys are wonderful." Hope choked back tears. "I just feel guilty accepting all of this help. Alvin has been out here every Monday for two months from sun-up to sundown taking care of David's boat, chopping lumber, clearing out the underbrush around the lodge, caulking windows, cleaning out the garage..."

"Alvin is a good man," Sharon said. "You could do a lot worse than Alvin."

"See, that's what I'm afraid of," Hope said. "If I keep accepting help from Alvin, people are going to start thinking that he and I are a couple. And I really don't want anyone, especially Alvin – "

"It's been two years, sweetheart," Molly said, stacking a pile of rose-colored triangles. "No one will think any less of you if you're ready to start dating."

"But I'm not," Hope said. "Alvin is a very nice man, and he's been so helpful. I just don't..."

She didn't think ill of Alvin, never had. She'd never been attracted to him either. But then, she hadn't ever been attracted to anyone except David, hadn't wanted to be attracted, even to Tommy Love. It had just happened. Now that Tommy was gone, it wasn't like she was in the market to find someone to replace him. She hadn't wanted that – him – it, in the first place. Tommy had been a minor distraction, a short-lived blip on the screen of life. That's all. The sheriff's offer of help had been very welcome, but she didn't intend to repay his kindness with a date, or anything else.

"You and Alvin made a deal." Molly clucked like a mother hen intent on keeping a fox away from her chicks. "If he's confused about the terms of the arrangement, then he can deal with it like a big boy, or move on."

"I don't want to hurt him," Hope said. "Not when he's been so good to me."

"Helping out around here has helped Alvin just as much as it's helped you," Sharon said, putting more paper in the printer. "All Alvin Turppa has ever needed is a little couth – and to get away from that crotchety old mother of his. You've taught him how to talk to a lady, how to act around women. You may not have noticed, but Alvin has really come out of his shell since he's been helping you out."

"There you go," Molly said. "You've given him a gift, whether you realize it or not."

Hope smiled, and snipped the ends of thread dangling from the block she'd just sewn. "I don't know how to thank you guys."

"One more thing you can cross off your list of things to worry about," Molly said, grabbing a pale yellow polka dot fabric from the pile of fat quarters.

"Any other problems you'd like us to solve?" Sharon said.

"Either of you want to call Tommy Love and ask if he'd be willing to testify against his old friend, Billy Bjorklund, in a court of law?"

Molly looked at Sharon. Sharon looked at the floor.

"I'm afraid you're on your own when it comes to Tommy Love, sweetheart," Molly said.

Chapter 21

Tommy stretched out in his royal blue Adirondack chair, looked down at the piece of paper in his hand, and tried to ignore the sensations swirling through his body. Hope Anderson had called him – jumped through quite a few hoops to get to him, too, if he knew his answering service.

He'd received word that she'd called the night before, but it had been late even in California – too late, he'd decided, in Minnesota.

His anticipation had simmered all night, while the song he didn't want to write raced through his veins.

Hope for Every Tomorrow, the melody his sub-conscious had written, had two verses, a chorus, and a riff. *Junk It, Punk. It's A Lot of Bunk* was all of 4 lines long and going nowhere fast.

A wave of pleasure swept past the barriers he'd so carefully engineered to keep Hope Anderson out of his thoughts. For a second, he allowed himself to remember her smile, the lilt of her voice, the way her hair teased her cheeks.

Junk It, Punk. It's a Lot of Bunk, he told himself. No way was he going to be Hope Anderson's handyman, groundskeeper, and entertainer in residence for a bunch of old fogies, their nuclear families and two point five children. Vary the job description and nothing changed. There was still no way he would ever agree to be a stand-in for a dead man.

He pushed his emotions aside with the ruthlessness of an army sergeant until any remnant of the pleasure he'd indulged in was so unrecognizable that he couldn't remember what he'd ever seen in the woman, or Rainbow Lake Lodge for that matter.

He dialed the number, steeling himself against the sweetness of the nectar she unknowingly emitted. He had the House at Rainbow Bay, the whole Pacific Ocean, and a state full of California girls at keep him happy now.

The Loveman was back.

"Hello. Rainbow Lake Lodge. Hope speaking," she said, the

sound of her voice blasting around his ankles like a rogue wave, sucking the sand out from under his feet and washing him out to sea.

"It's Tommy." He'd wanted to be confident, bright and star like. His voice sounded small and uncertain.

"Thank you for returning my call," she said, suddenly stiff and formal and totally unlike the woman he'd snuggled with under the quilts in front of the big fireplace in the middle of an ice storm.

"How have you been?" he asked, trying to thaw her iciness.

"Fine," she said. "Tommy, I didn't call to chit chat. As I'm sure you must know, Billy has called my note at the bank and started foreclosure proceedings against me."

Tommy froze in the balmy, California breeze. What now? Did Billy expect him to lie for him? If he said nothing, she would interpret his silence as a lie. Unless he was prepared to tell the truth, and how could he, he might as well tell an outright whopper.

Answer a question with a question. He wasn't evasive by nature, but he'd learned how to handle uncomfortable questions thrown at him by pushy members of the press when he least expected or wanted it. It wasn't really lying. At least, that's what his agent always said.

"Tommy? Did you hear what I said?"

Crap. Now all he had to do was think of a question. "Did you know I'm calling from California?"

"No." She sounded flustered – a coup d'état he took no pleasure in.

"It's not like Billy and I are in regular contact. If my memory is correct, I've only spoken to him once since I left Minnesota."

"Just long enough for him to say, 'Plan in motion, the widow doesn't have a clue, the place should be yours in sixty days?'" She fired back at him.

"I don't remember any of those words being spoken," Tommy said, mirroring her hostility even though she was right.

"Tommy, please," she said, her voice soft and pleading now. "I'm begging you. I need your help. I've poured my heart and soul into this place. You know how much it means to me. It's the only thing left that David and I..."

She was crying. Damn Billy. This whole mess was his fault. Tommy had never wanted to hurt anyone. He never would have participated in Billy's scheme had he known the facts.

"He's my friend, Hope. He may be... but he's my friend. I can't just... he's my friend."

"I have an attorney," she said, in a quivering voice, trying to be threatening and failing miserably. "If you won't help me, he can subpoena you."

"If it goes to trial," Tommy said. "Which it won't if your attorney can't prove probable cause." Which they both knew he couldn't without Tommy's help. "Please don't put me in this position, Hope."

"You can say that, knowing the position you and Billy have put me in?"

She had lost all respect for him. He could hear it in her voice. It hurt him so deeply that he wanted to cry along with her.

"Let me talk to Billy," he said. "I'll try to get through to him."

"And if you don't?" she said.

"Trust me," he said.

"Been there, done that," she said.

"I'll be in touch," he said. "I promise."

"Tommy?"

"Yes, sweetheart?"

She moaned out a sob. "Please don't call me sweet..."

David.

He didn't know what to say, what to do. So he started to sing. It was what he did, who he was, the gift God had given him. Him. Not David.

The words that he'd tried to push out of his head came flowing out in a gentle gush of emotion.

"You are my Hope for tomorrow,
I love you more with each day.
Ev'n in the dark night of sorrow
Light for each step of the way.

"Peace on the path when we're walking
Even through sadness and pain,
Stars in your eyes when we're talking
Sunshine and Joy after rain.

"You are my Hope for tomorrow..."

He could hear her tears in the background as soon as he stopped singing. His heart thumped to the bottom of his chest cavity. It wasn't fair. He was trying to write hip-hop. He was trying to think new generation. He really was. Yet here he was, falling in love with the original old-fashioned girl.

"Hope?"

"Yes?" she said.

"Trust me," he said.

"I'm trying."

He loved her. How had he shown her how he felt? He had hurt her. Just like she hurt him each and every time she made it clear how much she still loved David.

"I'll be in touch," he said, setting the receiver back on the phone.

He'd fallen in love with Hope Anderson.

Not that it mattered. He'd bought the House on Rainbow Bay so he could have the privacy and seclusion he needed. Hope would never abandon her dream of reopening Rainbow Lake Lodge, of filling it with love and laughter, noisy, messy children, people, and more people. Hope would never leave Rainbow Lake Lodge – not unless Billy had her evicted. Which Tommy had to talk him out of. Now, before it was too late.

Chapter 22

Hope held on to one end of a full-sized quilt her great-grandmother had made and helped Molly fold it into a square that showed off the prettiest part of its design.

"This one is made from feed sacks." Hope wiped a tear from her eye before it could drip on the quilt. "During the Great Depression, when they couldn't afford to buy fabric, Grandma and Great Grandma would go to the feed store with Grandpa and dig through the pile of feed sacks until they had enough matching bags to sew dresses, quilts, aprons – whatever the family needed."

Molly leaned closer to examine the tiny stitches. "It looks like it was sewn on an old treadle sewing machine."

"I can remember Grandma working the foot pedals while she guided the fabric through the machine. She sewed on that old machine until the day she died."

"Are you sure you want to part with these, Hope?"

"Yes," she said. "I mean, no, I don't want to. But I will to save the Lodge. I would never have used these anyway. I probably never would have even hung them on the wall. I'd have been too afraid they would fade."

"That just proves how precious they are to you."

"They're not doing anyone any good taking up space in the cedar chest," Hope said. "It's not like I'm cheating my son or daughter out of their inheritance."

"You could still end up with children," Molly said, sounding as protective as a mother bear.

"I'm more likely to get struck by lightning than to end up with a baby in a world where divorcees and widows have less than a five percent chance of remarrying," Hope said. "My age doesn't increase my odds."

"Funny thing how those odds never take into consideration that we have a God who works miracles," Molly said, raising her eyebrows at Hope.

Hope laughed and grabbed the end of a Ring of Roses quilt she'd made for the rose cabin. "Point taken."

"I'm sure it's hard to keep looking up when you're going through what you are," Molly said.

"I'll be fine." Hope ran her fingers over the violets she'd cross-stitched in the center panel of another quilt done in lavenders, blues and yellows. "I can make more quilts," she said, more to remind herself than to reassure Molly.

"I just hope they bring what they're worth," Molly said. "I wish we could wait until spring when the tourists start to arrive. A few of the Californians who come up here for the summer could make a big difference when it comes to bidding. People around here can be so tight."

"A friend of mine from Minneapolis is going to distribute fliers to quilt shops and fabric stores around the Cities. If the weather cooperates..."

"Maybe we should list a few of the quilts on eBay," Molly said. "I've set up several on-line auctions for antique dealers or private owners with particularly precious pieces."

"Not a bad idea," Hope said. "But it would be kind of sad to think of my grandma's quilts going to strangers. They could end up anywhere in the world. I'd have no way of knowing whether or not they went to a good home."

"If Tommy Love would just come clean and admit what he and Billy were up to, your lawyer could put an end to all of this and you wouldn't have to auction off the quilts," Molly said.

"It's been a week since I talked to Tommy and I haven't heard a word," Hope said. "That can't be good."

"I can't believe he wouldn't help," Molly said.

"I respect Tommy for being a loyal friend," Hope said. "I just wish it was me he was being loyal to instead of Billy."

"Did you two really get that close when he was here?"

"He and Billy go way back," Sharon said.

"I thought we connected," Hope said. "It felt like I had found a new friend."

"I guess old should trump new." Molly sighed. "Just like your quilts. Beautiful as the ones you've made are, I'm guessing the old ones will go for twice as much."

Hope added some notes for the auctioneer about a white, yellow and spring green quilt with a daisy pattern. "What I can't wrap my mind around is the fact that Billy doesn't deserve Tommy's loyalty."

"And you do," Molly said.

"My cause is worthy, noble and above board," Hope said. "Thousands of people will benefit if I reopen the Lodge. Billy's out to make a fast buck, of which he already has plenty. And if I've got things figured out correctly, Tommy is probably going to bulldoze the lodge and build some sort of private compound with a big fence around it so no one will be able to enjoy the place except for him."

Molly laughed. "You make it sound like he's going to put a mine field around the perimeter to keep people out."

"Well, if getting through to him on the phone was any indication of how he lives his life, he wasn't exactly planning to put out a welcome mat," Hope said. "I could never live that way. I know to some people, owning a lodge would be like having constant company, but I enjoy it. It's a wonderful feeling, knowing you're making people happy and helping them relax and reconnect with nature, and each other."

"Tommy makes a lot of people feel happy and relaxed in his own way," Molly said. "He's probably had to learn to guard his privacy and his affections."

"Still," Hope said. "If I had two friends, and both of them needed help, one because she had been wronged, and one because he had wronged someone, I know who I would choose to help."

"That's not how loyalty works," Molly said. "Or love."

"But..."

Molly added another quilt to the stack. "Loyalty, or love – parental, romantic, spiritual – doesn't happen because we've earned it or because we deserve it."

Hope took the last quilt from the cedar chest and placed it on the pile.

"I've put Tommy in a horrible position, haven't I?"

"If he's a man of honor like you believe he is, he'll find a way to make things right," Molly said. "Be patient. He'll find a way."

Hope squeezed Molly's hand. "I wish I had as much faith as you do."

"It's okay to be angry, Hope. I'm sure everyone who's been through what you have has moments, days, even months when their faith wavers."

"It's easier to be angry at Tommy Love than at David," Hope admitted.

"It's okay to be mad at David, Hope. He let you down when he died – disappointed you, left you in a terrible predicament."

"Not by choice. David didn't want to hurt me."

"I suspect Tommy doesn't either," Molly said.

"David didn't want to die," Hope said.

"But he did. And while you may know in your head that he didn't want to die, in your heart, it feels like he bailed."

"I feel like such an awful person when I think things like that," Hope said, deciding to refold the quilt a different way, and then a different way yet.

"Unless you work through your grief – and that includes letting yourself feel angry at David, even at God – you'll never be able to love again," Molly said. "Worse yet, you'll never feel worthy of anyone else's love, even God's."

"The whole time Tommy was stranded at the lodge, I was comparing him to David. I've done the same thing to Alvin."

"You've got David on a pedestal so high that no one will ever measure up."

Hope smiled. "Just the other day, I remembered something David used to do that really irked me. I felt so ashamed for even thinking about it that I almost cried – like admitting he wasn't perfect somehow dishonored his memory."

Molly looked at her square in the face. "Hope, are you sure – absolutely sure – that you even want to stay at Rainbow Lake Lodge? Is this really the way you want to spend the rest of your life? Is it your dream, or do you feel obligated to carry on out of some sense of guilt or duty to David?"

"When David's parents died, it was me who pushed David to move up north and take over the lodge. He would have been perfectly content to stay in Chicago and to keep teaching until it was time to retire," Hope said, wrestling with the quilt. *It wouldn't lay right. What was wrong with it?* She wanted to scream.

"The land this lodge sits on is worth a lot of money, Hope. If you sold the place, you could start over, do something you love. You could open a quilt shop, adopt a couple of children, travel the world – anything you wanted to do."

"But I'm the one who..." She threw the quilt and watched it fall into a graceful heap on the sofa. Right where she and Tommy Love had... "Renovating Rainbow Lake Lodge was always more my dream than David's," Hope said. "It was me who talked him into coming up here. I'm the one who..."

"Oh, Hope." Molly put down the quilt she was folding and hugged her. "You blame yourself for David's death, don't you?"

"If we'd never moved up here..." Hope cried softly. "It never would have happened. David wouldn't have been where he was when he was killed. If we'd stayed in Illinois like he wanted to..."

"Oh, sweetheart." Molly hugged her again, this time so tightly she could barely breathe. "You have to let go. You have to let go. What happened was so not your fault."

"I've tried."

"Hope, David was happy here. If he had any reservations about quitting your jobs and moving up here at the beginning, he had long since forgotten them. He loved this place, and you. He was so proud of the work you'd already finished. Every time I look at that beautiful new dock, and the canoes he made with his own two hands, I can just see him out there in those awful, too short shorts he always wore, shirt off, looking so happy he could burst. He told Bert one day when they were golfing that until you moved up north, he hadn't believed it was possible to be so happy."

She clung to Molly, crying, and let her tears cleanse away the hurt and guilt.

"Tommy Love sang me a song when we talked last week. The most beautiful song I've ever heard," Hope said. "It was about having hope for tomorrow, and believing that there's sunshine and joy after rain."

"He wrote you a song?" Molly said. "Oh Hope. That's so romantic."

"It wasn't for me. The first line just happened to have the word hope in it. I'm sure it wasn't about me."

"Of course it was, silly." Molly picked up the quilt she'd tossed aside and folded it with a few quick flicks of her wrist.

"I was so angry with him," Hope said, realization dawning slowly in her brain. "I was so focused on my own problems that I didn't even acknowledge how lovely the song was. Do you really think the song was about me?"

"Faith." Molly gave her another quick hug, grabbed her keys, threw her a kiss, and headed out the door. "You've got Love. Hope. All you need now is a little faith."

Chapter 23

Billy had guzzled three beers – so far. With a slap of his bare hand, he squashed the cans until each was as flat as a pancake.

Sharon would have moaned about the scratches he'd put on the stupid countertops for a week. That's why he was divorced, why he'd sooner shoot himself than hook up with another woman. One was as whiny as the next if you asked him.

You'd think Tommy would have learned that after not one, but two escapes from the death grip of marriage. Tommy had always claimed wife number two had only been in it for the money, but that he'd really loved wife number one. It had broken Tommy's heart when she'd slept around on him. Too bad that one hadn't stuck – she may have been a slut, but at least with her, Tommy had proof positive she hadn't married him for his money. Tommy hadn't had a cent to his name back then.

He was snapping the ring on another can when the phone rang.

"Yep?" he said, reaching forward to snag the receiver from three paces back.

"Stan Paulsen," the voice on the other end said.

Crap. He should have trashed his piece of junk phone and bought one with caller ID a long time ago.

"You there, Bjorklund?" Paulsen said.

"Just preparing myself for the good news," Billy said, biting back an explicative.

"If you'd clean up your act, I'd have no reason to call you. Wouldn't that be nice?"

If there was anything Billy hated more than cocky politicians, it was smart-ass lawyers. It was only after he bared his heart and told Stan how he really felt that he found out why Stan had favored him with a phone call.

"She gave you a good faith payment – a fairly sizable one given the low interest rates. If Hope's payment had been applied to the interest like it should have been instead of the principal, she wouldn't even be in arrears."

"Yet," Billy said. "Listen, Paulsen. You can let your heart bleed for this chick all you want, but it won't change a thing. The handwriting's been on the wall on this one for months. Hope Anderson is the only one in four counties who doesn't realize the gig's up."

"She didn't anticipate having to put in a new kitchen. She's had a run of hard luck with the inspectors. She's gone a little over budget. Who doesn't have a surprise or two when they're undertaking a quarter of a million dollar renovation?"

"No can help." Billy took another swig of beer. "You're forgetting. I just do what the Board of Directors tells me to do."

"Two of your uncles and three of your cousins were on the board last I knew," Paulsen said. "Don't tell me you have no pull."

"Pull, I have no time for." Billy burped into the receiver. "Push and shove, I understand perfectly."

He waited for Paulsen to speak for more than a minute.

"This isn't one more asinine football game," the attorney finally sputtered, sounding only fractionally mean on a scale of one to ten. "This is a woman's life. This is a local legacy. This is your chance to stand up, be a man, and do the right thing."

"Ah, this is Billy Bjorklund. Dudley Do-Right lives down in Duluth."

"I know who I'm talking to, Junior," Paulsen said. "Just as I know your daddy would never have treated Hope Anderson this way."

"My daddy may have chosen to bankroll every loser in two counties, but I run a business," Billy said, trying to bite back his anger and not succeeding. "A bank. Not a charitable institution."

"We've been in touch with Tommy Love, Billy. We know all about your little plan."

Billy's heart nearly cracked in two. *Dirty, rotten, backstabbing Judas.* He'd known three-fourths of the town hated him. He'd thought the one person he could still trust was Tommy Lubinski.

"You're right about one thing." Billy spat the words into the phone. "I have a buyer with cash in hand. A buyer I spoke to and met for the first time exactly one week ago. So you can put the idea of some grand conspiracy theory out of your puny little pea-brain and get used to the idea that Rainbow Lake Lodge is going to be under new ownership."

"Don't count on it, Bjorklund. Hope Anderson is one determined lady. She won't go down without a fight."

"There is absolutely nothing illegal or immoral about foreclosing on a loan that's in default, nor about reselling the property once it belongs to the bank. The fact that a qualified buyer came along midway into the process is my good fortune."

"You'll get yours soon enough."

"What I'll get is an owner who can afford to live at Rainbow Lake Lodge. Hope Anderson needs to wake up and realize that she doesn't have a hope in heaven of ever being able to make a living running that place. Her in-laws couldn't even make it cash flow. If it weren't for my foolhardy daddy and his compassionate heart, they would have been ousted two decades ago. If they hadn't died when they did, we'd have foreclosed already. David and Hope would have been out in the cold three years ago."

"If you knew all this, why did you loan Hope more money?" Paulsen said, sounding like he was finally getting it.

"My mother was still president of the board of directors when Hope applied for the loan. Mama never did have a backbone. Her only criterion for dispersing money was to stop and think about what my Daddy would have done. And we all know how generous dear old Dad was."

Paulsen laughed. "You got it so bad, Billy. Sounds like a twisted version of Little Red Riding Hood where the big bad wolf is afraid of the little old grandma."

Rage surged in Billy's chest. "I'm in control now. And don't you forget it."

"Oh, I won't," Paulsen said. "I know exactly who I'm dealing with, and so does Hope Anderson."

Billy slammed down the receiver, grabbed another beer and stormed out into the night.

Chapter 24

Alvin Turppa was practically dizzy with hunger – no wonder, after driving the ten miles from Rainbow Lake Lodge to Embarrass with warm-from-the-oven Swedish meatballs, mashed potatoes and gravy on the seat beside him. The scent of cloves and nutmeg teased his stomach to a frenzy – if he hadn't been the sheriff, hadn't known and seen the dangers of eating and driving firsthand – he would have unfolded the quilted casserole warmer, lifted the top, and popped one of the meatballs into his mouth right then and there.

His stomach was rumbling so loudly he could hear it over the Country Moose. He sighed, and tried not to dwell on the homemade oatmeal butterscotch cookies, banana bread, and carrot cake riding in the back seat. Or, the fried chicken and biscuits, safely encased in their Tupperware carrier. Even the freshly trimmed, ready-to-steam-and-top-with-cheese-sauce broccoli florets sounded good. Hope had really outdone herself this time.

He glanced longingly at the casserole of meatballs and ran his fingers over the top to make sure they hadn't jostled open when he'd hit the railroad tracks. Even if he hadn't been the sheriff, his conscience wouldn't have allowed him to eat in the car. His mother had raised him better than that. The last thing he needed was a grease stain on the front of his jacket, or heaven-forbid, the seat of his car. He'd never hear the end of it.

He smiled. Life was good. He couldn't wait to get home, have supper, and enjoy a nice, relaxing evening. He'd bought a DVD of the first three seasons of Mayberry RFD last week – an early Christmas present from his mother that he'd selected himself, knowing she wasn't well enough to shop. Unfortunately, he'd been so busy ever since that he hadn't even opened the box. Now that he finally had a free night, he could think of no better way to spend an evening than in his recliner watching Andy, Opie, and Aunt Bee. Especially now that he had a car full of Hope's homemade goodies. There was nothing worse than watching Aunt Bee dish up a good, home-cooked meal when you were staring at a frozen pizza from Quick Trip."

That didn't mean he was planning to eat dinner in front of the TV. His recliner was only five-years-old and as new looking as the day he'd brought it home from the Furniture Mart down in Hibbing. He intended to keep it that way.

He rounded the corner of Fourth and Main and pulled slowly into his driveway, minding the meatballs. It wasn't until he'd punched the car into park and leaned over to lift his precious cargo from the seat that he saw the white cloud of smoke swirling inside the picture window on the west side of the house.

"Mother!" he yelled, jumping from the vehicle and running to the back door.

He could hear the smoke detector bleating before he had the door open. No flames. But no mother either. He had to find her. The cold air from outside parted the smoke just long enough for him to get a glimpse of the stove. A red-hot burner glared under a saucepan that had held God only knew what. All that remained of whatever his mother had put on to cook was two inches of black, charred residue.

He flicked the burner off, grabbed a hot pad and threw the pan out the back door into a snow bank, then fumbled through the haze to his mother's reclining lift chair. She was there, either dead or sound asleep, with her hearing aids off. He shook her shoulder. "Mother, wake up."

She snapped to with a start. "What's wrong? Where am I? Is that you, Lars?"

"It's me, Mama. Alvin," he said loudly, knowing she couldn't hear him, knowing that it didn't matter. In her mind, he was his daddy.

He reached up and removed the battery from the smoke alarm. Mama wasn't even coughing. He'd arrived just in time to avert disaster.

He handed her her hearing aids, helped insert the pieces into her ears and adjusted the volume.

"What were you cooking, Mama? I told you I was bringing dinner home from Hope's."

"Rice. I was cooking rice. Didn't I add enough water?" She sniffed the air and evidently smelled something burned, although he didn't believe she could comprehend the full magnitude of the stench. Her sense of smell was about as far gone as her hearing.

"I have Swedish meatballs in the car, Mama. You don't have to cook anymore, remember? Hope sent a whole carload of food for us."

"Stay away from that hussy, Lars. I'm telling you, all she wants is your money."

"You remember Hope from church, Mama. She's a nice lady."

"She's trying to steal you from me, and I won't have it," she said, reaching for her walker, trying to get up, and plopping back down on the recliner.

"Use the lift. Remember, Mama?" Alvin pushed the control button and the chair began to rise ever so slowly.

"Why is the air so thick?" she said. "Where did all this dust come from? They must be plowing across the road. I'll be dusting for days."

"It's smoke, Mama. You left something cooking on the stove and fell asleep."

"I was hungry," she said. "If you'd give me the keys to my car, I could go uptown and get something at the Dairy Queen when I'm hungry."

"The Dairy Queen is closed until spring. And you know you can't drive anymore."

"If that young whippersnapper of a banker hadn't put the stalls at the drive-through so close together, I wouldn't have hit the blasted machine in the first place."

"Mother, you don't need to drive anywhere to get food. I left you a ham sandwich and some cottage cheese."

"You did?"

"Yes, I did." The smoke was starting to clear out, but he couldn't leave the door open indefinitely. The temps were getting down into the low teens at night.

"You're so good to me, Lars."

"I've always tried to do the right thing by you, Mama," he said, moving to the telephone and flipping through the pages until he found the section listing fumigators. He'd have to pay a fortune to have someone drive all the way up from Hibbing, maybe even Duluth, but he'd helped clean up after enough fires to know that odors this strong didn't just go away.

Calling a fumigator was easy compared to the next decision he faced – what to do about Mama.

He patted his mother's shoulder, turned up the heat a couple of degrees, closed the back door and opened the window over the sink. The Embarrass Care Center was still on his list of recently dialed numbers. He'd known the time was coming, and soon. Tonight, Mama had pretty near burned down the house, gotten herself killed, or both. It was time.

"Mama, I'm going out to the car to get the Swedish meatballs Hope sent for supper. After we eat a bite, I'll take you for a little ride." Hopefully, the room he'd looked at last week was still open.

What other choice did he have? He hated doing this to her. No one deserved to rot away in a nursing home for God only knew how many years, until they'd slowly, painfully, wasted away to nothing but a shell of the person they'd been. He'd seen his share of accidents, and witnessed first-hand the grief when someone died unexpectedly from a heart attack, but rough as that seemed, he'd always thought that maybe they were the lucky ones. Compared to what lie ahead for his mother, going quickly, before life had lost its luster, didn't seem all that bad.

He stepped out the back door, turned and looked at the house that had been his home since he was three days old. He couldn't help but think that if he had stayed to chop the rest of the firewood at Hope's like he'd planned instead of rushing home to watch Andy Griffith, his mother might have been spared the indignity of having to live in the nursing home once and for all.

He took the meatballs from the car and walked slowly back to the house. "Come sit up to the table now, Mama. Look what I brought us for dinner."

Chapter 25

The Kit Kat Lounge looked to be exactly what the name implied, at least on the outside. Cheesy, tacky and cheap. Tommy Love locked the Lexus, set the alarm, and wished he'd never agreed to come. Sure, Big Ben was a friend, and Tommy wanted to be supportive, but the place was so... seventies. The outside was downright depressing. The particleboard siding was so seriously crumbling and rotten that there was moss growing between the planks.

When Tommy walked in, Big Ben was singing his only hit, *Bop Till You Drop*. The big guy looked more like he was six feet under than a one hit wonder. Tommy hadn't seen his friend in three or four years, and in that short time, the guy must have put on fifty pounds. His face was covered with sweat. Droplets dripped from his chin to his belly as he sang. His hair was a long, stringy gray mop that hung from a bald, white top. The man seriously looked like he was about to drop from a heart attack brought on by a severe lack of bop.

Ben took a break as soon as he finished the song, leaving Tommy wondering if the rest of his act included Ben's non-hits, songs by other artists, or new material.

"Hey, man. Thanks for coming," Ben said, pumping his hand.

No surprise there. Who wouldn't be deliriously happy to see another face in the crowd? He's increased the size of Ben's audience by a whopping thirty-three percent just by walking in the door.

"Hey, man, yourself," Tommy said. "So what happened to you? You're supposed to be Big Ben because you're British, not because you're big."

"Divorce number three hit me hard," Ben said. "I had a thing with a groupie that I met on the internet and... oh well."

"Sorry," Tommy said.

"Hey, man, I really owe you for tipping me off to your agent," Ben said. "Things were pretty dire for awhile, but Jack's got me back in the money now. He's the greatest."

"No prob," Tommy said.

"I've only been with Jack for a month and he already got me this gig," Ben said. "And you should hear the line-up he's got booked for the next six months."

"Opening acts?"

"No. Headlining," Ben said. "I've got the Surf Ballroom in Clear Lake, Iowa, in February for Buddy Holly Days, the Leapin' Lizards Festival in Lawton, Oklahoma, in March, Tip Toe Through the Tulips Days in Little Holland, Michigan, in April, and the Mississippi State Fair sometime this summer. And all kind of clubs in between."

"Really," Tommy said, thinking Ben's idea of heaven was his worst nightmare.

"I am so jacked," Ben said. "I'll get to see the whole United States and then some. Pretty radical, huh?"

"Definitely," Tommy said, sticking his hands in his pockets and wishing someone would come along and put him out of his misery.

"Hey, aren't you Tommy Love?" A wisp of a waitress with black, spiky hair and skin so white she looked half frozen sidled up to him with a pad in one hand.

"See, I told you I had a following," Ben said.

"A regular stampede," Spiky Do said. "The place is bursting at the seams. You got so many fans I'm gonna need bigger pockets to hold all the tips." Her pale face scrunched into a smile. "What can I get ya?" She asked Tommy.

"Diet coke, please." Tommy smiled. She couldn't be older than twenty-five. And she knew who he was.

"You still gonna do your Tommy Love set now that he's here or do we get to hear the real thing?" Spiky Do asked Ben. "Cuz, if he's gonna sing, I wanna call my girlfriend." She twisted and tugged a spike to new heights and smiled at Tommy. "Her parents have every album you ever made."

Fine, so she only knew who he was because she knew some old dudes who were fans. Someone from the younger generation had still recognized him. It was a start. "Say, you don't know of any clubs in San Luis Obispo that play some hip-hop or a little R&B, do you?"

"Sure," Spiky Do said. "I'm supposed to meet some friends at this club called Bump and Grind after I get off work at nine. You can come if you want."

"Isn't that a little late to be driving all the way to San Luis Obispo?" Ben asked.

Tommy thanked God he had freshened up his hair with a little Just for Men earlier that day. Ben was acting so old it was embarrassing.

Spiky Do flitted off to help another customer and Ben went back to the stage to sing another set while Tommy sat at a table by himself. He was finally ready to admit that he just didn't have it in him to write punk. It had made sense to go that route – punk dated back to the late seventies, his era – and had recently had a resurgence in popularity. It was by its very nature a statement about being different, counter to what he'd been before, un-accepting of the status quo – the exact message Tommy wanted to send to his fans, his agent, his producer, and anyone else who thought he should spend the rest of his life rehashing old songs, playing reruns on a career and a life that hadn't been that great in the first place. Not only had he been there, done that, he'd done it again, and again, and again so many times that he wanted to scream.

But even with all those intense emotions, even with a passion that demanded that he do something different, he still couldn't write punk.

He was going to keep trying to write hip-hop. It was closer to the soft rock he was known for, yet vastly different. Younger, more energetic. Decidedly un-sappy. He found a pen and diddled a few rhyming words on his napkin, biding his time until he could blow the joint and take off for greener pastures with Spiky Do.

Chapter 26

Hope took a seat across the desk from Stan Paulsen and slid the dog-eared ledger she'd brought from Rainbow Lake Lodge in his direction. "This is all I could find. I still don't understand..."

"I spoke to Billy yesterday. There have been a few new developments," Stan said. "That's why I need to see the books. All the books."

"I loved my in-laws," Hope said. "They were wonderful people. But from my quick glance through these records, it appears that bookkeeping was not their greatest strength."

Stan grimaced. "That's what I was afraid of."

"David always tried to get them to show him the books when we were up during the summer. I mean, he was a business professor. It was natural of him to think he could help." She looked at Stan's face and felt her stomach twist into a knot. "The Andersons were very private. They never wanted to worry us – they always said that it was blessing enough that we gave our summers up to come and help at the lodge, that we should be able to relax and enjoy our time up north without having to worry about a bunch of nitty gritty numbers."

Stan didn't look appreciative of the Anderson's thoughtfulness. "From what Billy said, Rainbow Lake Lodge didn't cash flow in all the years the Andersons owned it. They were mortgaged up to the hilt, and missed far more payments than they made."

The thought yanked at both ends of the knot in her stomach until her insides felt as taut as a high wire. "So why didn't the bank foreclose years ago? And why in heaven's name did they loan me more money?"

"William Bjorklund, Sr., and the Andersons evidently had an agreement. I guess Billy's daddy had a big heart. He knew what the land was worth, and because the value far exceeded the amount of the loan, he knew he'd get his money some day."

"Like when? When they died?"

"Precisely. It had been discussed and agreed upon verbally. When the Andersons died, the property would be sold and the bank would get their money plus interest. You and David were to get the rest, of course."

"But we—"

"I take it you and David didn't decide to move back to Minnesota and renovate the Lodge until after the Andersons had both passed away."

"No. I mean, we kicked the idea around every summer when we came up to help, but we never thought... We had a good life. David was a full professor. He loved his job. The fact that we had our summers free to come up north made it perfect. It was only after Dad died and we realized that Rainbow Lake Lodge would cease to exist unless we moved up here and ran the place full time that we made the decision to sell our house in Chicago. By that time, there had been so much deferred maintenance that we really felt the wisest thing was to close down for a few months while we made some major improvements, then reopen. We had some money saved up, plus the profit from the sale of our home. The Andersons had a small life insurance policy. You know the rest."

Stan nodded. "I'm hoping that a quick look at the books will ascertain whether or not Billy is telling the truth."

Hope tugged on one of her curls. "Why did Billy loan me more money if he knew all of this?"

"Billy didn't. His mother did. Billy was nothing but a figurehead during the period from the time the Andersons passed away through the date of David's death two years ago. His mother was still presiding over the Board of Directors and had controlling interest. All she ever cared about was honoring her husband's legacy, and that included showing a great deal of mercy to a great many customers just like William Sr. had for so many years. That, and the amount you requested was still far below the projected value of the land, which you were increasing even more by renovating the structures. She had no fear she was making an astute investment in the long run."

"The very long run. If it weren't for David's accident, we would have lived here until we died, or retired at the very least."

"I'm just speculating based on what I know of Billy and his mother. Billy's mother isn't the type of lady to kick a person when they're down. There was no way she was going to lay all of this on David when he'd just lost his parents, or on you, when you'd just lost your husband. And, she firmly believed you were going to make your payments, which put her two steps ahead of the previous arrangement."

"She was trying to do me a favor."

"She did you a huge favor."

"I've heard rumors that Rose Bjorklund is in a nursing home and wondered if her health took a turn for the worse, or why she suddenly abdicated her post at the bank. I mean, did she initiate the change of policy on my loan, and if so, why did she change her mind? Was it something I did? Something I should have done and didn't?"

Stan stroked his chin. "A few months ago Billy had his mother declared incompetent and moved her into a nursing home against her will. In light of the somewhat overly generous loans she was approving, he had plenty of ammunition."

"Is she really crazy?"

"Most people believe she's more rational than Billy. From what I've gathered, Rose Bjorklund is just a nice old lady with a very kind heart. But she is eighty-five, so she wasn't going to be able to work that much longer anyway. I think Billy tried to wait until she gave up control on her own. And conversely, that she clung to the position long past the time when she should of relinquished control because she knew what kind of man Billy is."

"So now that Billy is in control, is he wreaking havoc on the whole community, foreclosing willy nilly on all the generous loans the elder Bjorklunds made, or does he have something personal against me?" Hope asked, feeling more scared by the minute. "Doesn't he feel any compassion?"

"Billy is a lot harder to peg than his mother. I'm not sure if he's trying to prove something to the board of directors, or if he simply acts because he can. Some people have a strong need to be in control. And Billy has had virtually no power until now. Or, it could be greed."

"Greed?"

"Hope, the Bjorklund's original agreement with the Anderson's was to put the lodge on the market when the time was right, pay off the loan and disperse the rest of the profits to you and David. That agreement has now been superseded by the loan agreement you signed with the bank, which says that if you default on your loan, the lodge becomes the property of the bank. Billy may have kept mum about the previous loan agreement when you came in to borrow money because he thought he could strike a bargain that would be more to his advantage."

Hope's mind raced at the speed of light. She heard every painful word that Stan was saying, but it was just so inconceivable that someone could be so spiteful, so cold, so evil. "I understand that this is going to hurt my case. I mean, the fact that the Andersons were in arrears for years, and that the woman who approved my loan has been declared incompetent by the courts."

"If Billy's telling the truth, you don't have a case," Stan said. "The way things stand now, you don't have a prayer of keeping Rainbow Lake Lodge."

No! "Even if Tommy Love comes around and testifies on my behalf?" Hope said, trying to wrap her head around the things she'd just learned.

"Anything he might have to say is pretty much a moot point right now," Stan said.

"This might be a stupid question," Hope said, feeling so cold and unable to breathe that she might have been trapped under the ice out on the lake. "But if Billy forecloses, takes the Lodge, and sells it to pay the notes on the property, who gets the balance of the money generated by the sale?"

"If the bank is granted a foreclosure motion, Rainbow Lake Lodge becomes the property of Embarrass National Bank, to do with as they wish. That's why Billy wants to foreclose. If the motion is granted, he'll have quadrupled the amount of the bank's original investment, which is just the kind of coup he needs to prove himself to the board of directors."

Stan rolled a pen between his thumb and first finger. "If the motion is denied, his next move will be to call the note, which would force you to sell the property to pay back the bank's money. Billy won't make as much money that way, unless he's the realtor for the buyer, in which case he'd at least end up with a hefty commission."

"So if I can't fight him on ethical grounds, what can I do?" Hope said.

"Well, you can sit around and hope the motion is denied, in which case, the worse possible scenario is that you'd lose everything, and the best, that you'd still have to sell the lodge to satisfy the debt."

"I can't take that kind of risk. I don't care about the money, but I can't lose the lodge."

"Hope, unfortunately, I think the time has come to face facts," Stan said.

"Saving Rainbow Lake Lodge is the only way I know to preserve David's legacy."

Stan winced. Which was not a good sign. "That's why you have to sell the lodge now. Before we go to court."

Hope's throat tightened and her heart fell seven or eight floors to the caldron of bubbling acid jostling around in her stomach. "No."

"If these books substantiate Billy's assessment of the situation, you have no other choice."

"It's over, then." If she hadn't been sitting in a lawyer's office, her first thought would have been it's time to call in the attorneys and let the wars begin. It wasn't fair. She'd been so close. Less than six short months from opening. She could almost see the disappointment on the faces of the little boys and girls and parents who would have come to stay.

"I'll get back to you in a day or two," Stan said, looking worried about the books and about her.

She sat. Stunned. Deflated. Empty. Alone.

"My next appointment will be here in just a few minutes," Stan said, standing to get the door.

She couldn't believe what was happening.

Chapter 27

Tommy looked at the wax statue on the dashboard and laughed. "Can I touch it?"

"You can do anything you want with it," Spiky Do, whose real name had turned out to be Nadia, said. "I am so over him."

"So let me see if I get this," Tommy said. "Two days ago, this blob of wax was shaped like a man."

"Eyebrows, arms, legs, a belt – the works," Nadia said.

Tommy stretched his legs out and wondered if he should feel righteous anger or pity for the poor little glob. "And you're supposed to set it on your dashboard and watch it melt into a puddle of unrecognizable goop."

"If the guy was really a jerk, you can bite his head off, twist his arm until you hear the screams, squash him flat with your fist... whatever. That's the whole point," Nadia said.

"So this melted blob of wax represents your ex, whose relevance in your life diminishes and eventually fades to nothing as the statue melts away."

"When I bought him, he even had black hair like Slate's. Two days later and he's gone," Nadia said. "Out of sight, out of mind. Kaput."

"So what'd the guy do?" Tommy asked her.

"Should've asked me a couple days ago when I was still looking at his ugly face."

"The melty thing really works that well?" Tommy asked.

"Who you trying to forget?" Nadia asked. "I gotta get gas. We'll buy you one."

"Her name's Hope," Tommy said.

"Blond, brunette, or red head?" Nadia said. "Tall, short, fat, skinny? White, brown, black?"

"There are that many options?"

"They gotta come in all flavors for the mind set to be right."

"I get ya," he said.

A few minutes later he was back in his seat with a three-inch tall, slender redhead in his pocket. Except that it wouldn't do to keep her in his pocket. Having the sun destroy the target of your previous affections was one thing – having the one you loved melt in your pocket from body heat was another thing entirely.

"So what'd the girl do?" Nadia asked.

"Hope?" Tommy said stupidly, trying to ignore the rush of heat, regret, passion he felt when he thought about her. "She's in love with her husband."

"Married dudes are bad news," Spiky Do said. "Not that I don't do one every once in awhile, but you gotta know there's no future in it."

Tommy tried to hide the shock in his eyes and said, "Her husband is dead. Two years and she's still not over him."

"Maybe you should have gotten *her* a melty."

Tommy sighed. Spiky Do pulled over to the curb of a red-brick building with a turret, stained glass windows and soft, neon lighting. He had a feeling the night was going to be a study in contrasts about as diverse as he and Spiky Do.

* * *

"So let me get this straight," Hope said, facing Stan Paulsen in his cramped, shabby office. This man held her life in his hands, and he was telling her that she was going to have to move away from her home and leave everything she held dear. That she had failed.

Stan pursed his lips and looked as uncomfortable as the cheap, straight-backed chairs sitting up to his desk. "By the time they both passed away, the Andersons had taken second, third, and fourth mortgages on the lodge. Apparently every time they had a financial shortfall, a slow period, or had to make a major repair, they would add to the loan. They made sporadic payments when they could, but it wasn't enough to make a dent in the principal. So the interest kept compounding and compounding until..."

"And David knew," Hope said, trying to stop her hands from shaking.

"According to the records at the bank, he was notified. At what point, I'm not sure. But, yes, he did know," Stan said.

She clenched her fingers into fists so tight that her arms ached. "So David knew that the original loan was still outstanding. David knew that the payments were in arrears. David knew that the lodge was so heavily mortgaged that we'd never be able to dig out from under..."

"I'm afraid so," Stan said. "Would you like something to drink?"

"David knew," she said numbly. "David knew, and he didn't tell me." Fury coursed through her veins. "He should have told me. He should have trusted me with the information, no matter how dire. He should have told me."

David was dead and he was no guardian angel. There was no perfection in hiding the truth.

"It's hard to imagine what his reasons might have been at this point," Stan said, looking appropriately sympathetic.

"He didn't trust me," she said. "He obviously didn't think I could handle the truth."

"Well," Stan said, with that one word, shattering the perfect, idealized version of David that had kept her going for two entire years. Because there was nothing else to say.

David had lied to her. He had taken the truth to his grave. Except truth had a way of rising again.

Well. She knew the truth now. She had learned the truth from Billy. Her husband had deceived her. She might have been kept in the dark forever, except Billy – Billy – had told the truth.

* * *

Tommy scribbled a few more lines on his napkin and let his body groove to the beat.

> Bop till you drop. Can't let the hip-hop stop.
> Don't wanna be a flop. Gotta make it to the top.
> The sun is beatin' down. What's that little frown?
> Revenge is sweet. Now it's gonna melt your meat.
> *Melt me. Squeeze me. Feel me. Tease me.*

He hadn't had so much fun in years. The music bombarding his ears was wild, and totally not to his liking, but in an amusing, energetic kind of way. The words of the hip-hop songs bouncing off Bump and Grind's old brick walls were so ludicrous they could have been the basis of a comedy sketch on Saturday Night Live. But just about the time you assumed the song writer was so full of it, so hokey he should die, out would pop a truth or insight so painfully honest that you almost hurt with the brutality of it. Hip-hop was an emotional roller coaster ride and, baby, he was hanging on tight.

He could do this, he really could. He might not like the music, but he could write it. He had a rhyming dictionary, a sense of humor, and an occasional significant revelation to share. He'd felt their pain, he could jive with the tribe, he was cool. He jotted a few more lines.

> The past is over. You're on the dash of my red Range Rover.
> So you'll melt faster, you blanking bastard.
> I'll be befuddled, till you're all puddled,
> Then I'll move on, and get a groove on.
> *Melt me. Squeeze me. Feel me. Tease me.*

So it wasn't exactly great literature. Nor his best work ever. It was a start. A new start.

Bad Bling, the female vocalist who was on stage, was dressed in a modern version of what Tommy's dad would have called bib overalls. The shorts were no more than a half-inch lower than her crotch, and the bib was so low-slung that her barely-covered breasts swung free for all to see. An LED sign behind her blinked with the message "If you thought you knew what bling was before, wait till you see the GRILLZ that just hit the site. More gangster than any accessory on the market, GRILLZ are more than just Gold Teeth, they help all your homies know that you are the ultimate pimp. All the ladies will want to see your grill!" A poster to her left read, "Which kind of fashion image are you rocking on your hoodies and tees? Guns, skulls, money, crowns? We're got what you want at PurpleTurtle.com."

He listened to the words of the song Babbling Bad Bling was singing, if that's what you wanted to call it, and realized he'd never known there were so many words that rhymed with the F word. Just because she did it didn't mean he had to. Maybe it was her choice of words that put the bad in Bling.

He squinted at the words on the T-shirt Babbling's bass guitarist was wearing. "Music is our weapon." Strange. To him, music had always been a balm, a salve, a comfort. From the time his mother had held him in her arms and sung him lullabies, his soul had been soothed by music – its words, its gentle rhythms, its melodic strains.

Hip-hop was more than a different genre. It was a different vocabulary, a different frame of mind, a different look, a different world. A world he was going to become familiar with if it killed him.

The thought that he would look like a big, half bald, overgrown fool performing hip-hop occurred to him briefly, but he brushed the notion aside. Positive thinking. That's what Jack always stressed. Which was why he was such a good agent.

He scanned the room until he saw a man with an Armani suit coat on. It was of a different cut than anything Tommy had ever owned, and the shirt underneath it was form-fitting and not tucked in. But it was a look he could handle. With the right clothes, and a stylish hat, he could do this. He could practice the walk; he could talk the talk. He was cool.

"Come dance with me, Tommy Pooh," said Spiky Do, who'd come up with the nickname after he'd told her his for her.

He looked around at the gyrating sea of bodies and tried to identify a few moves.

"Pretend you're a puppet," Spiky Do said, getting the picture pretty quickly. "You're going after total body balance, in-beat and out-beat, extreme moves. The lower you are, the funkier you are."

"Easy for you to say," he said, thinking about his knees while he attempted a few clunky steps.

She frowned. "No sliding. And please stop pointing your toes. Don't think about the beat. Feel it. And loosen up. You're a puppet dangling from a string."

"Does it have to be so complicated?" Tommy said, doing a couple of moves that had always made the girls go wild when he was performing on stage. "I do know how to dance."

"This is worse than I thought," Spiky Do said. "The mashed potato, or whatever that was, is so not hip-hop worthy." She stood back and looked at him like she was trying to block out the abhorrent sight she'd just witnessed. "Lift your arms. Believe me, I'm just going for the basics here. No electric boogaloo. No break dancing. If you can just get some basic pop, lock and jam down you'll be passable."

And he'd thought she'd be impressed.

"Here," she said, demonstrating with perfect ease.

"Fine." He tried to imitate her. "Crap."

"Why'd you stop?" She yelled over the music of a new band that had started to play.

"My back," he said. "I have a catch in my back."

He stumbled to their table, held on to the edge, and flopped down into the nearest chair. Who was he kidding? It felt like a sharp knife was poking through his left shoulder blade. Sitting was worse than standing had been. He tried to get up. What was with the armless chairs? Didn't anybody but him like to grab the arms of a chair and push your body up and out?

Pretend you're a puppet my foot, Tommy thought. Would that he were – a strong puppet master with a set of strings strong enough to pull him to his feet and out to the car was exactly what he needed about right now.

The words to a song started to form in his mind. Not hip-hop, but Hope.

There's a hope for every tomorrow,
shining at the end of the day.
There's a light at the end of the tunnel,
growing brighter each step of the way.
There's a hope for every tomorrow,
shining at the end of the day.
There's a rainbow after every storm,
sunshine to keep you warm...

So much for getting Hope out of his system.

"So you're Tommy Love."

He looked up into the breasts of Bad Bling. In the flesh. Lots of flesh. A second later, she'd plunked her barely covered bottom in his lap and draped herself around his neck.

"My back," he said, struggling to untwist his neck.

"Poor baby's damaged himself," Bling purred into his ear, her lips grazing his neck. "I've got something that will make you feel all better."

He tried to twist his neck away from her kisses.

"Better than you've ever felt in your life," Bling said.

He heard the cackle of laughter in the background.

"Ecstasy awaits us in the back room. What it won't do to make you feel good, Nadia and I will," Bling said.

"I just wanted to see what went on..." Tommy started to say.

"Oh, he likes to watch," another woman said. Except that she was

143

a girl, a very young girl. There was something terribly, terribly wrong with the picture.

"No prob," Bling said, motioning to the child woman. "You, me, and Nadia. Now there's a ménage he'd never forget."

"You can join in once you've seen the show," the nameless one said, rubbing against him.

His adrenalin surging, Tommy rose to his feet, plunked Bling off of his lap and on to the table, and beat it out the door.

He stopped to rub his neck when he'd reached the safety of the parking lot. His car was twenty-five miles away in Morro Bay. He dialed information and called for a cab on his cell phone. Tommy guessed he'd rather be an old fogey, has-been than to sink low enough to fit in at the Bump and Grind.

He was humming the song he'd been working on before the evening had turned sour when the cab dropped him off at the Kit Kat.

> I want some action. Not a fraction of attraction.
> I want passion. Not your smart-mouth sassin'.
> I want a girlfriend. Not a big dead end.
> I want your juices. Not some lame excuses.
> *Melt me. Squeeze me. Feel me. Tease me.*

So it was a little sleazy. It was nothing a good shower or a hot bath wouldn't rinse off when he was done recording it. Just because he sang about it didn't mean he had to live it. If it accomplished his goal, it was worth it.

Chapter 28

The next night, Tommy finally connected with Billy. And got exactly nowhere. The only good thing that came out of their conversation was finding out that Billy's younger brother, Pastor Brian Bjorklund, had recently accepted a call to a church in Paso Robles.

Maybe it was the bad taste he'd had in his mouth ever since he'd been at the Bump and Grind, the bad vibes he'd gotten from Billy, or the feelings for Hope that were constantly swirling around in his belly. Maybe it was a general feeling of homesickness for Minnesota – which didn't even make sense – he hadn't lived there for years – but whatever the reason, he knew he needed to see Brian. It didn't take a genius to figure out that the best way to do that was to go to church.

Tommy turned off Highway One on to Green Valley Road and headed for Paso Robles. He hadn't been to church since he'd moved to California and some time before that – maybe that's why the idea was so appealing. Wow. He really must be getting old if he thought going to church sounded like more fun than hanging out with Spiky Do, having a threesome, or even staying home and sleeping half the day.

He wound his way over the pass, through the vineyards that filled the valley, and to the center of town. When he found the church, he turned off his engine and looked up at a stained glass window set in a wall of cedar shakes. He could probably attribute his sudden thirst for the holy for the simple reason that at the moment, church seemed like an uncomplicated, peaceful place to be. Especially when compared to the sticky wicket he'd met up with at the Bump and Grind. He hadn't been able to relax and have fun with Spiky Do even though he'd wanted to. His stupid conscience hadn't let him. Well, if he couldn't manage to relax at church, or afterwards, to enjoy a lighthearted conversation with a friend / minister he'd known since he was six, something was really wrong.

Brian was just taking a seat in a large, carved wood chair on stage.

Tommy opened the program they'd handed him when he came in and listened as a band comprised of a drummer, a keyboard player, a flutist, a guitarist, a bass player, and three vocalists started to play. They weren't half bad.

Tommy didn't know any of the songs except *Great is Thy Faithfulness*, which they sang to an upbeat tempo with drums, and *Marching to Zion*, which the band played with a lilting Celtic rhythm. The other numbers were easy to pick up, and he found himself singing along, at least on the choruses. A few people glanced at him now and again, maybe because he was Tommy Love, maybe because he was a new face in the crowd, maybe because he was singing too loudly. He couldn't tell. It really didn't matter as long as he felt welcome, which he did.

The script for Brian's monologue was based on Luke 13:6-9 and was very easy to digest. The kid was a natural. His talk was about gardening and what to do when you had manure dumped on you. Tommy could relate – if he hadn't known better, he would have thought Brian was talking about Hope. It was raining manure at Rainbow Lake Lodge.

A crowd of people gathered around him the second Brian ended the show, the service, whatever it was called.

"What a lovely voice you have," an elderly woman who'd been sitting two rows in front of him said. "You should join the worship team. Do you play an instrument?"

Tommy smiled. It was kind of cool being just another guy with a nice voice for a change.

"Betsy, Betsy, Betsy," said a man who'd evidently overheard her suggestion. "Tommy Love is one of the most talented guitarists ever born. Not that we wouldn't love to have him play for the contemporary service." He turned to face Tommy and offered his hand. "Playing with our little worship team might not be the big times, but it would give you a way to use your talent now that you're not recording any longer."

Tommy frowned.

"I mean, since you're not in a band anymore."

Oh well. It was obvious the guy meant well. And this was church. Not a good place to be thinking ill of someone just because they didn't read the fine print on their CD cases.

The whole band headed in his direction as soon as they'd finished their closing number. By the time they left, he'd been talked into playing with them – the worship team that was – next Sunday.

When Brian had finished with shaking hands with his fans, he suggested they have brunch at a local café a few blocks down from the church. They set off on foot.

"I'm glad you came," Brian said when they were finally away from the listening ears of the audience. "I've been getting some extremely disturbing reports from my aunts and cousins in Embarrass about Billy, and I hear you've been in touch with him recently."

Extremely disturbing sounded much too deep and serious for the relaxing repast Tommy had in mind, but he went with the flow and told Brian about his last conversation with Billy.

"At least he'll talk to you," Brian said. "Since Billy had Mother declared incompetent and deposed from her position at the bank, he's refused to pick up when I call."

"He what?" Tommy asked.

"You didn't know?" Brian said, his voice no longer light and uplifting, but dark and sarcastic. "From all reports, Billy is running the bank like a crazed despot. According to my Aunt Mildred, Billy's become a greedy, money-hungry tyrant who has no qualms about crushing anyone who stands in the way of his self-serving agenda."

"Harsh words from someone who was talking about the loving gardener in the sky a few minutes ago," Tommy said, thinking that the last thing he wanted was to be a contestant on the Family Feud Reality Show.

"Aunt Mildred's words, not mine," Brian said. "Which makes it even more frightening. Aunt Mildred is not one to exaggerate. That's why I'm so concerned. Billy and I weren't raised to tromp on other people's dreams to achieve our own goals. From what I'm told, Billy is foreclosing and seizing properties right and left. It's unconscionable."

Brian steered him to the left. They entered a building that looked like it had been patched back together after one too many earthquakes and sat down at a table for two in the front window.

"Even if my mother is starting to lose it on some level, I can't justify what Billy did to her," Brian said, glancing at the menu. "As far as I can tell on the phone, she's as cognizant as you and I, maybe more so when it comes to financial matters. Aunt Mildred believes Mother's as sharp as a tack and has a memory like an elephant."

"I haven't seen your mother in years. She made the best chocolate chip cookies," Tommy said. "And I have very fond memories of your dad. He used to stand for hours, pitching to Billy and me so we could practice hitting balls. My own dad was always working... I was so jealous of you and Billy."

Brian had tears in his eyes. "He was a very special man."

Tommy nodded and patted Brian on the back. "When my little brother got sick, your father either made a loan to my family, or out and out paid for many of the medical expenses, probably the funeral, too. I have no idea if my dad was ever able to pay him back."

"Sounds like my dad," Brian said. "Always giving. I'm sure he would be considered a horrible banker by today's standards, yet he died a very wealthy man. God blessed him. That's why it's so hard to sit and watch Billy do what he's doing. He's making a mockery of everything my father stood for."

A waitress appeared and they ordered two of the daily specials.

Tommy cleared his throat. So much for light-hearted conversation. His stomach churned. There were no women doing lap dances in his arms, no raucous music playing, no lewd temptations to be had, yet he felt every bit as uncomfortable as he had two nights ago. Maybe more so. "I know ministers of your persuasion don't take confessions, but I should tell you that I unwittingly got involved in one of Billy's schemes. I'm still trying to make things right. I'm sorry to say without much success."

Brian raised an eyebrow.

"Rainbow Lake Lodge," Tommy said. "I wanted it for all the right reasons, but I was so intent on getting what I wanted that I didn't see, wouldn't let myself see, who Billy was running over in the process."

"What are we going to do?" Brian said.

"I don't know." Tommy shifted in his chair.

"The sad thing is that what goes around, comes around. Billy's going to go too far one of these days – if he hasn't already. I can't just sit back and watch him self-destruct, but I honestly don't know what I can do from here."

The waitress appeared with their food a few seconds later.

"Hi, Pastor Brian," she said in a shy voice, then turned to Tommy. "I saw you in church this morning."

Tommy nodded. He hadn't noticed her, but there had been a lot of people there.

"I've been a fan of your music since the eighties," she said, setting down two plates of scrambled eggs, bacon, Danish pancakes, and a mound of hash brown potatoes done up "animal style" as they liked to call them in California.

"I wanted to tell you," she said hesitantly, "that one of your songs saved my life when I was a teenager. I had just broken up with my boyfriend and I was so depressed that I thought about committing suicide. I was all ready to..." She knitted her eyebrows together and looked like she was going to cry. "*Walk on Water* just happened to come on the radio, and I..."

Just happened, huh? "Thanks," Tommy said. "I'm glad that my music was able to help you through a tough time."

"I'm always checking on the internet to see if you've released any new songs," she said. "But I haven't seen any for a long time. You should write more songs like that one. You know, about hope." She gave him a modest but grateful smile, told them to enjoy their meal, and went on her way.

"She is so getting a huge tip," Tommy said.

"Karen always leaves during the closing hymn so she can get here for her shift. She usually compliments me on my sermon," Brian said. "Guess I need to get used to playing second fiddle when you're around."

"Don't expect a lot of positive feedback on your monologue when your subject matter is manure," Tommy said, thinking about hope. Hope. The hope that Hope would be a part of his every tomorrow.

Chapter 29

Hope left Duluth Superior National Bank via a fancy revolving door thinking that it would be a miracle if the door didn't hit her butt on the way out. That's how dejected and rejected she felt. Sure enough, there were two kids behind her, pushing and shoving each other as they entered the next slot and, no surprise, bonked her good just before she exited onto Canal Street. Like she wasn't humiliated enough already.

She faltered, almost wrenched her ankle, and clutched the leather portfolio that contained her snazzy, new, computer-generated graphs, spreadsheets, and luminous photos a little tighter. She never should have worn heels. They were so not her – definitely not a good match for the jagged cobblestone streets of downtown Duluth. She'd only worn them to appease her mother, whose voice still told her what, when, and how a good southern belle should talk, dress, and act even though she'd been gone for over a decade.

Hope jutted out her chin and refused to give in to the urge to cry. Two banks down – very down – one to go. She was desperate for someone to validate her plan. Even if she hadn't needed the money, which she did, she was at the point where she simply needed someone to say, "I believe you can do this."

But no one did. Not her friends, not her enemies, certainly not the banker whose office she'd just left. The collective result was like a broken record in surround sound. "Sell the property and move on. Sell the property and move on. Sell the property and move on."

She squared her shoulders and tried to navigate the sidewalk without snagging her heel on a brink. A brick. She was on the brink. She tried to clear her brain of doubts, tried to find the wherewithal to smile, convince, exude confidence.

This should be it. She craned her neck so she could see the sign and rechecked the address painted on the heavy glass doors. She tried not to interpret the screech of the sea gulls behind her as a bad omen, but it was almost as though they were crying, "Don't go in. They're going to say no."

Merchants Bank of Duluth. Even the name was an assault to her confidence. Who was she trying to kid? She was no merchant, no businesswoman. She was just plain Hope, a good homemaker, a good cook. David Anderson's wife. Or had been. She would have made a very good mother, too. She'd been a good daughter, granddaughter, daughter-in-law.

Ouch! She nearly tripped over another jag in the sidewalk. She should have worn her favorite pair of chukka boots.

But all of that was in the past. She loved Rainbow Lake Lodge. She really did. She firmly believed that she would be a warm hostess; that guests would flock to the inviting, romantic retreat she'd create; that she could help those people make new memories – memories as precious as the ones she held of David.

She pulled on the gleaming brass pull and entered the bank, her heels clicking conspicuously against the marble floor.

She smiled, removed her gloves, and tried to emit the aura of old money. Old money that had been lost in war. She still had a trace of a Southern accent. She arched her neck, struck a regal pose, and called forth her best Scarlett O'Hara voice. "Hope Anderson to see Preston Witherspoon the Third, please."

The receptionist smiled and pushed a button on the phone board. "Hope Anderson to see you, sir." She placed the phone back on its cradle. "Please have a seat."

Hope chose the chair opposite the loan officer's door, knowing she painted a pretty picture in her calf-length, flowing, hunter green skirt and lacey, cream colored blouse. She believed with all her heart what her mother had said about first impressions being worth a million dollars – which seemed apropos since that was about how much money she needed.

Hope crossed her ankles and tucked her legs demurely under her skirt. Her mother always said charm was a woman's greatest asset.

Five minutes later, the door to Preston Witherspoon's office opened. She looked up at him and smiled, and for a few seconds, everything seemed right with the world. She was at her best, and the look in Preston Witherspoon's eyes said she wasn't the only one who thought so.

That was when she stood. And fell flat on her face. Literally. Pain shot through her legs and through her heart. What was happening?

Why? Why her? Why now?

Mr. Witherspoon and his secretary both came running. Or so she assumed. Her face was shoved into the carpet so tightly that she couldn't see what was happening. For all she knew, her butt was hanging out of her skirt. Talk about life's most embarrassing moment. Too bad someone hadn't had a video camera on her – she probably could have sold it to one of those amazing video shows and made enough money to renovate the lodge.

She heard herself moaning and felt someone slipping off her heels. If only she'd been knocked unconscious so as to have been spared the terrible humiliation – as if it were possible to feel any more mortified than she already did.

"What happened?" she finally uttered, once they'd righted her and gotten her back to the chair.

"The heel of your shoe was caught in the hem of your skirt," Preston Witherspoon's secretary said.

She thought back later on what Mr. Witherspoon's first impression of her must have been – a big splat, squirming around on the floor trying to untangle herself without losing her skirt. Which turned out to be very appropriate when Preston III turned down her request for a loan and advised her to sell the property and move on. Not only had she lost her pride and very nearly her skirt - she'd lost her shirt. She could only imagine the discussions that would fly around the coffee tables at the businesses and cafés on Canal Street about the woman from Embarrass who had embarrassed herself beyond belief – and walked away penniless.

Chapter 30

What was wrong with him? Tommy hadn't been on a guilt trip this bad since he was sixteen and went too far with his girlfriend. Seeing Brian and confessing his misdeeds should have cleansed his conscience, but he felt as guilty as ever. Guilty about what he'd almost done to Hope. Guilty about the fact that he'd refused to help her when she'd called. Guilty that he'd been dumb enough to fall for Billy's line of crap.

Admitting the whole sordid tale to Brian had made it even worse. Before, it had just been he and God who knew what a fool he'd been. Now his mistake was out there. Brian knew. Tommy had seen Brian's eyes glaze over with disrespect when he'd told him what he'd been a party to. Sure, Brian was a man of God, trained to forgive, not to judge. But the man was human, and hardly an objective listener when it came to plots involving his brother.

He tried to ignore the bad taste in his mouth so he could work on his song, but as he'd learned most graphically of late, feeling ashamed was not exactly conducive to creativity.

He pulled the paper he'd been writing on out of the trash, uncrumpled the creases and tried to think of a word that rhymed with crap. Flap was good, strap even better. Trap might work. Hmmm. Lap had all kinds of interesting possibilities.

His conscience flared with renewed guilt. Sleaze, innuendo, downright filth – *Melt Me* had it all. If he kept the words the way they were, there was no way they'd let him sing it on a family-oriented Christmas special broadcast from a National Park. Once it hit the radio stations, Brian probably wouldn't want him to sing with the worship team either.

He hated this. Sweet didn't sell. He needed to sell. If he wanted a hit, he had no choice but to write what the public wanted – even though what they wanted was crap.

He crumpled up the paper he'd been writing on, went to his backpack and flicked through the stack of Christian CDs Brian had sent home for him to listen to. The worship team had scheduled oldies only for the coming Sunday so Tommy could join in without having to learn a bunch of new songs. Ironic that he'd been typecast – again – as someone who could only handle oldies. He couldn't escape his reputation anywhere – not even at church.

He wanted a new hit so badly he could taste it.

He got one more line down on paper before the cell started to ring. Great. Billy.

"Hey man, you know what?" Billy's voice was loud, belligerent and on the verge of being slurred. "You lost your chance to buy Rainbow Lake Lodge for good. I got a new buyer. Richer than you, and a lot smarter, too."

He was so eager to put his association with Billy behind him that his first thought would have been good riddance – if it hadn't been for Hope.

"That shrew is getting exactly what she deserves," Billy said, railing into the phone so loudly that Tommy had to hold the receiver away from his ear.

"What have you done now, Billy?"

"You don't know how happy this makes me, Tommy Boy." Billy snapped into the phone, sounding bitter instead of happy. "The smug little witch turned my own mother against me. You're on her side, too. Even Brian's rooting for Hope Anderson, and he's never even met her."

Tommy thought of the two men. Brothers. Raised by the same parents, but so different.

"It's gonna drive her wild when she finds out what they're doing inside her precious little cabins," Billy boasted. "And the best thing is, it will be open to the public, so if she misses the place, she can go visit any time. As long as she doesn't mind being served by a topless waitress or a waiter in a G-string." Billy laughed.

Tommy resisted the urge to hang-up. He owed it to Hope to get as much information as he could.

"My first choice would have been to have my good bud Tommy Lubinski back in town, but since Little Miss Sunshine ruined all that, I figure a little adult entertainment and X-rated pleasure pursuits will go a long way to ease my lonely nights."

"Hope is not the one who's responsible for this whole fiasco," Tommy said, trying to keep the defensive edge out of his voice. The more he tried to protect Hope, the more Billy seemed to want to hurt her.

"Bitch. The only bright spot in this dreary little town is thinking about the day I finally get her to kick her out of her precious little lodge and take what's rightfully mine."

"Her lodge. That should tell you something right there," Tommy said, flailing for an intelligent response, and finding none. It was hard to fight an irrational drunk, especially one with venom oozing from his pores.

"That property should have belonged to my family a long, long time ago," Billy sputtered. "It would have, if my father had foreclosed when he should have, or if my mother had taken the property when the Anderson's died."

Tommy eventually hung up. His efforts to defend Hope only seemed to fuel Billy's anger, and the last thing he wanted to do was to make things worse.

Guilt. Remorse. What had been a heavy weight on his heart threatened to overwhelm him completely.

He wanted to undo what he had done when he'd aided and abetted Billy more than anything in the world. He couldn't stand thinking that he'd had anything to do with Billy's hateful vendetta.

In the old days, he would have slept with a groupie, gotten a quick buzz from whatever alcoholic beverage or drug was closest, and flown high until he'd forgotten what he'd done. But things had changed. He was a man between worlds. Compared to Hope and the saintly David, he might look downright degenerate, yet his own particular moral code – flawed as it had sometimes been – prohibited him from partaking in moral debauchery with Spiky Do and Bling. No matter what he did, he was screwed. Hope Anderson had basically ruined him.

With a grunt of frustration, he looked up and started to rail at God. He couldn't do this! No matter what he did or didn't do, he would never be good enough for Hope. No matter how he tried, he could never live up to the image of her late husband.

He wasn't even good enough to be singing with the worship team. He was a fraud, a loser. Not fit to walk in the doors of the church. He couldn't do sweet – he was rotten to the core. But he couldn't write smut either, because all he could think about was Hope – the way she looked and smiled and moved – and what she would think of him if he stopped so low as to publish *Melt Me*.

His eyes wandered to the list of songs Brian and the worship team from church had chosen for Sunday. It read like a list of Greatest Hits... a jazzed up version of *Amazing Grace*, *Just a Closer Walk* sung Southern comfort style, an old bluegrass standard called *I'll Fly Away*, a funky version of the old hymn *Power in the Blood* sung to a rollicking, finger-snapping beat, and *How Great Thou Art* styled into a medley with a chorus called *Awesome God* that was on one of the CD's they'd given him. The only other song they'd selected was a relatively new one called *I Can Only Imagine*, a crossover hit that had received so much play time on country radio stations that Tommy knew it by heart.

He'd really been looking forward to singing with the band. Worship team. He loved old gospel. Comfort food didn't interest him half as much as comfort music and the melodies and memories the songs evoked. He closed his eyes and remembered... singing in church for the first time when he was seven, harmonizing with his Grandma Lubinski seven rows up from the back on the left in the pew that might as well have had her name on it, choking back tears at his mother's funeral, solemnly parading down the isle behind his father's casket while the pipe organ surrounded him with music.

He'd heard Amy Grant sing on several occasions, Michael W. Smith, Chris Tomlin and Casting Crowns, too. The words, rhythms and melodies of their contemporary Christian hits were beautiful. But he really loved the old hymns he'd grown up singing as a boy back in Embarrass.

He scowled and chased the last remnants of his foolish sentimentality from his mind. This was the reason he was embarrassed to be from Embarrass. Everything there was old hat, boring, behind the times, archaic, outmoded, hopelessly old-fashioned.

He rapped his fingers on the body of his guitar and tried to catch the quick, upbeat tempo of *Melt Me*, then strummed a few chords. Hip-hop was his future. Time to move with the groove.

Then why was his hand moving so slow? His fingers stopped as realization washed over him. He loved the old favorites, all right – even though he'd heard them a million times. They were near and dear to his heart, precious – the same way his old hits were to the fans who kept requesting them, over and over and over again.

Crap.

That was when he saw the last song on the list for Sunday worship

- one more oldie but goodie. He remembered his mother singing it to him when they were out picking green beans in the garden. *"Spirit of the living God, fall afresh on me; Spirit of the living God, fall afresh on me. Melt me..."*

A chill washed over him. He stuttered out the rest of the chorus. *"Mold me. Fill me. Use me. Spirit of the living God, fall afresh on me."*

There was a second verse he'd never heard before. *"Spirit of the living God, move among us all; make us one in heart and mind, make us one in love: humble, caring, selfless, sharing. Spirit of the living God, fill our lives with love."*

Tommy Love. What a joke. He'd called himself the Loveman for years, but he didn't have a clue what love even meant. He hadn't been truly loved by anyone for over a decade, not since his mom and dad had died.

"I love you." A still, small voice spoke to his heart. He brushed it aside. *How could you, after the things I've done?*

"I love you. My grace is sufficient, even for you." The voice was louder the second time, heavy on bass, lots of reverb.

So God loved him. What good did that do him? It might keep him out of hell, even though that was probably what he deserved. But it didn't change anything on earth. He didn't have a clue how to love. If he was even capable of the emotion any more, he sure didn't know how to show it – how to be humble or selfless, how to care, how to share.

"My power is made perfect in your weakness."

God wanted to talk? Fine. He'd listen.

He ripped open a jewel case of a CD by Peder Eide, a musician from Minnesota that Brian had thought he'd enjoy. He popped it in his boom box, hit play, and peeled open the cover so he could look at the words.

"Teach me to trust, teach me to pray; teach me to walk in the faith to obey. Teach me to stand, teach me to fall, down on my knees in response to your call. I know that I have a long way to go until I'm made pure and true. But 'til that day, this Lord I pray; help me to be like you."

He thought back on Brian's sermon – aside from losing his little brother way back when and his ugly split with Jenny, his life had been pretty golden. There hadn't been much - if any - manure spread in his garden for longer than he could remember. Maybe that's what was wrong with him. A lack of crap. Baby, don't fall in. It's a trap, he thought, still thinking in hip-hop-ese.

For the most part, his life had been pretty smooth sailing. The flip side of few trials and no difficulties to speak of was no growth, no maturity, no wisdom, no nothing. Brian's words floated back into his head. When he'd spoken about geraniums in his sermon, he hadn't been talking about Hope, he'd been talking about him.

Brian's theory was that geraniums blossom more often if they're dry – that their thirst somehow causes them to put forth a greater effort to produce fruit, which in turn, causes them to flourish. Too much of a good thing, which in this case would be water, made them yellow, limp, weak, prone to infestation, and unable to sustain blossoms.

His problem precisely. He was weak, so accustomed to getting what he wanted, exactly when he wanted it, that he'd been a prime target for a leech like Billy.

"My power is made known in your weakness," God said again, speaking from the recesses of his brain, a verse he'd memorized in Sunday school when he was nine or ten.

For the first time in years, he saw himself with amazing clarity. He knew what kind of a plant he wanted to be from now on, even if it meant getting some manure dumped on his head once in awhile. He picked up the jewel case and punched in the number of *Be Like You* to play one more time.

"Teach me to trust, teach me to pray; teach me to walk in the faith to obey. Teach me to stand, teach me to fall, down on my knees in response to your call. I know that I have a long way to go until I'm made pure and true. But 'til that day, this Lord I pray; help me to be like you."

The song became his prayer as he worked, alternately exerting his will, giving in to God, and mentally wrestling with the demons who would have stopped him from doing what was right.

He finished the song two or three hours after midnight. Hip-hop that was sweet. A love song. Hip-hop about Hope.

It was midnight in the moonlight,
When we went walking, and we were talking.
You sang a love song, made my heart long
To simply kiss you, Oh, how I miss you.

Love Notes

When it's misty in the moonlight...
Hope comes calling. It's clear I'm falling –
A love so true blue, in love with you.

It was Monday out on Moonstone Bay
The waves were spiking when we went hiking.
You said some sweet words, made my heart purr,
I want to hold you, to just enfold you.
Will you be mine, sweet? In the sunshine?
You are my Hope for, every tomorrow.
Little sweet thing, you make my heart sing.

A melody chased the words through his subconscious like a breeze blowing the fog out to sea. It was good. He smiled. Maybe this was it. Maybe there was hope for hip-hop after all.

Chapter 31

"What's he doing here?" Billy said into the receiver, thinking that if he barked at his secretary loudly enough, maybe next time she'd think twice before interrupting him with news that someone like Dirk Westola was outside his door.

"He says he needs to talk to you. He's been calling every day for two weeks," Janice said in a hushed voice. "Maybe if you had returned his phone calls—"

"I didn't think he'd come to town," Billy said. "I thought he ordered everything from catalogs so he didn't have to risk leaving the compound. What if a nuclear bomb were to detonate while he's in Embarrass? He'd never make it back to the gopher hole in time."

"He'll be free in just a few minutes," he heard Janice say in a too cheerful voice.

I'm sending him in," she whispered. "The other customers are leaving."

Billy slammed down the receiver, turned the papers he'd been working on upside down, and stood to open the door.

Dirk looked over his shoulder twice before he entered the office, bringing the stench of unwashed body, gunpowder and who knows what else with him.

Billy debated leaving the door open, but opted to close it in the end.

"You needed to talk to me?" He headed back to his chair.

"About a loan."

"You have some source of income I don't know about?" Billy asked. "Because last I knew, this was a bank, and banks don't make loans to people unless they have a verifiable way to pay back the money."

"I have funds. But they're tied up at the moment, and I want to start building immediately. All I'm asking is for a short term loan."

"I don't see any of these funds deposited in our bank."

Dirk looked at him like he was an imbecile.

"Then I assume you have collateral."

Another look.

"What are you building?"

"A earthquake-proof, bomb-proof bunker."

"From what I hear you already buried your cabin in dirt. You know something that I don't?" He laughed.

"We're sitting on the Mississippi fault line. When the big one comes, it'll make California look like a kiddy ride at Disneyland. It's only a matter of time before the Iranians or some other terrorist group start nuking us. It could happen any day. I got the hole dug and I don't want to wait. If I don't get it done right now, before things totally freeze up, I'll have to wait until spring."

"Crazy old coot," Billy said.

Dirk balled his hands into fists. "I just need enough to pay the cement company and the lumberyard until I can free up some gold. You've got my word for collateral. That's it."

"Your word means nothing."

"If what they say you're doing to my neighbor is true, my word means more than yours does."

It was downright creepy the way Dirk fastened his beady eyes on him. But not creepy enough to make Billy back down.

Wait a minute. Billy's brain clicked into high gear. *Maybe... What if...* "Meet one condition and you've got a deal."

"I'm not signing away my land."

Billy scowled. "I'm not asking you to. Here are my terms. Do whatever it takes to get your pretty little neighbor to leave Rainbow Lake Lodge once and for all and the money is yours. Collateral free. And interest free."

Dirk's eyes met his. "I don't hurt people."

"Then don't hurt her. Scare her. They don't call you Creepy Survivalist Guy around town for nothing. You're scary. Scare Hope Anderson off her property and the money is yours."

"Do your own dirty work. I'll find my money elsewhere." Dirk turned to go.

"You're just like a weasel out there in the woods, aren't you, Dirk? Living under a pile of dirt, burrowing in and out of your hole in the ground like a dirty rodent..."

He could see the muscles rippling across Dirk's back, his stringy hair swaying from the momentum of his movement. Dirk paused, as though deciding whether to fight or flee.

"I'll see you in hell, Bjorklund."

Billy laughed until Dirk Westola turned to leave, then followed him to the door and watched him leave with a concerned look on his face.

Janice, the queen of gossip, was close behind, not wanting to miss any juicy tidbits ripe for the passing. If he knew her, her curiosity would get the best of her in ten seconds or less.

"What did he want to see you about?" Janice said.

Perfect. "He's worried about Rainbow Lake Lodge reopening in the spring." Billy twisted his face into a model of concern. "He bought his place for the privacy. The last thing he wants is a whole swarm of people and kids hiking around in the forest surrounding his little compound." He raised his voice a few decibels to make sure everyone in the reception area could hear. "Dirk doesn't mess around – he said he's going to do whatever it takes to make sure his rights are protected. The scary thing is, he's got the ammunition to back up his words."

"Someone should warn Hope about him," Janice said.

"I don't want to alarm anyone," Billy said, still speaking loudly, "but a threat is a threat. These survivalists are all kooks. Mark my words. Dirk Westola will do whatever it takes to make sure that Rainbow Lake never reopens."

Chapter 32

Hope had set up an appointment with a Christian counselor in Duluth not because she had anticipated that three different banks would turn down her loan request, but because she didn't get to the city all that often and was trying to make good use of the gas it took to drive so far.

She'd seen Doctor Hill once before, about a month after David's death. It was easy to look back over the past two plus years and realize that she should have continued to see him on a regular basis, but nothing had been regular since David died, including her schedule. For starters, there had been days early on when she could hardly get out of bed.

Well, that was something to count as a small victory anyway. Wasn't it? She thought about how far she'd come and waited for the thought to cheer her up.

There. That was much better – or a good start at the very least. What had she been thinking anyway? Bankers weren't known for their nurturing qualities any more than attorneys were – a counselor was what she needed. She wanted encouragement, didn't she? She looked around Dr. Hill's reception room at the comfortable, overstuffed chairs and vividly painted works of art and felt sure she would find it here.

A moment later, the receptionist motioned her into the inner sanctum of Dr. Hill's office. Pleasantries were exchanged. She was already starting to relax by the time Dr. Hill finished conducting a quick review of her situation.

"It would appear that you've worked though the greater part of your depression," the doctor said, after listening to her assessment of how things had changed since their initial meeting, including her current financial woes. "I think you experienced a major break through when you finally got mad at David and his parents for not telling you how heavily mortgaged the lodge was. Is." He smiled and rapped his pen against the edge of his desk.

"Thanks," Hope murmured, again feeling proud of the progress she'd made. At least she'd done something right.

"However," Dr. Hill began.

Hope sighed. "Howevers" were just as bad as "buts".

"Each person processes grief differently. While you've worked through much of your loss, I believe you may have skipped over some very significant stages."

"Like what?" Hope asked, not wanting to hear that she had more work ahead of her.

"Often times, people believe that they've accepted the death of a loved one, when the reality is that they can be caught in a web of denial for years, even decades. Especially when the death in question is untimely or unexpected like David's was."

"But denial is the very first stage," Hope said. "I may have been in denial...in shock for the first few hours, okay, maybe days, after I was told that David was dead, but by the day of the funeral... We buried him. Lowered him into the ground. There's no denying any of that. Believe me. It happened. I know full well it happened."

"Denial can take many forms," the doctor said. "David's death changed your life, narrowed your options, cut short many of your dreams and aspirations."

The overstuffed chair that had wrapped its arms around her a few minutes earlier threatened to swallow her whole. She stiffened and looked away from Dr. Hill's piercing eyes.

"There's a difference between having faith that things will work out the way they're supposed to and living in a dream world," Dr. Hill said. "I'm a firm believer in miracles, but at times, God prompts us to be realistic. It's a fine line – having hope for the future versus accepting the way things are and being content with what we can and cannot do."

"You think I should sell the lodge and move on," Hope said, barely finding her voice.

"I think you should be open to whatever God has for your future."

"So you're saying that I'm not open to whatever mysterious thing it is that I'm supposed to be considering for the next forty or fifty years of my life."

"I'm saying that I'd like you to examine your options."

"I don't want options. I want Rainbow Lake Lodge." Like it used to be. The warmth, the spirit of love and family that had always pervaded the place, the security of the familiar.

"Fine," Dr. Hill said. "Let's go at this from a different angle. Another of the stages of grief is bargaining. When you attempt to bargain with God, you lay a deal on the table. If I can get the money to restore Rainbow Lake Lodge, if I can keep the business going, then everything will be fine, and I can go on believing that I am fine."

"I am fine," she said.

"Let's talk about your options," he said. "You must still have friends in Chicago."

"I have no desire to go back to Chicago," she said. "The only reason I was in Chicago at all was because David was there. The only reason I was in Virginia was because my family was there. Now that they're gone – even if they weren't – the last thing I want to do is to go back in time."

"Isn't that exactly what you're doing at Rainbow Lake Lodge?" Dr. Hill said, cutting to the quick. "It looks to me as though you're desperately trying to recreate the good times you once had with David and his family."

She sat, stupefied, unable to speak.

"Can you honestly tell me that you're willing to risk everything to hang on to a lodge that will require you to work day and night while reaping very little in terms of rewards, monetary or otherwise, because this is what you want to do? Is this really what *you want* to do, Hope?"

"It's what..." She faltered. "It's what we..."

"You won't be working side by side with the man you love. You won't be striving together to fulfill your dreams. You won't be growing old together doing something you both love. Do you understand that, Hope? You'll be alone, clinging to the memory of a man who no longer exists."

She felt the tears stinging her cheeks before she was conscious that she was crying. Her eyes burned. Her nose clogged up. She couldn't breathe.

"I'm sorry to be so blunt, Hope." The doctor's voice finally pierced her haze. "But David's been gone for two years. I'd be amiss if I stood by and let you die with him. Your identity was and is still all wrapped up in David. Yes, you were his wife. But he is gone, and you are still here – a wonderful, talented, vibrant woman with so much love to give. What a waste to save all that for a dead man when there are so many people in this world who need to be loved, so many people that God can love through you."

He was asking her to let go of David. She hadn't been able to hear it from her friends, she hadn't been able to hear it from Tommy Love. She hadn't been able to hear it when Billy and almost every banker in Duluth had all but beaten her over the head with it. But now she was getting the message loud and clear. It was time. Time to move on.

Chapter 33

There was only one thing Tommy could think to do. He'd tried getting through to Billy. He'd tried to pressure him into making things right. Nothing had worked. If anything, he'd just fanned Billy's fire into a hotter frenzy.

Tommy looked at the telephone. He hated putting more pressure on Hope. She had enough to deal with already without having the agony of knowing what Billy's plans for Rainbow Lake Lodge were. Billy might be his friend, but he couldn't condone what the man was doing any longer – by his actions or inaction.

He dialed Hope's phone number as cautiously as a one year old taking his first steps. He had almost blown it with Hope. He couldn't risk making things worse. But he had to do what he had to do.

She answered on the first ring, almost as though she'd been sitting by the phone.

"Hope?" He stretched back in his recliner and tried to relax.

"Tommy?"

It felt good to know she recognized his voice. Dare he hope that she thought of him the same way he did her? "Do you have time to talk?"

"Yes," she said, her breath ragged, like she'd been hurrying. Or crying.

"I need to talk to you about Billy."

"I've been meaning to call you, too," she said.

He sucked in his breath. Something had changed. "I don't want to add to your stress level, but I've learned something that may affect your situation at the lodge. And with Billy."

He could hear her breathing. That was it. No smart comments, no quick comebacks, no insinuations about where his loyalties lie. Something was wrong. "Hope?"

"Go ahead," she said. "I'm listening."

Lord, she sounded tired. What was going on? How could he tell her what he had to say when she already sounded so defeated? "I never came right out and admitted the details of the plan Billy and I cooked up to get Rainbow Lake Lodge away from you." He didn't try to sugarcoat it, minimize his involvement, blame it on Billy or make excuses. Once he'd apologized and they'd put this behind them, he wanted her to know he'd been completely honest, a hundred percent above board.

"No, you didn't," she said, implying by her lack of emotion that it no longer mattered.

"You may no longer need or appreciate my willingness to try and undo the wrong I participated in," Tommy said, "but regardless, I owe you an apology. I want you to know how sorry I am that I ever got involved in this mess, Hope. I was so enthusiastic, so eager to get my hands on your property that I spurred Billy to action that he might not have taken otherwise, and for that, I am very, very sorry."

"Thank you," she said, crying softly. "I respect you for being able to admit you were wrong. It's more than I've been able to do."

"You haven't done anything to be ashamed of that I know of," he said, trying to envision what she might be talking about.

"I've been stubborn and bullheaded. I've refused to listen to reason, I've been—"

"Determined. Focused on your goal, confident," he said. "You've had faith. You have to keep having faith. You have to keep believing."

"It's over, Tommy. I didn't know it, but the Andersons had the lodge mortgaged to the hilt. The bank was meant to sell the property all along, as soon as they were gone. David found out at some point, and when he died, Billy's mother tried to protect me, but when Billy took control of the bank, she couldn't do it anymore, and..."

Crap, he thought, wishing he could hold her and soothe her instead of telling her the worst news he could imagine.

"So I guess what I'm saying is that I want you to have the lodge," Hope was saying. "It's not just that I have to sell it, it's that I've finally realized that I can't take care of this place all by myself."

"But – " he said, trying to tell her why he couldn't.

"All that's important to me now is that I know you'll take care of the Lodge and look after it the way it needs to be looked after. I can't think of anyone I'd rather sell the lodge to. You'll respect the history and the memories that are wrapped up in her nooks and crannies. And I know you won't bulldoze the lodge, or cut down all the trees. And I know you'll let me come and visit every so often."

"Hope. You need to listen," he said, lowering his voice once he had her attention. "First of all, I can't help you, not that way. I bought a house on the Pacific – it's a monstrosity, way more space than I need, but I fell in love with it, and, to be honest, with the new mortgage, I'm stretched a little thin right now."

The line was dead quiet.

"I know you're desperate, honey, but selling to me because I'm the lesser of two evils can't be the best solution for anybody."

"What would you suggest then?" she said, her voice hovering between brokenness and sarcasm.

Much as he was dreading it, it was time to tell Hope the rest of the story – time to be frank with Miss Hope for Every Tomorrow.

Chapter 34

Hope looked up at the stuffed bear in the corner of the room and wondered what she'd done to deserve the roller coaster ride that was her life.

Don't look at me, the bear seemed to say.

"What you need to do is to get serious about raising some money," Tommy said. "You need to find a way keep the lodge and do whatever it takes to make it work."

Hope rolled her eyes and tried not to laugh. Or cry. "You know, if my heart weren't breaking right now, that would be very funny, Tommy. Because it's the exact opposite of what every single person who knows me, and a lot of people who don't, think I should do."

"But you can't let Billy—"

"I know. That's the crux of it. If I don't sell the lodge now, before Billy has a chance to foreclose, I'll lose everything to the bank. Not just the lodge, but the balance of its net worth. Which is exactly what Billy wants. That's why I offered to sell you the lodge. I basically have to shoot myself in the foot to – "

"Selling to me would be like shooting yourself in the foot?" Tommy asked, sounding hurt.

"Well," she said, not wanting to jinx her chances of selling to Tommy because of some stupid expression when the truth was, she was so distraught she hardly knew what she was saying.

"Sweetheart, I wish I could help you. I really do. But that ship sailed when I signed the contract on my Pacific Paradise. That's why you have to come up with enough money to keep the lodge yourself."

"If you don't want it, I'll sell it to someone else," she said, thinking this was just her luck, and wondering what on earth was God trying to tell her now, when she had finally given up as gracefully as she could and acquiesced to the popular belief that she had no business trying to hang on to the lodge. "I'm sure there are plenty of people who would be interested in my property. I'll put a sign out and contact some realtors in Minneapolis and – "

"Billy already has another buyer." Tommy interrupting her again. "From what I hear, he's prepared to outbid any and all interested parties. And, as the man has no scruples, I'm sure he'd just as soon buy it from you as the bank. From what I'm told, the man will do anything to get what he wants."

This was not good. "What, one of your rock and roll, movie star friends?" she asked, trying to imagine who could afford to spend that much money and wondering how she could find out if he were a suitable buyer. "I'd rather it was someone I'm familiar with, but as long as he's not planning to bulldoze the place, I guess I can live with it. And if he has no loyalty to Billy, that's to my advantage, right? I mean, if you know who he is, then I can approach him and get him to sign something before Billy knows what hit him." She felt a surge of excitement flowing through her veins, the first glimmer of hope she'd felt in days. "Tell me about him," she demanded.

"He's very wealthy, but not because he's famous. He's a business man," Tommy said. "And he's willing to pay whatever price he needs to to acquire the land because he believes the property has unlimited earning potential."

"I know I'm not a born manager," she said, "but I watched the Andersons work their tails off to make a success of this place, and they weren't able to cash flow. I visited three banks in Duluth earlier this week and none of them thought I could make a go of it. What's this man's secret?"

"He has a secret all right. A dirty little secret," Tommy said. "Billy's new buyer is from Minneapolis, and he's planning on using the lodge for an adult entertainment business with a strip club. And if what I hear about him and his kind of business is true, he'll probably rent the cabins by the hour."

No. Her heart started a freefall.

"Because of the lodge's remote location, he wouldn't be subject to zoning laws, and his customers would have the anonymity they desire. Everything would be very discreet."

The bungee cord broke and what was left of her once proud little world came crashing down around her when her heart hit bottom. Not only had she failed to keep alive the legacy of the man she had loved so dearly, she had opened the door to the vilest fate imaginable. "I can't let that happen. It would make a mockery of everything Rainbow Lake Lodge stands for."

"Which is why we have to find you a financial backer. You have to fight, Hope. I know you, and you believe in Rainbow Lake Lodge. If your business plan wasn't good enough to dazzle the bankers in Duluth, then you need to come up with a new one. New ideas. New strategies. New goals. New ways to make the business thrive."

"I've already done everything I know how to do. I went over the Anderson's records line by line and tried to come up with every possible alternative to maximize income and minimize expenses within the framework of what they'd been doing."

"Forget the Andersons," he said.

Anger flared inside her like a match to tinder. She couldn't believe what he'd just said. "The whole reason I'm doing this is so David and his parents will always be remembered. I don't want to forget them. Ever." But she already was, and she knew it.

"Not a good reason," Tommy said, sounding unfamiliar, almost ruthless in his role as devil's advocate. "Resting on their laurels, or lack of them, isn't cutting it. Do this for yourself, or don't do it at all."

His words cut through her, not like a knife, which would have been entirely too quick and neat, but like a chain saw, leaving rough, coarsely splintered gashes in its wake.

"Think outside the box, Hope. I know it's become such a catch phrase that it espouses the very thing it sought to condemn," Tommy said, "but you need to do it. Now."

"I don't think I know how," she said, wanting to curl up in a little ball and die along with David. But even as she said the words, her mind was searching for answers, swimming with ideas, batting around options. She could do this. She had to do this.

"I'll talk to some people in similar industries out here," Tommy said. "I'm no business major, but you have my undivided support."

Business major. David had books full of notes from the business classes he'd taught.

"Start with winter activities," Tommy said. "There's no way you can make a living off this place if you're only open for six or seven months out of the year. People are willing to pay top dollar to snuggle up in front of a fireplace or bask in a private Finnish sauna."

Just like we did, she thought, fighting the feelings that welled up inside her. "None of the rooms in the main lodge have fireplaces. I told you they were more like bunkhouses. I did insulate the cabins when we were updating them this summer, but they don't have heat. I doubt the wealthy clientele you're referring to are going to pay top dollar for what we have to offer. The Anderson's believed that offering lower rates is what attracted so many families to the lodge."

"Forget families," Tommy said. "The kinds of customers you need are baby boomers who don't have to spend all their money on kids – singles, childless couples, and newly-retired empty nesters who have money and the freedom to get away. Young, adventure seekers are a hot target group as well. I did some research online last night, and there's a whole new generation of people looking for extreme vacation opportunities."

"Extremely nice? Extremely cheap? Extremely what?" she asked, hoping Tommy wouldn't pick up on her extreme frustration and extreme cynicism and lecture her even more.

"Extremely exciting and dangerous enough to make it seem extreme. Did you know the town of Ely is the worldwide center of dog sledding?"

"Sounds extremely cold," she said, not even trying to hide her skepticism.

"I'm serious. You need to capitalize on the dogsled idea. Talk to the outfitters. On the internet it said that they offer day trips where people get to interact with the dogs. The ad said 'Feed, handle, and learn to mush a team. Some overnight trips include stays at cozy lodges.' You get the picture. They've got the dogs. You've got the cozy lodge."

Something finally clicked inside her brain. "What about ice fishing? I told you about the first time I came up here for Christmas and saw people driving on the lake, and this huge snowplow out there making a road. I couldn't believe it. That's extreme, isn't it?"

"You got it, babe," he said.

A shiver of some indefinable emotion ran down her spine as she listened to Tommy talk. It had been so long since she'd felt anything but grief, numbness, and despair that it took her a minute to realize that she was excited. Excited how, why, or because of what stimuli, she didn't care to explore – but it felt wonderful. Joy and optimism had become foreign concepts since David's death.

"I wish I could do more to help," Tommy said.

"You've already gone way above and beyond," she said.

"I wrote a new song last night," Tommy said. "If I can get it released in the next couple of weeks, I'll funnel some of the profits your way. I want to help in a tangible way if I can. More than just words."

"You don't need to do that, Tommy. This is my problem and has been all along. I know you feel responsible, but the wheels of this monster truck were in motion long before you ever came into the picture. There's no reason for you to – "

"There's every reason in the world," he said. "If you hadn't opened my eyes to my need to have faith, if you hadn't taught me about hope, there would be no song."

"Fine," she said, and smiled, genuinely smiled, for what felt like the first time in weeks. "You've got great stage presence. Maybe you can teach me to be as inspiring when it comes to presenting my business plan as I apparently am when it comes to new songs."

Chapter 35

Hope crouched beside a blue plastic tub David had labeled *Marketing Your Business 301*, brushed aside a layer of dust and a few dozen cobwebs, and rifled through a file entitled *Creating a Buzz: Where to Start – The Snowball Effect of Social Marketing*.

If there was any doubt in her mind about whether or not God meant her to stay at Rainbow Lake Lodge, Tommy's news had settled it once and for all. She couldn't leave the lodge now even if she wanted to. They'd have to pry her fingers loose from the center support that held up the roof beams and drag her out by her hair before she'd let Billy bring in a bunch of buzzards intent on remaking her precious lodge into some sort of sleazy pleasure palace.

Thinking outside the box was just the beginning. She was determined to revamp her business plan, come up with a better marketing strategy, and set-up as many more appointments with as many more bankers in as many more cities as it took to save the Lodge.

The notebooks from David's business classes might not exactly be love notes, but she felt a renewed connection with him as she gave herself a crash course. Studying the words he'd written so long ago, penned in a voice that was so uniquely his, made her feel closer to him than she had since he'd died. Yet with every document she studied, she felt a growing sense of independence and assertiveness. She could do this! She could run this business more profitably than the Andersons ever had.

The future of Rainbow Lake Lodge was not simply going to be an extension of the past, it was going to be better in every way – a whole new beginning.

Her cheeks felt flushed with excitement as she jotted down idea after idea, snuggled in front of the fireplace. She could offer quilting and scrapbooking retreats for ladies, cooking classes for guests, live music in the restaurant. Tommy Love might not want to do it, but she felt sure there were plenty of talented locals who would love to have a venue in which to sing or play. She'd heard there was a barbershop quartet in Babbitt that was excellent and had a large following. If she could get them to sing at her grand opening, she could muster all kinds of word-of-mouth enthusiasm.

She'd also done a little research of her own on the internet and decided to join a bed and breakfast association. It would mean delivering a breakfast basket to the cabins or serving a free breakfast buffet at the lodge every morning, but according to the formula she'd found in David's business lessons, the return on a few homemade cinnamon rolls, some scrambled eggs and a little fresh fruit should be substantial.

Church retreats and business getaways also looked to be a virtually untapped market, and Tommy's ideas regarding outdoor sports had prompted her to contact several well-known boundary water canoe outfitters. The lodge would be a great place for their customers to shower, regroup, have a good meal, and go through a recap or debriefing session before they went home.

She had gone back to the computer and was just finishing a written description accentuating the lodge's features for an online B&B directory when the doorbell rang.

The last time someone had shown up at her door without phoning, it had been Creepy Survivalist Guy. She peeked out the front window. She didn't recognize the car, but the two people bundled up in snowmobile suits and parkas had familiar faces.

Her visitors were none other than David's Aunt and Uncle Wolfe from California.

"What a surprise!" She opened the front door and called out a greeting.

"Thank goodness you've got a fire going." Suzie hustled toward the lodge, rubbing her arms through her furry white parka until she was safely tucked away in Hope's spot under a quilt. "We're chilled to the bone."

"I can't believe you're here," Hope said, hugging David's uncle.

"We could say the same about you." Hank said. "We never expected you'd still be in town."

"We assumed you'd sold the place and moved on a long time ago," Suzie said, a slight shiver still in her voice.

"How on earth are you managing out here all by yourself?" When Hank had shed his coat, he looked tanned and fit and relaxed just like she remembered him.

She took two mugs from the buffet. "I've spent the last two years trying to finish all the renovations David and I started before he died. I'm slated to reopen in May if all goes well."

Hank frowned, tilted his head, and caught Suzie's eye over Hope's left shoulder. "You're kidding."

"No," Hope said. "Just waiting for warmer weather to finish up the last few projects. Speaking of, what brings you two up north this time of year?"

"The Wolf Pack Reunion," Hank said. "The annual *Let Your Pack Meet Ours* event."

"The International Wolf Center sponsors it," Suzie said. "People whose last name is Wolf or Wolfe come from all over the world to spend Thanksgiving weekend dancing with the wolves."

"I've never even been to the center," Hope said. "I guess David and I were always so busy helping out when we were up here that we never took the time to play tourist." She gave Hank another hug. She'd always thought David resembled him, and given that Hank had only been ten when David was born, he had always been a harbinger of what David would like a decade down the road, when he caught up to his uncle. Except now, he never would. "I wish I had known you were going to be here. You could have stayed here with me."

"We had no idea you were still up here," Suzie said.

"We just assumed..." Hank said.

"I haven't been very good about writing Christmas letters since David died," Hope said, hoping that if she smiled brightly enough they would drop the subject and let her keep her pride.

"We had a choice between winter camping and Whispering Pines Lodge when we signed up," Suzie said, winking as if to say, *you know me*.

"So you're at Whispering Pines." Hope ducked into the kitchen and returned with two packets of hot chocolate, a small whisk, and some whipped cream.

"We figured we'd get our fill of living on the wild side when we were out howling with the wolf packs, dog-sledding through the forest, and hanging around the campfire eating s'mores and telling wolf tales," Hank said.

"Wow," Hope said. "You guys are so adventurous."

"I don't think we've got anything up on you if you're brave enough to try to manage this place single-handedly," Suzie said.

"Bravery is one thing," Hank said. "Stupidity is another."

Hope would have pinched herself to see if she was dreaming, or more appropriately, having a nightmare, but at the moment, she was pretty near frozen with shock.

"Hank," Suzie said. "I'm sure Hope knows exactly what she's doing. It's not our place to – "

"Then whose is it?" He demanded.

There was an uncomfortable silence while Suzie glared at Hank, Hank glared at Hope, and Hope tried to get over being mortified and find her voice. "I'm doing this in honor of David and the Andersons. To keep their memory alive."

"My sister and her husband wouldn't need to be memorialized if they hadn't killed themselves working night and day at this place. They'd be alive. If it weren't for Rainbow Lake Lodge, we'd have her and John instead of their memories," Hank said. "David, too, for that matter."

"Hank," Suzie said. "Please. Don't..."

"I loved them, too," Hank said, turning away from both of them.

"Surely you don't really think..." Hope said in a quiet voice.

"It wouldn't be so bad if they'd at least gotten paid for all their hard work," Hank said. "But they never had a penny to their names. They couldn't afford to come out to California for Christmas with the rest of the family. They never took a vacation the whole time they owned this place."

"They worked as hard as they did because they wanted to," Suzie said. "And according to them, they *vacationed* all winter."

"Hogwash," Hank said, turning to stare out the window for a time before finally focusing his gaze on Hope. "There's nothing any of us can do to change the past, but I couldn't live with myself if I stood by and let you head down the same path without saying my piece."

"David loved you so much," Suzie said, taking her hands.

"I appreciate your concern," Hope said, wondering what on earth she was supposed to do with the emotions whipping around in her head.

"It's more than concern," Hank said. "Suzie and I have been talking about coming to this wolf reunion for twenty years, but something has always kept us from being here. Until now."

Hope looked at Suzie who looked resigned.

"I'm not saying I'm a Moses or an Elijah or anything like that,"

Hank said. "But messengers come in all shapes and sizes. There's got to be some reason we ended up here, at this particular moment in time."

"Ignore him," Suzie said. "He's been watching reruns of *Early Edition* and *Touched By An Angel* again."

"You really think that my staying here is going to bring me plagues, pestilence and misfortune?" Hope said shakily.

Suzie looked at Hank. "You know, your heart is in the right place, sweetheart, but you need to stop and think about what you're saying. If God were going to pick the perfect time to send you out here all the way from California to prevent something disastrous from happening, wouldn't He have done it before David got hit by a drunk driver?"

"Fine. Forget I said anything," Hank said.

"Maybe it's just me," Hope said, "but dismal tidings and dire predictions are pretty hard to ignore – especially when they come from someone who seems to know more than I did about the day to day operations of the lodge." She looked at Hank and Suzie. "I just found out how heavily the Andersons had mortgaged the lodge a short time ago."

"Get out while you can," Hank said. "It's not worth the toll it will take. You're young and beautiful – you have options. David wouldn't want you to sacrifice your life trying to do something that his mom and dad couldn't even do without jeopardizing their financial security, and eventually, their health."

"You've given me a lot to think about," Hope said, thinking about how quickly she'd slid from mountaintop to ravine.

"Hank will always have his opinions," Suzie said. "In the end, you have to follow your heart."

Hank grunted.

Suzie pulled the quilt a little tighter. "Much as we hate to put a damper on things and run, we probably need to get back to the pack."

"I never even asked if you've been enjoying the wolf, um, thing." So she was flustered. She'd just been attacked by wolves. She was entitled.

"We were just saying we hadn't had so much fun in decades until... well, there was an accident," Suzie said.

Just hearing the word gave Hope a chill.

"We were ice fishing near the bear sanctuary when a young man from Maine fell through the hole and got trapped under the ice. They called the sheriff to mount a rescue – "

"To recover the body," Hank interjected.

"And then the sheriff ended up in the water, and – "

"Alvin?" Hope said. "Was his name Alvin?"

"Tarp something," Hank said.

"Turppa," Hope said, her insides shaking, her heart breaking for the parents of the boy who had drowned. "Was the sheriff okay?"

"They took him to the hospital in an ambulance."

"I should go to him," Hope said. "He's been helping at the lodge. He's been a good friend."

"We'll take you," Suzie said, burrowing out from under the quilt. "We can finish catching up on the way."

"Just so you know," Hope said when they'd gotten into Hank and Suzie's car. "I wasn't planning on resting on the Anderson's laurels, or making the same mistakes they did. I've been researching adventure trips, bike rentals, motorized watercraft rentals, dog sledding excursions, ice fishing house rentals, Finnish saunas and all kinds of year-round activities."

"Yeah," Hank said, driving toward the hospital. "Do away with the off-season and you can work yourself into your grave by fifty-five instead of sixty."

"Good grief, Hank," Suzie said.

"Seriously," Hope said. "If I'm open year round, I can hire some good quality, permanent help instead of relying on seasonal laborers. Cabins with fireplaces go from $200 to $300 a night. With the upgrades David and I have already made and a few extra touches, I can make this place profitable."

"I've been ice fishing a couple of times," Hank said, his voice softer. "It's very relaxing – low tech, boat-free, casual. It's a good escape. You and a couple of buddies, good conversation, shooting the breeze," he said to no one in particular. "I went with a friend of mine. This guy gets out ice fishing at least a couple of times each winter. It's perfection – you can sit around and play a round of cards or listen to a game while you wait for the rattle to let you know there's a fish at the end of the line. This place was heated, carpeted, furnished with a table and chairs, and built around seven holes in the ice. The ice house next to ours was a sleeper with bunks and a cook stove."

"It almost sounds appealing," Suzie said. "At least, until the image of Alvin breaking through the ice and falling into the lake pops back into my head."

Hope said a silent prayer that Alvin would be all right. "I'm supposing people can be injured doing a lot of the active adventure vacations that are popular right now. But then, they can also be killed simply driving home from town."

A car whooshed around the curve and slid by Hank's rental car, inches from where Hope was sitting, far too close for comfort.

"I guess nothing is without risk," Hank said. "That doesn't mean you stop putting your self out there and doing what you want to do. The health benefits of being active far outweigh any dangers –"

"Exactly," Suzie said, looking over her shoulder to give Hope a triumphant smile.

"So even if I sell the lodge and use the money to move to Charleston and become, say a receptionist, I could still end up dead before I'm sixty-five," Hope said, trying not to gloat, and really not wanting to – she knew better than anyone how short and unpredictable life could be.

Silence.

Hank steered the car into the parking lot of the hospital. "Touché."

"I'm not putting all my eggs in the extreme adventure basket anyway," Hope said as they all climbed out of the car. "Next year, I'm going to donate a free stay to Autumn Apple Daze Festival at the Nelimark Homestead and the Boundary Waters Blues Festival in Ely to generate awareness of what I offer. I'm also going to contact businesses in Duluth and offer a corporate rate for business meetings, retreats and brainstorming sessions. I listed the lodge on wedding sights on the internet this morning and hope to start hosting weddings. I've already been in touch with a florist and a photographer I know from Embarrass, and this woman who makes the most sensational wedding cakes." Now I just need to find a musician, she thought, thinking of Tommy, and wishing, really wishing that he were less star and more normal.

"She'll do just fine. Won't she, Hank?"

Hank still looked skeptical, but he mumbled, "We can hope."

A candy striper at the front desk gave them Alvin's room number and pointed to a bank of elevators down the hall on the right.

Chapter 36

Tommy had just gotten back from an appointment with the chiropractor when the phone rang. His neck was finally feeling halfway normal, no thanks to sad sack, Bad Back Bling.

He glanced at the caller ID, acknowledged that sometimes God's timing was actually pretty perfect, and exchanged greetings with his agent. He could hardly wait to tell Jack about *Misty in the Moonlight*. First, because he was just plain excited about it; second, because if he had any hope of raising enough money to help Hope out of her predicament, he needed to sell the song, record it, and start raking in some serious cash like yesterday.

"The song is pure gold, Jack," Tommy said, trying to sound convincing – which wasn't hard. He was totally jacked about his new song. No pun intended. "It's got a hip-hop beat, but the words are pure Tommy Love. I'm telling you, it's going straight to the top of the charts. It's going to make me a teen icon all over again."

"Please don't take this the wrong way," Jack said, evidently trying to be diplomatic, "but I'm still a little worried about what your old fans are going to think."

"You make them sound like a bunch of moldy old dinosaurs," Tommy said. "They may not be teenagers anymore, but they're young at heart. They've got kids and grandkids they want to relate to. I'm telling you, this song is the perfect bridge between the generations."

"Well, I suppose it's better than punk," Jack said, still sounding unconvinced.

"Trust me," Tommy said. "When I debut *Misty in the Moonlight*, you'll think you were nuts for ever doubting me."

"I guess it can't hurt to try," Jack said, sounding like Tommy was forcing him to take a sip of arsenic and hoping it didn't kill him. "I'll start looking for the right venue for the debut as soon as I get this Yellowstone special behind us." He paused. "Think you can have it ready by spring?"

"Actually, I'd like to do it at Yellowstone," Tommy said. "The lodge would be the perfect setting – the whole park is a multi-generational phenomenon with cross appeal to young and old. The whole reason they're doing the show is because they want to put a new spin on Old Faithful, start attracting a new generation of visitors to the park. What could be more perfect?"

"Not going to work, Tommy," Jack said so quickly that he obviously hadn't given Tommy's ideas one iota of credence. "They requested specific numbers when they contracted you to perform. Nothing was ever mentioned about debuting a new song."

"I told you months before this invite came in that I was done performing shows that only included oldies. I was very specific about the fact that from now on, I would only perform my hits if I was also allowed to do my new stuff."

"Well, until ten minutes ago, there hasn't been any new stuff." Jack sounded as huffy as Tommy felt. "So obviously, your stipulation wasn't of the greatest concern at the time."

"You knew I've been working on the new songs all along."

"It's been more than fifteen years since you wrote anything. You didn't seriously expect me to make business agreements based on mythical songs that hadn't been written yet, did you?"

"When have I ever let you down?" Tommy said.

"You haven't," Jack said. "But that's beside the point. The producers of this particular television special have designed an old-fashioned Christmas show. They want you to sing *Moonlight and Mistletoe, Another Sweet Noel* and *Jenny's Song*. That's it. No room for discussion."

"*Jenny's Song*? You never told me—"

"I know you don't like to sing it," Jack interrupted.

"I have to pay her $10,000 every time I perform it," Tommy said. "Which I had no problem agreeing to during the divorce settlement because I never intended to perform it again. I won't sing it."

"You will if you want this gig. And I shouldn't have to remind you that this is the biggest thing that's come your way in a very, very long time. $10,000 is nothing given what they're paying you."

"I've been doing just fine with the work I've been getting," Tommy said, trying to reign in his fury.

"Doing background vocals and guitar riffs on other people's albums. You say you want to put your name out there – well, they're not going to see it in the tiny print on the back of somebody else's CD."

"They will if they're wearing their bifocals," Tommy said, then laughed. It was the only way he knew to diffuse the tension. "Listen to us. We haven't fought like this since the old days."

"I have no desire to be at odds with you, Tommy," Jack said. "But you have to listen to me on this one."

"I'm happy to do *Moonlight and Mistletoe* and *Another Sweet Noel*. At least they're associated with some good memories. But I won't dredge up my past with Jenny."

"You'll lose the whole gig if you don't," Jack said. "This producer is not known for his flexibility. And your fans love *Jenny's Song*."

"Then maybe we should invite Scott to play the drums. Jenny can do back-up vocals. Recreate the whole messy affair," Tommy said, not even trying to mask his bitterness. "Sounds like a perfect old-fashioned Christmas to me."

"Please don't be this way, Tommy."

"*Jenny's Song* is non-negotiable. Tell them they can take *Misty in the Moonlight*, or nothing at all. On second thought, tell them the new number is called *Hope's Song*. They can take it or leave it."

"I'll talk to them," Jack said. "But I wouldn't get your hopes up if I were you."

Too late for that. "Hey, you're the miracle worker," Tommy said. "Just do it. Isn't that what you always tell me?"

"When you have writer's block and can't get a new song out."

"Well, I finally found my voice," Tommy said. "Now it's your turn to shine."

"I'll do what I can," Jack said, sounding more dull than shiny.

Tommy made one last effort to pump Jack up and said good-bye. And then he prayed. Prayed like he hadn't prayed in three decades. After faltering through a lifetime of glitz and fame and fortune, he finally knew what was important – so important that he couldn't depend on Jack alone, good as he was at his job, to get it done.

He looked up and nodded. He wasn't used to trusting God with anything – even the big things. He'd always had enough clout, enough power, enough pull to take care of himself.

Even now, it wasn't as though he were desperate for divine intervention. In a sense, he felt almost guilty asking for God's help when there were so many people in the world whose circumstances were so dire, whose needs were so all-encompassing that they truly had no other option but to plead for God's mercy.

But for him, it was an important step. Sure, he could take care of things himself if it came down to it. But for the first time in his life, he wanted God to be a part of things – his life, his future, his relationships. For the first time, he was able to acknowledge that God would do a better job of directing his life than he – or even Jack – could. It was time to let go of his youthful arrogance and have a little faith.

He continued to look up while he consciously gave in, let go, turned over control. "Thanks, man," he finally finished. "I mean God."

Chapter 37

Hope re-stoked the fire and watched it sizzle, flames licking, branches igniting, energy pulsing.

She'd spent the morning going over the Anderson's reservation book. It had been her idea to write personal notes to each of the guests who'd visited the lodge in the last ten years, and inviting them to return for a grand opening. Good as her plan had seemed, she couldn't help but wonder how many of the envelopes would come back undeliverable – after nearly a decade, how many of their former guests had moved away, or worse, died – just as David had.

She'd been on the phone non-stop since noon, rounding up future clients so she could include them in her business plan, which she had to have ready by Monday, when she had scheduled a second round of meetings with a banker and some investors from Minneapolis. They'd told her "No deal" unless she could find a co-signer, which she didn't have. What she did have was a plan – to wow them with an even-better-than-before business plan – thereby stripping any doubts from their minds.

She was exhausted. She'd survived a Wolfe attack, although just barely, and not without some scratches and tears in her hide. And in her humble opinion, bankers were worse than wolves. She really needed to hear a friendly voice.

She dialed Tommy's cell phone number slowly, tempted to hang up even when it started to ring.

"Hello?"

"Hi Tommy," she said, hoping he would be happy she'd called.

"Hope?"

Good. He sounded pleased to hear from her.

"I did what you said," she said, trying to speak in the confident, I-can-do-this voice she'd used on bankers all week, and not the timid, who-am-I-trying-to-fool voice that reflected the way she really felt.

"Good," he said. "You probably came up with ten times as many ideas as I did. Do you think some of them will work out?"

"Yes. Thanks. You really got my brain going. I don't know how good I'll ever be at thinking outside the box, but at least my box isn't as tiny as it used to be."

Tommy laughed. "I'm sure you'll fill it with all kinds of things you didn't even imagine were possible a few weeks ago."

He sounded sleepy, mellow, soft, like he'd just awakened from a nap, and it made her want to touch him, cuddle up in his arms, feel her body pressed to his like it had been the night they'd spent on the sofa in front of the fireplace.

"I'm sure I will, eventually." She looked down at her knuckles, white, clamped tight, tense. "It's been a hard week." She told him about Hank and Suzie, and Alvin's close call, and the new rejections she'd amassed after talking to the bankers she'd visited in Hibbing and Duluth.

"But Alvin is okay?" Tommy said, his voice hesitant in a way she'd never heard it.

"His fever spiked a couple of days ago. He's been released from the hospital and the doctors have assured him that the antibiotics will have his pneumonia in check before long. He's going to have to take it easy for a month or more." She paused. "I was so scared for him."

"I'm sure you two have gotten close since he's been coming out to work at the lodge."

"I don't know what I would have done without him."

"Do you have feelings for him?" Tommy said after a few seconds of silence.

"No," she said. "Not that way. He's been a friend, and I appreciate all he's done for me, but that's all."

"Good," he said, not saying why it was good.

Because, really, it was bad. What would have been good would have been if she could put her fantasies about Tommy Love out of her head once and for all and learn to be content with someone like Alvin, who might not ever be the love of her life, but was a good man, which should have been fine, since she'd already had the love of her life.

"I know you believe in me," she said, "and I know I've made a lot of progress, but the more I try, the more I learn about what it's going to take to make this happen, the more terrified I am."

"You can do this," he said. "I know you can."

"It's not that I haven't tried. You know how hard I've worked to make this happen." An almost completely burned stick dissolved into a mass of red-hot ash and fell to the grate below. "I'm exhausted."

"You can't give up," he said. "Not now. Not when you're so close."

"I should have acquiesced months ago. I was a fool to chase you away when you wanted to buy the lodge."

"You were following your heart."

"I know you've moved on and I know you've bought a house in California, but if you would just think about... You could sell it again – I know you could. You could be happy here. This is where your roots are."

There it was. She'd admitted defeat. It didn't exactly feel good, but it hadn't been all that bad either. In a way, it was freeing to finally admit that she was in over her head.

"I don't know what to say." Tommy said, suddenly sounding very far away.

"Neither do I," she said, obviously having said too much already.

"You know I love Rainbow Lake," he said. "But California is, well, it's been good for me. I've made friends here, gotten involved with a church. I've been writing, and I really like my new house. Granted the walls are a little bare, but the view is beautiful, and it's mine."

"I didn't realize," she said, hating that she had said anything.

"All I know is that I'm happy," Tommy said.

"It's okay. Don't worry about it. It's not your problem," she said.

"What would you do? If I did sell this place, moved back to Minnesota and bought the lodge?"

"Now I don't know what to say." Her stomach started churning at the very thought of moving away from Rainbow Lake.

She'd packed up all her quilts without shedding a tear. It was what had to be done, and most of them were replaceable, and the ones that weren't... Whether or not her cedar chest was empty or full wouldn't affect the daily, nitty-gritty, what-really-mattered part of her life one way or the other in the end. But leaving Rainbow Lake Lodge was all wrapped up in who she was, and what she'd been for a very long time.

"Hey," Tommy said. "If you get to put me on the spot, turn about is fair play."

"Maybe I'd go back to Virginia. Or start out fresh someplace else. Or take an extended vacation to Europe."

Her heart was breaking here. Much as she wanted to sell the lodge to Tommy as opposed to any of the other options before her, she couldn't envision it being his home. The Lodge needed people - hordes of them, every age, shape and size. It needed laughter – babies cooing, little girls giggling, teenagers smirking, old men snorting. It needed happy feet pattering back and forth, and to and fro, up and down the trails, tracking in grass and bringing in warm humid air from the lake, even mosquitoes.

Tommy didn't say a word.

"I've been here so long that it's hard to envision being anywhere else," she said.

And then she thought about being there with Tommy, the two of them running the lodge together; he, traveling when he needed to, but always coming home to her; she, doing what she loved, making people happy, providing a place of refuge in a storm. Tommy, singing for the guests; the two of them snuggling in front of the fire, working together, making her dream come true.

Her dream. Not his. The antithesis of everything he wanted. Privacy. Seclusion. Solitude. A place to write. A quiet haven. A getaway from the world and everyone in it.

"Okay, so I don't have a clue," she said.

"California's not even on the list?"

"I hadn't even thought..."

"I'm telling you, you'd love the central coast. Think blue skies and flowers all year round and the endless ocean stretching on as far as you can see, and beautiful sunsets every night. All it would take to make it perfect would be for you to be here," Tommy said.

Her heart thumped in her chest. Tommy was in rare form – oozing charm, gently persuading, toying with her in that too-light-hearted-to-take-him-seriously way he had.

"I'm serious," he said. "Think of me as your Plan B. Consider this an open invitation to come to California and stay with me. You yourself said that your gift is to make a house into a home. Well, this place definitely needs a woman's touch. You could make some quilts, help decorate the house, you know, do what you do best."

"Fine, so I'm a good little homemaker. I can't earn a living doing that," she said, feeling facetious and breathless all at the same time.

"Hey," he said. "You have a gift – a gift that millions of people do not have. Even if I had it, I wouldn't have the time – that's why people like me hire people like you to do that kind of stuff. Really. I think a lot of people would be interested in the kind of thing you do. Hiring people to do things for you is the cornerstone California is built on. Why not jump on the bandwagon?"

Her mood plummeted the second he said the word hire. At least she knew where she stood. A chill ran from her head to the pit of her stomach. Tommy Love thought of her as one more potential employee among the entourage he paid to take care of him. She should have realized that he didn't take her seriously. Which meant she couldn't let him think for a minute that she had thought he did.

"It's not that I don't appreciate the invitation," she said, trying to sound as light and flip as he did. Banter was what Tommy Love did. "But taking on another renovation project so soon after what I've been through at the lodge? It makes me tired just thinking about it."

How she wished she could feel bubbly and optimistic and hopeful again. But that part of her, that wonderful, joyous, energetic part of her, had either died with David or been killed in the avalanche of negativism, loneliness and disappointment she'd suffered ever since. She felt like a rusted-out, old car sitting in a field of weeds with a dead battery or a starter that wouldn't turn over.

Tommy was talking double time trying to un-offend her, telling her how talented she was, laying it on as thick as he knew how.

She supposed she should be grateful for his invitation – glib as it had been. She supposed it was nice to know that Tommy Love would hire her to decorate his new house before he'd see her tossed out on the street, but it was little comfort when all she wanted from him was his love.

Chapter 38

Tommy scraped a swath of stubble from his beard, held his razor under the faucet, and made a second stripe next to the first. Women. Hope, in particular, but it wouldn't take much to include each and every one of them if he started thinking about it. What was wrong with her – besides the fact that she was still in love with her ex-husband? He'd all but proposed to her, and what had she said? That the very thought of being with him made her tired.

Great, just great. He'd gone out on a limb for her – practically bared his soul to her, and she'd rejected him. The worse thing was that she hadn't even thought about it. She'd said no before his heart had even stopped pounding from the adrenalin rush he'd gotten when he'd finally found the nerve to get the words out.

Ouch. The sting of blood and salty sweat and shaving lotion pricked his neck and pierced his consciousness. He laid down his razor, grabbed a tissue, brushed at his eyes and tried to cough away the ache in his chest. Couldn't she see how much he loved her?

In the old days, all he'd had to do to get a woman was to give her a look, crook his little finger, and wink once or twice. Countless women had come running, no clamoring, to fall into his bed. A look. That's all it had taken.

Was he really so decrepit that he had to beg for it like some shriveled up old coot?

He replayed the night he'd been at the Bump and Grind with Spiky Do and Bad Bling and tried to console himself with the thought that someone wanted him. Problem was, he didn't want them. Hope had ruined him for any other women. It made him furious. He was still fuming – mourning – when the phone rang.

"Hey, Tommy." Brian's now familiar voice greeted him. "Just wanted to tell you that we're going to practice for contemporary worship at 5:30 tomorrow night. Work for you?"

"Sure," Tommy said.

"We're doing one that's probably new to you called *The Joy of the*

Lord, so thought I'd better run the rehearsal time by you first."

"Should be fine."

"The sermon is the last one in the gardening series I've been doing," Brain said. "This one is on the verses about fig trees not bearing plums. Kind of a *Do what you're meant to do, be who you're called to be* theme, the tie-in being that when you're where you're supposed to be, you'll experience the joy of the Lord.

"Sure," Tommy said. "Got it."

"Something wrong?" Brian asked.

"Women," Tommy said.

"Oh. That. You're talking to the wrong person if you're looking for advice."

"You're a pastor, you dweeb. You're supposed to have a line for everything."

"I have a few pastoral-type adages I routinely share when the occasion calls for it, but to be perfectly honest, they're pretty lame."

"I was trying to talk Hope into moving out here, you know, to be with me. I tried to approach things from an angle that would appeal to her. I mean, Hope isn't just any woman," he said.

Brian snorted. "What did you say?"

"Nothing that should have offended her. I mean, she's a lady, and a Christian. I couldn't tell her I'm hot for her body."

"So what did you say?"

"I told her how gifted she was. She really has this knack for making a place homey, you know? She sews quilts and curtains and she makes these pillows that really make the house look classy, although I will say that they're a pain in the butt when you want to sit down and can't because there are pillows everywhere."

"What did you say?" Brian said again, this time, sounding a little too hellfire and brimstone for Tommy's tastes.

"That I was sure lots of people would be willing to hire her to fix up their places."

"Lots of people, as in you?"

"Well, someone has to give her a start. That's how these things work. She does my place, then I have a housewarming or some big shindig for the neighbors so everybody can see what a good job she does, and before you know it, her phone is ringing off the hook with customers who want her to make their places look as good as mine."

"So you offered to hire her to fix up your place."

"Well, I guess in a way I did. She needs money. I really stressed the part about how talented she is."

"Man," Brian said. "You're worse than I am."

"Not such a good idea?"

Brian grunted.

His other line was ringing through. "Bry, can I call you back? Someone's on the other line – it could be Hope."

"Let me think about this until tomorrow night. See if I can come up with something," Brian said.

It was Jack. "Hey, man," Tommy said. "This better be good news. I'm in the middle of something important."

"We lost the gig at Yellowstone," Jack said. "When they heard you refused to sing *Jenny's Song*, they decided to go with Vince Gill, who by the way, has no qualms about singing songs he wrote when he was with his first wife."

"Crap," Tommy said. "I didn't think they'd really..."

"I told you this would happen," Jack said. "I know these people."

"And I know you," Tommy said. "You're the best negotiator in the business when your heart is in it."

"You just don't get it, do you? Nobody wants to hear Tommy Love doing hip-hop. I've tried to be diplomatic. I've tried to be supportive, but you just won't listen. If you're really that determined not to get old, then do what everyone else does – buy a red convertible, find a twenty year old girlfriend, and get hair implants. But don't do hip-hop, or punk rock, or even R&B. You're too old."

He was shaking like a leaf when he got off the phone. Shaking and agent-less.

He called Brian about a half hour later, when he could finally talk without choking up, and got his answering machine.

Figures. "Hey, Bry," he spoke into the machine. "I'm going to have to pass on worship team this Sunday. No good excuse except that the *Joy of the Lord* is escaping me at the moment."

Chapter 39

Billy knew what Sharon wanted the second he saw her pull into his driveway and jump down from the driver's seat of her Dodge Ram. Sex. He and Sharon would have eventually killed each other if they'd stayed married, but just because they weren't good at marriage didn't mean they weren't great together in bed.

Exes who were good at sex. Between the two of them, they'd kept each other company in bed when the need arose, and sometimes just for the fun of it, through four marriages. From the looks of it, they weren't done yet.

He looked out the window and took note of Sharon's quick paced clip. She had it bad all right. She even looked hot. If he knew her, and he did, she'd have half his clothes off before he even got the door closed.

He opened the storm door and watched her swing up the steps. "Babe," he said, pulling her into his arms. Previous experience had proven that the less he and Sharon talked before they did it, the better it was for both of them.

"Get off me, you pig," Sharon said, pushing him away. "If you think that's the reason I'm here, you're crazier than everyone thinks."

So she was going to play hard to get. It was only one of the little games they liked to indulge in.

"Is that a new dress?" he asked, whipping out his sweetest voice.

"No." She looked downright miffed. "And you can cut the crap. I didn't come for – "

"That's what you always say." He lifted one eyebrow – their little signal for "Let's take it to the bedroom, shall we?"

She huffed and looked at him with disgust oozing from her baby blue eyes. "The fact that I haven't been by to see you in over five months should tell you something, Billy, but in case that's too subtle for you, let me spell it out plain and clear. I wouldn't sleep with the mean-spirited creep you've become if you were the last man on earth."

"So why are you here?"

"To drop off Hope Anderson's armoire." She looked over her shoulder at her truck and gave him another dirty look.

What the...? Billy bit back his words and tried to look like a man who thought Sharon coming by his house with a piece of furniture that belonged to Hope Anderson was the most normal thing in the world. He wasn't an idiot. If he said what he was thinking, it was all over. If he kept his mouth shut and managed not to do anything else that offended Sharon, he might still get some.

"Hope is so desperate for money to pay off a certain loan at a certain bank that she asked me to sell her great-great grandmother's armoire to raise some funds," Sharon said, clearly choosing not to climb on board with his few-words-more-sex approach.

"So what is it doing in my driveway?"

"I told Hope I sold it to one of the people who was in town for the Wolf Festival and gave her a bunch of money less my supposed commission, just like we agreed. It's in your driveway because I can't keep it at my house. Hope might stop by and she'd be furious if she found out I didn't actually sell it."

The last thing he wanted to do was to have something of Hope Anderson's at his house, but he followed Sharon out to the pick-up and pulled down the tailgate regardless because he was still hopeful that if he was cooperative, he might get what he wanted.

Sharon knew it, too. The woman was like a cat playing with a mouse, sashaying around as provocatively as she needed to be in order to get what she wanted.

"What if she drives by while we're unloading it?"

"The roads are too slippery. Hope won't be in town today."

"Admit it." He pulled the blanket back from the armoire slowly, easing the fabric down past each drawer like a striptease until it was lying in the back of the truck, totally exposed and buck-naked. "You brought it here because you were looking for an excuse to come over and do what we do best."

He pulled a drawer out just far enough that he could slip his hand inside and grasped the framework. Sharon did the same on the other side, and together, they glided the armoire from the truck.

"I brought it here because this is the one place in town I know Hope will never set foot," Sharon said, grunting from the weight of the chest. "And because I want you to look at it every day and remember how horribly you've treated her."

He leaned back and opened the door while supporting the chest with his body. "But as long as you're here..." Billy said, raising an eyebrow.

They were halfway into the living room.

"Right over here," Sharon said, straining to turn toward the wall opposite his recliner. "So you have a nice, clear view of it every time you sit down to watch television."

"Baby," Billy said, sliding the armoire against the wall. "Stop teasing me. You know you want it as bad as I do."

Sharon lifted her shoulders to a height as erect as he was and glared at him from eyes so black with fury that he wouldn't have been surprised it they sprouted laser beams.

"I abhor you, Billy Bjorklund. I'd sooner die than have sex with a loser like you."

She was out the door and back in her truck so fast that he didn't even get there in time to slam the door behind her.

Rage boiled up inside him. Hope Anderson had stolen his best friend, made him look bad in front of everybody he knew, including his employees at the bank, turned his own mother against him, and cost him sex. Great sex.

He went to the garage, lifted his ax from the nails that held it on the wall, and returned to the living room. With one crushing swing after another, he slashed into the armoire, pulling the head of the ax from whatever drawer or door it happened to lodge in and swung again, sinking it so deeply into the wood that it went in on one side and came out the other.

He looked down at the pile of broken wood and shattered splinters at his feet. The armoire would remind him of Hope Anderson all right.

He stood back and tried not to gloat. Served the bitch right. When the dull sliver of metal caught his eye, he assumed it was part of a hinge, a drawer pull, or even a square nail. But when he bent to pick it up, he discovered it was a key – the key to safety deposit box 229 at Embarrass National Bank. His bank.

Chapter 40

Hope gripped the steering wheel and prayed that she wouldn't skid into the ditch. The roads were passable for the first time in a week, but just barely. Between the new snow coming down, and the old snow blowing around, visibility had been near zero for several days. The wind had finally gone down, leaving so many icy spots in its wake that driving would be treacherous until spring unless there was a mid-winter thaw.

She wouldn't have tried to get into town in the first place if she hadn't been desperate for groceries. She was out of milk and eggs, fresh fruits and vegetables, and several essential toiletries. Plus, she needed to go to the post office to mail another payment to the utility company and get some things at the drugstore and the hardware store. Thank goodness the armoire had finally sold, or she wouldn't have had the money to get what she needed. Still, she looked for bargains and used the coupons she'd snipped from the sale fliers.

She should have headed back to the lodge the second she finished her errands – the days were so short this time of year that the sun seemed to make it only halfway up the sky before it set again – but there was someone she wanted, needed, to talk to.

When she reached the nursing home, she climbed out of her car, dodged an icy patch wider than a bear rug, and made her way to the front entrance, where she had to punch in an entrance code to prove she wasn't a senile resident trying to escape.

She'd wanted to speak with Mrs. Bjorklund for weeks, but she'd assumed that if the older woman was in such dire straits that she'd been deposed of her leadership at the bank and forced into a nursing home, that she was in no condition to have visitors. Then Alvin had seen her and spoken to her, and told Hope that she seemed perfectly cognizant.

She stopped at the nurse's station and checked in before starting down the hall to Mrs. Bjorklund's room. Billy's mother was the one who had agreed to fund Hope and David's renovation of Rainbow

Lake Lodge three years ago, the one who had given Hope a hug after David's funeral and told her to be brave and to keep her chin up, that the bank was still behind her, 100%. Her hope was that Mrs. Bjorklund could shed some light on Billy's motives, help her understand, perhaps even give her the ammunition she needed to fight Billy.

She poked her head around the corner of the door marked Rose Bjorklund and said, "Hello? If you're up for a visit..."

Mrs. Bjorklund was sitting in an easy chair, dressed in a soft pink sweater and a plaid, wool skirt in grays, white, black and pinks. "Hope. Please come in, dear. I'm always happy to see you."

"I wasn't sure if I'd be welcome since I only know you from the bank."

"Of course you're welcome. I've always treated, and thought of our customers as family," Mrs. Bjorklund said, her eyes gazing apologetically at Hope.

"I've missed seeing you there," Hope said, trying to feel her out, see what she knew. One hated to disillusion a mother when it came to her own son, and Hope certainly didn't want to be a tattletale, but this was Billy, and something had to be done.

"No need to pussyfoot, dear. Plenty of folks have told me what Billy's been up to since the day he ousted me from the bank."

"They're calling it Black Friday around town."

"I'm so sorry you've been caught in the crossfire, Hope. I never intended for any of this to happen. I've felt just awful ever since that horrible day when David found out about the second mortgages his parents had taken." Rose leaned forward in her chair. "When I heard about the accident, I couldn't help but wonder if his state of mind played any part in what happened."

Blood surged through Hope's brain until her head was swimming in it – hot, sticky, sickening waves of it.

"...to impart that kind of news and then hear that David had died before the day was out," Rose said, clutching her handkerchief. "I felt awful. I know I probably should have told you what had happened, but the last thing I wanted to do was to compound your grief or be the cause of any additional stress. Besides, it really didn't matter. I didn't care if those old mortgages were ever paid off."

"That's when David found out about the second mortgages? The day he died?" And she'd been mad at David for not telling her. Anger swirled inside her body, looking for an outlet. Certainly not this frail, old woman. David? David had always driven fast and wild when he was upset. Had he been killed because he was going too fast, distracted? If he hadn't been wondering how to tell her about the mortgages, would he have seen the drunk driver before it was too late?

Hank's words flashed through her mind. "My sister and her husband would be alive if they hadn't killed themselves working night and day at this place. If it weren't for Rainbow Lake Lodge, we'd have her and John instead of their memories," Hank had said. "David, too, for that matter."

For a second, Hope was filled with hatred for Rainbow Lake Lodge – the very colors it was painted in, the very timbers and stones it was built with, the very ground it stood on.

"I'm so sorry, dear," Rose said.

Kind, sweet, motherly Rose.

In the end, she and Mrs. Bjorklund made their peace. But Hope left without any more insight into Billy's behavior than she'd come with. Fortunate or unfortunate as that might be, it was fine – she really didn't care anymore.

The only reason she didn't floor the engine and drive home like a bat out of hell was because A, half of her hated the place and didn't even want to go there, B, the roads were still slippery, and C, she didn't want to end up being one more fatality courtesy of Rainbow Lake Lodge. The truly scary part was that she didn't much care about that either. What if she did die? Who would care? Rainbow Lake Lodge was irredeemable anyway.

Tommy might not get his house decorated, but he'd survive.

When she finally arrived at the lodge, she went directly to her bedroom, *her* bedroom, and started cleaning out David's side of the closet. His professional clothes and suits went in a box for Goodwill. There had to be hurricane or earthquake victims somewhere who could use a nicely tailored suit and some crisp, white shirts. His sweaters, polo shirts and golf clothes went in a different box. She could sell them on consignment at Second Hand Rose in Embarrass. A third box was filled with things so old or worn that no one would want them. Trash, she wrote on the side with a black marking pen.

The only thing she saved was a few of his old, flannel shirts. She needed work clothes, and her breasts took up the space his chest and shoulders had filled out.

The wind had come up again. She could hear it howling angrily against the side of the lodge as she worked. But she was undeterred. For the first time since his death, she found herself thinking about David's body without feeling ill. She'd had nightmares for weeks after he'd died, thinking of him cold, alone, buried in the damp, musky earth. Dust to dust had held no comfort. Neither had heaven – it had been too hard to imagine him happy without her, sitting around all day long on some stupid cloud, playing a harp and singing to the Lord when he should have been here, helping her. She'd been feeling too sad, working too hard to even think about that.

But now... She could finally envision it – David in heaven, full of joy, his face radiant with wonder. Suddenly, it all made sense. If David was happy, why shouldn't she be, too?

Chapter 41

Tommy was glad there were people in the world who didn't mind old folks. He wasn't one of them – never had been. He had nothing against nursing homes in general, but he'd never spent any time at one, and was hugely uncomfortable with the whole concept. One of his grandmas had died of a heart attack walking out to the mailbox to get the newspaper at age 98, the other, of an aneurysm when she was ninety-two. His parents had gone the way of his grandfathers, dying young of common maladies – that's the way it was when you were poor and didn't have health insurance.

He didn't have anything against Mrs. Bjorklund either. Nor did he think of her as being old. The only reason he was here was that he'd promised Brian he would check on his mother. And although he planned to keep his word - no matter how unpleasant the task – he also intended to get in and out quickly.

He walked through the front door with the eagerness of a man about to walk the gangplank. "Excuse me. Do you know where I might find Mrs. Bjorklund?"

"Room 24," the receptionist said. "But I think she's in the activity room, over that way, behind the piano, waiting for the music to start." She batted her eyelashes at him. "You're Tommy Love, aren't you?"

Figured she would know him. Judging by her gray hair and crow's feet, she was probably about sixty. He reached out his hand and took hers.

"Tommy Love."

He might wish he had younger fans. That didn't mean he didn't appreciate each and every one of the old ones.

"Jessie Campbell. I was several years ahead of you in high school, but my brother Jake is about your age. He would have been a junior the year you graduated."

"Sure," Tommy said, although he didn't really. "Tell him hello next time you see him."

"Wow, you showing up right now is so cool. We have a piano

player coming to play in about ten minutes," Jessie said. "I'm sure he knows some of your old hits. I mean, if you'd be willing to sing something, I'm sure the residents would love it."

"Sure," he said, wishing he could sink into a hole.

It wasn't that he thought he was too good to sing in a nursing home. He just felt so out of his element. Of course, if he didn't generate some admirers from amongst the younger generation pretty soon, he'd be playing retirement communities on a regular basis – that's where all his fans would be.

Mrs. Bjorklund had evidently noticed the commotion and seen him, because she was up and walking toward him now, her face alight like the sky on Easter morning. Quite a reception considering he hadn't even been sure she would recognize him.

Brian had talked to her to the day before Tommy left California, and according to him, she was as sound-minded as ever. The way Billy told it; she was so senile she didn't know her right foot from her left. Normally, Tommy would have put more credence in Brian's opinion than in Billy's, but Brian had a blind spot where his mother was concerned. He'd assumed Brian's assessment of his mother's mental state was more wishful thinking than fact given Brian's tender heart.

She sure didn't look ill. Mrs. Bjorklund's grey wool skirt, red silk blouse, and herringbone scarf made her look just as pressed and proper as he remembered. "Hi, Mrs. B."

Mrs. Bjorklund wrapped her arms around him and gave him a hug that would have been worthy of a bear if she hadn't been so frail. "Little Tommy Lubinski. My, my. You've certainly grown up to be a fine looking young man."

"Thanks. You look good, too."

"Brian said you'd be coming," she said, obviously delighted to see him.

Okay. Score one – she'd remembered his name. His real name even. And she definitely got a point for awareness of current events, another one for short-term memory.

"So, how are you feeling?" he asked, hoping it was okay to bring up the subject of her health.

The feisty glint in her eyes was his first clue that Mrs. Bjorklund was as sane as he was. "Depends on who you're reporting back to," she said. "It it's that low-down rascal, Billy, you can tell him I'm still madder than a wet hen, and that he'll have to answer for what he's done to me and half the town on judgment day. And because he's my son, and because I still love him, you can also say I hope he repents of his wicked ways before it's too late." Her fury softened to a smile. "If it's Brian, you tell him not to worry. I've never been better. Who wouldn't with a whole host of people eager to tend to your every need? I've never felt so pampered."

"You don't seem... I mean, I thought you'd be at least a little..."

"Demented?" she suggested, her voice mingling coyness and bitterness. "Babbling nonsensically? Sitting with my head hunched over, drooling out of the corner of my mouth like old man Johnson?"

Didn't humor involve utilizing one of the most refined parts of the brain? If so, the old gal had just scored another point. "Brain wanted me to check on you. He's really beating himself up over what Billy's doing, and thinking he should be back here taking care of you."

"There's nothing he can do. Billy never would listen to Brian anyway. Their personalities are so different. Billy has always believed he was king of the hill, even when they were small. And Brian, well, Brian has such a gentle soul. He always idolized Billy. That's why seeing Billy behave this way is so hard on him. He wants so badly to believe that his older brother is a good man."

"I don't know how parents do it," Tommy said. "Even I feel torn. I care about both of your sons. I really do. But Billy's gone too far this time."

"See, now, if you told him that, it might make a difference. You should talk to him," Mrs. Bjorklund said, moving toward an armchair. "He's much more likely to listen to you than to Brian."

"I really don't think I should get involved," Tommy said. "This is about family, and I'm in an awkward position since I know both Billy and Brian. I've been trying my best not to take sides – I mean, I certainly don't approve of what Billy's been up to these last few months, but I can't go against him. He and I go back to grade school."

"Ah, Mr. Love." A young nurse's aid in white scrubs tapped him timidly on the shoulder.

Tommy looked from Mrs. Bjorklund's wrinkled face to the peaches and cream complexioned girl and thought once more how much things had changed. The younger woman didn't have a clue who he was. Women used to faint to the ground, or at least manage a loud swoon if they were lucky enough to touch him, or even his jacket.

"Um, Jessie said to tell you that Mr. Jenkins knows how to play

Jenny's Song. She wants to know if you would sing it for the residents."

"Sorry. No can do," Tommy said, feeling like a double jerk. "Long story. How about *Walk on Water*? Or *Moonlight and Mistletoe*?"

"I'll go ask him," the young woman said, still not showing any signs of recognition.

A few minutes later, Mrs. Bjorklund was sitting front and center to the piano and Tommy was standing in front of a rickety old microphone that was perched atop a podium slash pulpit, singing to a slightly off-key piano accompaniment.

"Why don't you sing *How Sweet It Is To Be Loved By You*," a man yelled from the audience of walkers and wheelchairs.

"That's a James Taylor hit," Tommy said. "I'm Tommy Love."

"How about *Copacabana*?" another woman said. "My Earl used to love that song."

"Ah, I think you've got me mixed up with Barry Manilow," Tommy said.

"What?"

"That's a Barry Manilow song," he said, almost yelling into the mike. "I'm Tommy Love."

"We don't care who you are as long as you sing some songs we know," an old woman in her bathrobe and pin curls said.

"Sing *Bicycle Built for Two*."

"How about "*Tie a Yellow Ribbon Round the Old Oak Tree*?"

"My favorite is "*In My Merry Oldsmobile*."

Suddenly, they were all yelling. Some of the men were pounding their canes on the linoleum floor. Who would have guessed a bunch of old people could cause such a racket? And what choice did he have but to comply?

Forty-five minutes and two-dozen oldies but goodies later, and he meant really old, he was finally released from his tour of duty and talking to Mrs. Bjorklund in her room.

"You've always stayed with Billy when you've come to town before. Have you been to see him yet?" Mrs. B asked.

"I was holding off until I saw you. Brian said you were fine, but I thought he was in denial. I didn't want to believe that Billy would stoop so low." He took Mrs. B's weathered hand and held it gently. "At least not where you're concerned."

"We've all tried to be understanding when it comes to Billy. I've even spoken to a psychologist about him." Mrs. B looked at him expectantly. "You must try to get through to him. If not for my sake, then Hope's."

Tommy nearly choked on his own spit. He would rather do almost anything than to have to have it out with Billy. But Hope had already asked for his help; now a woman he respected very much was asking him to intervene. He had no choice.

"I know you can't see your face," Mrs. B said, "but the look in your eyes when I mentioned Hope's name was quite telling."

He lowered his head. "I love her."

"All the more reason to stand up to Billy and fight for what's right," Mrs. B said. "If there's any hope for the two of you, you must help her to save the lodge."

"Sometimes I think there'd be more hope for us if she didn't have the lodge," Tommy said. "She's still in love with David. As long as she's at the lodge, he'll be there with her – in her thoughts, in her mind, a part of everything she thinks and does."

"She needs you, Tommy. Whether she knows it or not," Mrs. B said. "I know you'd like to stay neutral. You always did want to keep everyone happy. But this time there's too much at stake to remain passive."

He'd never thought of himself as passive, but he guessed between agents, secretaries, personal assistants and attorneys doing practically everything for him, he probably had gotten a little rusty at taking care of certain uncomfortable matters on his own. Tommy lifted his eyes to meet Mrs. B's and came face to face with Alvin Turppa.

"Alvin?"

"I was walking by Mrs. Bjorklund's room and heard voices. And the ladies out in the lobby said some rock star was singing with the piano player." He looked at Tommy suspiciously. "I thought you were in California."

"I was," Tommy said.

"How nice to see you, Alvin," Mrs. B said. "Your mother said you're feeling much better."

"Yes, ma'am, I am – stronger all the time. Thanks for asking," Alvin said, turning back to Tommy. "Here for the auction, I suppose."

"Auction?"

"Hope's quilts. To raise money to pay off her mortgage at the bank," Alvin said. "No offense, ma'am."

"None taken." Mrs. B sighed.

"The quilts she sewed for the cabins?" Tommy asked.

"And a couple of cedar chest full of antique quilts made by her relatives."

"But she shouldn't have to—"

"She's just being realistic," Alvin said. "If she doesn't raise a lot of money, and fast, she's going to lose everything."

"Is she doing okay? I mean, is she handling this all right?"

Alvin looked like a proud parent. At least, that's what Tommy hoped he looked like, since he didn't want him looking like a proud suitor.

Alvin looked at Tommy as if to remind him that Hope's progress was no thanks to him. "For the first time since the accident, she really seems to be taking the bull by the horns and getting on with her life. She even cleaned out David's closet the other day. Had me haul a dozen boxes of his things down to the Goodwill."

"Really," Tommy said.

"The rest of the things went on consignment at that used-a-bit shop over on Third Street," Alvin added.

Tommy rubbed his temples. "I'm glad she was able to... sorry she's having to..."

"So if you're not here for the auction..." Alvin said, still looking distrustful.

"Just here for a few days to tie up some loose ends," Tommy said.

Alvin looked even more skeptical. Mrs. B smiled. The lady was sharper than a tack and then some.

"I'd appreciate it if you don't mention to Hope that I'm in town," Tommy said. "I'll contact her before I leave, but I'd like to talk to Billy about a few things before I see her, and I'm not sure when that will happen."

Mrs. B nodded. "Alvin?"

"I won't say anything," Alvin said. "But a word of advice for next time – if you don't want people to know you're in town, I wouldn't be giving concerts at the nursing home."

"I'll do my best," Tommy said, fully intending to try.

Chapter 42

Billy was sitting in his recliner when he heard a loud engine, probably a truck, in his driveway. He smiled. So Sharon had come to her senses and decided to take him up on his offer after all. He plunked his beer on the glass-topped end table in the middle of a maze of round circles left over from previous cans and looked across the room to the spot where the armoire had been.

Crap. If he'd gotten out the vacuum cleaner last night before he'd gone to bed like he should have, he could have told her he'd moved it to the basement. But with shreds and splinters still littering the floor, he could hardly invite her in, expect her to overlook his fit of rage and have sex.

He stood quickly – too quickly, judging from the woozy feeling in his head – and pulled the drapes shut. He wouldn't put it past the nosey bitch to start snooping around if he didn't come to the door fast enough to suit her.

That was when he saw Tommy's Porsche. Great. All the trouble and no possibility of sex. Just what he needed.

He grabbed his coat from the davenport, slid into it on his way to the door, and stepped outside on the front steps before Tommy could ring the doorbell.

"Hey, man," he said, trying his best to sound upbeat.

"Billy," Tommy said, looking stiff and foe-like instead of relaxed and friendly.

"What brings you back to Minnesota?" Like he didn't already know it was H-O-P-E.

"Just tying up some loose ends after my last visit," Tommy said. "Can I come in? I'd like to talk to you about some things if I could."

He inhaled deeply through his diaphragm. "The fresh air feels good. The house gets so rank this time of year with all the windows closed up."

"The wind chill is ten below," Tommy said. "It was eighty degrees when I left LAX. I'd rather be warm if you don't mind."

"What don't we take a spin in the Porsche then?" Billy said, brushing Tommy with his shoulder as he moved down the steps. "Nothing like a little direct heat from the old heat vents blowing right on you to take the chill off."

"Ah, because the roads are either snow-packed or glare ice everywhere in a fifty mile radius," Tommy said, taking a step toward the door. "Not a day when I want to be driving and talking. Besides, gas isn't exactly free these days."

"Neither is fuel oil," Billy said, scrambling to get back up the stairs and by Tommy so he could block the door before Tommy saw what was left of Hope's armoire.

"What wrong with you? You have a woman inside?" Tommy said.

"Just a bad case of cabin fever." Billy leaned against the door and tried to look like nothing was wrong. "Usually doesn't set in until mid-January, but we've had a doozey of a winter this year. Even started out with a bang – as you know."

"Fine," Tommy said. "I'll say what I have to say and hope I don't freeze to death in the middle of a sentence."

Billy grinned sheepishly.

"Brian asked me to visit your mother at the nursing home while I was in town. I did. And miracle of miracles, she's as lucid as I am, maybe more so at times, because she sees you for what you are and I keep thinking my friend Billy Bjorklund would never participate in the underhanded kind of stunts you've been pulling."

"Spineless little wimp thinks he's perfect just because he's a reverend." Billy kicked the concrete step and winced in pain. "Let Brian try living in this God-forsaken town all of his life, deal with my parents, put up with what I've had to put up with, and see how sanctimonious he turns out to be."

"You know, if this was just between you and your brother and that sweet little old lady down at the nursing home, I might – might – back off and chalk it up to one more episode of Family Feud, but this isn't just family anymore.

"From now on, you mess with Hope Anderson and you mess with me," Tommy said. "You stop treating women with so little respect, or you answer to me. You use one more person I care about to accomplish your greedy ends, and you will suffer the wrath of Tommy Lubinski in a way you didn't think possible."

The wind whipped up a scathing mixture of ice pellets, dirt, and grit from the asphalt and blew it into Billy's eyes. "You're barking up the wrong tree if you think I'm going to apologize to that little witch. And I don't need advice from you when it comes to my turncoat of a mother or my pea-brained little brother."

"That's what you have to say for yourself then," Tommy said, looking dangerously close to losing it.

"One more thing. You can take our so-called friendship and shove it." Billy slipped through the door and slammed it behind him.

His heart was pounding as he leaned against the inside of the door. It was more than losing his best friend. It was more than having his brother, his mother, his ex-wife and lover and half the town mad at him. It was knowing that it was all Hope Anderson's fault.

He hadn't done anything to her except to enforce the various mortgage agreements the bank held on her property – all legal agreements. He was perfectly within his rights, and would have been absolutely insane not to proceed exactly as he had. Any other banker in the State of Minnesota would have done exactly the same thing.

Hateful, venomous thoughts raged through his body. If the bitch didn't leave town of her own volition soon, he'd have no choice but to take matters into his own hands – before she turned anyone else against him.

Chapter 43

Hope stood by the back wall of the elementary school gymnasium and looked up at her quilts – the ones she'd made, the ones made by her mother, grandmothers and great-grandmothers – hanging from the bleachers. Hung out to dry in an otherworldly sort of way.

She could do this. She had to do this.

The scene before her was cheery and welcoming – small town America at its best. She looked past the throngs of people milling about, laughing, chatting, and checking out her quilts to the opposite side of the gym. The smells of dirty sneakers, stale lockers and freshly lacquered wood floors were almost overpowered by the scents of cinnamon and cloves wafting up from the freshly baked apple and pumpkin pies. A cocky rendition of the Baby Elephant Walk started and stopped while a group of excited children scrambled to find the magic seat, each one wanting to win one of the homemade cakes lined up on a long table behind the cakewalk. Another table, heaped high with sloppy joes, and turkey sandwiches cut, buttered and stuffed by the middle school youth, had a winding line a half block long. Jell-O salads glistened side by side with glass bowls full of bright green pickles and carrot and celery sticks waiting to be eaten.

The auctioneer's voice boomed over the PA system, urging people to look at the quilts, get their food, and have a seat.

Hope had been to the benefit they'd held for Jack Hawthorne when his cancer had spread to his bones, the fund raiser they'd held when the old swimming pool cracked and needed to be replaced, and the school carnival the tenth graders had staged to raise money for a class trip to New York City and Washington, DC. Never had she dreamed that she would be here today, selling things she didn't want to part with and accepting help, charity, really, from friends and neighbors.

She swallowed the lump in her throat and took another sip of water. The auctioneer, who had donated his services, had been a friend of the Andersons. He'd asked if she would be willing to say a word about each quilt as it came up for the auction – who had made it, its historical significance, if any, an antidote that might result in a higher bid. Piece of cake, she thought, trying to psyche herself up for one of the most difficult things she'd had to do since she'd buried David.

What if nobody bid on anything? What if the only ones to bid were antique dealers? If she had to part with her quilts, she at least wanted them to go to good homes. Not that they might not end up in good homes if they filtered on down through the antique dealer circuit, but she wouldn't know who was snuggled under them, who had them on display in their home, who they were keeping warm on cold, winter nights.

It was bad enough she didn't know where her armoire was.

She hated this. It was so humbling, so humiliating that she would have liked to disappear under a rock and not come out until it was over. But as the auctioneer had so astutely put it, she didn't have the cancer card going for her, nor an armful of adorable "young-un's" in danger of being evicted. The only chance she had of having a successful auction was her winning smile and what he'd called the widow factor. *Ugh.* She buried her face in her hands and tried to breathe deeply to calm her nerves.

"Hi, Hope. How ya doing?" Alvin approached her from the direction of the wishing well the kids from St. Olaf were operating. "Looks like quite a crowd. That should make you feel good. The bigger the crowd, the greater your chances of having a good auction."

"All I really care about is that the quilts go to people who will appreciate them," she said, scanning the crowd for familiar faces before she settled back on Alvin's smile. "How are you feeling?"

"Good. Better all the time. Still a little tired, but other than that, I'm great," Alvin said, holding his cap in his hands and shuffling his feet. "Um, the nursing home brought over a van full of residents. Mother is here."

"I'll have to say hello," Hope said.

Alvin's face turned beet red. "That might not be such a good idea. Oh, and please ignore anything offensive she might say. She's not herself these days."

"I'm sorry to hear that, Alvin. I'm sure it's been hard for her to adjust to being in the home."

"Hard for both of us. It's pretty quiet around the house without her there. But after the fire..."

"You didn't have a choice," Hope said, feeling guilty all over again, because she did have choices. And because there were so many people in the world who had far worse problems than she. People who had no options. No one to turn to. No where to go, which she didn't either, really. Unless she gave up and sold Rainbow Lake Lodge.

"Maybe I wanted her gone, you know, on some sort of subconscious level." Alvin capsized his hat in his hands. "I feel so guilty about putting her in the nursing home that I can't even relax and enjoy my own home. I feel guilty when I watch an 'R' rated movie because I know mother wouldn't approve; guilty when I don't open a can of peas or beans to eat with dinner; guilty when I leave the lid of the toilet up."

"You can't blame yourself for moving on," Hope said, "but I know what you mean. When I started clearing David's things out of the closet, it made me feel just awful. Like I was taking advantage of his being gone and grabbing all the space for myself."

"I'd be the first to admit that it's nice not having to check on Mother all the time," Alvin said. "Or do her laundry, or worry about what we should have for supper. That's why I feel guilty. In the end, I'm no better than Billy. He had an agenda, and his mother was keeping him from it, so he dumped her in the nursing home."

"You're bound to enjoy having the house to yourself," Hope said. "The freedom, not having to check with someone before you do something or go somewhere, is kind of nice once you get used to it. That doesn't mean you're like Billy."

"I bought a new weed whacker last week without even thinking twice. Put it on my credit card instead of paying cash. And I haven't dusted the house in three weeks," Alvin said. "Mother would have a cow if she knew."

She smiled. "After David died, people told me – still do – that I needed to look for the silver lining, the rainbow after the storm." Hope stepped back to get out of the path of two rambunctious children flying toward the cakewalk. "But sometimes, even when it's been raining so hard that I can hardly see the tree on the other side of the road, I get a glimpse of the rainbow, and all I can feel is guilt."

"You didn't send David away. What do you have to feel guilty about?"

"Same silly things as you do," Hope said. "Except for the part about having to ask someone before I spend money. No need to fret about that one when you don't have two nickels to rub together."

"Speaking of, I think the auctioneer is trying to get your attention," Alvin said.

Showtime. She pasted on a smile and squared her shoulders. She didn't want anyone's pity. If the quilts simply brought what they were worth, she'd be more than thrilled.

The auctioneer welcomed everyone, explained the procedure for bidding, and said both the new quilts and the antique ones were of as fine a quality as he'd ever seen. "I knew this little gal's in-laws for years. Their son, David, played football with my boy back in the eighties. So let's bid high on the pretty lady's quilts and help keep Rainbow Lake Lodge open."

Hope climbed the steps to the stage at the end of the gymnasium, went to the podium and leaned forward to adjust the microphone. "The first quilt was made by my great-grandmother, Pearl Fox. She taught me to sew when I was eight-years-old on an old treadle sewing machine. The pattern is a traditional log cabin."

"Who'll give me a $100?" the auctioneer barked. "That's the way. Number 87. Gimme three, three, three. Okay, I got three. Who'll give me four? Five? Okay, people," he said, his voice growing more and more excited, "I've got an offer for $500 from the lady in red in the front row. Now, who'll give me six?"

Hope finally remembered to take a breath. By the time she looked back at the board, it was up to $1000. She'd known the antique quilts would go for more than the new ones, but she'd no idea how much more. The auctioneers strategy was to start with a few of the higher-end quilts so they would think they were getting a bargain when they got to the new ones.

A man at a computer on the far side of the stage motioned to the auctioneer. "I've got $1200 from an online bidder," the auctioneer said. "Things are starting to get interesting."

Heads turned this way and that as the other bidders digested the news. Thelma Jones, a woman Hope knew from church, leaned over to consult with her husband.

"Twelve hundred. Who'll give me lucky thirteen?"

Thelma nodded.

"We've got thirteen. Who'll give me fourteen?"

Thelma shook her head, but a new bidder, Carly Rottingham, a nurse who worked at the clinic in Ely, raised her card just high enough for the auctioneer to spy.

"Fourteen, fourteen, I got fourteen, let's jump to sweet sixteen," the auctioneer chanted. "Sixteen, sixteen, sixteen."

The man at the computer nodded. So did Carly.

"Seventeen it is, now eighteen, eighteen, eighteen."

Carly leaned over and whispered to her mother-in-law.

Hope's stomach flip-flopped and landed as neatly as a pancake on a griddle – a sizzling hot griddle. If she'd gone down gracefully when Billy had first tried to take the resort, Tommy Love would own the lodge by now and she wouldn't be in the position of having to have an auction, or defend her kingdom against the Sleaze Master.

The auctioneer was in the two thousands by the time she refocused her attention. Carly was shaking her head. Another nod from the man manning the online auction. The crowd collectively hushed.

"$2500," the auctioneer said, his voice reverent with appreciation. He scanned the crowd, looking for a nod, a hand, a look. But the sea of heads were down, defeated. "Going, going, gone." He plunked the gavel on the table.

Gone. She should have felt joy – she'd never dreamed a single quilt could bring so much. But the flip side of the welcome news was that the quilt was gone. To someone, somewhere, who she didn't know. She couldn't envision it hanging in the vaulted living room of that nice lady from the hardware store, couldn't know that it was on little Susie Q's bed, couldn't see it hanging on the log banister at the Hinkle's cabin next time she went to Bible Study. Gone.

The auctioneer was motioning to her. She stood and went to the microphone. "The next quilt is called Ring Around the Rosie. I made it about two-and-a-half years ago for Rose, the cabin on the west side of the peninsula." David had helped her pick out the fabric. One wintry night he had also cut squares with the rotary cutter he'd bought for her at the fabric store in Duluth. He'd been wearing his old jeans and blue striped sweater – the one that had made his shoulders look so broad.

She left the stage and went to watch from the sidelines. It was too hard, keeping her face impartial, having to smile and look overjoyed.

"This one has a lot of appliqué work," the auctioneer said, his rough, Norwegian voice stumbling over the French word. "Let's start this one at two hundred."

The truth was, she almost wished this one wouldn't sell, but it was one of the most beautiful of the new quilts, and she couldn't imagine it wouldn't.

Someone in a pink sweater upped the bid to $500.

What was wrong with her? This wasn't about being able to make her loan payments until spring anymore – she needed enough money to buy out the various mortgages the Anderson's had put against the lodge. All of them.

The bidding was at $1000 and climbing. She couldn't believe this. For a few seconds, she felt a surge of excitement. And then it happened again – the locals dropped out one by one while the man sitting at the computer calmly nodded, again, and again, and again.

Sally Conner stood and wormed her way through the crowd. "Sorry," she said. "I was going to redo Gloria's room in pink roses, and thought this one would be beautiful mounted on the wall beside her bed."

The auctioneer's voice rang out from the podium. "Sold to an anonymous online bidder for $3000."

Sally shrugged. "You know I'm behind you 100%, but we just don't have that much to spare right now."

"No one does." A rumble of frustrated voices washed over the room.

Hope rushed to the stage to say a few words about the next quilt. A few minutes later, the Amish Bars quilt she'd made of strips in traditional petunia pink, purple and peach sold for $1550 – thanks to an anonymous online bidder.

Sure the colors were nice, but she'd put the strips of Petunia's quilt together in less than a day. It should never have gone for more than a thousand.

The antique dealers sitting in the front row put their heads together, whispered to each other, and sat watching, their faces stony.

Some of the crowd got up and began to leave when her Daisy Chain, Ivy Manor, and Bluebell quilts also went to online bidders for outrageously overvalued prices.

"Please don't get discouraged," she said from the microphone just before she told them about the antique feed sacks from Charleston she'd used to sew the quilt that was supposed to have graced Magnolia's bed. "I'm sure not every quilt will go to online bidders. If I had my druthers, I'd rather see every single one go to a local buyer. It's important to me that they go to good homes. Good people." She looked out over the crowd, which had already dwindled by a third judging by the empty chairs. "If you'll just stay awhile and be persistent, I'm sure there will be opportunities to pick up some of the remaining quilts at reasonable prices."

Then, online bidders claimed not only Magnolia, but the crazy quilt her grandma had sewn from old wool suits, the afghan her mother had crocheted before she died, and the quilts she herself had sewn for Violet, Lily, and Fern.

More and more people left. Who could blame the bidders for being disappointed when they kept losing? These people knew her. They had come to help as best they could. Whoever was outbidding them was cheating them of their chance. The thrill of the hunt, the joy of victory, the pleasure of seeing who got what quilt – the online bidder was robbing them of it all.

"The quilts sure are bringing in a lot of money," Alvin said, coming along side her.

"Too much," she said, fighting back tears, frustration. "It's all so cold and impersonal. I envisioned myself handing over the quilts to the new owners personally, almost like a blessing, if that makes sense. That's how I was going to deal with parting with my quilts. Now..."

She followed Alvin's eyes as they wandered over the crowd and landed on his mother, who looked to be preoccupied talking to an old neighbor. He put his hand on Hope's arm and gave her a quick squeeze. "You need the money."

"I know. Desperately," she said. "But I can't deal with this just being about the cold, hard cash. I've felt so out of control ever since this whole mess started. The auction was the one thing I could do to save myself, the one thing I was in charge of. Today was supposed to happen on my terms, and instead, I feel like a puppet on a string."

Alvin cringed. "And I was going to tell you to *hang in there*".

She smiled. "Thanks for being a friend, Alvin. I don't know what I would have done if you'd ended up at the bottom of that lake."

"There are plenty of guys around here who would do most anything to eat one of your home cooked meals and see that smile of yours. You'd have gotten along just fine," he said.

"Seriously. I really appreciate everything you've done to help out at the lodge."

"From the looks of this windfall, you won't need my help for much longer."

"That's not true, Alvin. I'm thrilled to have raised so much money, and flattered that people think my quilts are worth these kinds of prices, but I owe the bank much, much more than will ever be raised here today. In the end, it all comes down to Billy, or some other banker, and whether or not he or they are willing to keep extending me credit." She smiled at Alvin and blinked away tears. "Besides, there's no substitute for friends. All the cash in the world can't buy a friend. Or the goodwill of a community."

Alvin's ears turned red. "Thanks. I'm pretty glad I ended up on the top side of the ice, too."

She nodded and looked up at the stage. The auctioneer was playing to the computer now, having dispensed with her folksy antidotes, starting the bidding in the thousands of dollars instead of the hundreds, and barely looking at the audience.

Molly rushed over from the far side of the gym. "Oh, Hope." She threw her arms around Hope's neck. "I'm so sorry I ever came up with the idea of live internet bidding. I mean, the money the quilts are bringing in is amazing, but I've never heard so much mumbling and grumbling from an audience in my life. I never meant to make anyone angry."

A woman Hope knew from the bank walked by and held up her empty arms. "Oh, well. We tried."

"I know you wanted to go home with one of my quilts," Hope said. "I'm sorry it didn't work out."

"I hope these rich folks with the fancy computers appreciate the love that went into these quilts they bought," the woman said, heading out the door.

"I feel so awful," Molly said. "I know a lot of people are into eBay, but I never thought that all the quilts would sell online."

Hope shook her head. "It's not your fault. Who could have guessed this would happen?"

"You obviously did a great job publicizing the event for so many out-of-towners to find out about it."

"I mailed out fliers to every big quilt shop between here and California. But I never thought... When I planned the auction, I envisioned the people of Embarrass, Ely and Babbitt collectively rising up and rallying behind you," Molly said. "I'm afraid we've managed to alienate them instead."

Unfortunately, Molly was right. The whole thing felt terribly, terribly wrong. What Hope needed, even more than the money she'd raised by selling the quilts, was for the townspeople to feel a kinship with her, to take up her cause, to give her their undying support. If she had been able to unleash that power, there would have been no way these folks would have stood by and let Billy take the Lodge from her, say nothing about allowing someone to open a topless nightclub and sex store.

Molly hugged her again.

"I'm sure the online buyers who nabbed all my quilts think they were doing me some sort of favor by bidding so high, but instead, I've estranged the one group of people who truly could have made a difference in the outcome of this whole fiasco," Hope said.

"Don't take it personally," Alvin said. "They'll get over it."

"It feels personal," Hope said. "I poured my heart and soul into those quilts."

"Let's go have a bite to eat," Alvin said. "My treat. I think you could use a little de-processing before you head back to the Lodge."

Chapter 44

Tommy couldn't wait to see Hope's face when she walked into the lodge and saw all of her quilts. She was going to be thrilled. He could hardly stand the anticipation. He looked at the pile of quilts beside him on the car seat and glanced over his shoulder at another two mounds in the back seat. No matter how much she loved Rainbow Lake Lodge, he knew that parting with them had to have been awful for her. He could only imagine how relieved she was going to be that he'd been able to purchase them and return them all to her.

He pulled into the driveway and wound his way down the snow-covered lane, through the forest, to Hope's back door. With waist deep snow everywhere except the driveway, there was no way to hide his Porsche. She'd know he was there the second she drove in and saw his car, but he'd still get to see her face when she saw the quilts.

He parked the car, grabbed an armful of quilts and trudged through the snow to the back door, which he knew she never locked. Thank goodness he'd come prepared this time – his new boots were warm and waterproof.

He made two more trips to the car for quilts, then went back for his guitar, which was part of the surprise he had planned. Next, he got a fire going in the hearth.

When she arrived home from the auction, he wanted her to find him sitting in her living room, playing his guitar, surrounded by her quilts. He really wasn't looking for glory, yet he couldn't help feeling pleased with himself – his plan had gone perfectly. That gave him the right to gloat for a few minutes, didn't it?

In the end, that's all the time he had. Hope was coming down the driveway. He settled down into the sofa and started to strum his guitar. Hope was going to be the first to hear *Hope for Every Tomorrow*. He hadn't even played it for his agent. Of course, he didn't have one at the moment.

He was just finishing the riff he'd written for the intro when she opened the door. For as long as he lived, he'd never forget the look on her face when she saw him, heard the music he was playing for her and looked into his eyes. Eyes full of love and longing and tenderness. Eyes full of joy and laughter and love.

And then she saw the quilts.

"What?" she asked, her face turning flame red with what he could only suppose was gratitude.

"What have you done? Oh, Tommy," she wailed. Her words should have been fraught with relief, except that her tone that didn't exactly sound pleased. Or happy. Or any of the positive emotions he'd envisioned her having.

"You were the online buyer? You're the one who bought the quilts?" she said, her voice getting louder with every syllable. "What were you thinking?"

"That I'd done a wonderful thing by saving your quilts?" he asked, somehow knowing that it was the wrong answer. Worse yet, he didn't have a clue what the right answer might be.

"Oh, Tommy." She wailed again. "They were all so disappointed and sad that they couldn't help, and bitter because they went home empty-handed." She looked at him like he was the most clueless man on earth. "They felt unnecessary and shunned. They went with their hearts and pocketbooks open and left without a thing to show for their compassion. And, yes, they were angry – they got totally skunked. It was horrible."

"I didn't think about it that way."

Her look said, *yeah, right.*

"I'm sorry. Like I said, I just didn't think."

And then she lost it.

"You never think. If you'd have thought things through before you got in your Porsche in the middle of an ice storm, if you'd thought just once before you got in cahoots with Billy Bjorklund, if you'd thought before you kissed me, I might not be in the mess I'm in now."

"But you're still glad you have your quilts back, right?"

She didn't say a word. And then her lip started to quiver, and her eyes got all teary, and her chin puckered up, and... Oh, man. Was she crying because she was happy or because she was sad? How was he supposed to know?

He laid down his guitar and went to her, put his arms around her and hugged her.

"I came up with this plan all by myself," she finally said. "I felt so powerless. I was at the mercy of Billy, all of the banks in Ely and Hibbing, and almost every bank in Duluth. And the Anderson's poor decisions were affecting me, and Billy's problems with his mother were affecting me – even David's dying was affecting me, and there was nothing I could do except make quilts. Sew quilts. It was the one thing I could do by myself."

"Oh, sweetheart," he said with his mouth pressed to her hair.

"I wanted to be independent, and capable, and self-sufficient for once in my life. If it wasn't enough, then it wasn't enough. I just wanted to go down trying."

"And all I could think of was how hard you worked on those quilts, how much of yourself you poured into them, how much they mean to you," he said.

"I know you meant well, but I needed the town to be behind me, and now they're all mad and frustrated and a person doesn't get second chances in small towns. I've blown it."

"You didn't blow anything," Tommy said, holding her as tightly as he could. "I did."

"Did anybody see you pick them up?" she asked frantically. "Because you have to take them away. To California. We can put them in dark trash bags. No one will ever know if we – "

"I bought them for you," he said. "They belong here." He was beginning to think he did, too, but he didn't want to muddy the waters by saying it.

"But if they see them, they'll think I planned it. That it was all a ruse. That I deliberately..."

"Stop," he said. "I caused the problem. I'll find a way to make it right."

"I haven't made it easy for you, have I?" Hope said. "First, I didn't want you to help, and then I did, and then I didn't, and then I changed my mind and begged you to put me out of my misery, and then you tried to help, and now I let you have it."

"You said my kissing you was part of the reason you're in such a mess," Tommy said. "And I'd really like to know why, because I'd like to do it again, and I don't want to make things any worse than I already have."

He finally got the smile he'd wanted from the start.

She looked at him as though she was trying to decide whether or not she could trust him with a secret. "I said that?"

"Yes."

She pulled away. "I'm not sure what I was thinking."

He dropped his arms. "So I shouldn't kiss you?"

"I didn't say that," she said.

"I don't want to cause you any more agony." Hmmm. Watching her squirm was kind of fun.

"Kissing you is not agonizing."

"What is it then? I'm trying to understand here."

"Confusing?" she said.

"I don't want to confuse you," he said. "Confusion is one area where you don't need any help from me."

"That's not fair," she said. "I wouldn't be confused in the first place if it wasn't for you."

He grinned and took a step toward her.

"I thought you weren't going to..." she said, backing up a step.

He didn't move a muscle. "I'm willing to risk it if you are."

She nodded once.

And he kissed her. Long. Hard. With all the love he had in his heart.

When he finally let her go, her face was shining with a mixture of tears and smiles. "You didn't seem confused when we had our lips locked," he said. "If you're crying because I let go, I'd be happy to reconnect."

She laughed, and it was like a million drops of sunlight scattering in the breeze.

"I feel so at home with you," she said.

He turned away from her and scanned the room. When he'd been here before, he'd almost had the feeling that the Andersons were there watching. David's presence had been so strong that he'd felt like an intruder invading someone else's territory.

"What are you looking for?" she said.

"You've finally let go." He turned to face her again.

"Of the lodge?"

"Of David."

She nodded. "Part of me will always love him – a part of him will always be here with me."

"I can't begin to know what it's like to lose someone you love the way you lost David. But I do know that our past experiences help make us who we are today – good and bad. You can't disconnect yourself from the things that make you who you are any more than you can breathe without air."

She looked up at him. "I don't know how to describe it except that for the last two years I've felt like all my rooms have been booked. Now, I can finally say there's room at the inn again."

"Even for a quilt-pilfering, old fogy, used-to-be-hot-stuff musician like me?"

She looked at the quilts and grimaced. "The quilts are a problem. But from where I'm sitting, you look hotter than ever."

"You must either be up in the nose-bleed section or have really, really bad eyes." He laughed.

Her face took on a serious look. "Am I dreaming, Tommy, or is something happening between us?"

He stroked the sides of her face. "I'm wide awake, sweetheart, and so are you. If dreams have anything to do with it, it's only because from now on I want to be the one who makes all your dreams come true."

"You and Billy have been fodder for more nightmares than dreams the past few months."

"I had a long talk with Billy last night," Tommy said. "He knows where I stand and where my loyalties lie."

"I never meant to come between the two of you."

"Billy's made his choice. It has nothing to do with you," Tommy said, hoping he was right.

She gazed at him wistfully. "How long can you stay?"

"I'll be here for Christmas. But I have to be back in Minneapolis by tomorrow morning."

"To fly to Yellowstone?" she asked.

"Cancelled."

"But I thought Jack – "

"Simultaneously fired and quit," Tommy said.

She took his hand and pulled it to her lips. "Maybe you should tell me what's going on."

"You know I've been going to Brian Bjorklund's church out in California. When Brian found out I lost the Yellowstone gig, he called a pastor in Minneapolis who's a friend of his from seminary and lined up a concert for tomorrow afternoon. I'm doing a holiday show called *Discovering Hope* at a big mega-church with an auditorium that seats two thousand people."

Her eyes lit up.

"It's not sold out yet. It was kind of last minute since it didn't get scheduled until Yellowstone fell through. They're hoping that if I attend all three of their church services tomorrow, sing with the worship team, say a few words, sing kind of a teaser for special music, and personally invite them to the concert, that we'll pack the place out for both performances."

"And you're okay with this? A church auditorium is pretty small potatoes for a big name like Tommy Love."

"My pride has taken a few hits these last couple of weeks. If that's what the Big Daddy in the sky thinks I need, then who am I to argue?" Tommy said.

"Do you have to leave right away, or do you have time to sing a few songs for a certain adoring fan?"

"Hey, if I've learned anything in the last few weeks, it's that you have to give your fans what they want."

"Except when it comes to quilts." She smiled. "Because while they may want them, they really shouldn't have them."

"Except when it comes to quilts." He picked up his guitar and began to strum.

"What's that noise?" she said.

"Noise?" he said. "You call my music noise?"

"No, not that, silly," she said. "Right before you started to play. I heard something. Listen."

"You must have a drippy faucet." Tommy stood and headed for the kitchen. "I'm pretty good at fixing things."

"Except when it comes to quilt auctions," she said, smiling.

He tried to scowl and laughed instead. "Seriously. If you have a wrench..."

But the sinks in the kitchen and both bathrooms were dry.

"It's like dripping, but quieter," she said. "More muffled."

"Shhh," he said. He walked to the window as quietly as he could and motioned her over with his hand. "It's the icicles hanging from the roof. They're melting."

The sun peeked out between a narrow patch of trees just as Hope approached the window, touching each droplet of water until the whole snowy landscape sparkled with radiance.

Chapter 45

Billy bent down, grabbed the waistband of the faded fatigues that were pooled around his ankles, and pulled. He fastened the snap at the waist and zipped the zipper three-fourths of the way up. The Dirk Westola look to a T.

He hadn't showered since the night before, when he'd used a black rinse on his hair. The natural oils he'd sweated overnight paired with the dye made his hair look remarkably like Dirk's. With scary survivalist guy's signature dirty baseball cap perched on his head, he'd be a dead ringer.

He smiled, pleased with the results of his efforts. He'd never be able to brag about what he was about to do, but after his recent bout of deals-fallen-through, he liked feeling that he'd exceeded at something.

He leaned over and tucked the bottom of his pants into his boots. "Mother would be so proud."

Yeah, right.

Not that it mattered. Hope had raised an obscene amount of money at her little auction. He had to scare her away now, before she got the funds and made a loan payment. The buyer he had lined up wanted to start bulldozing trees while the ground was still frozen so he could break ground first thing this spring and be open by July when the tourists descended in force. It was time for desperate measures.

A half hour later, Billy had stowed his truck in a densely wooded area well off the road, and was hiking toward Rainbow Lake Lodge from the direction of Dirk Westola's place. He brushed aside a branch and ploughed through a thicket of raspberry cane, not caring that the thorns ripped at his pants. His mind was a caldron of hatred. She'd pushed him to this. She was the one who'd been so unreasonable. She was the one who had dug her heels in and refused to budge. She was the one who had left him no choice but to retaliate.

The snow was thick and wet around his ankles, but he bulldozed through the muck with the energy of a twenty-year-old, making no effort to cover his tracks.

A deer reared up in front of him just as he was about to ford a stream turned to ice. Without thinking, he lifted his rifle and put a hole in its head as neatly as if he'd been stalking it for hours.

The shot rang through the forest and the deer crumpled to the ground. It crossed his mind briefly that he shouldn't have announced his presence, but he brushed the thought aside. What was one more shot in the north woods? Gunshots were as much of a non-noise here as they were in the inner city.

He looked at the deer and felt a surge of pride. "Not bad, Billy, old boy. You've still got the touch." He kicked the carcass and laughed as a spurt of blood oozed out of the animal's forehead.

He felt his eyes glaze over for a second as he envisioned another lifeless form crumpling, falling to the floor.

Too bad getting rid of the bitch at Rainbow Lake Lodge couldn't be so simple. Or maybe it could be.

He knelt and made sure the deer was dead, stood, took his knife from his pocket, and cut through the roe's skin and ribcage with one forceful motion.

Fresh blood spurted up at him as he cut the heart from the animal. He held it in his hands like a cat with a dead bird in its mouth, coming to get approval from its owner.

He cradled the heart in one hand, re-shouldered his rifle and resumed his course.

This was turning out even better than he'd hoped. If all went as planned, she'd get a glimpse of "Dirk" slipping away through the woods, find the bloody mess on her doorstep, and get the message loud and clear. Maybe he'd write it in blood: "Leave the lodge closed!"

If she called that Barney Fife, Alvin, all the better. Billy would be long gone by the time Alvin got there. Besides, the dweeb was probably more scared of Dirk than she was.

Of course, Dirk would deny everything, but the evidence would all point back to him. With the help of the rumors Billy had started, no one would ever look further than Dirk. While the deed might be reprehensible, there was nothing illegal about it. A good thing – he wanted Dirk around for the duration to keep the whiny little bitch in a constant state of fear until the day she finally gave up and left town.

He only wished he could see her face when she got her little present.

He smiled at the realization that he no longer thought of her as Hope, or even as a woman. To him, she had become evil personified, the source of his troubles, his woes, his loss of respect from everyone he cared about.

He picked his way around a fallen tree blocking the path in front of him. He was like a tall tree in the forest. To be truly great, he had to weed out the smaller trees growing around him – trees that hindered his growth by blocking the sun and not giving him enough space to spread out his branches and thrive.

Christmas trees weren't harvested from a cramped, overgrown, dark forest. They were chosen from a meadow where the tree had received plenty of sunlight, a clearing where a tree could grow straight, even, and perfectly rounded.

She was crowding his space. She'd taken the niche he'd carved for himself in this community and toppled it like a row of dominoes. She'd ruined everything.

Chapter 46

Hope ducked under the overhang of the roof of the front door of Rainbow Lake Lodge and listened to the water drip off the eaves as Tommy drove away – which was absolutely fine because this time, he was coming back! She returned his wave and laughed out loud even though she knew he couldn't hear her with his windows rolled up. She was happy – ridiculously, gloriously happy.

She'd been so horribly angry that Tommy had bought all of her quilts. But that's also when something had clicked, and she'd realized that she never would have reacted so intensely, that she never would have felt such deep emotions about him and his actions – unless she'd been in love with him.

She turned to go back into the lodge only when his car had disappeared from sight.

"Thank you, Lord," she whispered, letting the door fall closed behind her. Once again, God had surprised her – in a way that surpassed her wildest dreams, hopes and expectations. Although in this case, there had been no place to go but up. She'd had no expectations, no anything since David's death. She'd been lucky to get her shoes put on and place one foot in front of the other.

She was happy! And so preoccupied that she almost didn't hear the gunshot. Odd this time of year, she thought, going to the window and looking outside at the woods. The ground was as speckled as a calico cat, with fresh patches of dirt and pine needles showing through the snow. She hadn't watched the weather report and didn't know how long the warm spell was going to last, but it didn't matter. Spring-like weather suited her mood perfectly.

The only bad thing about a mid-winter thaw was that you knew it couldn't last. As opposed to what she was feeling, which she felt sure would last forever. Neither she nor Tommy had gone looking to fall in love, which in her mind, was a firm sign that God had planned the whole thing.

A chill fell over the room as she stepped back from the window.

She went to the west side of the lodge and looked out from the living room window. The sun had gone behind a cloud. That was all. The days were so short this time of year that the sun barely had time to clear the treetops and shine before it sank again. She hoped Tommy had allowed enough time to get back to his plane, take off, and reach the Cities before dark.

She was just turning away from the window when something caught her eye. She peered into the woods, expecting to see a deer scrounging for food in the patches where the snow was gone. The deer were probably just as thankful for the thaw as she was.

She let her eyes slide over the landscape. If there had been a deer, it must have hidden behind a tree, because that's all she could see. Trees. Hundreds of them. They always had given her a sense of calm. When she looked out at the forest, she felt as though God was touching her, enveloping her with his love. She gazed out the window contentedly.

She was just ready to turn to go back to the kitchen when, again, she saw something out of the corner of her eye – or thought she did.

What was wrong with her? The sun had shifted behind another cloud, a puffy, white little thing that she wouldn't even have noticed if she hadn't had the weird sensation that she was being watched.

A shift in the shadows can do that sometimes, she thought – take what's shiny and lovely and bright and make it look all troubled and worrisome, when the reality is, nothing has changed in the slightest.

Without another thought, she turned and went back to the kitchen. Tommy Love had written her a love note. No need to be fretting over minor worries when all was finally well with the world.

She smiled and straightened a photo hanging askew on the wall as she walked by. It felt so good to be happy for a change. She meant to make a habit of it as of right now.

She tilted the picture, stood to the side, then tilted it back just a smidgen – and heard something. Now *that* she was sure she hadn't imagined. It sounded like it was coming from the front door.

Her heart thudded a little faster. Before she'd taken the sign down, she'd occasionally been surprised by people who hadn't heard the lodge was closed for renovations, looking for a place to spend the night. But this time of year? Her friends always called to make sure she was home before they made the long trip out from Embarrass. Tommy was probably already in the air and on his way out of town.

He hadn't wanted to dally, knowing he had to sing at an eight o'clock service the next morning.

She went to the front entryway, listened for a moment, then went to the closest window and looked out.

The gunshot pierced the quiet of the woods with almost as much clamor as the ear-splitting scream that followed. She froze in her tracks like a startled deer.

The shooter was at close range now. She couldn't imagine who would be so foolhardy. Her fear turned to anger – at least she assumed it was anger. None of the hunters she knew would dare be so careless. The bullet was probably lodged in the masonry or wood trim of the lodge itself. Someone could have been killed. She could have been killed.

Her hand shook like a leaf in a stiff wind.

When the gun didn't fire again, her heartbeat finally started to slow. The shock was beginning to wear off when she remembered the scream. Had she been the one to scream without even realizing it? If it had been someone else, they could be hurt.

She opened the door slowly and saw someone in hunting camouflage crawling through the snow as if in great pain with a trail of blood following behind. She swung open the door and dashed outside without even grabbing her coat. In the middle of the front step was a bloody glob of who knew what. Her stomach revolted. She'd almost stepped on it.

"Dirk?" she yelled. She heard a muffled whimper and the figure came to a halt. "Dirk? She ran toward the person, knowing she had to help.

"Don't come any closer."

The voice was a man's and familiar, but didn't sound like Dirk's.

"Are you hurt?" she asked.

"Get back inside the lodge." The man twisted into a sitting position and leaned against a tree while she ran toward him.

"Billy?" The man in front of her was dressed like Dirk Westola. His face was unmistakably Billy Bjorklund's.

He lifted the rifle and pointed it straight at her.

"What are you doing?"

Billy winced, fumbled the gun and recovered it just before it hit the ground.

"I twisted my knee. I leaned down and tried to straighten it out. It was hurting so bad I... I'm not sure what happened. I must have shot myself in the foot. It hurts like hell."

"The way you're waving that thing around is making me nervous," she said, trying to sound chatty and matter-of-fact and as nonplussed as if she found a bloody man dressed in someone else's clothes pointing a gun on her in her front yard every day. "Why don't I take it for you and lay it down right over there?"

"No! Stay there or I'll shoot," he said. His eyes glazed over like a wounded animal's.

A roar filled the air. They both looked up.

Tommy. He dipped his wings, flew just above the treetops and roared by for a second pass over.

"No," she cried, knowing what he was going to do even before he brought the plane around to the end of the lake to line it up with the long strip of ice where people had been driving – until today, when the temperatures had gotten so warm that...

"Do something!" she yelled at Billy. "Put the gun down. He can see the clearing from the air. The ice is too thin. Stop him!"

Billy said nothing, but kept the gun trained on her.

"He thinks you're Dirk." She looked at Billy's face and saw his eyes – haunted, cold, unfeeling – and wished that it was poor, eccentric, slightly scary but basically harmless Dirk.

"The plane will fall through the ice," she screamed at Billy, trying to break through his stupor as the roar of the plane filled the air and Tommy came closer and closer to killing himself trying to save her.

"Do something!" she screamed, at God, at Billy, at anyone who might be listening. She was pleading now, desperate to stop this madness. But the terrible truth was, there was no way Tommy wasn't going to land the plane and come to her rescue – not with Dirk's image and the blood and a rifle pointed at her staring him in the face.

He was cutting back the engines, coming in for a gentle landing, gliding down over the last of the birch trees as light as a butterfly, except that his plane must weigh as much as three cars or two snowplows and the ice was melting.

She was still looking up, half paralyzed, praying, watching the plane as it hovered over the lake, inches from the ice, when another shot rang through the forest. She crumpled to her knees; too numb to know if she'd been shot, or if he'd hit the plane, or if the noise she'd heard had been the ice cracking when Tommy landed. The plane had disappeared from sight as it dipped behind the trees, too close, but so far, and she could only hope on top of the ice and not under it.

Another sound – this one the one she'd been dreading – the same one she couldn't wait to hear come spring, the sound of life returning, a sound of life ending for anyone in the wrong place at the wrong time. The ice was cracking. There was no denying it now. Crack after ear-splitting crack. The sounds of ice moaning and Billy moaning merged into one.

She hugged herself and cried.

"Are you all right?"

She looked up to see Dirk – the real Dirk – standing over her.

"I'm not sure." She said, doing a mental inventory of her body parts. "I think I'm okay. What did you do?"

"Grazed Billy's shooting arm. Scared him so he'd drop the gun," he said. "I have it now."

"Tommy landed the plane on the lake," she said, struggling to get up. "We have to help. The ice is breaking up."

Dirk was halfway to the lake by the time she was able to get to her feet.

"Get a rope, a chain, a heavy extension cord," Dirk yelled over his shoulder. "Whatever you can find."

"Lord, please." Dirk thought Tommy was in the lake. She tried not to panic as she raced to the house, grabbed the extension cord David always kept hanging from a nail by the back door, dashed out the door and ran after Dirk. It was hard to trust a new love's fate, even to the Lord, when she'd barely come to terms with losing her old one.

Chapter 47

Tommy didn't move a muscle for the first several seconds after the plane landed. It was clear his situation was precarious and he didn't want to do anything to make it worse. The only reason he'd taken such a foolish risk in the first place was that Hope was in trouble. She was still in trouble. He had to get off the plane if he was going to get there in time.

The ice was eerily shiny up close. *Swell, just swell.* He looked up. *You wouldn't be in the mood for an arctic blast about now, would you? It would sure be appreciated.*

He stepped down from his seat as gently as a six-foot two inch, two hundred twenty-five pound man could and grabbed the seat cushion to use as a life preserver, which would do him absolutely no good if he was caught under a plate of ice.

His odds didn't look that great right about now, but neither were Hope's unless he got to her fast.

A shot. The gunfire echoed through his head like a surreal, slow motion animation.

He was helpless. Not a good feeling. Brian kept saying that when stuff like this happened, maybe God was trying to teach him about patience, grace, or even faith. He hated thinking Hope had to suffer just so he could learn some stupid lesson.

Okay. Not a good time to get mad at God. Especially since God was the only one who could protect Hope until he got there.

If he wasn't already too late. Fear rippled through his body. He couldn't even go there.

The ice under the plane creaked as he opened the heavy door between the cockpit and the tail. Lowering the steps could punch a hole right through the ice. But the full weight of his body hitting the ice if he jumped could be even worse. He lowered himself backwards over the edge of the emergency exit, stretching his legs down inch by inch until he'd alighted as gently as a moth on the shade of a lamp.

None of which helped him get to Hope. The ice had to hold his weight. Had to.

Ice over shallow waters melted faster than ice over deep waters. The closer he got to the shore, the worse it would get.

He resisted the urge to let loose and run. Thanks to the sunshine, the ice was covered with a thin glaze of water, and so slippery he could hardly stand up. He inched toward the shore half sliding, half gliding.

Hope. He tried to think about something other than her. It was the only way he could keep from breaking into a fast jog.

He was going to have to find another way to get to Minneapolis. That was a sure thing. He listened for more cracking noises, and slid a few more feet. Maybe he could borrow Hope's car. He almost slipped and put out both arms to regain his balance. He crept around a pool of water and eyed the shore. Still a long way off. Maybe Hope would go with him to the Cities. He inched a little closer. If she was still...

He looked down just in time to avoid stepping on a crack. Okay. It was obvious that he hadn't sought divine advice before he landed the plane – if he had, he wouldn't be in such a mess. But if there was ever a time to seek a little intervention from above, it was now.

His mind searched for the right words. Those dudes the Lord had hung out with had walked on water. If Jesus could help them out over open waves, keeping Tommy Lubinski walking on the top side of some half-thawed ice shouldn't be too hard. Bottom line, it was all water. They all needed to stay on the surface so they didn't drown.

"Stay where you are." A man's voice, one he didn't recognize, called out from the shore. Tommy looked up and froze. A man in army fatigues and a baseball cap – the same man who'd been holding Hope at gunpoint – stood at the edge of the lake

"I'm not armed." Tommy held up his arms, feeling doubly helpless.

"I'm Dirk Westola. It was Billy with the gun. He was dressed like me."

"Billy?" Tommy took another step. "Is Hope...?"

"Tommy!" Hope was running down the hill, her arms open, dodging snow banks and outcroppings of rocks and puddles of water.

Alive! "Are you all right?" He yelled over the distance that separated them.

"I'm fine. Are you?" Her face fell from happy to worried. "Oh, Tommy."

"I'll be out of here in a few seconds," he said, wondering if it was true. "Don't worry about me."

"Did you bring a rope?" Dirk asked, looking at Hope.

He could see a clump of orange dangling from her arm. "Good girl," Tommy yelled. "Westola, you willing to walk out as far as you can and toss the end to me?"

Tommy took a few more steps, but stopped when the ice started to moan underneath him.

"Tommy, please wait," Hope cried out, her voice high with fear.

Dirk took the cords from Hope, tied them together, chose a solid-looking route, and started toward him. He'd only gone a few feet when the ice cracked. The sound reverberated through the air like a sonic boom.

"Stop," Hope said. "I weigh the least of anyone. I should be the one to go."

"No," Tommy said, hearing Dirk's voice in synch with his own.

"Dirk will never get out far enough to get the cord to you," she said. "I can do it. I'm the one who's most likely to get there."

"Likely is not a great word when it comes to your odds," Tommy said.

"Forget odds," she said. "Have a little faith."

She was a brave one all right; he'd give her that. And it was amazing that she could have faith when she knew how quickly an accident could change an entire life; even end it, faith or no.

"God will get us through this no matter what happens," she said. She was either reassuring herself or reading his mind.

He watched silently as Dirk backed up, tied the middle of the cord around Hope, and coiled up the rest of it so she'd be able to slide it across the ice when she was close enough to get him the other end.

If anything happened to Hope...

His brain flitted to a subject he could deal with.

His plane. Dusk was coming, and the temperatures would start dropping. Once the lake refroze, he could fly her out, simple as could be, although the landing gear would probably be stuck to the ice like superglue.

Hope was inching closer and closer. "I love you," he said, watching her face – the intense concentration, the awesome determination, and, yes, the pure and simple faith.

"I love you," she said, just loudly enough that he could hear her voice over the remaining distance that separated them.

"You should be able to reach him now," Dirk yelled. "Throw him the cord."

She threw, but the cord skittered to a halt just a few feet in front of her.

"Try again," Dirk said.

"Crouch down and pretend you're throwing a Frisbee," Tommy said, "or skipping a rock."

She re-coiled the cord, tossed it out again, and watched it slither across the ice and come to a stop right before him.

He took the end, tied it securely around his waist, and gave it a little tug. A chill that was so intense it made his spine tingle ran through him as he assessed what might be the safest route. They were connected now, he and Hope, tied together by an unbreakable knot. The theory was that if he fell through the ice, she would pull him out of the water before he went under. His fear was that he could just as easily drag her down with him. He weighed a third again as much as she did. Dirk looked strong, but if Tommy went in, there would be a lot of slack to take up, and the thought of Hope being caught between them was not something he wanted to think about.

He had taken two steps in Hope's direction when he heard it – ice cracking, plates shifting, water whooshing. He looked over his shoulder. The plane tilted at a forty-five degree angle. Another crack split the air and reverberated under his feet like thunder. There was no time to waste.

"Run!" he screamed.

Water splashed under his feet as he ran, slid and stumbled toward the shore. All he could see or think about was Hope, getting back to Hope, being with Hope, which he couldn't do if he were twenty feet under.

He caught up with her just before they reached the shore. She was moving almost as fast as he was. He grabbed her hand and pulled her along. And then they were safe, and together again, and her hand was tucked in his. After a second, his arms were around her, too. He could feel her shivering though his jacket.

"Where's your coat?" he asked.

"I didn't have time. It all happened so fast."

"If you'd fallen in the lake..." he said.

"I didn't."

"Thank God."

"Definitely," she said.

He was so into hugging her that he almost didn't see the plume of water shooting into the air. The metal skin of the airplane screeched against the ice and tore. The lake made a few mournful noises like it didn't want the plane to fall in any more than Tommy wanted it to. The wheels disappeared. The wings went next, and finally, the cockpit. A final geyser of water erupted from the lake and his plane sank from sight.

Hope stared at the water and watched as a few stray bubbles floated to the surface. "Your guitar."

"Major bummer," Tommy said.

"We'd better go look after Billy," Dirk said, looking ill at ease. "Sorry about your plane."

"Better the plane than me," Tommy said. "Thank you for that."

"Thanks for believing me when I told you it was Billy who had the gun and not me," Dirk said, starting up the hill.

"Speaking of, one of you needs to fill me in on what's going on," Tommy said, jogging to catch up.

"I wish I knew," Hope said, following close behind. "Billy injured himself. Other than that, all I can say is that he has a lot of explaining to do."

Tommy caught up to her and squeezed her hand. "I'm just glad you're okay."

"Thanks for coming to my rescue."

"I could say the same," Tommy said. "Dirk, you're the hero here."

"Don't be spreading it around," Dirk said. "I'm not a people person and I got my reputation to protect."

He was glad people were afraid of him. "Well, you'll always be a welcome sight to us." Tommy grabbed Hope's hand. "Guess we'd better go find out what Billy's up to."

Chapter 48

Hope was getting more frustrated by the minute. All she wanted was a few quiet minutes alone with Tommy.

He'd said he loved her. As a friend? As a phone buddy? As a cohort in crime-solving and extreme adventures? Did she dare hope that he wanted all of her the way she wanted him?

Grateful as she'd been for their assistance, this was not the kind of thing one discussed in front of Dirk, or Alvin, who had shown up minutes after the plane had sunk in response to Dirk's call to 9-1-1.

She hadn't even had the satisfaction of finding out what had prompted Billy's mysterious behavior. Billy was gone. His tracks, paired with the drops of blood he'd left behind like Hansel and Gretel's crumbs in the forest, had led to a clearing lined with two sets of tire tracks – one coming, one going. Solving the mystery of what he'd been doing and where he'd gone to was up to Alvin and his men now.

She and Tommy had left for Minneapolis together shortly after Alvin had finished questioning them, mostly because Tommy had been afraid to leave her alone until Billy's whereabouts were determined.

She'd hoped they could talk in the car, but Tommy had spent the entire three-and-a-half hour trip on his cell phone, lining up another guitar, and making sure he would have internet access so he could download copies of the songs he'd lost with the plane. Since he no longer had an agent and his manager wasn't around, it also fell on him to make sure the sound system was adequate, that there were sufficient amps and high caliber microphones, which had also been in the airplane.

The next order of business was to report the incident with the plane to the Department of Natural Resources, the Fish and Game Commission, and the Federal Aviation Administration.

By the time he'd called ahead to cancel his dinner reservations, let his hotel know he was going to be late, and secured her a room, they had reached the Cities.

They'd both been exhausted. She'd gone to her room, showered, and fallen asleep the second her head touched her pillow.

* * *

Hope suspected Tommy had been up half the night printing up new copies of the songs that had sunk with his plane and scribbling chords and notes in preparation for his performances Sunday morning. She hadn't seen him since he'd kissed her goodnight outside the door to her hotel room.

He'd arranged for the concierge to phone with a wakeup call, and a driver to pick her up and take her to and from the church as needed. Flowers had been delivered to her room, along with a note apologizing that the ride he'd arranged for her was in a church van and not a limo.

The flowers were incredible, and it wasn't that she wasn't flattered to be on the receiving end of the Tommy Love treatment, but all she really wanted was Tommy Lovinski – the Tommy who'd fixed her generator, the Tommy who'd brought her gas on the back of a snowmobile, even the Tommy who'd embarrassed her by buying all of her quilts.

When she arrived at the church, she was ushered to a special seat on the isle, a few rows back from the front, beside the head pastor and his wife. They were at the church all day long, with a quick break for lunch with the church's music minister and his wife at a nearby restaurant. She sat through all three services, a long rehearsal, and two concerts and enjoyed every second. Tommy sang a beautiful repertoire of praise songs, original tunes and classic hymns. Each one delighted the audience, and her, more than the last. Tommy knew where she was sitting, and sang to her like she was the only person in the room except God.

Too bad she hadn't been. Between organizers organizing, reporters interviewing, techies tweaking, fans clamoring and people wanting autographs, she'd barely seen Tommy until they were in the car on their way back to Embarrass the next morning.

"Sorry about all the craziness," Tommy squeezed her hand when they were finally alone.

"I understand," she said. But she really didn't. After two years of relative seclusion, living and working by herself at Rainbow Lake

Lodge, Tommy's life style was as foreign to her as Japanese was to an Englishman.

"I'm always pretty peopled out after a concert."

She nodded. She could see why. Really, she could. The whole concert had been a zoo. But she was 'people'. Did he mean her, too?

"Now you know why I want to live in a place where I can be totally secluded. It's the only way I can tolerate the hectic pace of my public life." Tommy steered the car up an entrance ramp and got on the interstate.

Disappointment clutched at her heart. "I can see how a person would get to that point." But she didn't have the same need. "I guess I'm just the opposite. The only thing that's kept me going these last two years is dreaming about the day when the lodge will be full of people again – families, children, staff members, whatever kind of interesting person happens to come through the door."

"You don't find that exhausting after a while? It sounds like having company 24 by 7, months and years on end." Tommy said, his voice sounding stilted.

Unless she was imagining it. Unless she was projecting her own rigid attitude on him. "People rejuvenate me. I may get tired, but not tired of, if that makes sense."

"But if you remarried and had someone to be with, don't you think that would fulfill your need to be around people?" he said hopefully. "Or if you had a baby? I mean, I've always been told that women are wired to be caretakers, and that if they don't have that need met by being a mother…"

He must have glanced at her and seen her expression, because he stopped mid-sentence.

"A person's personal life and their career goals are two different things," she said. "Sure, I'd love to be married again, even have a baby. But that doesn't mean I'd want to give up all the joy and fulfillment I'd get from serving my guests and knowing that what I've done at Rainbow Lake Lodge has made people happy. Surely you can understand that."

"The feeling of making people happy, sure," Tommy said. "But there are a lot of ways you could do that. Teaching school, working at a hospital, being on staff at a nursing home."

He looked at her and evidently had enough sense to change gears. "You could open a fabric shop and give quilting lessons."

A rush of disappointment assaulted her senses.

"Aw, c'mon, Hope. Don't look at me that way. I'm just trying to find some sort of happy medium here."

"We want totally different things for our lives. How could we ever be happy together if the only way to accomplish that is for one or the other of us to give up everything that's important to them?"

"People who merge lives don't give up the things they love, they make trade-offs," Tommy said.

"So now it's a merger?" She swallowed hard and fought back her anger. "Maybe when you hire a new agent, he or she and my attorney can work out all the details and let us know when it's a done deal. Assuming they can come to terms."

"Hope, please." Tommy steered around and passed a semi pulling a trailer. "I love you. But this is not going to be like when we were twenty-years-old. It's complicated when two mature adults go into a relationship."

"I know that." And she did. That didn't make it any easier. She and David has forged a new life together at a time when neither of them had had a care. She and Tommy both had vested interests, past scenarios, baggage galore.

"We're not exactly blank pieces of paper anymore," Tommy said, slinging his right arm over the back of her seat and squeezing her shoulder. "We're scruffy and tattered around the edges. We have lots of scribbles and black marks written on our hearts."

Her shoulders stiffened, and her heart took a nosedive. "Your ex-wives may have left black marks on your heart. David left a beautiful, hand-written love note on mine."

Tommy looked at her, his eyes the only part of him that revealed how deeply she'd wounded him.

"And here I was thinking that's what made getting a second chance at love so exciting," he said.

She didn't want to hurt Tommy, she really didn't. But she missed David so much. The idea of starting over, having to relearn the little kinds of things she'd known about David for a quarter of a century was not only intimidating, but downright unappealing. She just didn't have the energy, or, right now, the desire.

When she and David had started dating, there had been nothing to merge except two hearts, so hungry for each other that nothing mattered but their love.

"How did we get on this anyway?" Tommy asked, with a laugh that made it sound like someone was strangling him, namely her. "All I was trying to say was that the only way I can tolerate being *on* all the time when I'm Tommy Love is to take it down a notch and let good old Tommy Lubinski chill when the concert is over."

"Lubinski?"

"Ah – yeah," Tommy stammered.

"It's not *Lo*vinski?"

"Um, no. Does it matter?"

"No. Of course not."

But it did. She didn't need a heartthrob. She needed a helpmate.

They traveled the next few miles in silence. And then, the tears she'd been holding in for over a day finally seeped out. Silent tears for silent fears.

"It's just that from the very beginning, our relationship was built on secrets and lies and misconceptions," she said quietly. "I don't know anything about you, Tommy. Not really."

"It's just a name," Tommy said, sounding old and tired and resigned. "People in show business change their names all the time."

"Sure," she said. If he didn't get it, nothing she could say would make a difference anyway.

They spent the rest of the ride engaging in safe, chit-chatty conversations about the concert, speculation about Billy, or silence.

They took the scenic route so they could have lunch at Grandma's in Duluth and dessert at Betty's Pies, a few miles north of Two Harbors. The North Shore Drive and the back roads they traveled to cut back over to Embarrass were as beautiful as always, the weather clear, and the pavement free of snow. It was late afternoon when they finally pulled into Embarrass. Thank goodness, her old tires made the trip without popping a leak.

"Well," Tommy said. "I don't know about you, but I need to get some sleep. I don't know if I should set up camp in front of your fireplace just in case Billy shows up or head back to my motel."

"I don't mind going the rest of the way by myself. Alvin said he or a deputy would be staked out somewhere near the Lodge to keep an eye on things until Billy is apprehended. He said he'd call if he thought there was any need for concern. I just checked my cell and there are no messages."

"Are you sure? I could drive you out to the Lodge, but then you'd be stranded out there without a car. We could see if the hotel has another room."

"There's no need to spend money on a room for me. I'll sleep better in my own bed anyway," she said. She definitely was ready for a nap.

"I guess if Alvin's got things covered..."

They pulled up in front of the hotel and she took Tommy's place behind the wheel.

"Is there anything else you need before I go?" Everything he'd had with him was in his suitcase, which was now at the bottom of the lake. "Are you sure you don't want me to take you out to the airport to get your car now?" She hoped not. The Ely Airport was another 30 miles to the north.

"I'll find someone to run me over later," he said. "I'm pretty tired."

"Me, too."

"Well, you've got my number if you need anything," he said, looking like a caught fish struggling to get off the hook and back in the water. "If you keep all the doors locked..."

"I did, before we left. And I will. I'll be fine," she said.

"I have no doubt," he said, looking relieved and unhappy at the same time.

"You sure you don't want me to come into town later tonight so I can give you a lift out to the airport?"

"Let me see what I can do first. I hate to make you come all the way into town." He closed the car door, gave her a quick kiss goodbye through the open car window, then turned toward the hotel before looking back at her. "Billy always hauled me around when I was in town."

"I know," she said. "Things change."

Tommy gave her hand a squeeze. But when he turned a second time and walked toward the Nothing To Be Embarrassed About Motel, she was alone again.

Chapter 49

The cemetery was deathly quiet except for the sound of Hope's footsteps crunching against the brittle pieces of last fall's grass. A few pebbles poked out between the patches of snow that had melted earlier in the week, before the temperatures dropped again.

She pulled her parka a little tighter and nuzzled her chin into the wide turtleneck of the sweater she wore underneath. She'd never been to David's grave in the wintertime. Deep snow normally covered the ground and swirled around the tombstones, making it all but impossible to visit. Rightly so – it was hard being here when everything was either dead or hibernating. Springtime's wildflowers, green grass and budding trees made it infinitely easier to see the cold, granite headstones and carved-in-stone dates dotting the hillside.

She knelt beside David's grave and pulled away a clump of sod wedged so tightly against the stone that the gardener's weed whacker had missed it. She heard a sigh echo through the cemetery and assumed it must have been hers. There was no undoing death, at least not on earth. It robbed you of what was loved, precious, and familiar, and left you with nothing – unless you were willing to start from scratch and build a new life.

She didn't want a new man in her life any more than she wanted a new house, a new job, or new friends. Right or wrong, the only way she'd made it through the last two years was to cling to the familiar – in her case, Rainbow Lake Lodge.

Anything else was too terrifying, too risky. She would sooner re-sew exact duplicates of each and every quilt that had sold at the auction than open her heart up to the pain she'd felt when David died. That's what she'd learned when Tommy was standing in a puddle of water sixty feet offshore with ice cracking around him like an eggshell hitting the side of a bowl.

It was already too late. She loved Tommy. Really, really loved him. She squeezed her eyes against her tears for fear they would freeze to her face.

"Let not your heart be troubled, neither let it be afraid." She'd chosen the words for the inscription on David's tomb – it wasn't like she was seeing them for the first time. But she was. Caring for Tommy – caring about someone who was vibrantly, joyously, stubbornly alive – had changed her, changed everything.

The second line of the inscription read, *"For lo, I am with you always."*

It was God who was with her always. David had gone. God was still there. And now, Tommy wanted to be, too.

"I can't do this."

"You most certainly can," David's voice taunted her. *"You think you can't, but you always do in the end."*

"That was when I wanted to. I don't want this."

"You wouldn't be here if you didn't," David's voice echoed inside her head.

She sucked in a breath of ice-cold air. He was right. She had come to say good-bye.

"It doesn't mean I'll love you any less." She looked at the headstone. Cold. Solid. Safe. Familiar.

"You have so much love to give, sweetheart. You can love God, and me, this new guy, and a handful of kids besides if you have the chance."

"I can, can't I?" She said the words, but it was still hard to wrap her mind around the concept. There was just so much she didn't understand.

How could heaven be heaven for David if she wasn't there?

She tried to envision him there. Aside from streets paved in gold, some harps, and a lot of angels, her concept of the great ever after was very vague. But one thing she knew – no felt – was that David wasn't in mourning – how could he be? The sadness and grief she'd been harboring were totally incompatible with eternal bliss. David was happy, rejoicing – gloriously so.

She had no clue whether he had duties and responsibilities, or whether he was spending eternity praising, worshipping and adoring. But she felt sure he wasn't moping around and thinking about the past, or her, all the time. David was gone — to another realm, another life, another existence entirely. She would always love him, always remember their time together, always cherish her memories of him. But David had moved on. It was time for her to do the same.

"Don't look down," David's voice said. *"Promise me that you'll keep looking up."*

She lifted her eyes to the clouds, the hills shimmering in the distance, the evergreens lining the ridge, the sun sinking slowly in the west like it did day after day, only to rise again.

Death had no hold on her heart. It couldn't, given what she believed. Life had to be about living, whether by herself, or with Tommy Love, whether at Rainbow Lake Lodge, in California, or wherever God wanted her.

She bent and kissed the cold granite stone that would stand forever as a memorial to David's love and looked up at the sky. Whether or not Tommy Love held the key to her future, she wasn't going to choose death to living in God's love.

Chapter 50

Alvin trudged up the sidewalk between the parking lot and the Alzheimer's unit at the nursing home. The lot was so packed he'd had to park on the back forty behind the home.

Christmas. Probably carolers, grandkids, long-lost relatives from who knows where. Christmas – it supposedly brought out the best in people. Only problem was the "good" never seemed to last past midnight on Christmas Day. If that long.

He picked his way through the maze of cars and wondered if it was being a sheriff that had made him so cynical, or having his mother lose her mind. Not that it mattered. The result was the same.

He rounded a corner and came out from behind a Nissan Pathfinder that could have housed a small family in many countries in the world. He looked up at the glow coming from the nursing home's windows. It was dark three-fourths of the time these days. Yesterday had been the shortest day of the year.

He reached the front door, punched in the code, and stepped inside. A rush of warmth tried to envelope him, but he pushed it aside. The heating bills at the home must be astronomical, outrageously hot as they kept the place.

A tinkle of laughter filtered out of the door to the room to his left. Sounded like they had about twenty people in there, except that he knew better. The rooms were so small one barely held he, his mother, and her walker.

The aides had promised to have her ready. Coat, hat, gloves, a satchel with the things she might need. Not that it mattered. He'd have her back before her diaper needed to be changed.

He opened the door to her room. She was sitting in her wheelchair in a thin cotton dress. No coat, no hat, no nothing.

"I thought the aide was going to have you ready," he said, dreading what lay ahead.

"Ready for what?" She sat stone still, staring out the window.

"Christmas. I said I would take you home to celebrate Christmas."

"Today isn't Christmas," she said.

"It's my day off," Alvin said. He'd offered to work Christmas so the men with families could spend the holiday at home. "I've got a nice meal in the oven and I put a little tree up with all your nice decorations."

"I suppose that hussy made the dinner."

Great. She couldn't remember what year it was or when it was time to go to the bathroom, but she would never forget her twisted version of the innocent arrangement he had with Hope. "Hope is not a hussy, mother. And she's a very good cook."

"You never would have sent me away if it wasn't for her. I won't have you cavorting with the likes of that woman under the roof your father and I worked hours to build."

"I'm not cavorting with anyone, Mother. Hope has never even been at our house. I picked up the food and brought it home just like I always do."

"Fine. You like her food. You eat it."

"Did someone say food?" Tommy Love poked his head in the door and grinned like there was something to be happy about. "Thought I heard a familiar voice."

"If you're here to spread Christmas cheer or sing Christmas carols, you can go away," Alvin said.

"Bah humbug to you, too," Tommy said. "I'm here to see Mrs. Bjorklund. Just trying to be neighborly."

"More likely to see if there's any more news about Billy," Alvin said.

"So is there?" Tommy looked over his shoulder, squeezed into the room, and partially closed the door behind him.

"No," Alvin said. "Not a trace. I've got sheriffs in six counties looking." He turned as far to his right as he could in the cramped space and scrunched his mother's sweater around her shoulders. "We don't want you catching cold."

"I told you I'm not going near that hussy."

"Hussy?" Tommy said.

"Hope," Alvin said.

"She thinks Hope is a hussy?"

Alvin rolled his eyes.

"Well," Tommy said. "I guess I'll mosey on down to Mrs. B's apartment and..."

"She's not there." Alvin struggled to get his mother's hands into her gloves. Mittens. That's what he should have gotten her for Christmas. She didn't drive. She could hardly move her fingers. Mittens would have been just the thing.

"Ouch," his mother said. "You're hurting me."

"Sorry," Alvin said. The word pretty well summed up his whole attitude about Christmas – and life in general.

"Any idea where she is?" Tommy asked.

"Probably at the bank, if I know her."

Tommy looked at him quizzically.

"After Billy disappeared, I got a warrant to search his house. Sharon brought Mrs. Bjorklund over since she was next of kin. I don't think she's been back here since. She was giving Sharon heck last time I saw them. Said she refused to set foot in this place again until she was at least ninety-five."

"How was everything over at Billy's then?" Tommy asked.

He cleared his throat. "I was afraid he might have done something stupid."

"It crossed my mind as well."

"We did find a mess, but not what I thought," Alvin said, shifting a little so he could start on his mother's left hand. "Hope asked Sharon to sell her great-grandmother's armoire a few months ago. Sharon thought Hope would regret selling it one day, so she gave Hope some money of her own, told her it had sold, and took it over to Billy's for safekeeping."

"I was over there the day before the incident at the lodge and Billy wouldn't let me in the house," Tommy said.

"Billy took an axe to the armoire. Turned it into toothpicks."

Tommy face turned livid.

Alvin lined up all five of his mother's fingers and pulled on the bottom of the glove. Success. "I thought maybe you would know where to find Billy," he said to Tommy. "Someplace the two of you used to hang out as kids – a secret hideaway or something like that."

Tommy shook his head. "No place that I can think of."

"You know where to find me if—" A rap on the door interrupted him. Probably the aide now that he had his mother almost ready. "Come in."

Tommy tried to move out of the way and ended up sitting on the bed for lack of a better option.

"Hi, Alvin." It was Sharon, bless her heart, looking past Tommy Love like he wasn't even there and focusing the prettiest pair of baby blues he'd even seen right on Alvin.

"Hi, Sharon," he said, hoping to God he wasn't blushing like some silly schoolboy.

"Merry Christmas," she said, like he was the only one in the room. "Merry Christmas to you, too, Mrs. Turppa."

"Hussies coming out of the woodwork," his mother said.

Sharon looked at him, her eyes big as saucers.

"She doesn't mean it," Alvin said.

"I do, too," his mother replied.

"At least you're in good company," Tommy said.

"Thanks for dropping by," Alvin said, trying not to act as mortified as he felt. "I don't know anything more about Billy than I did yesterday."

"I'm not here about Billy," Sharon said.

Tommy nodded at him as if to say, *Go for it, you idiot.*

"Are you having a nice Christmas so far?" Alvin said because he couldn't think of anything better.

Tommy tried to stand and couldn't find room for his feet. "Why don't I wheel your mother down to the activity room for some punch?"

Sharon smiled and backed out the door so Tommy could get up. Alvin kissed his mother on the top of her silver blue curls and ducked out after Sharon before his mother could object.

Sharon was waiting in the hall, her hair glowing around her face like a Christmas tree lit up with lights, her eyes shining like the disco ball in the center of the dance floor at The Northern Lights Bar and Grill on New Year's Eve.

Hmmm. Maybe Tommy wasn't such a bad guy after all.

Chapter 51

"Please come in." Rose Bjorklund stood behind an old-world looking cherry desk and smoothed her pale pink angora sweater down over her hips. "Thank you so much for coming, dear. I would have understood perfectly if you'd never wanted to set foot in this bank again."

Hope set her purse on the floor, took a seat, and motioned for Stan to do the same. "I feel perfectly comfortable now that you're back in charge."

Rose smiled. "The papers are all ready to sign."

"I'm sure you remember Stan Paulsen," Hope said, sinking back into the leather-covered wingback. "I hope you don't mind me bringing him along. I just want to make sure I understand everything I'm signing."

"After what we've both been through with Billy, it's best that everyone involved feels totally at ease," Mrs. Bjorklund said.

"Has there been any news?" Hope asked. The assumption was that Billy was miles from Embarrass by now, in a part of the state or country, or even Canada, where no one would recognize him. It would be next to impossible for someone as well known as Billy to stay hidden anywhere nearby. Still, it would set her mind at ease to know that he was somewhere safely away from her, and not lurking, waiting for a further chance for revenge.

"No." Rose fidgeted with her scarf. "I'm so terribly sorry for what Billy has put you through."

"It's okay," Hope said. "In a strange sort of way, the whole thing forced me to take a look at my faith. What I found out taught me some lessons I must have needed to learn. And if it hadn't been for Billy's scheme, I never would have met Tommy." No matter what happened, she would always be glad he'd come into her life.

"Yes," Rose said. "I'm so happy for the two of you."

"Thanks," she said, opting not to point out that Mrs. Bjorklund's good wishes were a little pre-mature, that she hadn't seen Tommy in three days, and had no idea if he were even still in the state or back in California.

"I know the reduction in the loan amount can't undo what Billy did," Rose said, her discomfort leaking through the somewhat regal, always stoic voice she used.

"You only reduced it by the amount of the Anderson's original loan, correct?" Hope asked.

Rose nodded.

"I appreciate your generosity," Hope said, "but I want to pay back the money I borrowed. I need to know that I've made a success of Rainbow Lake Lodge by myself."

"I understand."

Stan had been busy rifling through the loan paperwork while they chatted. "Everything looks to be in order. The terms of the new loan seem very fair, and the payments structure seems manageable enough. Do you have any other concerns, Hope?"

"No." For the first time in over two years, she really didn't. She reached across the desk to take the pen Mrs. Bjorklund offered and signed by each "X" Stan pointed to.

It was done. For better or for worse, Rainbow Lake Lodge was finally hers. Not the Anderson's. Not the bank's. Not even David's, but hers.

"There's just one more thing," Mrs. Bjorklund said. "Sheriff Turppa got a warrant to search Billy's house earlier this week and in the process, found something that we believe belongs to you. I'm not sure of the details, but Sharon believes Billy must have found it taped to the inside an old armoire that you had asked her to sell."

Surely she would have seen noticed if it had been taped to the armoire. And when had Billy had access to her armoire?

Mrs. Bjorklund pulled out a key. "We thought at first that Billy had taken out a safety deposit box. Maybe left a note giving us some sort of explanation for what he was trying to accomplish the day he..." Mrs. Bjorklund wiped away a tear. "But when we checked the ledger, we found the key was registered to David. We were able to verify his signature with bank records."

Hope tensed. More secrets. "If the box were David's, wouldn't I have gotten a bill?"

"David took out the box eight years ago and paid twice, each time, for five years. The last time he signed in to access the box was the day he died." Mrs. Bjorklund pushed a button on her phone. "Please send someone in to escort Mrs. Anderson to the safe deposit boxes."

Stan took her hand.

Mrs. Bjorklund stood. "Thank you again, dear. You'll be in my prayers in the days ahead."

"Thank you."

"I expect to be invited to the Grand Reopening," Mrs. Bjorklund said. "I've already got a dress picked out."

"The Lodge will be ready sooner than you think. The Justinen Brothers called yesterday. They're running ahead of schedule at the job they were working on in town and since the extended forecast is for mild weather for the remainder of the winter, they'd like to resume working at the lodge right after the first of the year," Hope said.

"In like a lion, out like a lamb," Mrs. Bjorklund said.

"It seems like we've gotten all of our bad weather out of the way in the first part of the winter this year," Stan said.

"Oh, there'll still be a storm or two before winter is done," Rose said, blinking away another tear.

Hope looked down at the key in her hand and wondered what surprises God had in store for her in the New Year. "I'm sure you're right," she said, clutching the key in her palm and lifting her eyes. She'd promised to keep looking up – no matter what — and that was what she was going to do.

Chapter 52

Tommy bunched the overly plump, plastic-wrapped pillow at the Nothing to Be Embarrassed About Motel under his neck and tried to go back to sleep. He'd been in bed for five or six hours, but he hadn't slept well, if at all. And it was all Hope's fault. He hadn't seen, contacted or otherwise spoken to her since she'd dropped him off the day after the concert, and it was haunting him.

Condemned men don't do sleep.

Guilt was eating away at his insides – guilt because he hadn't called; guilt that he'd led her along when it was clear they had no future together; guilt that he'd gotten her hopes up only to jump ship mid-stream. But bad as he felt, guilt was not a good basis for a relationship. He'd been there, done that, wasn't going to do it again – no matter how much he didn't want to hurt her feelings.

He loved her. That was the worst of it. Because, unfortunately, life wasn't just about love. He'd done that, too. Love alone just wasn't enough.

He attacked the pillow and tried to block out the crinkle of the plastic liner as he rolled over on his back. Why couldn't she understand that he needed his privacy? That he literally couldn't survive without peace? That without a quiet place to write, create and unwind, he would cease to be the very man she claimed to love?

He shifted his hips and tried his side. What was so hard about that? After a concert, he craved solitude so much that it hurt. Between gigs, he needed the refreshment that came from being alone. He had to have time to rejuvenate his soul. There was no way he could face the crowds that clamored around him when he was performing without the sandwich bread of quiet time on either side. Being alone was the buffer his trampled heart needed before it could rise up and sing.

He flopped over again, hoping the mattress would be more comfortable in a different spot.

Hope couldn't honestly expect him to write music surrounded by customers and kids, canoes and cabins, crews and cameras. Could she?

Hope's vision of Rainbow Lake Lodge might be warm and fuzzy, even noble, but to him, it was the stuff nightmares were made of.

He rolled to his stomach and threw the pillow to the floor. He'd always needed time alone. It was just the way he was. Even as a kid, he'd lived for the times he and his dad would go off by themselves to hunt, fish, or set traps.

His favorite spot had been an old hunting cabin on Little Leech Lake, a hut his Dad had built out of scrap lumber with an old, tar-patched, wooden rowboat for a roof.

Little Leech Lake was so far out in the boonies that most locals didn't even know it was there, a shallow, marshy lake so thick with cattails and water lilies that you could hardly get a canoe through in spots. Where the water was deep enough to navigate, it was the perfect place to hunt for duck and geese. Tommy's dad had fed their family off Little Leech Lake many a lean year.

In all the times Tommy and he had holed up in the hunting shack, they'd always been alone. Anyone else who had stumbled upon it at one time or another quickly discounted it as a worthless swamp and moved on to one of the hundreds of other deeper, bigger lakes in the area.

Billy. Tommy sat straight up in bed and swung his feet to the floor. Billy knew about the cabin. Billy was at Little Leech Lake. He could feel it. Why hadn't he thought of it sooner?

He brushed his teeth, threw on the jeans and sweater he'd worn the day before, slipped into his shoes, and grabbed his coat. He was out the door in under ten minutes.

Chapter 53

Hope's hands were shaking so hard she could hardly get the letter open. There had been seven thousand dollars in the safe deposit box and a card from David, which she hadn't wanted to open until she got home and had a little privacy.

She felt half-elated and half-grief-stricken as she pulled the card from the envelope. "Happy Anniversary with My Love" the front of the card said in a flourish of glittery blue calligraphy and pink roses.

It was sweet, absurd, and ludicrous all rolled into one, getting this now, over two years and how many days after the anniversary he hadn't been here to celebrate. Bittersweet and ironic and so very, very hard.

She opened the card, read the Hallmark-ese inside and tried not to cry. So like David. Tender, appreciative, loving. Or would have been, if he had been here. As it was, the words seemed almost trite, hollow. Heartfelt words never said, void of meaning. He had meant them at the time, she felt sure of that. But the time was gone. He was gone.

She thought of Tommy and wondered how she could move on when she still had so much unfinished business with David. She hadn't known these emotions were still so near the surface, but they were, or her heart wouldn't be pounding, her head wouldn't be throbbing, her eyes wouldn't be dripping tears she hadn't known still existed.

She unfolded the paper that was tucked inside the card and pressed the two-year old creases flat.

Dear Hope, It's still a week until our anniversary, but I wanted to get this written today while I had some time alone. The longer we're married, the better you know me and the harder it is to surprise you.

I wouldn't trade our first night together for anything in the world. It was perfect – you were perfect. I can still remember the sound of the water lapping at the shore as I made love to my new bride, snuggling under the quilt you made for our wedding night, the sweet smell of roses in the wind as we walked along the lake later that night, holding hands and watching the fireflies.

Precious as that night was, I've always dreamed of taking you on the honeymoon we couldn't afford twenty years ago. As you can see, I've tucked away a lot of tip money over the years. Knowing how busy we'll be once we reopen the lodge, I thought the time was finally right to surprise you with a second honeymoon.

You've worked so hard to make this dream of ours come true that I'm going to let you decide where you'd like to go. Sweden, Scotland, that cruise up the eastern seaboard to the Maritime Provinces and down the St. Lawrence Seaway to Quebec City that you talked about a couple of years ago before my parents died, the Pacific Coast, Oregon and Washington State, France, the North Pole. Wherever you want to go, sweetheart. I'll be right there beside you.

I love you, David

Except he wasn't here, and wouldn't be, ever again.

She'd never felt so wretched. She ached all over, from her heart to her fingertips. She'd been dreaming about a second honeymoon, too. With Tommy Love.

It was the morning before Christmas and she was alone. She had a husband who wanted to honeymoon with her and couldn't because he was dead, and a man who could honeymoon with her but wouldn't because his heart was dead. She didn't know which was worse.

Chapter 54

Tommy never would have known the car was there if he hadn't been looking for it. As it was, it was only the taillights that were visible. Had he not known exactly where to look, he never would have seen them glinting through the underbrush.

A shredded piece of his mother's old kitchen curtains fluttered in the only window that looked out to the road. Road was too nice a word for the overgrown, barely-there path that wound its way through the swamp. But he could see a fresh set of tire marks, etched in the mud, and tall grasses crumpled and matted in the center.

The hem of the curtain bobbed again. Billy was in there, all right. Alive. In what state of health and in what frame of mind, it was hard to tell.

Tommy stopped his Porsche a hundred yards or so back from the shack, got out of the car, and started walking toward his friend – if that's what you called a man who had tried to hurt the woman you loved.

"I'm alone," he said when he reached the door.

"Come in."

He barely recognized the voice. He opened the door and slowly peeked his head around the corner.

"Took you long enough." Billy was huddled in the corner, shivering, wet, hungry, white-skinned and weak from losing blood, his rifle propped beside him.

"Man," Tommy said, not knowing what to say or think. He hated what Billy had done, but seeing him like this...

Billy nodded at the rifle. "Thought about sparing you the trouble but I didn't have the guts."

"Billy." Tommy sighed.

"I thought you'd figure it out. This was our meeting place. If either one of us got into trouble..."

"Forty years ago."

The blanket Billy was wrapped in was threadbare and caked in dried blood. "I've got blankets in the car," Tommy said.

"Don't go," Billy said, gripping the shaft of his rifle.

Tommy wiped the corner of his eye and pretended to cough.

"Look at the bright side," Billy said. "I've found the perfect place for you to build your dream house. So secluded no one even knows where it is. The view isn't quite what it would have been on Rainbow Lake, but the water is so smooth it's like glass. When the sun sets, the whole damn light show reflects off the water. You'll love it here."

"You need help, Billy."

"It's a regular wildlife sanctuary out here." Billy tugged the blanket a little closer. "Loons, egret, cranes, bald eagles. It's like the most solitary place on earth. You'll have all the privacy you want, plus some. No neighbors for miles, no anything, or anyone. You'll be totally alone."

"Let me take you back to town."

"Hey, man. It's perfect for you. Just what you said you wanted. You'll have to be content with a canoe or a pontoon boat instead of a speedboat. Water's just as shallow as ever. But that's minor. Put in a long dock with a boardwalk and a Finnish sauna and you'll have the perfect place here." Billy laughed – a pathetic imitation of a man pretending everything was okay.

Tommy looked around the room. He could almost see his Dad, shotgun balanced on his knee, sights set on a mallard, or if they were lucky, a Canadian honker. Tommy had been the best caller in ten counties. His Dad had told him so.

A flood of memories assaulted his senses... laughter around the Christmas table, his mother roasting a goose his dad had shot over a spit on the fire, warmth from the hearth, hugs, playing games and cards, his first taste of hot chocolate, stockings stuffed with oranges, apples, and pecans still in the shell. Treats fit for a king in his eyes.

They'd had next to nothing back then. But they'd been happy.

"Just think," Billy said. "Nobody to bother you. Total peace and quiet. Your own personal retreat."

Realization clunked him over the head. It wasn't seclusion he craved, but intimacy. He'd been surrounded by people his entire life, but no one who loved him. Everyone wanted a piece of him – his fortune, his glory, his fame, even his music, but none of them had loved him like his mother and father and little brother had.

What he wanted was not privacy, but love. It wasn't fame and adoration from a new generation that was going to make him happy, but love.

Hope. Hope loved him unconditionally, loved him like he hadn't been loved since he was a penniless, run-of-the-mill little boy. Hope was his future. All he wanted was a basketful of tomorrows with Hope. Living anywhere. In the middle of Grand Central Station if it meant being with her.

"Crap," Billy said, trying to lift his rifle, only to have it clatter to the floor.

"Come out with your hands up." Alvin's voice rang across the swamp and ricocheted against the cabin walls.

"Stop." Tommy rushed to Billy's side before he could do something stupid. "He's hurt," he yelled.

Alvin booted the door open, strode across the room and wrenched Billy out of his chair. He re-pocketed his handcuffs when he saw how weak Billy was.

"Thanks, man," Tommy said, watching Alvin escort Billy to his car with the same gentleness he'd shown his mother at the nursing home.

"I can take it from here," Alvin said. "Why don't you head back to town, find Hope, and tell her we found Billy."

It was Christmas Eve. Not the way he'd planned on starting out the holiday.

"Hope told me she was planning on going to the vesper service at six," Alvin said, not even trying to be subtle.

"Cool," Tommy said, smiling for the first time in three days.

"Say a prayer for your friend here."

"I will," Tommy said, and headed back to his Porsche to go find Hope.

Chapter 55

The last two weeks had been so busy and Hope had been so preoccupied with the whole Rainbow Lake Lodge / Quilt Auction / Billy / Tommy situation that Christmas had nearly been relegated to the position of an afterthought. Which Hope knew was exactly the opposite of the way she should be handling her priorities.

She didn't have a single present under the tree. Nothing new there – it had been that way since everyone she loved had died. First her parents, then David's, then David – everyone on her gift list was essentially gone.

Still, it was Christmas. The year before, and the year before that, she'd done all the classic things – Christmas poinsettias in honor of the Anderson's, a heifer and a gaggle of ducks to some poor children in Ethiopia in memory of her mother and father, a quilt for a women's shelter in Minneapolis in a gesture that connected her to the larger, world body of fellow humans in need, care baskets delivered to needy families in the area, and Teddy bears for the children in the cancer ward at the hospital. She'd found ways to give even when her heart had felt gift less.

This year was different. She had no gifts for anyone, friend or foe, stranger or acquaintance. Ironically enough, she had money, but inside where it mattered, she had nothing left to give.

But she had promised to keep looking up, and there was a star up on the roof of the church, hovering over all of Embarrass, or so it seemed. And a baby in the manger.

That was why she got out of bed, put on her blue silk Christmas dress, bundled up in her coat and mittens, and slipped into town to go to the Christmas Eve service.

Perhaps it was the year to be given to, to simply accept God's gift and hold it in her heart.

"Hi, Hope." An elderly woman who had lost her husband to cancer three or four years ago greeted her at the door of the church, hugged her and pressed a candle into her palm. "Merry Christmas."

"That's a pretty dress, Mrs. Anderson," said a blond-headed little girl who had been in the Vacation Bible School class Hope had taught last summer. "You look beautiful."

"Thank you, sweetie. Merry Christmas," Hope said.

Gladys Bechtel shimmied over to her and smoothed her velvet skirt down over her too-tightly corseted form. "You must be so relieved that Billy has been apprehended. I've been so worried about you, out there in the middle of nowhere all by yourself."

A shiver ran down her spine. "They found Billy?"

"Yes. Early this morning. I thought you would have heard from Alvin by now," Gladys said.

"No." Hope felt more faint now that the danger was past than she had in the middle of it.

"Tommy Love found him out in some old fishing shack by Little Leech Lake. They used to play there when they were boys."

"And everyone is okay?"

Gladys tucked a stray wisp of hair back under her wig. "All I know is that Billy is back in custody and has been taken to the hospital to be treated for some minor injuries and dehydration."

"Thanks," Hope whispered, seeing the pastor coming toward them.

"How's my favorite widow?" Reverend McAllister said, his green eyes sparkling under bushy white eyebrows and his faint brogue light with mirth.

"Fine," Hope said, smiling like she always did when he teased her. He'd earned the right the day he buried David, and during the months after, staying beside her while she went through the worst days of her life.

"Do not think you need to feel festive tonight," he said. "The holidays will always be a wee bit rough. Just keep looking up at the Christmas star, and follow where God leads you."

She nodded, tucked his words away in her heart, and took a seat. The Christmas program had always been difficult for her, even when David had been alive, looking at this little one and that, thinking that if she had gotten pregnant when she and David had first started trying, that they would have had a five-year-old, or an eight-year-old, or whatever age, by now.

They sang *O Come All Ye Faithful* before the three and four-year-olds lined up on stage to say their parts.

Love Notes

"Wise men coming from afar, following the Christmas star," said a little girl with red curls.

Next in line was a tow-headed little boy. "Baby Jesus gave his life, to save us from our sin and strife."

That was when Tommy slipped in beside her and slung his arm over the back of the pew behind her like absolutely nothing was wrong. For a few seconds, it felt like nothing was.

Then reality hit. "This is my pew. David's and mine," she whispered. She sounded idiotic and she knew it. But it was how she felt, and because it was Tommy Love, and because he drove her crazy, she was powerless to keep quiet.

"So pretend you're playing a game of Musical Men. The music stopped, and guess what? There was an empty chair, so I sat down," Tommy said in a stage whisper barely softer than the kindergarteners and first graders who were filing onto the steps at the foot of the cross.

"You can't just... You pew-stealer, you."

He almost cracked a grin. She could see it flickering at the corner of his mouth, like it was tickling him almost to the point of exploding into a fit of giggles.

"The cattle are lowing, the poor baby sleeps..."

Giggles would not be good.

"Let's start over," Tommy whispered, evidently having come to the same realization. "Is this seat taken?"

"As a matter of fact, it is," she said quietly. "I'm saving it for someone."

"David?" Tommy tipped his head a little closer and looked at her incredulously.

"No. Of course, not. Don't be silly," she said, adding lying in church to the offenses of arguing and almost giving Tommy the giggles.

"I'm willing to share if he is," Tommy whispered.

"Don't be ridiculous. David is dead," she said.

"Oh, little town of Bethlehem, how still we see thee lie..." Good. They were singing. Camouflage for their conversation.

"But you still love him, and my guess is, you always will," Tommy said.

"Why couldn't I have sat in the back row?" she moaned quietly.

"Because he's here."

"No, he isn't." But he was. In her mind, he was, large as life even in death. "This is very confusing," Hope said.

"No, it's very simple. You'll always have David's love. Now you've got mine, too." Tommy leaned back in the pew and lopped both arms over the edge of his seat. "Get used to it, sweetheart. Most people would give anything to be bursting with love like you are."

"But what about...? We want such different things," she said. "Rainbow Lake Lodge is my dream and David's, not yours."

"Rainbow Lake Lodge will always be yours and David's. You and I are going to have a new house of our very own, built on the land I just bought from Dirk Westola. Close to the Lodge for you, secluded and private for me."

She smiled. How could she not? He'd clearly thought all of this out. "Where is Dirk going?"

"Little Leech Lake. Private. Secluded. Totally tucked away from the world. It's perfect for him."

"What about your house in California?" she whispered.

"I'm hoping we can live there for most of the winter. When we're in Minnesota running the lodge, my realtor will hire a property management firm to rent it by the month."

What could she say to that? "You're really willing to share me?"

"We can put it in our wedding vows if you want to. What's mine is David's. What's yours and his is everybody's. I'm willing to do whatever it takes to be with you."

"I don't have to run Rainbow Lake Lodge for the rest of my life," she said.

"You don't?"

"No. Someday a couple will stay there on their honeymoon and be so taken with the place that they'll want to stay forever and raise their children there, just like David's mom and dad did." She was sitting so close to him now, their heads so close together that she barely had to speak to convey her message.

He took her hand. "But you need to be the one to get it off to a good start. You're the bridge between the Andersons and whomever God brings along next."

She smiled. "Or, we might want to stay there forever."

"Wherever you are is where I want to be." He squeezed her hand.

"I'm a homebody at heart, but when it comes right down to it, I'd follow you to the ends of the earth," she said.

He grinned. "Can we put that in our vows?"

Love Notes

In the corner of her eye, she saw the fourth and fifth graders finish their parts and begin to file off the platform.

"Can I be Mrs. Tommy Lubinski?" she whispered.

He grinned. "I love you, Hope Anderson."

"I love you, Tommy Lubinski."

That was when they realized the sanctuary has gone dead quiet.

She looked at him. He looked at her. A round of applause broke out from the audience.

"Um, slightly embarrassing," Hope said.

Tommy smiled and took her hand. "Pretty much a typical day in Embarrass, Minnesota. Besides, you're the one who wanted to live your life surrounded by people."

She looked around the room, which was practically aglow with shining faces. "I did say that, didn't I?"

"Merry Christmas," said Reverend McAllister, looking down at them from his seat by the pulpit.

"Merry Christmas!" the congregation chimed in.

"I think now would be a good time for a little special music," Reverend McAllister said. "Tommy?"

Tommy nodded, picked up a guitar from the pew behind hers and went to the microphone. "I haven't sung with the Love Notes for quite some time now, but tonight I have a very special love note to sing to you all – a love note to the Lord in honor of a beautiful lady who I consider to be the best Christmas present I've ever received."

He sat down on a stool and started to strum the most beautiful melody she'd ever heard, eyes shining, heart singing, his voice velvety soft and full of love.

You are my Hope for tomorrow,
My reason for living each day,
Certain of finding at sunrise,
Love, peace and joy for the way;
Strength for each moment of weakness,
Faith for each moment of pain,
Comfort for every sorrow,
Sunshine and joy after rain.

You are my Hope for tomorrow,

Sherrie Hansen

The miracle God made for me,
Even in the darkness I see you,
Touch what my eyes cannot see,
Stilled by the promise of music,
Soothed by the touch of your hand,
Confident of your affection,
Knowing our life-path is planned.

You are my Hope for tomorrow,
Life with its changes may come,
With God behind and before us,
How can we ever go wrong?
Even when we're so sad and weary
We don't know which way to turn,
We have each other, and Jesus,
To teach us to love and to learn.

When he was finished, he started another, his voice so hushed and humble that it made her heart melt.

Hope, Joy, Peace, Love –
Gentle blessings from above.
A rainbow bright, a starry night
To warm our hearts – the gift of light.

Hope, Joy, Peace, Love –
A star to follow from above.
Shining brightly in the night
To warm our hearts – the gift of light.

Hope, Joy, Peace, Love –
The Son of God from heaven above
Came down to us on Christmas night
To warm our hearts – the gift of light.

The ground was covered with a light dusting of snow when they left the church, she wrapped in her wool tweed coat, her rainbow colored scarf around the collar, Tommy in his black leather bomber jacket. Tommy took her hand and they walked away from the parking lot to the courtyard where the bell tower stood. He stopped when they were tucked away in a stand of blue spruce, standing under snow-dusted boughs in the starlight.

He kissed her reverently. Like he adored her. Which he clearly did. "I love you, Hope."

She felt happier than she would ever have thought possible. Tommy, his song, the snow – it all seemed so fitting for a night of miracles.

Tommy was the first to speak. "Brian, Billy's brother – I want you to meet him – is a pastor out in California. He gave me a book of devotions a few weeks ago. It was almost funny – I was trying to write hip hop, but all I could think about was you. The first time I looked in the book he gave me, there was a quote by this Thomas Fuller guy from England. 'If it were not for hope, the heart would break.' I mean, I knew my heart was broken – had been for a long time. And that you gave me hope. But I guess I still wasn't ready to admit that I was in love with you."

She smiled, and hugged him.

"So the more I tried to get you out of my head, the more signs there were that God wanted us together. Every time I opened the Bible, the first verse my eyes landed on had the word hope in it. This morning it was '"For I know the plans I have for you," declares the Lord, "Plans to prosper you, and not to harm you, plans to give you hope, and a future."'

"Jeremiah 29," she said. "It's one of my favorite verses."

"And everybody in California – people who didn't know about you – kept telling me that I should write more songs about hope –"

"I can't say it a million different ways set to music, but I do love you, Tommy Lubinski." He was so dear to her. When she'd thought she was going to lose him...

"Those are the only words I need to hear." He looked into her eyes and kissed her again. "Will you marry me, Hope Anderson?"

And then she bent down to write a love note in the snow, tracing each letter with the tip of her finger.

Hope + Love + a little faith = Joy + Peace.

"Joy and peace and wedded bliss?" Tommy asked.

"Yes. Just like that. You want to make some snow angels?" She reached for his hand and gently tugged him to the ground.

"A whole heavenly host of them." Tommy smiled and looked up at the sky.

"Hope, Joy, Peace, Love"
Words and Music written by Tommy Love

Hope, Joy, Peace, Love –

Gentle blessings from above.

A rainbow bright, a starry night

To warm our hearts – the gift of light.

Hope, Joy, Peace, Love –

A star to follow from above.

Shining brightly in the night

To warm our hearts – the gift of light.

Hope, Joy, Peace, Love –

The Son of God from heaven above

came down to us on Christmas night

To warm our hearts – the gift of light.

To hear the music for Hope, Joy, Peace, Love, please visit www.BlueBelleBooks.com

Also available by Sherrie Hansen from Indigo Sea Press

http://indigoseapress.com

Night and Day

It's midnight in Minnesota and Jensen Marie Christiansen is dreaming of a rosy future. It's daybreak in Denmark and Anders Westerlund is waking up to a world full of stark realities. When parchment paper and faded ink meet computer screens and fax machines, the old-fashioned magic of a great-grandmother's letters sets the stage for a steamy Internet romance...

Stormy Weather

An ill wind is brewing up a storm and as usual, Rachael Jones is in the middle of the fray. If thelocal banker succeeds in bulldozing the Victorian houses she's trying to save, she's in for yet another rough time before the skies clear. The only bright spots on the horizon are her friendship with Luke... and her secret rendezvous with Mac... Is Rachael meant to weather the storm with Luke, who touches her heart and soul so intimately, or with Mac, who knows each sweet secret of her body? STORMY WEATHER... Stay tuned for the latest forecast!

Water Lily

Once upon a very long time ago, Jake Sheffield and Michelle Jones graduated from the same high school. Jake can't wait to take a trip down memory lane at their 20th class reunion. Being with his old friends is like guest starring in a favorite episode of Cheers. Everybody knows your name. Everybody's glad you came. The last thing Michelle wants to do is dredge up a lot of old memories and relive a part of her past that wasn't that great in the first place. Will the murky waters of the past destroy their dreams for the future, or will a water lily rise.

Merry Go Round

Everyone who knows Pastor Trevor, his lovely wife, Tracy, and their three children thinks they're the perfect family. But when Trevor leaves Tracy for a man, Tracy's whole world starts to spin out of control.

Barclay Alexander III's charmed life as the heir apparent of Alexander Industries screeches to a halt when his father gives him an ultimatum - move to Iowa, marry Lauren Humphries, and turn red ink to black, or see Maple Valley's woolen mill shut down forever. The unlikely romance Barclay finds with Tracy is the dream that gives him hope. Michelle and Rachael, Tracy's sisters, unite to help her get back on her feet. But powerful forces are pulling them apart - her children, his parents, her pride, his honor, the welfare of the entire town.

Heaven only knows if their love was meant to be, or if they will always be on opposite sides of the merry-go-round, riding round and round, never catching up to the other.

Made in the USA
San Bernardino, CA
26 April 2016